The Manor's Eyes

Patricia Petronella Balinski

ISBN: 0997051280

ISBN-13: 978-0-9970512-8-5

Portals Publishing
An imprint of Denouement Literary Agency, LLC
PO Box 973, Eagle Lake, FL 33839

PortalsPublishing.com
DenouementLit.com

DEDICATION

The Manor's Eyes is dedicated to James and Jean Kilgallon. They gave me the best gift of their love. Life.

CONTENTS

ACKNOWLEDGMENTS

In loving memory of my husband, Michael Balinski Sr., who encouraged me to follow my dream as a published writer beyond the stories I told our children. When life happens and you try to be creative, these adult children and several grand-daughters subtly and not-so subtly nudged me to see it to "The End". Thank you. Thanks to close friends for their encouragement. When I stalled with the ending, Francine Duet, my hair stylist, suggested I take a break and visit friends in Pennsylvania and Ohio. The sites and scenes gave me the ending to my first novel, "The Manor's Eyes". I recognize creative accolades to book cover designer, Susan Krupp and to Life Time Portrait Studio for my photograph. All is not complete without special recognition of my friend, agent, editor, and publisher, Evelyn Rainey at Portals Publishing. With her trust and confidence in me, dream fruition achieved.

CHAPTER 1
THE MANOR'S EYES

Following Mom's funeral service, the manor is now empty of guests. I retreat to my bedroom to cry without condolences from anyone. With a storm brewing outside, twilight comes early and tonight's weather produces a series of lightning bolts across the sky. Through my window, the repetitive flashes recall the frightening memories of Mom's boyfriend, C. J., when he took compromising pictures of me. The unpleasant thoughts give me goosebumps, and I rub away the echo feeling of her red boa's pin feathers pricking my bare skin. Mom, how I prayed, while you lived, you didn't know the photographs he took of me wearing only your neck piece. Although my room is warm, a cold shiver travels down my back. I wonder Mom, was your death worth the job. Was the move to a mansion, a place with so many windows, like they are the manor's eyes looking out and in, better than our life in the third-floor walkup?

Through the rear window, I watch the steel gray clouds race toward the western horizon and realize the worst is over. Below, ground puddles ripple from the shifting winds, and I arch my back before I lower that window half way. Without undressing, I lie upon the bed, close my eyes and think, maybe the sun will come out tomorrow, and life will be brighter.

A cool cross breeze filters through the windows and chills my body. I awake and stretch to welcome the incoming sunlight that filters through the sheer curtains. A glance at the clock indicates 11 o'clock. I've slept much too long fully dressed.

As I walk the second-floor hallway, I pass the housekeeper's favorite painted mirror, and I stop and look why a mirror has a name, for Clare said it is a Flora 200. Instead of pastel flowers, I stare at a pale image of lifeless lips and bloodshot eyes. I look terrible but don't care and hurry to the kitchen stairway. After several steps down, I hesitate in my descent because Clare is talking with the manor's owner, Katherine McCutchen.

"Did you ever wonder if Adam did it with Anabelle's mother? Her age is about right since Dorothy stopped comin' here." I can't believe that my mother had an affair with this Adam person and whisper, "Lord, give me patience because I'm losing mine. It's no picnic working with Clare's attitude of her way or no way. She's so perfect, a pint-sized know-it-all, and now adds my mother to her collection. Sorry, but this housekeeper speaks her mind too freely with Mrs. McCutchen. Why does Katherine keep her employed?" I proceed downward.

Now three stairs before I enter the kitchen, I back up one stair as Mrs. McCutchen troubled voice asks, "Clare? Why, would you even think that?"

"Once Dorothy told me that she thought Adam's life was so Victorian and mysterious. Well, I was thinkin' could Arabelle might be like her. With your son's unpredictable home visits and Neil secretive about his trips away from here."

"Clare, Neil is a man and entitled to his privacy. Keep him out of this conversation. I don't know nor would I gossip if Dorothy and Adam had a relationship. I only recall that Adam said that he enjoyed Dorothy's zest for life. Now instead of hashing the lives of the deceased, let us hope my friend found peace from her illness. The sooner we find Adam's will to know his rightful heirs, happiness shall reign in the manor. Do you know if Anson found anything after searching the carriage house?"

"Uncovered nothin'. Unless someone invents a hand-held x-ray machine or Superman pays a visit to help; it's a lost cause. Wait, did I hear someone?"

I take a breath. Lean against the wall and wonder. Who is this Adam? If he were my father, I could be an heir. If so, why would Mom say that my Dad died after I was born and say nothing about Mrs. McCutchen's son?

"Wasn't anyone.Katherine. Once I heard on a TV program, grief adds to depression. Not sayin' that's Arabelle's trouble, but worryin' about her is raisin' my blood pressure. Why it may even ruin my health."

With Clare's concern, I relax and listen.

"Clare, please don't worry. Arabelle suffered a significant loss. Let her rest. Don't know why I wear this cape, have such a time with these frog closures. Anson has the patience to forgive my delay in meeting you, but waiting fifteen minutes is time enough to drive me to the Civic Center. Please be patient and do not disturb her. I should be back in a couple of hours. Arabelle and I will discuss her circumstances later. Bye."

The back screen door creaks when it closes which gives me the courage to descend another step until Clang! Clang! The sound of metal, as it hits the stove, startles me. I fall back against the wall and once more hold my breath.

Clare grumbles, "Humph! Be patient! Let her rest! I don't agree with you, Katherine. You should've talked to her before you left, but you own the place. Okay. Okay. I'll back off from worryin'. Sure hope your decision has her stayin', I could use her help."

Clare's comments upset me. I exhale and retreat upward when a familiar voice cracks the air like a drill sergeant.

"Arabelle Lacey, I know it's you. So come down."

There is no way I want to face Clare. I ignore the rumbling of my stomach and make like lightning to my room. My rumpled quilt twists around me and in a low voice I confess, "Lord, don't want to be on my own without a job or a place to live. What if Mrs. McCutchen flips a coin to decide, how will I repay her for the funeral?" I lie down and hope for the best.

However, what seems like a short nap, my clock shows it is two hours later. I rub my stomach. With lunch over, I chance another trip to the kitchen. Once Clare finishes the dishes, she watches her Soaps in the living room. I flip my quilt to straighten the covering. With a brush, I untangle my hair. Wash, dress and to walk silently, I leave my room wearing slippers. Near the kitchen, the sound of water running causes me to peek around the stairwell's corner into the room.

On her stool at the sink, prim and proper in a blue housedress, Clare peels potatoes. To my surprise, Anson remains at the table and puts down the morning newspaper. Unlike his casual appearance of slacks and Tommy Hilfiger shirt, he wears gardening coveralls, and a beaten straw hat hangs on the chair to cover his red hair.

"Clare, Katherine surprised me yesterday. Not even half-way down the drive, when she had me use the car phone to call a cab. Said that you were upset. She was worried you might do something rash. I couldn't see it, but, she is the lady of the manor."

Yesterday? I thought. Did I sleep an entire day? Maybe, I shouldn't act surprised and just say "Hi, guys!"

I decide to stop viewing them from my vantage spot; until I see Clare turns to face him. His back is toward her, and she takes aim with a dripping potato. Several seconds later, Clare turns and suspends the potato mid-air. When she looks over her shoulder, I question her motives because her eyes remain too long over Anson's torso.

She drops the potato into the sink. "Anson, a few years ago, we talked to each other. What happened?" She pauses for his reply. "Anson, are you listenin' to me? Not sayin' that it tires me from doin' those stairs to check on her. Even though, it's natural considerin' she just buried her mother. But, it's the second day since the funeral, and she's still sleepin'. Anson, would you go now and see if she's up? Don't worry; she's dressed."

Anson lowers his head closer to the table and barely above a whisper says, "Katherine told me we treat her with kid gloves. She'll handle Arabelle's situation. Don't you worry that pretty little, blonde bun of yours."

"Anson, I'm well aware of how you change the subject. So, don't try flatterin' me. Only askin' you as I need to finish the laundry. Put down that paper and check on her."

My mouth falls open when he pushes aside his coffee cup. In one swift move, his towering six feet built is now exaggerated when he puts on his hat. This mountain of a man creates a showdown of temperament. I watch Clare, all five-foot stature, as she stands her ground, and Anson's face becomes red.

"Nag! Nag! Nag! Said I'd go in a minute. Quit goading me, woman. I'll go."

"Not naggin' you, Anson Redman, only askin' for a little help. Oh! Forget it; I'll do it myself."

"Now Clare, . . ."

Afraid and embarrassed if they knew I overheard them argue, I retreat to my room and ignore my hunger. Once there, I open the intercom. There is nothing but silence. After what seems like a lifetime, footsteps reverberate against the wood floor and remind me of a Clydesdale on cobblestone roadway.

I slide sideways under the quilt and pull it up near my ear. Anson's coffee breath almost gags me when he whispers beside it, "You rest."

I pretend to wake when he spoke. "Anson? Why are you here?"

"Sorry, didn't mean to startle you, Miss Belle. Though, I'm glad you're up. You had us worried." He presses the wall intercom, "Clare, she's awake and looks like she slept in her jeans. Here, you talk to her." His job is done, he leaves me.

I didn't, honestly didn't, want to speak to her. Instead in a flat tone, I say, "Clare?"

"Yes, Arabelle. It's important you come downstairs."

"Be there in a few minutes," I say. With no response, I cover my head. Then feel the quilt pull off of me.

"Your time is up," Clare says and removes my last layer of defense. "I send a man to get you up, and he doesn't finish the job. Instead, he leaves me to handle it. Never will I think Anson has something to offer a woman."

Am I'm supposed to ask something about Anson or is she blowing off steam because she had to climb the stairs? I sit up and nod.

"You're in agreement. Good. Now you see I'm standin' here. Only I see a poor example of a young woman, who changed clothes. However, she needs to take care of herself by comin' downstairs to eat."

Not sure why I ask permission, but I do. "May I say something?"

Clare nods and tugs at the bed sheets so I have to get up. I help pull them off into a heap onto the carpet.

"Clare, I want to thank you for all you did for me. What I mean is, you sang beautifully at the service. Plus, so many candles in the windows, I thought the manor was on fire when we returned from the estate's cemetery. And well, just everything."

"You're welcome, Arabelle. Didn't do it for you, did it for Dorothy. Your mom always treated me like I was her family. I knew she loved candlelight and thought it important to show my gratitude."

"Clare, would you know what instrument Anson played at the funeral? Thought it was a guitar, but that long frame tilted sideways on his lap confused me."

"Dulcimer. He played his dulcimer. Katherine returned and asked if you'd stop in to see her after you ate."

While I brush my hair, Katherine's voice comes over the intercom. "Clare, what is going on? I have some news to share and find you upstairs. Is there a problem?"

As Clare leaves my bathroom, she says, "No problem Katherine, just collectin' her laundry." Clare adds the bed sheets and totes my hamper through the doorway. As she nears the stairwell, her voice becomes faint. I hear her complain about her new eyeglasses, "Darn these bifocals, can't judge my footing. One. Two."

In the kitchen with the intercom on, Katherine sounds excited. I want to know why and get closer to the box.

"Neil called. There's some glitch with the connecting flight. Canceled his flight out of Pittsburgh and rented a car. Clare, Neil will probably be hungry. Would you have time to make a meatloaf and his favorite dessert?"

"Sure, dependin' on traffic, I figure Neil will arrive around seven tonight. With Arabelle's help, there's enough time for a lemon pie. Katherine, you have plenty of time to rest and freshen up before he gets here. I know, Neil can't wait to see you, as much as you are to see him."

"Clare, that is good advice. I'm excited to have him home. If you need any help, call me."

"No problem, Arabelle will help and I'll get the meatloaf started." Her footsteps on the tile floor tell me that Katherine has left the room.

A tap, tap sound comes into the room before Clare says, "Arabelle, I know the intercom was on. You heard the news. I'll see you here when I return from the carriage house. Got to tell Anson the news."

While she's telling Anson, I decide to upscale my appearance for Neil's arrival. I take a quick shower and put on a lavender shirtdress. With all the rushing about, the bedroom seems warm. Before leaving, I open the one window that faces the back drive about six inches. From out in the garden, I hear a bullfrog's greeting. "Croak! Croak!"

I return a croak and leave to await my fate in helping Clare. For once I enter the kitchen, her stern voice will boom in my ears. Today, she sounds contrite.

"I'm sorry Arabelle for your loss. Nevertheless, grievin' passes. You begin again. Neil will arrive this evenin'. Although he likes eatin' in my kitchen, I need your help settin' up the dining room table. Nor do I expect you to help on an empty stomach, so eat."

Clare points to a chair opposite her and hands me a dinner plate with hamburger, fries, and fresh fruit on it.

Several hours later every room is in readiness, and the smell of a finished meatloaf lets me know I'm ready to eat again. "Clare, any chance there is enough for a sandwich?"

She removes the pan from the oven. "Maybe for lunch tomorrow. Tonight, it's for them. However, meat needs to rest a few minutes." After adjusting the oven temperature, Clare adds the meringue, and the lemon pie goes into the oven.

I wonder. Will Clare notice if I wait and cut a sliver off the meatloaf? Maybe not, if I distract her. Could ask her some questions about Neil. Like, why aren't there any pictures of him in Katherine's office? Clare said he's lovable; why doesn't anyone talk about him? Is he near my age? Since Charlie Boyd and I split-up in tenth grade, it might be nice to have a new boyfriend.

"Clare? Katherine's son, how old is he? Any girlfriend? Will his father be coming with him? It sounds like both must travel a lot. Do you know where he goes?"

While I wait for her to answer, I forget the pie is

baking and open the oven door.

"Close that door or the meringue won't brown," Clare calls over her shoulder. "Don't you think I got eyes in the back of my head because that oven door has a slight squeak when you start to open it? Pay attention."

Carefully, I close the door and lose my chance for Clare to answer my questions. She's not talking and stalls with changing her apron for the third time. I wait when I smooth out the table cloth then eat a red delicious apple from the pantry.

Hands on her hips and a broad smile on her face, Clare surveys the room and says, "Arabelle, Neil is twenty-one. He's on the trim, lean side and I think he is a handsome young man. Father and son travel separately. The rest, you might ask him. Now, I want you to know that I've been hard on you because I saw me in you. I couldn't let this place change me, but it did. Before tonight, you've been doin' the same thing. With the way you helped, I saw you reconsider if given the chance. You are a survivor, street-smart and have a curious nature."

"Thanks, Clare. That means a lot to me." I want to hug her, but that's not the way with people like us.

"You're off duty, and we can relax until he arrives. Neil and Katherine, they eat together on the first night. That reminds me I need some cut flowers for the table. Be right back and there's no need for you waitin' for him."

Don't believe it. Clare is telling me to go, to leave. "He doesn't know about me, does he?" I said abruptly. "I'm a townie. So I'm not good enough to meet the mysterious man of the manor when he arrives."

"Not at all. We, Anson and I, exchange a few words when he arrives. Then, dinner and evenin' time are theirs to catch up. I'm not sure if Katherine mentioned you to him before today, so tomorrow mornin' you will probably meet him at breakfast."

"I'm sorry, Clare. Only wanted to meet him and not be left out of his homecoming."

"Apology accepted." She makes me a sandwich and removes the pie to cool. With a flashlight and scissors in hand, Clare goes outside.

I call over my shoulder. "Goodnight. Thanks for the burger." I take a can of soda from the refrigerator. Flex my shoulders and realize how stiff I am. While a massage would be nice, I settle for a couple of aspirins. After eating, I'm invigorated and do not feel the least sleepy.

I return to my room. While pills ease the ache, a hot shower and faint traces of lily-of-the-valley perfume on Mom's chenille robe comforts me. I toss bed pillows near the open window and raise it higher. The evening air is nippy and with such a soft seat, I yawn and enjoy the setting sun's red skyline. Beyond the estate, a soulful train whistle grows faint in its travel. When two lights shine out beyond the driveway's perimeters and approach the rear porch, my excitement builds.

To see who parks the car, I lean out as far as I can and balance myself beyond the window sill. Below, within the spreading porch light, Clare hugs a male figure.

"Neil! Welcome home scalawag."

Scalawag? Is this who Neil is, a mischief maker? Was this the real reason Clare didn't want me there when he arrived? Well, Clare, I can meet him tonight and say, "Hi, my name is Arabelle Lacey, Clare's assistant."

I pass the dresser mirror, and the reflection startles me. Mom's robe is too large. I change into jeans and a gingham shirt. A few minutes with brush and hair dryer gives me a decent, casual look.

CHAPTER 2
PINKIE PROMISE

It surprises me when I find the kitchen empty. Humph. If this is a homecoming, it's rather disappointing. I hope the dining room tube is still open from the wake. With the intention to make out Neil's voice, I listen. For a minute or two, conversations are, quiet; I don't understand who is who until a tenor's voice begins singing "New York, New York."

While accustomed to Anson bass, I presume the singer is Neil. He carries the tune but finishes it with an apology. "Sorry Clare, I sang for my supper because I felt guilty for having that club sandwich at the airport. I ate so little of your preparations. Should have known you'd have a meatloaf waiting. Hmm! But there's always room for another piece of your pie."

"I'll bring the pie plate in, and you visit with your mother. Katherine, pie?"

"No thank you, Clare."

"Hey Clare, you relax. I'll help myself. Mother, would you mind if we continue our visit in the morning. I need to submit a report over the phone and fax the paperwork tonight, after another piece of lemon pie. Therefore, with your permission Mother, I wish you a good evening?"

"Goodnight dear, I understand. It's wonderful having you home with us. I'll look in later and maybe we can continue our visit then."

His footsteps fade as he leaves the room and I dwell on what I learned. He is polite and has a good voice. He travels a lot and is three years older than me. Not much in the grand scheme of life, but what if he doesn't know I live here? Then I can't just pop in on him. That is one of my most stupid ideas especially with both of them returning here.

"Clare," Katherine said, "will you stay for a minute. I'd like to discuss an idea I have. Let us adjourn to my sitting room. It was a shame Arabelle couldn't meet Neil tonight. Make sure she joins us for breakfast. I'm certain Neil would like to meet her."

The room grows quiet, and I recall Neil left the dining room minutes ago. I've got to get out of here before he arrives. Steps, lighter than Anson's, come toward the kitchen. Without his hearing me leave, I won't make it to the second floor. I scan the room for a hiding space and focus on the kitchen's broom closet. Although narrow, it is two feet away and a perfect place for me to see him when he sits at the table. I enter the hideaway as the kitchen door swings open. Without closing the shutter door completely, I have enough space to see him enter the room.

While his trim body indicates he's played sports, his masculine physique and profile could lure me to see more of him in the moonlight. When he removes a plate from the cupboard. I take advantage of the overhead kitchen light to see his face. Even though Neil has a five o'clock shadow, on a scale of 75 to 100, his cleft chin is enough for me to tip the scales to 110.

The fight or flight hormone leaves, and I'm no longer frightened at being discovered. However, this isn't how I want us to meet. Until, the temptation to shock him outweighs common sense and I throw caution aside by opening the door and say, "Evening Neil."

He jumps and takes a side-step, losing his balance. When Neil stumbles forward, he knocks over a chair after he bumped into an antique metal boot cleaner. "Ouch! What the?"

I watch him hop on one foot toward the fluorescent light with his back to me. Now's my chance. Go. I dash across the tile floor to the stairwell's inner shadow. While I cringe at his misfortune, I peek around the stairway's opening. When I recall his fumbling, a giggle escapes.

Moments later, he throws his arms up in surrender. "Okay, whoever is laughing, it's not funny. Nearly broke my toe bone and perhaps destroyed a chair. Show yourself!"

Because he's agitated, I won't reveal myself and lean against the wall. Quietly I climb backward and wait in safety on the second floor. Eventually, the kitchen light goes off, and the creaky screen door opens and closes. I breathe easier and continue to my room.

Neil went outside. The butterflies within cannot help me to relax by the window. I search where the back porch light extends. He's not in sight. However, the garage section light of the carriage house is on, unlike the unlit kitchen where the memory of Neil's hopping around the kitchen makes me smile. I stare into the darkness beyond when the lyrics from 'Strangers in the Night' come to my mind. I find the North Star and say, "Star light, star bright end my worry and let me stay here for many a night."

After closing the window and drawing the sheer curtains across its width. I carry an armful of pillows to the bed. To help with breakfast, I set the alarm for five a.m. and retire.

ꟷ

I tap the snooze alarm so many times, and I sleep until seven. Dressing hastily, I race to the kitchen to find Clare busy frying bacon. I add bread to the toaster. "Morning Clare, will Neil be having breakfast?"

"Neil? He left sometime early mornin'. Don't know why. Remember, you don't even ask Katherine about it because it's none of your concern. Only this place knows their secrets."

I stand for a moment while my mind swirls like a whirlpool. Don't ask? What secrets go between mother and son are certainly none of my business. However, she might know more. "Clare, I . . ."

Clare puts a finger to her lips and glances toward the backdoor. "Katherine is lookin' forward to your get-together. She's waitin' on the terrace. Here's her tray. I added your cup."

"She eats outside for breakfast," I say and take the tray from Clare.

As she gives me a gentle shove out the door, she says, "Most times she and I enjoy breakfast in the kitchen. Sometimes, like today, she meditates there before havin' an early breakfast. If you'd been up earlier, you'd see the sunrise. Although there is a beautiful view of the garden, you'll enjoy."

"Thanks, Clare," I walk onto the back porch when

Clare appears and takes the tray away from me.

"Arabelle, I'll take this to her. You see whoever is always ringing the front door bell. Then, excuse yourself and join Katherine. Why anyone would visit at this hour?" She shrugs her shoulders and leaves me before I could offer a guess.

The door chime stops as my best friend, Decima Gordon, hugs me so hard, I get tears in my eyes. "Decima. Shalom. What happened? Whose car is in the driveway?"

"It's Charlie's. Anyway, I had to get this off my mind before work. Leaving early, not comforting you, and forgetting my mother's message. I've been . . ."

I interrupt Deci. She has to focus, or she'll take forever to tell me. "Come inside. Exactly what do you want to say?"

"Can't stay long, Belle. Need to return his car. It's a loaner. Mine's in the garage. Had to apologize. That Charlie is a great friend. Would you mind if we stay outside? Victorian houses are spooky."

"Decima, you're rambling. Yes, by all means, the wooden porch swing is fine. So, tell me, what is so important you borrow Charlie's car?"

"Not visiting sooner after the funeral. We're best friends and I should have, but my car is in the garage, transmission problem. Lucky for me, Charlie loaned me his until mine gets fixed."

"And you came all this way to apologize and tell me about Charlie Boyd's good deed. Girl, that's why we have telephones."

"Not exactly, my mother was upset that I didn't tell you that the family never thought of her or you being a shiksa. I know, you're not Jewish, but your mother was a mensch, a fine human being, and a blessing to you."

"Thank you. It means a lot to have you tell me this. Decima, I've known you forever. What's the real reason you are here?"

"Okay, I'm here because I want to know why the hottest couple at Emerson High went separate ways. Come to the funeral and see he's a casket bearer. How come?"

I clear my throat several times before I begin. "You are correct. We broke up before graduation. Since then, no communication happened between Charlie and me. Guess our romance wasn't meant to be permanent. After he read Mom's obit notice. Mr. Boyd got the phone number from directory assistance. Called and asked me if he could be a pallbearer. Mom liked him a lot, so I agreed."

"So, you have no feelings for him."

"Deci, at the funeral service, when our eyes met for a brief moment, he flashed me his wicked smile. Can't believe that it still makes me weak in the knees."

"Belle, suppose he does likes you and has second thoughts. Unless, he is still acting the part of a big brother. Since our freshman year, Charlie always acted as your protector. Maybe, he's thinking differently now. You remember how he started acting sort of grown up after his Dad died and he took over the construction business with his brother."

"Maybe. Decima Gordon, you keep on dreaming. However, I don't agree that the two of us will reunite. He thinks outside the box with his construction ideas, and I like roots in one place. Deci, I'm sorry I didn't see him leave the funeral to thank him. When you return his car, do me a favor and give him a hug from me?"

Decima begins with a giggle that becomes a snicker and is followed by soft meows under her breath.

"Stop the meowing. All right, already. I get it. Okay, okay! Only you'd remember that 'meow.' Yes, I thought he was freaking awesome. Still do. Unfortunately, Deci, my future doesn't show Charlie in it."

"That's all I wanted to know, Belle. So, care to go out for lunch?"

"I wished you'd call earlier because I should be meeting with Katherine now. What about next Wednesday? Here, at the manor, since I don't drive."

We exchange farewell hugs and Decima says, "Sounds great, except I drive and you pick the restaurant."

In the kitchen, Clare rinses the breakfast tray. "Sure glad, I didn't hold my breath waiting for you. Katherine still wants to see you. She enjoys chamomile tea. Take her another pot on that tray, if you want some, add a cup. There's sugar and cream if you add anything. Walk slowly over the flagstone. Some are still wet."

From the back porch, the view of the distant gardens becomes a colorful palate. While traveling along the terrace's walk, I see Katherine, and she appears to be resting. Foremost, I'd like to find out what she wanted to discuss. In bringing out her tea, it's an opportunity to thank her for the financial aid.

Although I tread lightly, my next step snaps a twig and the sound surprises Katherine. She sits forward.

"Arabelle. Good morning. How are you?"

"I'm okay. Katherine, the bright chrysanthemum colors within the garden are impressive. Who does the gardening?"

"Anson has the green thumb. You've been here a

short while, and soon you'll discover he wears many hats at the estate and for the company."

After I place the tray on an adjoining side table, Katherine reaches for my hand to sit beside her. From her gentle touch, I know she understands the emptiness I feel. She lets go. I continue holding her hand and force my lips to curl upward in an attempt to return her faint smile.

Wait a minute, she and Mom were best friends. Why didn't she cry during the service? I want to know. "Thank you for everything. You didn't know the day of the funeral I was in the hall when you mentioned to Clare about a doctor appointment. Hope everything is okay."

She puts down her cup and says, "Arabelle, you are more than welcome, and your concern is heartwarming. Doctor said that there were signs of glaucoma. There's some distortion and things are cloudy at times. Everything is fine. , and I and my eyes are okay. What I wanted to discuss with you is that I'd like you to remain here as my assistant and help me pull together my memoir. Will you accept my offer?"

I pour her tea and a cup for me. Okay, get a grip. With the money I owe her, I can't believe what she said. "Did you just offer me a job and a future in living here?"

"Yes, I did."

"Mrs. McCutchen, I'm indebted to you so much for Mom's funeral. Your assistant, yes, I would love to help. How soon? I mean when do I start? You did say a future here with a mob, I mean job." Good, grief. Gibberish! Arabelle, you're making little sense in conveying your gratitude.

"Arabelle, slow down. Your words are like bumper cars playing with each other. Please listen. I want you to inhale, pucker your lips, and exhale slowly. Good girl, take a deep cleansing breath. Pucker and exhale."

The softness and repetition of her words have a calming effect on me and my thoughts. I relax and let go of the viselike grip I have on her hand. "I'm okay." My words come slowly. "Mrs. McCutchen . . . Thank you for Mom's funeral. I promise to repay every cent."

Her fingertips lift my chin. "Dear Arabelle, look at me. So very long ago when we were teenagers, your mother and I made a pinkie promise to watch each other's back. You have my word that agreement covers any debt you feel you owe me. Though, I must ask a favor of you."

What favor did they make to seal a teenage pinkie promise? Mom could never have held up her end. I begin to cry, and Katherine draws me closer.

"Arabelle, I'm sorry. I do understand because I loved your mother, too."

The control and calm appearance I showed at the funeral was gone. I pull away from her. At this moment, I try to stop crying, but it sinks in, I've lost a special part of me. Grief overwhelms me. To avoid crying, I bite my lower lip. It doesn't help with the tears. My breathing becomes labored as I run back from the terrace with her words trailing behind me.

"It will get better, Arabelle. It will. . ."

CHAPTER 3
FAMILY HISTORY

I avoided Mrs. McCutchen for the remainder of the day with small jobs, namely laundry, watering plants, arranging the linen closet. Until Clare asked me to dust the figurines and furniture in the sitting room since she was out of the manor.

Clare's timing is off. As I dust the desk, I pick up a notebook and pen when Mrs. McCutchen taps my shoulder. "Arabelle, I see you found your writing tools. I apologize if I upset you earlier today. I thought your mother told you about . . ."

I interrupt her. "Your story was a shock. Until we came here, I didn't know who you were, or the friendship Mom shared with you. Although, sometimes she talked about Katie Greene and her two sisters. Are you Katie?"

"Yes, I am the youngest. Miriam was the oldest and Annie. . ."

"Mom told me about a sad Mir Mir, who didn't have any children and that another sister, Annie had a baby and left home."

"Dear Dorothy, your mother, called us by our nicknames. Mir Mir was Miriam. When Annie left with her son, Anson, I wasn't born. However, on a happier note, we went to the same high school. On Fridays, Dottie came here and stayed until Monday. Then, we'd go to school together. She would go home during the week."

"Well, that explains why she'd said that she liked visiting Katie, I mean you."

"It was a fun time. Mother was the housekeeper then, and Pop was a traveling salesman for Adam McCutchen. Years later, when Miriam was older, Adam married her. They almost adopted, but she died before it happened."

Mrs. McCutchen stops to sip her tea. I'm glad because I scribble reminders onto the first page. Too bad, she didn't think to buy a tape recorder for me because longhand sucks.

She places the cup down, runs her fingers back through her short bob of brown hair, and rubs the back of her neck. "Arabelle, Miriam was nineteen when Adam asked Pop for her hand in marriage. At seventeen, they faced the world alone for many years. "Her thoughts seem to relate everything as if it happened yesterday. I laid my pen onto the notebook.

"How can you relate the details so clearly? Excuse me, Katherine, are you clairvoyant?"

"No. I was born in 1941. I could never get enough of family history and learned a lot from Clare and Mother's diary. Following her death, I found and read it over and over. Mother missed her grandson. She wrote the house was empty without Anne's son."

"You said Miriam married Adam?"

"They did. According to her diary, Miriam wanted a baby. Unfortunately, their twins were stillborn. Adam also wanted an heir. After six miscarriages, Miriam's health declined. Adam refused to adopt. Several months later, Miriam got pregnant."

"Well, that Adam sounds selfish. Adoption would be one way to have a family. Did they?"

"Yes and no. Mother didn't write anything about that. Clare, now a housekeeper, knew of a two-year-old foundling at the Erie County Orphanage. She convinced Adam and Miriam when you secretly adopt a child, then who would know outside these walls that he wasn't an heir. When Adam took in the toddler, as his ward. Adam changed Cameron's last name to McCutchen. In time, an arranged marriage contract was agreed between Adam and my mother. I sometimes refer to Cameron as Miriam's almost child. Later when we married, Adam's lineage would continue."

"How could Clare say that? There is no way the secret wouldn't leak out to someone." I said and leaned forward in my chair.

"During the 50's and 60's period, Adam considered my family and Clare as his chattel. Yes, all of us were his property. As chattel, we had no choice but to keep his secret. You need to understand. Anyone, who worked and lived here, eventually signed a privacy contract."

"Mrs. McCutchen, slavery was abolished. People don't own people."

"While that is true, Arabelle, in Adam's mind state, his idea of chattel meant control over everyone's lives while they lived here. Clare said that he had everyone sign an agreement to keep this arrangement a secret. The guarantee to them was that they'd have the right to live here until they died with burial in the estate cemetery. When I was sixteen, I became Cameron's betrothed."

"Huh! Katherine, you married your nephew? That's

not right."

"No, no. He never was.Cameron isn't even an adopted nephew."

Either I'm becoming confused or does she know more than what she is saying? "So what you are telling me, your husband is your half-not-blood nephew? Am I right?" Maybe Clare was correct. I shouldn't have asked.

Katherine walks to the turret window and pauses before she continues. "Not even that, Belle. One evening, Clare pinky swears me never to tell Cameron that Miriam died before the paperwork became official. So Adam decided not to adopt him."

"Don't understand Katherine, you have the McCutchen name?"

"In Adam's business and social circles, he didn't need a scandal. Cameron became his ward. Adam legally changed Cameron's last name with the provision Clare agreed to raise Cameron. Therefore, he is a McCutchen in name only and by marriage, so am I."

Katherine walks over and sits across from me. Uncomfortable with her stare, I remain silent and wait. Whatever she has to say must be important. The lines across her forehead are noticeable, and she rubs her hands back and forth.

"Would you like some more tea? I'll get it."

"No, it's not the family history or my memoir. Arabelle, there is a major problem in my life. Adam hid his last will. Recall I showed the riddle to you and your mother that first night you arrived."

"I remember. 'Neither high nor low, but within is your treasure.' Confusing but it is a riddle."

"Yes, it is. Only an attached codicil is our life saver.

Until we find his will, naming Adam's heirs, the estate, and all its business holdings remain intact, as if Adam is still living. For fourteen years, we've lived in a state of limbo. Would you help in our search?"

"I'd love to help Katherine. Did you keep any record of where you searched?"

"I didn't, but Clare has. Why?"

"My friend, Charlie Boyd, you met him. He was a pallbearer, and he is a good contractor. I'll call him to see if original house plans are available."

"How wonderful." She said and moved away from the sunlight. In the shadow, without makeup, she aged. Her face has a gray pallor. When her hand begins to shake, Katherine rests it on the desk, and a vacancy fills her eyes before she says, "Arabelle, years after Miriam died, I found her love for him was diminished because of letters, and suggestive photos, that Adam was a skirt-chasing womanizer."

"Katherine, how? I mean. Didn't you sign a contract?"

"Somehow, he forgot, and I didn't remind him. I thought little of the actions he'd take when I confronted him with flinging the evidence in his face." Her voice becomes hysterical when she cries out, "In front of Clare and Anson, my witnesses, I accused him of touching me inappropriately."

"Katherine, Katherine. Are you okay?" My mind is numb by what she said and equally amazed that Katherine appears unruffled by her confession. We say nothing, only look at each other. "Katherine, where do you keep the smelling salts. Just in case, you faint."

Katherine smiles and runs her finger along her lip. "I'm okay Arabelle. What was I saying?"

"Sort of jumbled . . . like something about your sister and Adam's follies." How calm she became after her outburst. Was there any truth to what she screamed or was it a release from something deep within her?

"Yes, I found out he was a shrewd businessman. In 1939, Adam's business and financial ventures abroad kept the estate solvent. While many suffered and were destroyed by it, the Depression did not bankrupt him."

"Is that why Neil isn't here, family business?" I forgot Clare's warning not to ask about Neil as he was none of my business. I try backpedaling by asking, "Any more pens?"

Katherine hands me another from a heart-shaped lead crystal vase on her desk. "Arabelle, I've given you a bit of history, and you jump several chapters to my son's activities. However, before Neil's birth, Adam traveled on business to California to inquire about a new communication idea. Adam's fortune didn't come from his family's company. He gambled on investing free and clear 'seed money' to associates when it included a future gainful purpose."

"I don't understand business matters," I said.

"When the company went public, Adam could purchase stock. He bought 30 percent of the H.P. preferred stock as a birth gift for Neil with Anson receiving one-third ownership so long as he handled Neil's future investments."

"And Neil doesn't mind?" I drop my pen and take another one to continue.

"Neil has no complaints. Today, he is traveling for other estate interests. Unfortunately, whatever shares or additional agreements exist, I believe they are with the will."

"Jeepers, Adam was a player and a gambler. All this seems surreal Mrs. McCutchen. Almost like when Mom told me that this house should have been your parents' because of squatters' rights and with everything else that happened."

I must have hit a nerve for Katherine rises and heads toward the turret. After two steps, she turns around. When she looks at me, our eyes lock, and I squirm in my chair. Don't understand. She crossed arms defensively. That's not a good sign. Say something; her face is getting red. "What's wrong?"

Katherine places her hand close to her throat and with great self-control said, "My parents were never squatters. They were servants. Adam paid fair wages plus gave free lodgings in the carriage house. He insisted the family live in the manor after Anne's son was born.

In Mother's journal, she wrote that the baby's hair was red and suspected Anson was Anne and Adam's love child. But, do understand. My parents were not squatters. Paid house servants—not squatters no matter what circumstances were."

"Sorry Katherine. I guess I misunderstood. Please forgive me. Do you want to continue?"

Katherine clears her throat as she walks away from me to the turret window. "I must dry clean those draperies one of these days. Sorry, I digress. Mother's diary had short sentences. From what I read, she indicated that Anne called. She found a job, 25 cents per hour, and has free use of company nursery. She sent Miriam, a wedding gift, a tiny plane like Howard Hughes' plane. It used to be on the mantelpiece. Mother wrote,

'Like Hughes; Anne disappeared.' Until 1952, it was Anne's last communication."

Katherine returns to the wingback chair and sits. Alone in her thoughts, she gently dabs at the tears covering her eyeliner. Then softly blows her nose before she continues. "In '52, Adam bought a vacation cottage in the Poconos. He called it 'No Name.' I was eleven and found most things in life dull. With little to do on a rainy day, cabin life is twice as tiresome. So I snooped everywhere for something to read or draw on. There it was. Our Anne's picture lined a dresser drawer. The obituary notice indicated a fourteen year-old son, Anson Redman, survives."

"Sorry about Anne's dying, but you found out your nephew is alive." I hope my words are a comfort.

"My parents didn't know for sure. Mother asked, and Adam hired a private investigator. Months later, I answered the front door. There stood a red-haired teenager. He held an envelope and baseball cap in his right hand. He asked for Mr. Adam McCutchen."

"Yippee, it was Anson. What was in the envelope?" I'm happy Anson is included in her memoir.

"I never knew because Mother sent me to my room. However, that day's entry indicated that he wouldn't say his name. Also, she wrote that she saw Anne's blue eyes and her smile coming through in this young man. My Mother ended the entry with the exact words he kept repeating, "I'm too young and can't fight the Koreans. Need to see Mr. McCutchen?"

"Since Anson is here, I presume all went well with Mr. McCutchen."

"Mother wrote Adam came out of the library after an

hour. With his hand on Anson's shoulder, he said, 'Feed your grandson, he's hungry.'"

Even if I lose my job here, I've got to tell her my impression of Anson's mistreatment. I stand to give greater emphasis. "Katherine, Anson's job here infuriates me. He lives above your cars. As a chauffeur, at any hour, he answers to everyone's beck and call. Pulls weeds and mows grass no matter what the weather. Not much future in that for someone, who's smart, explains things and doesn't treat me like I'm a child. And besides, I like him!" Good grief, I'm shouting.

"Arabelle, I can't talk to you when you're so upset. Let's try putting your temper on a slow simmer. Anson likes independence and chooses to live in the carriage house's apartment. Yes, he chauffeurs and tends to the grounds because he enjoys driving classic automobiles and is a horticulturist."

"I didn't know that." I lower my eyes and return to the chair.

"I totally agree he is smart, a necessary asset to be the chief financial officer that handles Neil's investments and manages the estate and company business here and with Neil, in Europe."

I'm embarrassed and try to apologize for my outburst in judging the situation so wrong. However, a light tap on the door interrupts our conversation. It's Clare.

"Excuse me, Katherine; it is a beautiful day. I could set a snack for you and Arabelle in the gazebo."

"How thoughtful Clare. Thank you. Be there in a few minutes. Arabelle is sweet tea with a lemon wedge okay?"

"Sounds delicious. Thank you, Clare."

Clare nods and exits the room as quietly as she

entered it.

"Arabelle, I'll join you in a minute or two. Have a matter I need to handle."

"Let's make it five. I'll meet you there." I'm glad for the welcome diversion away from McCutchen family history. Although it is only a short break outside, it is what I need to sort through all I've heard.

I join Katherine in the gazebo where a tray of cucumber sandwiches is between glasses of sweet tea. The gazebo's location offers a panoramic view of lavender, gold, plum, green, pink, and scarlet flowers that stretch across the lawn before us.

"I'm sorry for the outburst earlier but would you mind if I call you Katherine? You've shared so much with me."

"Of course, I wouldn't mind in the least."

"Thank you. I've learned so much family stuff. However, Clare is still a mystery. She is good at her job but acts as if she owns the place. Her attitude breaks all the rules of being a housekeeper."

Katherine smiles. She takes a deep breath and bows her head. "Lord, we thank you for your bounty and forgive us when we express our exuberance and mixed confusion. Amen."

I add my "Amen." And take a long drink of the cold tea.

Katherine leans forward and places her hand over mine. "I'm delighted you want to know more about Clare. After lunch, I'll tell you what I know."

We finish our meal and true to her word, Katherine begins. "Her last name is Collins and to me, she is much more than cook and housekeeper. She is like having an extra pair of hands."

"But she wants to know everything."

Katherine laughs. "You are correct. Personally, I don't think Adam anticipated the impact she would have on him and my family. Yes, Clare manages our lives to a degree and keeps household matters under control. In Mother's journal, she considered her a teenage miracle worker. Pregnant with me, she delegated Clare all the housekeeping chores. Also, she cared for Miriam, then pregnant and required complete bed rest."

"Okay Katherine, guess I'm not used to someone managing my life. Do you want to start another of life's chapters because I'm ready? Or, do you have something else in mind?"

"We stop for today, Arabelle. I forgot about a meeting. Anson waits for me by the carriage house. Enjoy your weekend and we will continue Monday. "Katherine pushes her chair back and departs.

"T.T.F.N. Katherine. "I take another sip and wonder about what I'd do with two and a half-days of pastoral life? See if Clare needs help. Nope, that means cleaning. Visit Decima but Anson has left. Take a fresh air nap, maybe later. Or, organize what I have before my head explodes. I gather pick up my writing supplies and return to the manor.

Strolling through the vestibule, I meet Clare dusting the foyer's console tables. She did the same thing yesterday and the day before. "Thanks, Clare, cucumber sandwiches made a fantastic lunch. I've some serious work ahead of me, so I think I'll skip dinner. Know where I'll find typing paper?"

Clare raises her eyes. "Glad you enjoyed them. In the library, push the letter 'P' on the wall. The false door opens, and there is your paper. Would you like tea later?"

"Sounds wonderful around seven. Clare, thank you for asking. Oh, I forgot to clean up outside."

"No problem," she says and continues dusting.

Inside the first-floor library, the walls display a scattered random pattern of sixteen inch square alphabet tiles. When I press the P block, the tile swings out. Within the wall recess is paper. Try again and press the letter T. Inside is a portable typewriter with an extra ribbon spool. Happy with the necessary tools, I quickly organize my notes. In a cozy section of the room, I begin. Initially, the words flow for the first draft. Then, my fingers lie on the keyboard. Her life story comes to a halt.

"Ahem!"

CHAPTER 4
HIDDEN SHELF

I turn to the doorway and watch. Clare balances her tray and avoids the wadded paper balls as if they are land mines waiting to explode. She makes her way to a reading table.

"I thought a full teapot would last longer. Under the napkin, you'll find a ham and cheese sandwich or a hot turkey sandwich. With your new floor covering, I might have to invest in Hammermill stock. Will you need Anson to buy more?"

"Only used one ream of paper, that hidden shelf held six. That contractor had an excellent idea to use the recessed wall space. After I found the typewriter, didn't look any further. Did anyone?"

Clare pours the cup of chamomile tea and says, "Haven't found any. How's it goin'? Did Katherine mention the invisible will?"

"Yes, she did. Hopefully, we'll find it soon. She has a big dream waiting for an answer. Katherine said you wrote down where everyone looked? If you do, may I have it? After those hidden alphabetical shelves, I thought where else could Adam hide paper to keep it from yellowing or becoming brittle. My former boyfriend knows blueprints, and I'm calling him for help. Did anyone locate any clue?"

"Arabelle, we searched for two years, four hours a day, and gave up after findin' the paper and typewriter. We can't figure what he was tryin' to tell us with his riddle. Katherine agrees with me. Anson, he laughed and said that the old man probably had clues all over just to help or confuse us."

With the first bite of the ham sandwich, I realize I am hungry. "Clare, this is delicious. Thank you. Didn't think I'd want to eat, but I'm ravenous. I'm glad you brought that second sandwich."

"You're welcome. One thing I know is that food for the stomach also feeds the brain. Keep typing. She's a good woman and from the completed stack, she shared family history. Well if you need more backstory on her, I got a few secrets to tell. Good evening Arabelle."

"See you tomorrow Clare. Once I get a feel how Katherine wants me to go with her story, I shouldn't be so messy." Hurray, she's on my side. Wonder what stories she'd tell about Neil, the scalawag.

After Clare leaves, between bites I reorganize the plot outline until inspiration strikes. Fingers fly across the keys, and ribbon must be changed before midnight. With a revised first draft in a neat pile, I stretch out on the comfy sofa and rest my eyes.

When I awake under an afghan, the lamp's light is on and gives off a soft glow for darkness outside closed the manor's eyes. I feel refreshed, and the wall clock indicates 3:10 a.m. Holy smokes. The floor is spic 'n' span; even the dishes are gone.

I peek around the doorway. A soft light spills out from

the sitting room. I presume Katherine hasn't been to bed. With her office door ajar. I knock. "Hello. Hello Katherine, are you in there?"

"Yes Belle, please come in."

I push the door inward and notice the existing furniture was rearranged. A new marble-top coffee table now stands between the wingback chairs. Katherine sits in one and leans over an ottoman that supports an album. She opens it and bookmarks a section.

"Happy Autumn Katherine. By the way, how did the meeting go?"

"A joyous equinox Belle. The town council meeting was a waste of my time and taxpayers' money, as they postponed my proposal for another month. They can't seem to understand the importance of a home for single mothers. Anson and I had a late meeting about your sleeping in the library. He thought you might awaken when he covered you. You didn't. He left and I did some reading. With my light on, Anson brought back fresh donuts. Join me. Coffee remains in the carafe, and glazed or filled donuts are on my desk."

"You are kidding. Katherine, how much coffee did you drink?"

"Not a drop Belle. He joined me, and everyone knows that Anson loves his caffeine. Sometimes I feel as if I should try it someday."

"Okay, when in Rome." I go to the desk and select a blueberry filled. "Love it."

Katherine claps her hands at my apparent enjoyment. "Belle, I reviewed your notes and saw where areas lack continuity in search measures. I believe with you and your friend's help; we will find the heir or heirs. The property deed, you'll see my name is on it. Granting that, I need to know who else has a share in the legal ownership. Then I can request a zoning change to remodel this museum to help girls, like my sister Anne, get a fresh start."

"Katherine, I haven't figured how to do more than one thing at a time. All right, I can chew gum and walk. So tell me, what comes first? Do I search, work on your memoir, or finish this donut?"

"By all means, finish eating. However, I heard you clicking away on my Underwood. I'm curious what you put together from yesterday's ramblings. Is there any chance for a rough draft before you contact Mr. Boyd; or must I wait?"

"Yes, there is. I left the draft in the library. I'll get it." Within a minute, I return and hand her a sheaf of papers. "Katherine, it was amazing how it happened. I had a terrible time making sense with my notes. After Clare's snack, I relaxed while drinking the tea. Suddenly everything became clear. I didn't want to stop. Sorry, I disturbed you. After midnight, I fell asleep. Didn't even hear anyone clean the room."

I collapse onto the other wingback. Katherine does a fast read, sits back, and taps her fingers on her chair's arm.

Come on. It's a bummer sitting here. Say something. Patience is not my virtue. "Well, Katherine? The suspense is killing me, not knowing what you're thinking."

"Okay for a first draft. Some information is missing. I need to give some thought as to what the memoir should encompass. However more important, I have to shed additional light regarding Clare."

I throw up my arms and let out an exasperated breath. “Katherine, you described Clare being street smart. She got the job for being outspoken and helping two women. I included that. I think she’s nearing fifty and has been the housekeeper like forever. Is she retiring or does she need more help? I give up Katherine. What do I add because it’s your memoir?

“Arabelle, add that Clare will stay here. Forever, if she chooses because of the extenuating circumstances. My sister, after the last miscarriage, slipped into a deep depression. Yes. Adam unequivocally needed Clare to be Miriam’s caregiver until she died. After my birth, Mother retired. Clare became the housekeeper and young Cameron’s governess. Only a few years older than Anson, she’d shield him from Adam’s lifestyle. She has become my confidant. My memoir includes her in the best light of friendship.”

“Okay, okay. I apologize. Before she died, didn’t Miriam ever consider having a surrogate mother?”

"Arabelle, Miriam's health was fragile; she was willing. Adam convinced her it was against God’s plan.”

“I’m sorry. Can’t believe I could be so wrong about Clare. Did your mother ever write about Clare and Anson being a couple?”

“Mother mentioned them in one sentence. ‘What a shame, Clare is older.’”

“Katherine, age difference is insignificant when love steps in. You know, she could have a chance with Anson, if. . .”

“If what? Having a friendlier relationship between them would be nice. Not necessarily for the memoir, but for them."

"Well, Clare's clothes scream 'the fifties.' With some awesome threads, maybe then Anson might change his viewpoint."

"Matchmaker Arabelle, I don't think fashionable clothes would alter his feelings. Clare keeps to herself and knows almost everything that happens in the place. She holds her tongue and he safeguards all family circumstances. I love them both.

After Adam's funeral with their insight and companionship, my life became easier managing the estate and business. Between us, my husband lacks any business sense. Cameron spends his share of company profits wherever and however he chooses. Remains away from the manor until he runs out of money."

"A share? Why would Adam make life so difficult by hiding his will?"

"Adam McCutchen was a control freak. He took great pleasure in confusing people by his actions. Why did he hide it? I have no idea.Without the will, it was decided yearly profits are divided. Only Cameron receives his portion monthly. Anson and I receive our percentage at year-end. Clare receives a monthly salary. Anson manages all other expenses through income from the company. wasI have a suspicion there are more clues than just that one, which I believe solving his riddle might be the last clue versus the first."

Katherine walks from the room. I hear her laughing and have no idea what is happening to incite such an outburst. I follow her into the library where she pulls a book from the shelf and with a trembling hand throws it across the room, missing a Japanese vase. With stooped shoulders, she looks exhausted. We walk together to a nearby settee and wait until Katherine gains control.

"While I'd prefer to forget the past, I cannot. That time, according to her diary, was horrible for Mother. She was pregnant with me, when Papa died. On a business trip for Adam, he had a heart attack. She wrote that she dealt with this with Clare's help in handling Adam's demands. The next entry was when I was three months. Cameron was now Adam's legal ward. Anne no longer lived here, so Adam advised Mother and Miriam that I would marry Cameron in the future with the hope of having a McCutchen heir. Instead he . . ."

I watch in horror. Katherine leans forward and grabs a smaller book off the coffee table. Her aim is better, and she knocks an Edwardian milk glass vase to the tiled floor. Hobnail shards scatter.

Calm and collected, Katherine says, "There. I feel better." She stands and wipes her hands back and forth as if abolishing an unpleasant memory. When her composure returns, she asks, "Do you mind my calling you Belle? With such confidences I'm sharing, Arabelle is too formal for me."

"No, problem, Katherine."

She takes hold of my hands and continues. "Belle, I'm confident my behavior looked bizarre to you. I should explain. Adam McCutchen believed he was reincarnated from the Edwardian age. Consequently, in matters of satisfying his carnal needs, in guaranteeing an heir, he treated my family and me like chattel. When it concerned me, I spent a lot of time in his bed." Her grip tightens, and I feel her manicured nails piercing into my palms. She releases me and begins to laugh.

"Good grief, Katherine. It isn't funny when anyone

treats people as their personal property, to do with whatever they want."

Katherine took my face between her hands."Life is funny, dear Belle. For my spring wedding, I wore white and your Mom had a long red dress. This one time I didn't share everything with her. She knew."

CHAPTER 5
CLARE AND ANSON

I calculate the nine months in my head. Spring wedding? Neil's birthday is in September. She was already pregnant. "Katherine, may I ask how old were you when you got married?"

"I wouldn't be eighteen for three months. During that time and under Adam's control, Cameron agreed to no premarital sex in exchange for a Mustang. Cameron was so naïve. He never suspected it was Adam's child and not his when Neil was born, seven months later. My son and I were very much Adam McCutchen's property, and his payment to me was my son bore the McCutchen name."

I'm speechless and shake my head at the atrocious act.

"Belle, I need someone with a fresh outlook. I'm confident we missed something. Would you help figure the riddle and help in the search? Our wits are exhausted in whatever 'security within' means. Therefore, the memoir is on hold until a legal heir is found. What do you say?"

I hug Katherine and say, "Yes. Yes, I'll search for Adam's will, but I need something from you. Please, Katherine, tell me how Mom ever fit in with your life here. Was she dating my father then? Did you ever meet him? "

"In school, your mother and I were opposites. Eventually, we became the best of friends. Your father was two years older and a free spirit. Met him once, thought he was okay. To your mother, he was so hot that he'd melt an ice block if he stood beside it."

"Mom said my Dad died early, but she didn't tell me much about him. So I'd love if you could share something about him. Did you go to their wedding?" "

"No. I believe they eloped. After a while, she didn't come over as often. Then one night, she dragged me into the library. Between sobs, she blurted, 'I'm pregnant Katherine.' I wasn't sure I did hear what she'd said between her crying and the cheering from the sitting room."

"Someone is cheering because my mother is pregnant? I don't find that amusing." I start to rise from the chair.

"Oh, Arabelle, I do apologize. They weren't cheering about her condition. It was the early newscast. A chimpanzee had gone into space. Think his name was Ham. Strange to think, how far space exploration has come?"

I stand and get right in her face. "Katherine, stop. What bearing does a space chimp have to do with Mom's pregnancy?"

"Nothing. Nothing at all, please I sometimes get distracted. My world view was moving at a crazy pace. In the sixties, people talked of electing a Catholic president or what side they'd choose in the Civil Rights Movement. That night, my best friend's news put my world into a tailspin."

"What about my dad?"

"Don't know much, not even his full name. I had my suspicions about him in school, but personally, knew very little about him. I saw him at an assembly. Cute with a babyface but was still rugged looking, a regular James Dean. Like the actor, he'd wear a decorated leather jacket and motorcycle boots. Your mother liked that look."

"Katherine, please get to the point. Was he my father?"

"Funny thing, she didn't say yes or no. She only told me that without insurance, she'd be a charity case. But, she knew that he would take care of everything. My thoughts immediately went from the high school, unemployed rebel to Adam McCutchen."

"Was he?" Chills race down my spine. What if it were Adam, would I be a bastard heir?

"I had my suspicions but didn't want to leave your mother crying. I insisted she stay. The following morning, I took advantage of her not being awake. Although I was afraid of what Adam might to do, I found him admiring his new well. I accused him of getting your mother pregnant. He slapped my face and pulled out his wallet. He emptied all his cash, waved it in my face, and said, 'Here, $200.00 will cover her abortion.'"

"He couldn't be my father. Mom told me he died." I thought Katherine knows nothing. "Dad's identity is hidden like Adam's will. Tell me, how do I find the truth?"

"Belle, I don't know. I gave your mother the money and she threw it to the floor. She began to leave but stopped at the doorway. I remember her exact words, 'Tell him money won't change what he did. I'll always love you, Kate.' Then, like my sister Anne, your mother dropped out of her life visiting here."

In disbelief of her story, I pace back and forth until I stop in front of her, "If she disappeared, Katherine, how did she? I mean how did we, you know, manage to come here? What miracle brought you two together again?"

Katherine places her index finger over my lips. "Let's go onto the terrace. I think some fresh air will help."

I follow behind and go out the library's outer, glass doors. The air is brisk, and I rub my arms. Katherine motions for me to sit alongside her in the shade. I go over and stand with the sun at my back.

"Through a mutual friend, I learned of Dorothy's heart problem and placed an ad for a companion. Our friend saw to it that your mother would read and answer it. I was delighted as we made all the arrangements over the phone. I knew, but she never divulged her health problems. Her dying, so soon, was unexpected."

I gasp. "That's not true; she would have told me."

Katherine stands beside me. "Arabelle, you didn't know how sick she was."

"Once I asked her why she was so tired all the time. Mom only said that she had aches and pains from being on her feet most of the time. Or, she'd tell me not to worry that it was only indigestion. Never said what her pills were for." Now I'm crying and experience Katherine comforting me.

"Belle, the night you arrived, and went upstairs, Dottie and I discussed her health and your future. Neither of us thought her death was on the horizon. However, we agreed on a plan in the event she died before you married. Our primary objective was to assure you would have a safe place to live until you left on your own."

"Would you mind if we go back inside? I'm not dressed

for the cold air."

"Yes, I agree. Warmth is a priority."

We hurry along the short walk back toward the kitchen, where the smell of warming chocolate is welcomed.

"Clare, thank you. You anticipate our needs. However, this not a trick but a treat. I called the Galleria Outlet Mall. They are open late this evening. I also authorized either of you with identification to use my American Express. Clare, you are to get a new outfit, something cool and trendy. It's time for serious shopping and Arabelle, your job is to assist in coordinating her new look. Clare, I want no objections from you. Go change, I'll call for a cab because Anson had some plans while you girls have fun. Belle, here is enough cash for cab fare and a sweet treat."

Five hours later we return. To our surprise, we see Katherine pouring herself a cup of coffee. I get Anson to help with the boxes. He returns with packages under his arms and dangling from his fingertips and takes everything into Clare's adjoining bedroom. He returns to the kitchen and Clare closes her bedroom door.

Katherine tries to say something when Anson stops her with a finger to his lips and motions for her to sit. I wait beside her room for the prearranged signal to start the unveiling of Clare's new wardrobe.

Minutes later I hear a weak 'okay.' I extend my arm with a grand flourish and announce, "Ta da lady and gentleman. On the catwalk, I present Miss Clare Collins."

Clare is only a few feet from the doorway when a small whistle from Anson stops her. She gives him a big smile and resumes her walk.

I begin, "Notice how the vibrant colors of a fitted

gypsy top take your eyes down to the willowy skirt that accentuates her slender waistline. Her festive Cuban wedged pumps and the gold lame purse add the perfect touch for an evening out."

Clare adjusts the thin purse chain on her shoulder; and with a bit of boldness, twirls in front of Anson, flaring out her embroidered skirt. Katherine applauds and I give a wide-angle look at Clare and Anson. He gives a long whistle when Clare does another mini-twirl as she turns from him. His gaze follows her off-the-shoulder blouse to her dainty feet gliding across the kitchen's walkway.

In a surprise move, Anson is on his feet and dances her around the room. She laughs and follows his lead. They dance to a tune known only to them.

"Anson, I didn't know you still remember our first dance. Will the memory of that night be repeated?"

"Possibility, Clare. Shall we finish the dance?"

Katherine and I exchange glances and leave in opposite directions. Once in my room, I kneel beside my window and look upward. "Mom, if you're listening, lMife isn't what I expected, but it will be interesting when I find that will. Life is good."

Late autumn in western New York State brought October's gusts of cold weather and the spectacular display of fall foliage. For the past week I tied up loose ends in Katherine's story and today, I officially place her memoirs on a back burner behind the library's letter 'M'.

Afterward, I return to the kitchen and find Katherine and Clare waiting for me. In unison, I hear, "Good luck. Let your hunt begin."

I take a bow and leave the kitchen amidst a blending of handclapping. As I make my way to the gathering room, I think about Adam's logic in hiding. From their earlier searches, I eliminate the obvious findings. Now is the time to separate me from thinking about the hiding spaces and begin sorting the records Charlie brought over yesterday.

Except for Adam's obtrusive, black mural jutting into the room, the room's lighting and ambiance quickly relax me. In a half-hour, I separate the earliest original prints with any duplicates over several tables. Here and there a dotted line sets one blueprint apart from a previous copy and dates are highlighted. This doesn't make sense unless the room size changes and makes allowance for a hidden site. I call Charlie.His phone line is busy, so I can't leave a message. My last resort is to show Anson if he returned home.

The upper apartment's light is on. I walk upstairs and knock. "Hi Anson, thanks for coming down, these prints are confusing. I thought you might understand the squiggly lines."

"Miss Belle, I promised I'd be your backup in uncovering Adam's will. Let's inform the others; the search is back on track. If only, we had the original plans."

I agreed and called Charlie, hoping he can be of help. "Hi, it's me, Belle. Need a favor. Would you be able to get copies of the manor's earliest drawings, permits from the 1800's up to those you brought me? If there's any cost, Katherine will cover it and I'll prepare you a home cooked meal." -- "Yes, from me." -- "Great! I'll see you the day after tomorrow around lunch. Appreciate your help. Later

Charlie."

Later with Anson's help, we concentrate on what's been done before going any further.

"I find Clare's notes lack detail and uniformity in her search methods. Concerning the library, she wrote, 'Finger tapping done only on painted walls of the first-floor library resulted in a riddle and some legal document behind a wall letter. Swept under large pieces of furniture on two floors removed dust bunnies.'

"Anson, a legal document."

"That was the codicil and wasn't attached to any will. It allowed the estate and company to function as if Adam is alive."

"After so many years and no further clues, I think everyone relies on the codicil to keep matters continuing. Can't blame anyone's enthusiasm fading. Guess a second inspection wouldn't hurt. I could start in the library."

"Well, I started with this box from the basement. Clare's note indicated it contained t nothing but miscellaneous paperwork. I went through and found paid receipts and yellowed prints for the carriage house's construction. Used your grid and checked off the basement with the current date and description of what I found."

"I know how busy you are with the gardens, and if you don't mind, I'd like to have an outsider give an opinion."

"That would help. Someone, I know?"

"Before Adam's will comes into Katherine's hands, I decided we need someone, who thinks outside the norm.You know, like a secondary sidekick, as our eyes and ears for deductive logic, and that would be a former boyfriend, Charlie Boyd."

"Yes, the young man from the funeral. Excellent. With that info, I'll get you a step ladder for the library search and then onto my plants."

ꕥꕥꕥ

Until Charlie calls or shows up with the results, I create graphs and charts for the three limited areas previously searched or marked for future inspection. When his call comes, I agree to meet him at Denny's.

Inside the restaurant, in a back corner booth, I recognize his ash blond cowlick and walk to the rear. He sees me and smiles. I can't help but wish we never broke up. I sigh looking at his blue eyes. His sexy, long eyelashes cause a whispered meow to escape, and I must stay focused because puppy love belongs to children. I wave. He nods.

"Hi Charlie, find anything?"

"Nothing unusual Belle, with drawings and plans. There is one document that has cryptic notes in the margins. I got the impression Anson is a good man to have on your side. Have him look. There might be some history on what the jottings mean. Sorry, I can't stay. Have a job. How's your schedule for Thursday lunch or dinner?"

"Hey, lunch or dinner works for me and thanks for the documents. Cost?"

He shakes his head. "Consider it your tip for dinner."

"Can you make it around one o'clock at the manor? Or, would six be better for you?"

"Thursday, one o'clock at the manor, is fine. I'm there. Hope you'll excuse me. I must leave."

I nod my head. Charlie tips his baseball cap and goes. I gather everything he brought and left the restaurant.

Should have known, I'm nothing more than another job contact. It's obvious where I fit into his life. What was, is no more. The past is the past.

Back at the manor, I spread out copies of faded drawings against similar room prints. Tiny changes from the original are highlighted. Before tomorrow's search, I note the differences because I'll need help to measure the rooms. As I consider today's possibilities, Katherine's voice comes over the intercom.

"Arabelle, there's a meeting in my sitting room tonight. Please be here before 7:30. Thank you."

CHAPTER 6
ADJUST AND ACCOMMODATE

At 7:30 p.m., Katherine, wearing a purple ribbon sash, walks into the room. It can only mean one thing. Katherine has accepted some project.

"Exciting news, I was voted the Autumn Fest's chairwoman. If you think the position will overburden my typical schedule, you are right. Considered my options and knew it was possible if all of you will help me in whatever capacity during my reign."

She's out of her freaking mind. When will she consider what is important, finding Adam's will or delivering handbills for the festival? "Excuse me. Don't mean to be rude Katherine, but what about Adam's will? Think of the lost hours and tell me how do I schedule 'search time' if I'm volunteering so you'll have another ribbon?"

Clare steps forward. I look, and her icy glare generates disapproval at what I said.

"Arabelle, while everyone's search is necessary, it can be done as you find the time. This chair magnifies the network I'd need for a future dream. Remember, to grow in wisdom; we learn to adjust and accommodate others. Tonight with a clear vision, I'm certain this team will successfully meet whatever issues or challenges may be ahead of us."

"Okay Katherine, I'm on board." I do my best to smile, but it's hard when I don't understand her.

"Meeting adjourned."

ꙮꙮꙮ

For two weeks, I feel as if Clare glued roller skates to my feet and sewed on an extra pair of hands. I learn to blanch and freeze, preserve by hot or cold, and make freezer jam. However, I receive good news today. After breakfast, I'm free to continue the search and return to the gathering room. To my dismay, Clare blocks the doorway.

"Change in plans, Arabelle." She hands me gardening gloves and rubber boots. "Anson needs help. You'll be workin' in the gardens. You're already late, so hurry."

"I don't think so. Anson's gardens are in full bloom."

"Don't argue. Change. Take him the thermos and cinnamon buns. That'll put him in a good mood."

Instead of changing, I slip on Clare's coveralls from the utility room and the boots fit over my shoes. Dressed in minutes, I go outside, and see Anson is mid-garden. He waves a bushel basket in the air. I wave the thermos and hope he's not expecting too much from me.

When I arrive at the gazebo, Anson leans over a poster board covered with scattered colored squares, triangles, and circles. He smiles. "I see Clare dressed you for work."

"Oh, these, something I threw on. Besides the coffee and buns, Clare sends you her hugs and kisses. Oops, I mean, she sent a snack pack. What's with the colored shapes?"

Pointing to a green rectangle, he said, "This represents my greenhouse, and the others cover my garden plan. If I replant the gardens with these ideas, next year's roses would still be in bloom for the Fest."

"Wow! That's some presentation. Not sure how a weaved basket fits in with my helping you."

"In a minute." Anson takes two bites of the roll and washes it down with a quick swallow of coffee. "Okay assistant, choose either rose bushes or our tender gladiola bulbs. We'll plant them in another area next spring. Not sure if I'm replanting the hardy ones this fall."

I circle the pointed trowel high above my head. "Look out fragile flower source, I'm on a mission." I stop at the first drooping plant and dig up a precious bulb.

Hours later, the sun is lower in the sky, and I ease into an upright position. Twisting side-to-side to relax, I view more of the estate's landscape and acknowledge Anson's love of gardening. Dwarf conifers and ground juniper surround the Victorian manor. A beautiful backdrop for the remaining chrysanthemums. Beyond the gazebo is a trampled path. It extends from the cemetery through high grass to a small building.

"Anson! Hey, Anson!"

"Be there in a minute Miss Belle." He comes beside me and offers the last garden rose.

"Thank you. However, I have a question. See behind that high grass, is that a kid's playhouse?"

"Belle, you are curious, and that grass is called feather reed. A first-rate ornamental, it adds to the hideaway mystery of Neil's guest house. Its best feature is the wraparound porch. From any side, there's a magnificent view of McCutchen's stately mansion."

"Here, I filled it. Would you take the basket back and tell Clare I'm on a break? I'd like to take a closer look at this guest house."

"Sure." He says and from his hip pocket, he tosses me a worn rag. "Here, you may need this. Windows weren't cleaned in the past two years. Enjoy your exploring." He lifts the basket onto his shoulder and heads to the back porch.

I turn and race to the pathway and the bungalow. Anson was correct. The wrap-around porch creates several sites from sunrise to sunset for you to enjoy the estate grounds. Several hours pass with tiptoe viewing through semi-smudged windows. My inspection reveals a wonderful possibility. Come spring; it's mine. But how do I get Katherine to agree?

The sun sets on the treetops while I stroll back. I have to think of a plan on how to change my physical address. Within fifteen feet of the kitchen's open window, I freeze. Words, like bullets, ricochet out the raised window onto the porch. I move closer until Anson's shouting drowns out Clare's ramblings.

Off to the side and out of sight, I wonder what caused such a ruckus?

"You—you get under my skin, Clare. Always has to be your way or not at all."

"Not so Anson. I once thought you were so handsome, someone who lived and loved adventure but . . ."

"But what Clare?"

"Nowadays, I see a couch potato. Anson, once you made my blood boil."

Anson protests, "If I remember correctly, it wasn't that long ago."

As if defending herself to a jury, Clare's voice becomes deafening. "Don't change the subject. For instance, when I have to find you, I do. However, you're either drinkin' coffee or makin' pictures for some flower ideas. Those ideas will never happen unless you can convince her and you won't. Your ideas will blow away with the next wind because you do nothin' else to make things better around here."

All becomes quiet. I creep closer until an explosive scene plays out on the back porch before my eyes. I hide behind a large larch tree, a perfect location. Jeepers, he's shirtless and why is Clare attacking him with the kitchen shears?

Anson sidesteps Clare's unorthodox assault. His shirt protects his left arm while she waves her scissors under his nose and blocks his entry into the house.

"Woman, be reasonable. Put down that weapon and let me inside." He backs away when a red-faced Clare lunges forward and attacks. She shoves Anson out of her way and goes to hanging the herb basket. There she mutilates the unsuspecting oregano plant.

Anson takes the opportunity to go back inside but stops and turns around. Free of Clare's onslaught, I watch in horror when an angry Anson stomps his way over and kicks the bushel basket into the air and off the porch. Gladioli bulbs take flight or roll on the porch and steps. With a final well-placed punt, Anson's shoe connects with one that flies over my head. Their actions frighten me. Which one is becoming unstable?

Anson opens and slams the back door shut. "Bang!"

Then he opens the door, goes inside, and slams it again. "Bang!"

In protest, Clare waves the shears at him. With Anson out of sight, she appears calm. The worst is over. I'm glad the scattered bulbs are safe.

As if threatened by the floor's mess, she tramples every bulb in her way across the porch deck. Her shoe soles slide along the porch. Before she slips, Clare enters the kitchen. "Bang!" The door slams behind her.

I'm shocked when I tiptoe to the open window for a better look. Anson's fist is raised. Is he going to hit her? Or, is she going to use that frying pan she's holding? I watch as he puts his fist into the wall.

"Ow! That hurt. You know Clare, after finishing what I have to accomplish, I quit and rest. And you, will you stop poking me in the chest and lay down that pan. You could hurt somebody with it. Here and now, what exactly do you mean 'do nothin' else?'"

Clare lays the pan onto the counter. "I admit it. When you say you've work to do, you do. But, I made a mistake a long time ago."

My feet hurt after standing for so long on tiptoes. Therefore, I crouch beneath the window to relax. Now that Anson's voice sounds normal, I struggle to hear what they are saying.

"Can you be more precise? Speak up Clare, not like the unreasonable woman, who probably half the county heard. Don't preach to me. Talk? I'm listening, that is anytime you're ready."

Clare's voice has a tenderness when she says, "When we first met, you were a child, independent and so boyishly handsome. I felt you saw right through me. Like a man-child, you acted as if you were 19. That's not what I meant to say. I need your help to clean his place. Arabelle can't turn that mattress. Your muscles will. I got to make sure the bungalow is clean before he gets here. Anson, please help."

"Simply ask, Clare. Don't need to cut off my nose. After all, it's been ten years since I flipped your mattress. Remember my 18th birthday?"

There's no more screaming. Guess she liked him once upon a time.

"Anson, I do remember. What I can't recall is who kissed who first, and all of a sudden we were all over each other."

Whoa! I back away from my spot.

"Clare, when I saw your smile, I knew you were the one. That day, it and your birthday kiss signaled a green light to go for it."

"Wasn't right, Anson. Older than you, I should have known better."

"Clare, for me, there was no age difference when I held you so near. But a boy—nearing manhood, never knows if he's in love until he rests with her. When you pulled away from me, a polar ice cap settled on what I felt and everything changed between us."

What is happening? It's too quiet. I steal a look and see them embrace. To give them privacy, I do a hasty retreat to the gazebo and watch the sunset.

When I look over my shoulder, I'm surprised to find a fully-dressed Anson running toward me.

"Hi there," I shout.

Without a word, Anson grasps my hand and pulls me along with him. I'm panting when we arrive at the bungalow. Before I'm able to talk, he unlocks the door, flips the mattress in two directions, and hands me a key.

"All right Miss Belle, the rest is up to you. Think you can handle it?"

I do my best to act dumb. "I'm bewildered Anson, like what did you have in mind? There is no electricity."

"Miss Belle!" Anson stops. "Look, Arabelle, Clare wants the bungalow clean for Neil or his guest. Me? I finished my work here; but, I'd like to pass along a piece of good advice before you meet him anytime in the near future. Be yourself, and you'll have a husband within the year."

"Ha! Your advice poses a major problem; I don't want a husband."

"That's my advice. You do with it as you see fit."

I realize Anson means well and change the subject before he leaves. "Does Clare always make you so volatile or am I too nosey?"

At the doorway, Anson hesitates, turns back, and confesses. "Once I made a fool of myself. Guessed she wore a size four shoe, tiny feet in comparison to my size 11, double EE. I thought she'd be dainty and demure. I was wrong. A spitfire, whose look could set off a sparkler. This evening is another story. Learn from me. With Clare, you don't get too close, or you use asbestos gloves so that you won't get burned."

"Anson, maybe you haven't noticed. Her temper loses its edge when she gives you the sweetest smile behind your back. Who knows if she is warming up to melt the ice?"

"I did my job. See you in a few hours." Anson jumps off the porch and soon disappears behind the gazebo.

If I failed again at being a matchmaker, what are my chances of locating Adam's will or finding my father's the true identity? I go outside and get the garbage can. For without electricity, that is all I can do. After two years, the place needs a serious cleaning. With an overcast sky, I race back to the manor hoping I might locate the will here in the bungalow in the daylight hours.

Once the sun rises, I dress and go to the bungalow. Although I worked an hour and a half sweeping, dusting, and doing the windows last, no will was found. I lock the bungalow's door and hear a thunder clap. The sky remains overcast; and today, there are lightning flashes in the distance. I hurry back for a shower because I reek of ammonia. Once in my room, a hot shower and repeated yawns override thoughts of breakfast. I lie down.

The sound of a car's backfire disturbs my sleep. I open my window and lean far over the sill until I notice Anson give a man-hug to a hulk.

"With all these females around, Anson, I see that you still survive. One matter before I go, I need to discuss Hewlett's stock situation."

"Sure Neil, the report's done and ready for review. Come inside and join me in a house overflowing with estrogen. As to how I survive, that is another story."

Both men laugh heartily and go onto the porch. I start to back up when I hear Clare's voice. Instead, I lean out and listen.

"Welcome home, Neil."

"Clare, my love, care to share your thoughts about Mother's companion? According to her, this teenager is a cherub with a slightly tipped halo. What's up?"

"Neil, our Arabelle is hardly a cherub. Some call her a ball of energy with a happy-go-lucky outlook on life. Some say she's a mite curious. Belle took to hard work and tried my recipes. Unfortunately, can't even boil water without burnin' the pot. So, my job's safe."

Anson's voice comes to my defense. "Clare, you exaggerate. Maybe, she chars the kettle black but doesn't burn water. Personally, I find her to be an independent thinker. Neil, the truth is that she'll astound you in pigtails and jeans and have you whistle when she wears high fashion and leather boots."

"Humph sounds as if she fools everyone. If not, she's a stylish tomboy, relishing life; or, a modern day angel with spunk to keep you all on your toes. So where do you hide this self-reliant teenybopper?"

Clare's laugh answers Neil's question. "She must have finished cleanin' because there isn't a light on in your bungalow. She's most likely in her room, and I'm preparin' your welcome home dinner."

"Meatloaf?"

"No, a roast."

I hear footsteps cross the porch and the door close. I climb back inside and close the window.

Before I dress, I wash my face and hear someone calling my name.

"Miss Lacey, if you're there, come downstairs."

It's not Anson. Neil's? If it is, I'm shocked that he'd be so bold to enter my bedroom. I shut off the water and dry my face. Using the door as a shield, I take a glimpse and no one is there. "Excuse me, where are you? Never mind, I'm coming down." I cinch the bathrobe with a double knot. Then change my mind.

CHAPTER 7
NEIL MCCUTCHEN

Wearing a 'Go Bill' t-shirt and a pair of cut-off jeans, I finger comb my hair and race to the kitchen. Running much too fast on the stairwell, I'm stopped short at the bottom when I bounce off a man's chest into outspread arms. His dark brown hair is cut short to control a natural curl.

I do my best to avoid his noticing me giving him the once over. When our eyes meet, we exchange smiles. As he moves to the side, Clare stands in the background. With arms across her chest, she scowls until Neil turns toward her. Then, Clare smiles and comes forward. "Arabelle Lacey meet Neil McCutchen."

"Sorry, guess I exceeded the stairwell's speed limit. Mr. McCutchen, it's my pleasure meeting you. Let me shake your hand."

He surprises me when he kisses both my cheeks. A bit European, but who cares?

"Miss Lacey, on real authority I heard you were responsible for cleaning the bungalow. I'm very particular about my guest house. Without electricity, would you join me for a flashlight inspection? Or because you're wearing slippers, would you prefer it during the day?"

"No reason to fear a night walk, is there?" I say but wonder how his closeness can be so unsettling. It must be his patronizing manner that bugs me.

Neil shakes his head and goes to the back door where Anson waits with garden boots, a poncho, and his lantern. "No reason at all Miss Lacey. I'm ready whenever you are."

Anson leans over to assist me with the boots. "Clare thought a comb and these might help. There is very little moonlight and it looks like rain."

I turn my head and look over at Clare to mouth a silent thank you. She smiles back. I can't figure her out, but with Clare, I'll enjoy the good when it comes.

As I step over the threshold, lightning streaks across the skyline. "Well? Come on." I say and give Neil a side glance. "I don't plan on getting wet from an incoming cloud burst." With the poncho hood up, I take the lead and jog down the path toward the bungalow. I wonder if Neil suspects it was me, who spooked him the last time he visited.

With his long strides, Neil soon passes me as he walks backward and waves his goodbye.

What a showoff. He's so into himself that he doesn't see the tree root. I jump to the side to avoid his falling on me.

"Enjoy your trip?" I ask.

He laughs and says, "Yes. I was hoping you'd join me." While Neil struggles to free himself from the rain-soaked undergrowth, I run faster. Ten more feet and I'll be home free.

From behind, I hear, "Slow down Miss Lacey. It's not a race. Give a guy a break."

I pause to listen, and Neil surges ahead. He's on the porch and performs the wackiest dance I've ever seen. "Not a race, eh? Do you usually suffer from convulsions when you lie?"

"No, I like to win. The wraparound was my idea. After the contractor finished the porch, I'd come here to watch sunsets."

"You're right about the porch. It's perfect. I feel at home when I'm here. Only with three doors and a wraparound porch, maybe hide and seek, with side bets, could be promising."

Neil's laughter mocks me. "Miss Lacey, childhood games? How interesting. Thought you'd be a 'twenty question' game player. Say, questions about me?"

Clare told him. I ignore Neil and walk around the porch. As he follows me, his shoes slap against the soaked wood boards. A gust of wind whips water from a tall bush into my face. I turn and feel his hand against the small of my back and his arm holds me fast. Geez, I wanted his arms around me but not this way. Angry, I slap his face. "Mr. McCutchen, how dare you? Whatever were you thinking?"

"Turn around," he said.

Out of the corner of my eye, I see the shutter swing back and forth. With the wind, it hits against the bungalow, where I once stood. "Oh, sorry," I mutter.

"Not even a thank you, Miss Lacey. Lucky I grabbed you away in time before it smacked you." Neil releases his hold.

"No thanks when it's your fault," I snap back, "if it weren't for your inspection, I'd be safe and dry. Shutters come loose now and then. See you just push up, and it slips on." Gusting winds push and pull against my efforts and prevent me from lifting it high enough.

Neil stands directly behind me. "Shutters are made to withstand our weather. Therefore, if you won't chew me up and spit me out, allow me to help. If you would hold it steady from the bottom, I'll lift."

The unexpected pressure of his six-foot body against my back makes my breath come up short. He presses forward and lifts the shutter above my head. The wind gusts require our combined strengths to complete the task. Our breathing becomes labored and I see my breath in the chilling, night air.

"Good job. That's it, move to your right."

Occasionally I feel his warm breath come down against the back of my neck. This and his closeness triggers an unfamiliar excitement within me. Unlike, the nausea experienced when C.J. took his photos. I move forward a step. It allows a breathable space away from him because my emotions are unlike those when Charlie and I necked.

"Hey Lacey, quit moving. Hold it steady. Good girl, just a minute more. There, it's locked onto the porch. Well done, Miss Lacey."

"Any time Mr. McCutchen. If you don't mind backing up, we should go inside where it's dry."

With the shutter secure, he backs slightly away from me. I take a small side step to the left. I now inch my way to the door handle. He mimics my movement. Maybe, he's suspicious or is he playing cat and mouse? Come on, get yourself out of this predicament.

Without warning, Neil's chin rests on my shoulder. His head is cocked and near mine. His Chaps cologne has my heart beat faster. I should be in a state of panic when he nibbles my earlobe. But I'm not. The pleasure it brings is electrifying until he whispers, "Ever see a grown man tripping over furniture in the dark?"

When he reaches around my left arm, I'm immobile until Neil opens the living room's front door. As the door swings inward, the outgoing smell of ammonia gags me.

"Ah! I presume the cleaning essence remains. Next time Lacey, try vinegar and water. Would make it easier to breath afterwards; now before you throw up, tell me. Could you picture me making a fool of myself?"

He knows and I need time. Over there away from the doorway, the porch swing would give space between us. I need to think. I stagger a bit until I rest on the metal seat.

He says nothing more. With hands in his pockets, he stood there and shook his head as the rain stopped. I'm shivering under Clare's poncho and remove it because it's beginning to stick to my skin. I find the night air refreshing, until the wind shifts direction. The nearby branches shower me with the earlier rainfall. The wind blows strands of hair into my face and goosebumps appear when Neil comes closer.

"Great, now I'm sopping wet. Can this evening get any worse? "I look at him, and he's removing his shirt. I wonder. What does he think he's doing?

"Uh, hum." He clears his throat then laughs. "Young lady, your hair looks as if somebody dropped a bowl of marinara sauce over your head. Sorry, I don't have a towel. Want a shirt to dry off?"

"Kindness, Mr. McCutchen, or do you have an ulterior motive in mind?" Better be careful. Flirting can be dangerous if I believe Anson's warning.

Before putting his shirt around my shoulders, he winks. "Hardly Miss Lacey. Only a gentleman that comes to the aid of a lovely young lady. Who, I presume, might be cold."

A wink and now a mischievous smile, it's no wonder Clare called him a scalawag. "Thank you," I say and close the shirt around me, but I can't stop shivering. "Hey, how about some help. I'll open the kitchen's side door. Maybe you'd get us some cross ventilation from the rear door?"

"Makes sense, Lacey."

As he walks away, I notice his swagger and broad shoulders. My eyes linger on his buns, and I sigh. Maybe Anson had a point if I were interested in a mate. However, from the panties I found while cleaning, I wonder. Would Neil make a faithful husband? I open my door and go back to the porch swing until the inside air becomes breathable.

When Neil returns, he sits down on the top step with his back against a column. He doesn't move much while scanning the twilight sky.

"North Star. Look over there, ten o'clock high. Find it and make a wish."

It's not a star, too early. He's like a little kid, so I'll amuse him. "Star Bright, Star Light . . ."

Neil turns and smiles broadly. Dimples are his trademark. Rising, he extends his hand and gestures for me to enter the bungalow. I follow his lead until he becomes a physical obstruction to my crossing over the doorstep into the living room.

"I agree. It's warmer inside than outside. Now I insist you answer my question."

"Mr. McCutchen, I'd love to slug you for blocking my way. Although I wouldn't be a lady, if I did. So I'll take it down a notch. I'd like to go inside because that kitchen is the size of our apartment and without heat, this porch is colder. You may not believe this, but please, I'm freezing."

"You don't say. However, I insist. Could you picture me making a fool of myself?"

He's not joking so how do I answer him. Remember inside is warmer. "Yes, I could because you are doing it so well, now." Without a second thought, I push him out of the way and go inside to find the flashlight in the cupboard drawer.

I forgot this is his place, and he is familiar enough to remove an oil lamp from below the kitchen sink. When he lights it, I maneuver around him to raise a nearby iridescent glass vase to catch the lamp's light.

Staring deep into the light, I murmur, "Oh Jinn of magical rays, come forth and answer my questions." I respond with a cracking voice, "Acts old but not a man. Not a homebody, but a nomad. Foolhardy, he walks but does not look."

I turn around to keep the vase within the lamp's glow. I mumble under my breath until the voice utters, "Curiosity reveals a dark secret." I backup two small steps. "Ah yes, darkened room, a presence stumbles, chair falls, a giggle. Jinn's light fades."

Neil comes over and stands before me. He gently slides his hands from my shoulders down the length of my arms until his hands join mine. Neil takes the vase and asks, "Okay Jinn, tell me does the young girl know love?"

He kisses the nape of my neck and returns the vase. I must stay focused for his kiss excites me. I force myself to continue, "Jinn sees, one who seeks lasting love . . ."

Neil interrupts, "What about the man?"

"Pampered child, envied by peers, many female followers. Jinn's eyes grow dark."

Neil kisses my forehead. Because he backs away, I'm confused and place the vase on the table. He turns the lamp off. It takes me several moments to get accustomed to the semi-darkness. I stretch out my hand to touch him to get my bearing.

He moves and calls out, "Marco!"

After several steps, I bump into him, and a nervous giggle follows, "Polo."

"So it was you, Arabelle, in the kitchen when I. Oh shit, you know the rest. I believe additional illumination will eliminate a repeat performance." Neil moves out of sight and lights the oil lamp.

"Mr. McCutchen, I plead the Fifth, wouldn't want to incriminate myself."

There is enough light to see Neil pull out a chair and sit down. "Pleading the Fifth wasn't necessary. You are a young adult, who giggles and mother's employee. I'm interested. Tell me more of your thoughts."

He wants more. Here's my chance, because he does look interested. I sit across from him. "Well first that is before your recent arrival, Clare recruits Anson and me. After your two-year absence, we are to arrange furniture and clean the bungalow for your possible stay. Note, Mr. McCutchen, I said 'possible stay' because a firefly's light stays on longer than you stay home."

"You do me an injustice, Miss Lacey. Though, I am curious. What do you think about my guest house?"

"I admit, cleaning it was a job. In my opinion, the

kitchen's size is adequate. You have outdated appliances. Ice boxes and coal stoves are not in style. Interior walls require two coats of paint. The bedroom is so small even two elves couldn't sleep there. And that goes for the bathroom, too. Not sleeping, of course. Update your electricity. Burn the hide-a-bed. It sags, smells, and springs poke out. Only if a million pillows are covering it, I might allow you to keep it for viewing purposes only."

An amused look on Neil's face is enough for me to continue.

"Before I resume on what is necessary to have this bungalow acceptable for me to move into it, allow me to talk about a personal matter."

Neil nods and leans back in his chair. "Miss Lacey, there could be no explanation to say your request is most unusual. However, I am interested in what you have to say. Go right ahead."

"Thank you, Mr. McCutchen. Regarding your last visit, your departure was the meringue on Clare's lemon pie baked several hours before you arrived and disappeared several hours later. Your quick departure left Katherine depressed for several days. That was cruel to dash her hopes on your last visit. I lost my mother. You have yours."

"I did say to go ahead. However foremost, my Mother understands that I leave when I must. Second, don't interrupt me. Third, as her employee, her emotions should have no bearing on yours." Neil stands to leave.

I rose from my chair, went to his side and didn't know where my courage came. I started poking him in the chest, as I'd seen Clare do to Anson. "Hey! Sit down. Your leaving bothered me."

"That's promising. I'll stay. Please go on."

With Neil sitting, I notice his neck has a rising pinkness. I stand to face him and continue, "Not promising that way. You wouldn't understand. You're never here or only hear that the hunt continues for Adam's will. Outside the addendum, nothing bothers your life, as if Katherine couldn't use some of your moral support. For your information, Anson flipped the mattress; and first, I cleaned the bungalow. All trash, including a lace undergarment, found behind the dresser's secret panel, was thrown out. Although Mr. McCutchen, you lay claim for the porch design, and the residents here say this building is yours, I doubt it." I come closer and place my hand on his shoulder. "You don't appreciate what you have. Come and go without a care. My opinion is, it should be mine after Katherine agrees and you correct everything I mentioned."

Although he looks embarrassed, Neil sits with his arms across his chest while I'm ready to explode. He stands and says, "Stop fuming, Arabelle." Then, gestures for me to sit.

I collapse into a nearby chair.

He paces back and forth in front of me. "Look, Lacey, since my arrival, I learned you are opinionated and do interrupt. Especially to someone, who could have you fired. I agree you are industrious. Heard you can't boil water, but you don't look as if you are starving. Finally, you assume because you've cleaned my guest house it should be yours. Am I right?"

"Perhaps," I say and show him my pearly whites. Wonder what else he has to say?

"Also, if Mother approves, I agree to update

appliances, hire a painting crew and deliver a truckload of eye-catching pillows."

"So far, I believe all things are possible. Neil, what do you say if I give a counter offer?"

"A what? What is whirling around in that beautiful head?" Neil leans against the table. I suspect there's something brewing behind that idiotic grin.

I roll out my lip and pout. Then walk into the living room where I pat the back of the sofa and openly flirt. "A definite yes to painting and modern appliances, including heat. Instead of a zillion pillows, would you upgrade with one new sofa and two pillows? If you resize the closet, a standard bed will fit. Or . . ."

"Or what? Is there no end to your demands?" Neil asks.

"Well if you say 'yes' to being my sleepover guest on the new sofa, you save money. How? I'll buy the paint and roller coat the rooms. You'd eliminate the bedroom remodeling because I'm short." Shouldn't have offered that, although that's what I meant. Good grief, I'm throwing myself at him. He's too quiet. What if he doesn't know I was only flirting? What if he says okay?

CHAPTER 8
WELCOME HOME KISS

"Miss Lacey, enough is enough. Anson and Clare were both wrong. You are a mischievous child, cleverly disguised as a naïve lady. It is a shame you aren't a few years older; I might have accepted the cost savings. Regarding the bungalow and your invitation, I will make appropriate arrangements where and when to satisfy your needs."

His words squash any bit of sophistication I thought I had. What a disillusionment, instead of his thinking I'm a flirtatious worldly woman, he treats me like I'm a starry-eyed romantic. I step outside while he closes the bungalow.

"You realize listening to your complaints; I haven't greeted Katherine. So, little one, I must go. He pats my head and asks, "Are you coming?"

I can't believe he patted my head. Furious, I jerk my head away from his hand and push him down a step to do a face-off. "Look, Neil, for your knowledge, you're only a few years older. And, I'm not ashamed of anything I offered. I meant it. So put that in a pipe and smoke it."

"Miss Lacey, contrary to your expectation, I meant everything I said as well."

We seem paralyzed by what we have said to each other and stand in silence. He extends his hand to assist me going down the unlit porch steps. Over the damp ground, we walk side-by-side. The spongy surface creates a suck, suck noise until we near the back porch steps. With the sink light on, I presume the kitchen will be empty, and I've nothing to lose in the game I started at the bungalow.

I play my last card to an unsuspecting fellow and go up one step before I say, "Excuse me, Mr. McCutchen, would a 'welcome home' kiss be too bold of me?"

"Between friends, it would be appropriate." When he brings his head down to accept my kiss, I whisper in his ear, "Thank you, Neil. Remember, I gave you an open invitation." I kiss his cheek, wave goodbye and go inside.

He stands back and looks surprised. When I leave him, he scratches his head.

It's through the kitchen and a mad dash up the back stairs. I hope to pick out my loveliest outfit for tonight's dinner because from the stairwell; his tenor voice carries the tune 'Got You Under My Skin'.

I don't turn around or reply with a sound because the feeling is becoming mutual. After a warm shower, a blow dryer and curling iron work a miracle in a hairdo sure to impress Neil. A navy sheath dress and black pumps with two-inch heels should show him he doesn't need to bend to kiss me and that I am a woman.

Before I leave for dinner, moonlight exposes a small puddle under the bedroom's window sill. I dry the floor with a bath towel and close the window. In the distance, a car's brake lights flash before rounding a curve in the driveway. I'm not surprised as Clare often sends Anson on an errand.

Going downstairs, I smell spaghetti sauce cooking. I step into the kitchen and Clare sees me. From her set jaw, raised eyebrows, and a look to kill, I'm in trouble and don't understand why. "Gee Clare, now what did I do?"

"Infuriated Arabelle, that's what. That boy spends over two hours with you, then, he visits Katherine. I'm a little annoyed but have no problem with who he sees. What raises my pressure is he talks to Anson without a word to me. Imagine that; he drives away without a single minute for me."

I shrug my shoulders because I have no answer to please her.

"Why are you dressed up? Arabelle, what happened in that bungalow? What did you do to that boy?"

"Good grief, he leaves, and you're ready to take off my head. I didn't do anything. You know Neil has a way of coming and going and his not talking to you isn't getting me in hot water. Honest Clare, we talked, but nothing happened. We came back to the manor. I told him that I'd see him at dinner. That's all."

Clare stirs the sauce and turns to look over her shoulder. "Dinner together, that's what she told me. Think of it, all of us eating in the dining room. Now Neil's gone, and Katherine doesn't want to eat. Then, Anson drives off right after Neil left. I'm too upset to eat. The sauce is ready, and spaghetti needs to be cooked. You're on your own." Clare goes into her bedroom.

Instead of cooking pasta, I plate several meatballs to make a sandwich. Before taking a bite, I start to hum 'I got you under my skin.' Aagh! Good, grief! Even the song lingers longer than he does.

Later at my vanity, I play several games of Solitaire and listen for any car's tires on the gravel. It's approaching midnight. I shut off my dresser light and wonder where he does go without a goodbye to me. "Anson, if you're with him, stay safe."

ഇഇഇ

Morning light creeps across my bed. I dress before the alarm and join Clare and Katherine having breakfast. Neither one has heard from either man. Later we watch the morning weather report. Cold and flurries are expected. Clare leaves to take care of her cleaning routine. Katherine decides to finish her novel. I wander down the hallway to the gathering room and refresh my thoughts on where to check next.

The hours fly by, and the skies turn gray, as the air grows colder. For once, the forecast was on the spot. I find Katherine and Clare drinking tea in the sitting room and go toward the library. When the door chimes ring, I collect a message from Anson and give it to Katherine.

After opening it, she reads it aloud. "Sorry to worry everyone. Return next week. Neil needs help with a problem. He hopes to be home for holidays. Anson"

Katherine's head and shoulders droop. She takes short steps into the hallway. Turns and said, "I'll be in my room. Belle, please handle my calls today."

Katherine, how I'd love to tell you I share your disappointment. My hope is he returns sooner. I take advantage of the inclement weather outside to check another room. After several hours, I add the information to the mix and regrettably, another dead end.

ഇഇഇ

Three days later Anson returns in the afternoon. He

gives no explanation why they left or when Neil is expected. Living at the manor resumes under Katherine's routine. The search and her biography are at a standstill because her focus scatters among several committees. As her assistant, I tag along and nod my head in support.

It's mid-November and Clare leaves for two weeks to visit friends in Florida. Jack Frost's signature decorates the window glass, and a light dusting of snow covers the ground. With the fingerprints of early winter weather around me, I layer my outfit, including socks and shoes that replace sneakers. With Clare gone, I experience serenity knowing the household chores are in my hands.

Through the window above the sink, I see a yearling deer at the salt lick outside. A beautiful sight until I find a list taped to the windowpane. Tranquility flees because Clare left me a freaking schedule. "Oooh! I hate lists." Like an annoying splinter, I pull it away and toss it into the garbage pail.

Punctually at 7:30 a.m., I take Katherine's breakfast to her room. Within minutes, I return with the tray and her note regarding a holiday meeting in town. I finish my cereal and highlight Charlie's earmarked notes on the blueprints, especially those indicating a discrepancy in room measurements from actual size to newer print dimensions. I'm so absorbed in making notes on where to measure that I don't pay attention to my surroundings until a cold hand covers my shoulder. Startled, I drop the marker.

"Morning Miss Belle." Anson pours himself a cup of coffee. "You're up before the rooster. Ah, I see you found her note. She told me to order pizza for dinner."

"Yes, I threw Clare's schedule in the garbage can.

However, the house is clean and Katherine's note gives me the day off. Would you like banana pancakes or sausage omelet for breakfast? If not, I'll explore the library."

"No, thank you. Relax, may I refill your cup?"

I offer my cup. Sitting across from each other, his face shows he wants to talk, but Anson doesn't start conversations. Although, he does answer questions and I'm curious to know more about him.

"Anson, at 14, how did you manage? I mean back then when you came here." Oh no, his neck is getting red. Did I embarrass him?

Anson takes a deep breath. "Miss Belle, why such a personal question?"

As if Clare was still here, I look over my shoulder, lean forward, and whisper. "What I mean is, how do I go from there to here? You saw our third floor, one bedroom, walk-up, all 500 square feet. The nightmares that suck me back there persist. How did you manage to adjust when you came here? Please tell me."

Furrow lines stretch across his brow. Anson rubs his forehead and removes his steel-rimmed glasses. "Shortly after I arrived, Clare took me under her wing in learning the ropes to live here. Although bossy at times, she inspired confidence to accept, without question, everything Adam offered me. Adam told me the gardens were my responsibility. I thought it unusual for a businessman to love gardening. He worked beside me in plant propagation while grafting the roses. We shared a love of horticulture. It was then he taught me the barter system. Plus, associating my work to the estate's finances. Why I bartered my college education by agreeing to teach

Cameron the basics in running the company."

"I've nothing to barter. So what you tell me has no practical use."

"Miss Belle, after coming here, I put my past behind me. I accepted a new life of challenge and opportunity. Think you can do the same?"

"I guess so. You said Cameron learned to run the company. Katherine mentioned Cameron only returns when he needs money."

"I am surprised Katherine divulged family issues for her story. Let me explain. Before Adam died, he added a codicil to his will."

"Anson, how do you know so much? I mean about his will and the codicil?"

"Adam trusted my integrity. Although he never showed me either one, Adam confided in me that he did it. The man was many things but whatever he told me was the truth."

"I'm interested in learning more about Katherine's husband's liberal allowance. I'm confused how to write it into her story?"

"Cameron struggled for his legal right to the estate. Without a will, he lost his claim. After Adam's funeral, I told them what I knew. Cameron agreed to relinquish his claim to the estate, domestic and international holdings. Instead, we agreed that monthly payment came from his share of all profits until he dies. The amount depended on how well the businesses did the previous year. Katherine agreed."

"Anson, that's unreal. More coffee?"

Anson shakes his head and covers his cup. "The four of us use everything we learned from him or Adam's books."

"Because his library could be an obvious place, did anyone check his on the upper floor?"

Anson rises and walks around the table. "No. Why are you asking me all these questions? I thought you were doing Katherine's memoirs."

"Questions weren't strictly meant for her memoirs. What you've told time will fill certain gaps. Any communication from Neil, it might help me to know more about him."

"Don't know where? Neil will call when it is important. To tell you about Neil, I'll say he is an honest man and gifted. At eleven, he enters and wins a Chess Tournament. By fourteen, his business perception equaled a college graduate. At eighteen, he convinced Katherine to let him travel abroad for three months. Later, she encourages his involvement in the smaller foreign companies, where he does well."

"Thanks, Anson, I'll fit all this somewhere because Katherine's story has more turns than a corkscrew. I wonder about my life. Is it twisted, as well?"

Anson reaches for my hand. "Miss Belle, who you are or who you'll become, comes from within you. Before you decide to search among nooks and crannies, why not use your day off to return home for a visit. It may help end your nightmares. Want to give it a try?"

I nod my head. Put on my coat and meet Anson by the carriage house. With an hour's drive ahead of us, we descend the winding driveway. Anson exaggerates the shifting curves. I sway right, then left. It is then I notice his signet ring. "Anson, your ring. It's unusual."

Momentarily the car swerves. Once he gains control, I

squirm in my seat because he is upset when he turns his head and says, "Buckle up."

Afterward, the car's heater could not defrost the chill between us, until he arrives at the Interstate's rest area. I'm concerned because he stops, leaves the motor running and has me look at him.

"It was my thirteenth birthday when Mom hands me a small box. She said that the gift inside belonged to my father. I wore the signet ring around my neck. After Mom had died, I took her letter to Adam."

"I'm sorry Anson. Katherine told me that Mr. McCutchen hired a private investigator to find you."

"That's true. However, when I meet Adam, he fingers the ring hanging around my neck. I didn't say a word. Gave him Mom's letter and he didn't open it. Instead, he took me by my shoulders and offered me a job. Asked if I was hungry, I nodded. We went to the kitchen, and he said, 'Feed your grandson.'"

"So what you're telling me is Adam McCutchen was your father?"

"Legally, I don't know. My birth record indicated father is unknown. My grandmother said that I have mother's eyes. How I wished the same for my hair, jet black not red."

"But Anson, your beard is black."

"A freak of nature with red hair and a black beard that his genes gave me. Now it's a way into town. Do you need to use the facility?"

I shake my head, and Anson puts the car into reverse. He peels out from the empty rest area and enters highway traffic. Doing 70, he passes a fuel truck. At the next entrance by a hair's breadth, he misses a car entering the expressway.

Will I ever let well enough alone? Okay, how do I get him to slow down? Wait, he usually plays the radio. I turn it to the F.M. station. The classical music acts as a salve, and soon the irritating red folds on his neck become flesh-colored. He resumes the speed limit, and his driving allows me to shut my eyes and relax.

When traffic becomes stop-and-go, I awake and recognize a landmark. “Myrtle Oaks! Take next left, Anson. It’s two houses after Swan's Deli.”

My directions take us past a faded Deli sign that hangs from a single bolt. In the window is a yellowed FOR SALE sign. Next door, the once grassy lot is overgrown and littered. Broken furniture and six men surround a fire barrel.

“Anson, this isn’t where I lived. Please, turn around.”

Anson pulls over to the curb and turns off the motor. “Sorry Miss, we’re here.”

Overturned garbage cans offer food scraps for strays. It is the Thursday before Thanksgiving. Garbage pickup hasn’t happened. Across the street, near the alleyway, kids play football and ignore the snow and accompanying slush.

From a high-rise apartment window, a woman’s voice yells in our direction. “You there, in the car, move it. Garbage trucks use that side.”

I begin crying. This isn’t real. It can’t be.

CHAPTER 9
HAPPY UNBIRTHDAY

Anson turns toward me. "Miss Belle, the happiest people don't own the best that money can provide. Instead, they find joy in what they have. Visit your friend. I'll move the car across the street and wait there." He hands me a clean handkerchief. "Keep a spare; Katherine gets emotional now and then. Never know, you may need it later."

When I get out, a familiar aroma greets me. "Anson roll down your window and take a whiff. Mrs. Orsefski is cooking kaputsa for her cabbage soup. You know Anson; overall it's not a bad street, just worn out. When Mom lived, we had our good times."

I climb the front steps and press Decima's apartment number. I hear familiar, loud voices while waiting on the front stoop and think. That's got to be the Brown boys in Apartment 14. Still quarreling and you never know who'll win the argument.

When the vestibule door opens, my dearest friend greets me with arms extended and a warm smile. "Belle! Shalom. When I heard Mrs. Cohen yell that she saw a Beamer in this neighborhood, I knew it had to be you."

"Shalom, Deci." I turn and wave back to Anson. "Be

back in a few minutes, Anson." Then arm-in-arm, we enter the three-story row house.

Three hours later, I return with a steaming mug and a lunch bag. Anson comes out of the car to open my door and does a seventh-inning stretch before taking the food and drink.

"I couldn't believe how time flew. When we began to eat, I remembered you didn't have breakfast. Decima made you a pastrami on rye. She even packed a pickle and a big slice of cinnamon babka to go with your coffee."

"Toe-dah, thank you, Miss Belle. Now your visit, tell me did you enjoy it?"

"Bevakasha Anson, you're welcome. Didn't know you could speak Yiddish. Please, enjoy your lunch. On the ride home, I'll tell you all the news."

Anson wet fingers the remaining crumbs from the waxed paper and drinks the last of his coffee. "Excellent. Do convey my thanks to Miss Decima."

"I will. Oh, Anson, I had a supreme time. We hugged so much; we almost flattened each other. It was like old times, drank colas on the fire escape landing, and this is the best news ever. She's back in school."

"I presumed she graduated with you."

"She did. We graduated, and she went to work at the neighborhood clinic. Since she's attending a nursing school, she got a promotion and yesterday; she became Assistant Director. Would you believe when she saw the size of the manor, Deci thought she'd never see me again."

"That hardly seems the case, Miss Belle."

I take a deep breath and let out a slow sigh. "You know it. We'll be B. F. forever. Anson, guess what I learned?"

"Haven't the foggiest," Anson said and started the car.

"I want to go home, to the estate. Responsibilities, you know. I need to order dinner." I adjust my seatbelt and observe his grin is so wide, he reminds me of Alice's Cheshire cat. "Anson, what's so amusing?"

He glanced over and said, "Responsibilities? You mean ones that might help a young woman to grow."

"Yes!" I say as we drive away. I leave my past behind me and lift an imaginary glass. "Here, here, a toast to Decima and me, young women forging ahead. I wish us long life, love, and brighter futures."

"Here! Here!" Anson says and merges into the traffic flow. The surrounding sounds become intense. Over a cacophony of horns and rumbling engines, Anson is singing. "Grey skies are going to clear up . . ."

I join in the singing. ". . . Spread the sunshine all over the place and put on a happy face." The neighborhood trip gives me closure and the car phone permits a pizza pick up call.

When we arrive at the manor, I plate several slices, add beverages to the tray and walk to her sitting room. I know from the music that Katherine is watching 'Wheel of Fortune.'

"Belle, come in. The pizza smells delicious. But, if you'll excuse me for a minute."

"Is there something I can get you?" I put the tray on the coffee table.

"No dear, I have to talk with Anson. I'll be back shortly."

I wait and continue watching the next program. Five commercials later and Katherine has not returned. Shutting off the television, I wander into the vestibule.

Balloons float throughout the room, and a large banner extends across the interior front doors. Katherine, Anson, and Decima wear party hats. Anson holds a tray of lighted cupcakes. All begin to sing, "Happy . . ." Later they applaud as I blow out the candles.

"Decima told me your actual birthday is ten days away. Therefore, Anson checked with the DMV. If you study, you could pass your driving test on your birthday. Before she left on vacation, Clare prepared freezer meals so you can study."

"DMV? Driving test? I'm confused, are you giving me driving lessons?"

"No Miss," said Anson, "I'll be giving you lessons. Tomorrow, you go for your permit. You'll study the rules with Katherine. When it's test time, Decima will go with you."

"Anson? You didn't say a word. I'm so happy." I grab hold of Deci and we jump up-and-down, squealing like teenagers.

ꙮꙮꙮ

For the next ten days, Clare's emergency dinners relieve me of heavy kitchen duty. Because of Katherine's dedication to detail and pop quizzes, I know the driving manual word-for-word. Anson's driving course covers the estate's grounds and corkscrew driveway. Occasionally, strictly by accident, I create new country by-ways on the back acreage. Finally, the day arrives. Deci and I take off to the test center.

Three hours later, I drive towards the carriage house, and notice three people are on the terrace. I stop. Do a quick sprint and shout at the top of my lungs. "I passed! I passed!"

"Congratulations!" Calls Anson and to my surprise, Clare is in their midst.

"Congratulations, Arabelle. The kitchen looks as if I never left. You must have been studying and driving all the time."

"Congratulations, Belle. So what's it feel like now that you're a licensed driver?"

"Katherine, I aced the written test. When I start the driver's test, I put the gear into reverse instead of first gear. The DMV agent gives me this know-it-all smirk. Then I see Deci, and I'm okay. Thanks to the manor's driveway, the curved road on Elm was a piece of cake. In town, I didn't hit the oblivious jaywalker. Then he makes me parallel park, three times because I pass on the first try."

"Well, I think we should celebrate. Where would you like to go?"

"Gee Katherine, Deci asked me to chauffeur her to her new apartment. Was hoping to ask a favor?"

"Which is?"

"I thought you'd let me borrow a car for a double celebration with Deci. She's got the night off, and John Travolta is at the Majestic. Would you mind if we don't go out to eat?"

Katherine pauses and walks around. "Let me understand. You and Decima are meeting a boy at the movies, and you need to borrow a car. Why?"

"Not precisely, I need a car to drive us to see her apartment and the movie called Grease. It's a musical about rebellious high school lovers. Olivia Newton-John sings with Travolta. John Travolta! Katherine, I promise to bring the car back in one piece. Please."

"No."

"No?"

"No Belle, not until Anson fills the tank. I wouldn't refuse you on your birthday."

"Thank you. Thank you. Thank you! Can you imagine it, Olivia and John, in love, together on the screen? Thank you, Katherine." I dash off to call Deci with the news.

It's nine p.m. when I rap on Katherine's bedroom door and open it just a crack. "Hi, I'm back. Thanks again."

"You are welcome. Was Grease like an Elvis movie?"

"No, no. Better music, a fantastic love story. Well, goodnight."

"Goodnight Belle."

I take a shortcut to my room through the kitchen. See Clare sipping hot milk and hope she'll find excitement in her life. "Hi Clare, good musical, you might enjoy it. John and Olivia, their singing was excellent. Man, you'd love it, well night Clare."

"Good night Arabelle."

I'm half way up the back stairs and pause. Clare is humming. Nah, she wouldn't know their song. I continue to my room.

ജ്ജ

Next morning, I foresee an uneventful day when I find Anson washing the BMW that I used last night. "Anson, I have a terrific idea. The record store has the Grease album. We can get Clare that for Christmas."

"Can't. After I had heard her singing, I bought it. You want to partner in?"

"Would I? Anson, I'm in."

We both laugh, and I return to the house. Near the back door, I hear Clare place her Thanksgiving order with

Swan's. Not to disturb her, I go around the manor and enter through the front door, as Katherine leaves her office.

"Belle, there you are. If you have no immediate plans, I need a lift into town. Anson is busy, and you won't have to wait. I'll take a cab back. The holidays are approaching, and there's much to do at the Civic Center. Is that a problem?"

"No, I love to drive. Give me a few minutes and I'll bring the Beamer to the front. If you don't need help at the Center, I'll stop at Swan's for Clare's Thanksgiving order."

"No, we have plenty of volunteers. You continue your day."

ꟷꟷꟷ

Thanksgiving was a lost day for me. I ate too much and rested most of the time. Neil's arrival did not happen nor did he or Cameron send their regrets. I found this unusual, but I was the only one who thought that. I invited Charlie to assist in my search because too many measurement discrepancies are found in similar blueprints. He's coming this evening.

. The front chimes ring twice, and I suspect it's Charlie. When I answer the door, I'm surprised that he greets me with a kiss on my lips. "Hi beautiful Belle, I thought a kiss is a fantastic way to start the holiday season. Agree?"

"Charlie, a kiss on the cheek is okay. One on the lips better carry more than a hello. Now, Katherine and Anson are off to the tree farm for the perfect evergreen. Clare is busy with her recipe book. And, I laid out the questionable prints in the gathering room. Charlie, we should go over everything again."

"Why? We did that. I didn't see anything suspicious. Since you ignore my friendly kiss, what have you done to make my trip worthwhile?"

"Charlie, measuring is painstakingly tedious. With the exception of Adam's room, I finished all others on the second floor. Measured inner and outer to match the blueprint, tapped walls, checked and moved furniture and lifted carpets. Then, I lost the motivation to continue. It seemed like I fell into the bottomless pit. Anson helped get me out. We went back to the old neighborhood. That visit taught me sometimes you need to go back before going forward."

"That's great Belle. You're enlightened but what do you want from me?

"Your eyes, your brain, a pencil and measuring tape, that's all."

"You're funny. Where do I start?"

"Under the main stairway, and then we can review your notes against mine, against the earliest and last recorded."

"I'd be willing if she wasn't over there."

I turn to see Katherine in front of the terrace's storm door. Unaware of our presence, she draws her shawl closer and appears pre-occupied with the flagstone.

Charlie pulls me back and hands me a notebook. "Here, look over these notes on possible search sites. I think Katherine is not at the tree farm and may need you more than I do. I'll let myself out, call me later." He kisses my cheek and leaves.

I go nearer and wonder if her remoteness has anything to do with an earlier telegram she received. I'm within touching distance, and she is not aware I'm behind her. I clear my throat and say, "It's a beautiful snowfall. Don't you agree? I'm curious Katherine, have you received any word from Neil or Cameron about coming home for the holidays?"

She turns her head, then opens the door and steps outside. Katherine motions for me to come closer. "Dear Belle, I love the first snowfall. Everything has magic in it, wherever it falls. Yes, I got word from Cameron. You'll meet him when he arrives to collect his money. Thankfully, he won't be here for Christmas."

"And Neil?"

"His itinerary . . . " The telephone rings in her office. "Excuse me, Belle. We'll talk later."

How long before I accept this dysfunctional family's irrational behavior as normal? Rather than wait for her return, I decide to check Charlie's notebook. I walk back to the gathering room, her sitting room's door is open and the light brightens the hallway floor. Because she appeared withdrawn earlier, I enter her private office. "Good news, I hope. Katherine, are you okay?"

There's a smile on her face when she places the phone in its cradle. "Yes, excellent news. Neil plans to arrive home before year-end. Also, he mentioned you want to move into the bungalow. Do you?"

"Yes, I do. I could kiss him for remembering."

"Dear girl, if you want to, you have my blessing. Please tell Anson that I said to repair the heater. Here is my American Express card. I'll notify them you're authorized to use it. Buy whatever you'll need to transform the bungalow to your liking."

"Yikes Katherine, I've got three weeks to get it ready.

Thank you so much. I've had a make-it-mine list available since Neil left in October. Excuse me; I need to make a phone call."

"Of course, use my phone. I want to tell Clare the good news." She leaves as I dial Decima's number. After six rings, I'm ready to disconnect when she answers. I scream into the phone. "Deci, mission impossible is ready to launch."– "Yes, the bungalow. We got three weeks, you still available?" – "Fantastic, be there in about an hour. Bye."

I was glad Deci could take time today away from the Clinic. Our school friendship was almost twenty-four/seven. Nowadays, our personal schedules play havoc on getting together.

After several hours of shopping and traveling wintry roads both ways, I'm exhausted and glad that the ride back is uneventful. Arriving at the carriage house, Anson volunteers to unload everything into the bungalow while I go to share my fun day with Katherine. Eventually, I find Katherine on the terrace where accumulating snowfall covers her shoes.

"Katherine, come inside. You'll catch your death. I believe Neil's arrival is like waiting for the fallen leaves to go backward through the snow and reattach themselves."

"You are right. It can't happen soon enough, Belle. I do miss his not living here, and I also worry about his health. Let's go inside and you tell me your day."

Katherine gives an occasional nod while I relate my day. "I ordered Kenmore appliances. They deliver next Thursday. Brought the paint, small appliances, linens, and a couple of decorator pillows back with me."

"That's nice," she says and turns on the news.

I know Katherine's not entirely ignoring me, but I become concerned when she gets lost in her thoughts and becomes distant to her surroundings. Because of her health, I watch the six p.m. weather report with her.

"Good evening," the weathergirl announces, "Keep warm folks, blizzard conditions should drop six to eight inches overnight in the outlying areas."

"Well Katherine, the kids will enjoy it. No, school!"

Katherine clicks the remote and finds her station. "Yes, I'm sure they will. Look, 'Wheel' is on."

That's her secret. The program is her disconnect to daily stress. However, Cameron is due to arrive soon, and a gut feeling tells me something else is bothering her. We chit chat during commercials. Otherwise, I sit there, and my mind wanders to Neil's call. His time frame escalates my proposed facelift and every daylight minute must be put to good use.

༄༄༄

Ten days remain to year-end. On the weekend, Deci and I generate a whirlwind of fix- up activities at the bungalow. However, Anson can't locate a primary heat supply and without heat each weekday, I must return before sunset to the main house.

"Clare, the bungalow still lacks heat, any news from Anson?"

"Arabelle, don't worry. Before Neil arrives, you'll have heat. Now, the foyer's mirror has fingerprints on it. Would you please clean it?" I nod. She says, "Thank you."

CHAPTER 10
HEAD START ON SPRING

I get the Windex and head out to clean a mirror that I cleaned the day before. It finally happens. With the squirt of a bottle, I surrender to the mundane reality within this manor. As I wipe the glass, Clare's voice comes from the hallway behind me.

"Arabelle, Miss Gordon is on the phone."

"Thanks, Clare, I'll come to the kitchen."

"Hi Deci, what was I doing? I was cleaning a smudge on a mirror." – "Oh, you wouldn't believe it. If it weren't for the stained glass, the window panes would be invisible." – "I know Deci. Go ahead laugh, but no fooling, if you step one foot in the kitchen, Clare will hand you a dust rag. Hey, had a thought." – "This year, Chanukah comes during our Christmas. How about celebrating the Eve at my pad? – "Yes, you'll meet the elusive Neil. We'll end the old year together." – "Great! Love you too. Bye."

Re-entering the foyer, I notice the decorated tree blocks the front windows. Several ornament boxes are stacked against the wall. I flick the light switch and a profusion of colored lights add sparkle to the entry.

Without a coat, I go outside and quicken my walk down the driveway. Twenty feet off the veranda, I turn to view the panoramic picture Neil will see on his homecoming. The manor eyes reflect the entry's tree lights and glowing electric candles in each window to produce a sparkling reflection from the snow. I make a wish and picture him kissing me under the mistletoe.

Within the warmth of the mansion, I shut the front door. Through the sitting room's doorway, I see Clare and Anson standing beside Katherine. When I come closer, Clare takes hold of me.

"What's happened?" I ask.

Clare whispers, "Shush, she was about to tell us."

"Some of you may already know the Western Union called. With bad weather, the supervisor thought it best to call first and deliver later."

Clare's face whitens, and her fingers tighten on my arm. "Cameron?"

"Clare, it's not about Cameron. He's fine, just delayed in arriving. It's Neil. He won't be here."

I shake my head in disbelief. "I'm sorry Katherine because I wanted Deci to meet him. You see, I invited her to be here New Year's Eve. Is that okay?"

"Yes, it is. Belle, I didn't want you to think something happened to him. What I meant to say is a personal matter requires his immediate attention. He wishes everyone happy holidays. Sent me his regrets and love. Maybe your friend can meet him at another time. However, there is nothing I could do to change his decision."

Anson takes Katherine's hand and says, "I'll have a man-to-man talk with the boy when he does arrive."

ꟷ

Christmas passes, mistletoe comes down, and Neil's

gifts lay on his dresser. Without further word from him, I have a growing concern for his safety and cannot hide my feelings. When the midnight toll of the grandfather clock ends, it's followed by the sound of clinking champagne glasses and weak 'Happy New Year' wishes are heard. Deci and I sip the bubbling drink and make our way outside.

"Let's do it." Deci shouts and without our coats, we dash to the bungalow's snow-covered porch. Inside we stomp our shoes and Deci says, "Brrrr! Belle, I thought you said there was a heater. It's cold out there, but it's freezing in here."

"Give me a minute. There. Anson forgot to set the heater on high. Deci, I should have said something, but didn't. I thought about it but hoped someone else would make a New Year's resolution to find Adam's will. It's hard to continue when I've lost the desire to look."

Desi rubs her arms and looks for something to wrap around herself. "Belle, you tell me Katherine asks for help but finds more than one excuse for you not to search. I think, and it's a shot in the dark, the disinterest is because no one wants to disturb the status quo. If she finds the will, Clare might lose her job. Anson is possibly secure but to what extent. Katherine owns the improvements but not the property. Without the land's heir, they continue here without any significant change. That makes sense to me."

"Deci your reasoning hit a home run and I'm checking that thermostat."

"Glad to help, so where is that graph map you told me about last week? Hey, is that heater, at least, working?"

I hold my hand on the top and front of the heater.

"Feels like it. Here is Charlie's notebook. He did a graphic sketch of each room. Except, I haven't followed up on where he thinks might have a hidden space."

Deci cups her hands and blows down on them. "Belle, I'm glad we're here in your new pad. But be honest, would it make an Eskimos feel right at home?"

My teeth are chattering. I nod. "You're right. We aren't Eskimos. Anson said he fixed the heater. Must be on its last legs and, speaking of feet, I'll race you back to the kitchen. Hot chocolate sounds like a winner."

Inside the kitchen and with Clare's bedroom door closed, I quietly make and fill our mugs. I blow down onto the cup's surface as I go upstairs. Deci covers hers with marshmallow islands and sips the hot liquid while climbing the stairs. Shedding our shoes, we get comfortable under the down comforter and finish our drinks.

Then Deci asks, "Belle, think this Neil likes you?"

"Maybe . . . if he does, I sure can't tell by his absence."

"Do you like him?"

"I doubt if his presence would make my heart any fonder? Guess it's possible to love a will-o'-the-wisp, even a little." I shut off the lamp.

Deci says, "Happy New Year, Belle."

"And a prosperous one to you and the clinic, Deci."

Snow! Snow! Snow! January's snowfall continues through the month. Boredom moves life slower than a slug's pace. With Katherine not chairing the Guild's Valentine Dance, we ignore attending the function. For me, there is light at the end of non-discovery. Clare and Anson put projects on hold and like Katherine, they vanish somewhere in the manor. Their absent presence keeps me busy checking out Charlie's graphs. There is great joy when I discover the space behind and under the central stairwell has a compact exit to the basement. Then comes a letdown. There isn't any paperwork only cobwebs and a rickety ladder. I continue my singular search.

ഇഇഇ

It's the Ides of March, and time for me to type Katherine's article about Italy for the Guild's Newsletter. This morning, Katherine gathers us into her sitting room. We look at each other, and no one knows why.

"Everyone, I decided it's time to enjoy some travel. I told the Guild's board that my term is over, and I wasn't running. Nor, was anyone here at the manor doing any additional work for them either. Anson, if you've no plans, would you drive me to the travel agency? So, anyone answering the telephone, give the message, Katherine will call you ASAP. Is there any question?"

"Do you want us to write who, at what number, with what call is about?" I smile back.

"No. Only say, Katherine will call you ASAP and hang up."

I give her a thumb's up. She leaves and I take advantage of her 'no interruptions' with a measuring tape to graph the first-floor common library, using the handwritten notes from Clare and Charlie. He believes with so many dimensional changes; there are hidden spaces somewhere between the blueprint lines. Cameron and Neil are missing from this equation. I decide to confront the others after dinner.

"Clare, the roast was delicious and Arabelle. Didn't

know you could bake bread."

"Well, Clare helped. Katherine, I have a hard time understanding how everyone shows indifference to the whereabouts of your husband or Neil. Doesn't anyone here ever question their long absence? Would it be foolish of me to display 'dead or alive' pictures at the post office?"

"Arabelle!" Clare's look tells me this is a family matter and then rolls her eyes towards Katherine.

However, Katherine says, "Belle, it's not unusual for them to miss the holidays or to travel this time of year. Isn't that so, Anson?"

"Have to agree with Katherine. The fiscal year ends at different times. Everything is as it should be. Cameron's time frame is open to his need for funds. Neil will be contacting us as the showers bring May flowers."

I'm concerned about them because they accept their absence as usual behavior. Will any motivation help them to get out of their same old, same old patterns?

ຣ໑ຣ໑ຣ໑

The following week, sub-zero weather comes and goes. Because of unpredictable lake effect snowstorms, the estate resembles an ice palace, and within the walls, I notice a declining outlook on life.

Katherine without committee meetings spends hours reading fictional romance. Anson spends time in the carriage house recording his dulcimer music. Clare's culinary skills are now her, Nov. 20, '78 emergency frozen meals.

I walk aimlessly over the frozen ground and ice-covered plants. It begins to snow, and I shiver as flurries hit my face. Soon I become a snow queen and stomp my feet to shake off the light covering of white crystals. Doing that, I feel better as if shedding a part of the darkness I feel inside.

I stop and think; it's not me. It's not any one of us. The manor's depressing interior and the estate's bleakness is the reason for our lack of inner vitality. I make a mad dash back for I have a solution.

Without regard to snow traces through the hallway, I hurry to her sitting room. She's there, reading. "Excuse me, Katherine; this can't wait. The entire estate, including the manor's interior, exposes us to a depressing attitude that causes an infectious, dismal outlook in us."

She looks up and is about to say something.

I interrupt. "No, I don't need a trip to a psychiatrist, and you shouldn't stop me until you hear me out."

"Okay." She said and closes her book.

"Great. Today, this very afternoon gives us the necessary prescription to shatter the blahs with a head start on spring."

"Belle, tell me, what is going on in that brain of yours? You have my utmost attention." Katherine gets comfortable and leans back in the wingback chair.

"Well, it started when I saw the snow mounds over the gardens. I thought about how a white sheet covered that monstrous wall hanging at Mom's funeral and how many people fit into the gathering room without the furnishings as a reception area."

"Yes, I do but what . . ."

"And last year, you chaired the historical society's fundraiser, right?"

Katherine nods, but, the confused look on her face remains.

"Right, and think what a fundraiser this year could be

if you vary tours of the manor. One could be your private library with its Japanese artifacts or the west-end historical gallery. Or a Spring walk through the garden's early blooming trees and flowers. Or, where they turn around, they'll see the manor's stateliness. Cost discounted for members and a set fee for public admission. The Guild could raise a chunk of change from group or personal tours."

"It amazes me, Belle. You got all that from looking at snow mounds."

"Yes, I did Katherine. Another option, forget tours and hold an antique auction with your donation of that carved wall mounting and contributions from the other members.

Third, rejuvenate the estate. Coat of fresh paint revives a room. Modernize the kitchen. I know Clare has some marvelous ideas for it. And, Anson spoke about reinventing your rose garden. What'd you think?"

Come on Katherine. Give me something. Don't sit there. Okay, you're tapping your fingers on the desk. Wheels are in motion.

"Belle, as a fundraiser for the Guild, I'm not sure about tours with potential liability. However, by all means, we should work toward an early spring. I love the concept. If you coordinate your idea with Clare and Anson, then, get back to me. Your idea springboards several of mine, which should alleviate my cabin fever. Thank you, Arabelle."

Katherine said yes. I'll need Anson's and Clare's support to help to pull this off. I remove my wet shoes and hurry to the kitchen.

Anson sits in his usual chair with a coffee cup in

hand. “I cleared a pathway for you from the carriage house. In case you need to use the Beamer.”

Okay, Belle, get them motivated. “Not today, Anson. What I want to know is if you have your gardening ideas on paper? Clare, your kitchen ideas you showed me. May I have them?”

“Why?” They said in unison.

"Well, I mentioned something to Katherine, and she asked me what it might cost to renovate the kitchen and the rose garden."

“I can find my drawings. Are you sure, Katherine said the word renovate?”

“No. She said ‘I love the concept.’

Clare appears hesitant at first, Until she says, “Always thought we could use maybe a dumb waiter or another powder room.”

“Whatever you think of is fine. Will you both go for it?”

They look at each other and give me the nod.

Anson comes closer and says, “Arabelle, what do you have up your sleeve because you’re acting out of character.”

“Yes, I am. I’m so excited about Katherine’s willingness and have an ace in my pocket. Charlie Boyd is a contractor, and I know he’d do a super job. Pool your ideas and later, I'll present them to Katherine. Cost estimate; that's Charlie's job. I want your ideas on modernizing the manor’s interior and the grounds. Anson, along with your drawings, add whatever extra you’ll need.”

“No problem,” Anson said. “But, Arabelle we all know Katherine is a stickler for a time and place for everything.

May I ask, what was so important to interrupt her?"

"A way of getting rid of my blahs with a fundraiser or for updating the entire estate including the gardens—that's all. Besides your drawings, add any ideas that pop into your head."

"Have a few from Gertrude Jekyll."

"Anson, you're telling me 'Dr. Jekyll had a sister?"

He burst forth with a loud, belly laugh. "No, that Jekyll was fiction. Mr. Stevenson named that character after a family friend. Miss Gertrude Jekyll was a British horticulturist, garden designer among other careers. She died in 1932. Today, people might call her a Renaissance woman. When her eyesight failed, she took her art outdoors. Here and in England, her gardens are famous. I own her book on rose gardens."

"You want to paint live roses, as in 'Alice and Wonderland'?"

"Miss Belle, she never painted flowers on bushes. Gertrude used her sense of color in garden landscaping. If I solely used Miss Jekyll's ideas in the rose garden, Katherine might win this year."

Eureka! Anson's got an angle. "Expensive, huh? Like how much to have Katherine win?"

"Belle, with what exists here at the estate, more labor than cost outlay."

"Fantastic Anson, get with Clare sometime today."

That evening, Anson brings me Miss Jekyll's book. A cursory glance helps me understand his love for gardening. Before going to bed, I spend time in the library putting my ideas on paper before I meet with Katherine.

Eleven chimes, I know she's watching the weather report. Afterward for a short time, I'll have her attention.

I close the library door and walk toward her sitting room.

"Arabelle, come in. Barometer and television weather report match. We'll have a cold morning and showers all day. Now, how was your day? Yes, from the paperwork in your hands, I see Clare and Anson had a few thoughts on the coming of spring."

"Well, these papers are my room grids. Anson told me about Gertrude Jekyll. Lived a long time ago and wrote a book about landscaping. Ever hear of her?"

"Somewhat, I believe an artist in her day. But, how does her book have an effect on my gardens?"

"Well, Anson believes you'll win some rose show with her ideas. And, Clare is in a 'do-over' mode for the kitchen, adding a powder room and hiring some dumb waiter. Tomorrow, you'll see their ideas.

'Speaking of seeing, Katherine, I'm concerned because you saw the optician."

"It was because of glaucoma. Yesterday's appointment eased my mind and prescription eyeglasses are on order."

"That's great. Oh, I made a call to the Historical Society, and the Director likes the auction idea. So I scheduled your meeting with them on April 16th. Katherine, the only problem I could foresee with all this, would be your husband giving thumbs down."

"Whoa, Belle, you filled my plate. However, I did ask about your day. Didn't I?" Katherine goes to the turret window and pushes away the draperies.

With her back to me, I'd typically see the determined stature of a woman of power. Now, she lowers her head and stares into the darkness outside. Uneasy with the silence, I wonder if I should leave the room.

When Katherine turns around, she looks past me as if

someone was standing there. "I don't need Cameron's approval concerning the buildings or any part of the Estate. My name is already on the deed."

"Okay, I didn't know that. So you're alright with the garden makeover."

"Are you sure Anson thinks our roses would win? How I'd love to have the manor in this year's Rose Festival's map of homes. Between Clare's and our ideas, we will bring a new look to the outdated house. I'm eager to start, Belle, and precisely what auction item were you thinking of donating?"

"Sure, it's that black mural or you hosting a special house tour once the gardens are in bloom."

"That meeting on the sixteenth is unacceptable. The ninth is better for me. I'll get back to you on your donation suggestion."

For the next three days, periodic cloudbursts erase any trace of winter and increase our fantastic four's participation in making dreams become realities. Katherine chose the gathering room, now renamed command center, to lay out Anson's drawings and greenhouse blueprint. It's a hub of excitement when Anson explains his proposal and details his drawings to us.

Her usual passive role of sipping Earl Grey tea and listening falls away as Katherine examines Anson's book. It outlined his goals to create a Jekyll's rose landscape. This brings a smile to her face.

I've come a long way from a frightened teen. Wait, I forgot my search for Adam's will, but, who knows what inside changes might reveal. It's a matter of time until someone finds it.

CHAPTER 11
PLEASE DON'T LEAVE

"Belle, stop whatever you're doing. Please come to the command center."

Katherine's intercom message sounds urgent. "Are you okay?" I respond.

"Yes, I'm fine."

"Be right there," I say and go downstairs.

Katherine is surrounded by quotations, brochures, and blueprints. Plus, two other tables are loaded with unopened envelopes and mailing tubes. "Belle the majority of the contractors won't bid on a restoration portion. To them, they want the full job with the option of subcontracting portions of it. I don't care to do business with them. Please see if you can make any sense of this mess."

"Katherine, what do you expect I keep from this clutter?"

"Number one, organize this mess. If something meets or is lower than my figures, keep it alphabetical. The rest, dispose of it in the round file."

I begin with the unopened replies. Eliminate bids higher than her projected figure. Keep blueprints or drawings for later inspection or reuse. Eventually from the opened mail, I uncover three competitive bids. Two are identical in cost. The other is slightly above her figure.

"Katherine, I kept these three. Although this one is slightly above, the proposal indicates their discovery of earlier remodeling not found on original house prints. In some circumstances, it was noted additions exceed current building requirements."

"Resubmit to them and indicate their quote is on specific project or complete package with limited use of subcontractors. Phone, fax, or deliver the new request to those local contractors before noon. Emphasize, time is of the essence."

"Katherine, it might cause confusion if two or more are working at the same time. Whose project goes first?"

"I believe their timelines should consider the growing season. Anson's project is first. The kitchen is next. Finally, squeezing in smaller projects, like painting, between the other two. The room colors haven't changed since 1901. Highlight the following. Final completion date is crucial. Each project begins within five days of my acceptance. Completion dates, weather and permits considered, will not exceed ten days. If compliance is not met, I will enforce and deduct a daily fifteen percent penalty."

"What if . . ."

"Go Belle. There are no 'what ifs' or 'buts'. Time is of the essence."

ഌഌഌ

Before five p.m. the next day, one refusal is received. Two faxes are received with an additional Courier delivery from one of them. Both quoted complete package with greenhouse and grounds structures for the same amount. The kitchen's quotes are close. Room to negotiate on smaller projects are indicated. I want to do the foyer's interior and seize my opportunity for Katherine to view a chandelier I found.

"Katherine. Between the two contractors, would you be willing to submit a tie breaker, since they offered room to negotiate. It will include the kitchen package complete with dumbwaiter plus the powder room and an entry chandelier in the foyer. If you like the concept, I'll phone in your request."

"I notice you add an item. If you can convince me on changing the front light fixture, I may consider it. I'll invite Clare. She and I will meet you at the carriage house within an hour."

"Super fantastic! If you see Anson, please tell him I'll drive." I hurry to change clothes.

We arrive at Carter's and leave Clare in the bath and kitchen section. We are two aisles away from overhead lighting when we hear our names.

"Mrs. McCutchen! Arabelle, stop!" Clare is running and waving brochures to get our attention. "There are too many people. I have a migraine. Katherine, please get me out of here."

As I drive back, Katherine comforts Clare in the back seat. By the time we arrive, Clare's color returns and her headache gone. I take Clare to her room and look around. It's the same size as mine with a floral border against light blue walls. A Danish modern chair is beneath a shelf where a reading lamp and several books gain support by pineapple bookends.

Katherine places a wet cloth over Clare's forehead and eyes. Lying under a white blanket, she almost appears angelic. Alongside her daybed, a boudoir lamp, and a clock radio are placed atop a small end table. So like her, everything is simple and direct.

Katherine closes the blinds and draws the curtain. "Clare, you will remain in bed. The day after tomorrow, I'd like you and Belle look over the brochures. Pick your cabinet design, appliances, and countertop. Arabelle, you're to organize everything and keep the job within budget, any questions?"

The silence is deafening until Clare lifts her towel. We exchange stares then shake our heads back and forth.

"Good. Clare, enjoy a good night's rest. Arabelle, devote time with Clare on her projects. It's time for my program, so ladies, adieu and good night." She gives us a slight smile, turns and leaves.

I look back at Clare. Start to say something but notice she places the towel over her eyes and lies back onto her pillow.

ຣາຣາຣາ

The following morning, we have breakfast together. Then, Clare refuses to decide on anything. Her projects will soon become dead in the water unless I get her interested.

"Clare, I don't understand. You were delighted to have a new kitchen and now nothing. Explain yourself, or I leave." I push away from the table and stand. Can't believe she's throwing her dream away.

"Please don't leave. Arabelle, I have a social phobia. As a child, too many guests at my birthday party and my face got all red. I scared the other kids. Avoided pep rallies in high school. An unfortunate incident happened. I couldn't hide my stomach getting bigger. My classmates would snicker and point at me. Left school when not only my face but whole body got red. I looked like a ripe tomato ready to pop and left the baby at an orphanage. After that, I ran away from home and came here. Here I had privacy and seclusion from crowds. I was safe. If I went with Anson to the A&P, I'd push the cart with my eyes glued to the floor. He'd get the groceries and talk to the people. Gradually, I recognized the workers and some of the other customers. Eventually, the fear went away. Thought I conquered being afraid of embarrassing myself."

"But you went with us to look for information. What happened?"

"Until the designer came from behind me, I was okay. Then she began asking questions like I was the homeowner. I couldn't see either of you. Became anxious, and that's why I went looking for you."

"I'm so sorry Clare. If I'd known, we would have stayed with you. I'm sorry." I take her hands and felt a slight tremor while holding them.

"Arabelle, you know the truth, and I'm glad."

"Clare, the past is just that. Now it's time to realize your dream. We finish it together." We complete the proposal before midnight and deliver everything to Katherine while she watches the Tonight Show.

Katherine shuts it off and asks, "Are you satisfied with your handiwork?"

We respond with a nod, and she says, "Congratulations. Arabelle, please fax copies to B&B Construction and Repairs Made Easy. Good job ladies and good night." With the remote, she finds her channel.

ଚଚଚ

Two days later, Clare confirms phone calls from both contractors. Katherine's conditions are acceptable and indicate time frame is doable. Let spring arrive early.

Knowing Clare's secret, our relationship results in workable meal plans with using Schwann's phone-in orders or our taking an occasional drive to support local produce stands. Clare now has time to learn how to make pottery.

Released from kitchen duty, I'm glad for the extra time to measure the east wing's rooms. I find doing solo searches has a drawback. I can't share my frustration in not locating the will.

I pull out Charlie's prints and create a new graph of the east wing. At lunch, a courier brings the quotes Katherine wanted. With lunch over, Katherine has time to review both bids. Three of us wait in the command center for her decision. I watch her. She scribbled something on her pad erases it, then circles a figure. We look at each other when she picks up the telephone and makes a call. I hold my breath. Will the manor see a brighter future?

"Everyone, there is only one company for both contracts, if Clare is willing to cook our meals on the bungalow's stove? Clare?"

"I'd cook for their crew if they get my kitchen done. Who won and when will they start?"

"That phone call was to Repairs Made Easy. They begin this weekend. Anson, here take his plans. Your project starts tomorrow, and I would like you to review his drawings against your ideas. If there is any change, coordinate with the owner. His bid indicated he's willing to work with us. After getting his permits, the owner will arrive tomorrow for my signature. Well fantastic four, the meeting is adjourned. Spring comes early."

In turn, we extend a high five to each other.

The work crew of carpenters, electricians, and masons come and go without disturbing my search within the manor. I only know of their presence by the rat-a-tat-tat of a hammer. Installing power lines for the electricity extends the greenhouse construction time into twilight hours. Foundation drains, and concrete floor once poured allow the operation of automatic sprinklers and water line connections to function.

ᢒᢒᢒ

After three days, fresh dirt and dust continually fill the air, landing at times onto the back porch terrace and in time into the manor. At lunch, I learn from Clare when Repairs Made Easy's CEO sees the mess; he comes to the rescue with a sea of green tarps.

"If he smiled a bit more, he could be good looking," Katherine said. "Too serious, reminds me of you, all work and no play I'd like to introduce you, but when I look, you're somewhere poking around in another room."

I look forward to meeting this owner.

Clare welcomes the disruption of her old surroundings and appears to enjoy cooking in Anson's apartment above the carriage house with our meals served in his kitchen. Tonight he fidgets and plays with his favorite meal.

"Anson, even I can tell something is worrying you. What is making you so jumpy?"

He pushes back his chair and points to his spare room. With parade-like precision, we stand and follow him into the room. Exercise equipment is against the outer wall because a white sheet covers a large pool table.

"Ladies, may I present this year's entry and winner in

the Rose Parade of Homes." With a hand fanfare, he lifts the covering.

The three-dimensional scene of greening the gardens with rose tea pergolas dividing the various rose categories is on display. Tiny strategically placed topiaries add accent to walkways. I point beneath a trellis to a bench with cushioned seats.

"Golly Anson, your scale models are incredible. Look, Katherine, there in the corner, it even includes Anson's greenhouse."

"Katherine, here the diorama shows what I hoped my drawings indicated. I scatter pergolas throughout the estate's gardens. Each one will separate the many varieties including hybrid roses. With these separations, a refreshing light scent will reinforce the rose theme but not overwhelm them.

Belle, glad you noticed the cushions for resting along the way. Here the judges can relax, appreciate a spectacular rose array, and view the manor's additional display of supporting, non-fragrant, colorful annuals."

Katherine scrunches down to eye level and considers the entire miniature floral representation. Standing, she gives Anson a hug and a kiss on his cheek. "Anson, order your plants and whatever you need. Check with Mr. Boyd on the greenhouse's completion and installation of your arched trellises? Need help, please let me know. I wouldn't mind planting a few rose bushes."

Mr. Boyd? Repairs Made Easy? Charlie never said anything to me? Is he missing me intentionally? "Excuse me. I forgot an appointment I made. Okay to use the BMW?"

"Of course, drive safe," Katherine said.

I call ahead to make certain my ex-friend Decima will be there for I have to straighten a misunderstanding. When I drive into town, I rehearse what I want to say to her.

Decima answers the door. "Arabelle, Shalom."

I push her aside and walk into her living room. "Decima Gordon, how could you stab me in the back by not telling me about Charlie's business? You're a low-down person, who sank to earth's inner core. We used to be friends. No, best friends. No more. Goodbye. Don't even think of calling me ever again."

She looks puzzled when I verbally attack her and she remains standing there.

"But you knew he took over his dad's business. Therefore, I thought you knew that he changed the name when his brother became a partner. And F. Y. I., I wouldn't count on his being at the manor too often."

"And why, may I ask?"

"Well next couple weeks, he's renovating exam rooms at the Clinic."

"Oh?" I say.

"So, are we still not friends because you need to cool off, and tea is brewing. Want some?"

"No tea, maybe a cup of forgiveness."

"Sure Belle, I'll make it a large one. Whatever gave you the idea I'd backstab you? I'm a nurse. I'd go straight for your heart."

CHAPTER 12
CHARLIE BOYD

It is the first week in June and the carriage house garage and Anson's apartment overflow with rose bushes and annual plants. His diorama sets a precedent with the Rose Committee in using accent plants and viewing sites. With the greenhouse operating and pergolas installed, gardening becomes a joint activity.

While we wait for Katherine, Clare is busy with frosting the cinnamon buns. However, Anson must be sick as he stares out at the terrace without his coffee cup. I walk over to check why he looks depressed.

"Anson, Katherine is pleased you utilized the gazebo for a mini green view of the gardens. The location worked so well for your diorama and gave bonus points to your presentation."

"Thanks for the pat-on-the-back, Belle. Unfortunately, I overheard one of the judges."

"And . . ."

"It was a smart demerit to my display, although she didn't say anything. However, I noticed she wrote in the Review's margin 'plagiarized idea.' I didn't copy Gertrude's ideas. I created the layout, selected the annual plants and rose varieties. Yes, I landscaped in color. She recommends that in all her books. A recommendation is not plagiarism. I was tempted tell her but, thought it unwise."

"Okay, you better relax and let's not disclose that bit of info to Katherine. Her hopes are high, and even a tiny leak will deflate the humblest soul. Let it be our secret."

"You are right. It'll be our secret. Is that why you wear a gloomy face?"

I shrug my shoulders and attempt a fake smile. "That's not the reason Anson. I find it disappointing and crime that with all the interior remodeling, nothing revealed a hiding space. At this rate, I wonder if it even exists."

"In time Belle, you'll figure it out. Forget the will and let's tell her the good news."

With the McCutchen Victorian residence added to the 'tour of homes,' Katherine's spirits sky-rocket and I hope to motivate her for additional change in the foyer. Instead, she wants me to join a committee meeting and run several errands in town.

I back out from the garage and pick up Katherine, who waits in the front driveway. Unfortunately, our departure is delayed because we are blocked from leaving. When the elusive Contractor gets out from his truck, Katherine insists we get out so I may meet him.

"Arabelle, Mr. Boyd, our contractor. Mr. Boyd, this is Miss Lacey."

Charlie smiles broadly. "Arabelle Lacey, with your permission I've waited since tenth grade to give you something more than a big brother hug."

He's asking permission for what? Before I can speak, my face is between his hands. I feel the soft touch of his lips that he confirms with a firm, solid kiss. An electric shock runs up my back, and it seems my heart skips a beat. I enjoy the sensation and try my best to sound upset. "Charlie Boyd, what got into you? Kissing me like that, in front of our employer?"

"Wanted to do that for a long time, never had the nerve until today. Hope I didn't offend you, Mrs. McCutchen, because I'd like to continue working here once the job is done. You know, whenever you need a contractor."

"Mr. Boyd, there is no need to apologize. It appears Arabelle is none the worse for it, and your personal life is yours. Since you mentioned continued employment, I might have something in mind. Come with me; I would like to discuss a project I'm pursuing. Come along." Katherine takes Charlie by his arm onto the terrace.

Without concern for me, they leave. I shake my head bewildered about his secret wish.

Shortly after Charlie leaves, Katherine decides not to attend the meeting and has Anson do her errands. The morning is disrupted, and I join Katherine in her office. From my past intrusions, I know well enough not to question what she discussed with Charlie, so I skirt around the subject.

"After dinner tonight, Clare wants a grand unveiling of her kitchen. You're not going to believe her kiln and new laundry room. Wait until you see them."

"He did both. That's wonderful. Tell me more, Belle."

"It happened after Charlie converted the outside shed into a kiln. Next, he used a small section of the kitchen, plumbed the broom closet, and lo and behold; Clare has an indoor laundry room."

"Interesting, when we return tonight, I must see these changes."

We walk around to the carriage house, and the Beamer is ready. "Katherine, how would you like to ride 'shotgun'? I'll drive, and it'll give Anson a break."

Anson tosses me the car keys. Although she sits beside me, her attention is given to the blueprints, and I hum along with the radio's tune of 'Let's fall in love.'

"Very enjoyable, Belle. However, both contractors submitted two sets of drawings. Like yours, one is without changes and one indicates possible directional changes that could conceal a hidden passage or opening. I realize you are doing your best, but I'd like you to involve Anson after we return from seeing the light fixture."

"Katherine, lunch is a priority. I'm starving. Then, we head over to Lighting Extraordinaire. The perfect chandelier awaits your approval because it is so, so lovely.I promise you; it will be the foyer's most spectacular illumination ever."

"I sincerely hope it is as fantastic as you say."

I glance over to her, and she looks doubtful.

After lunch and dessert, I take a shortcut, which takes a little longer due to construction. When we arrive, I push the shopping cart to the store's rear where only one luminary hangs, brightening the corner. I watch Katherine stand back, with her eyes fixed on the elegant black and gold crystal fixture.

"That one, I presume." She said and shook my hand.

"Yep, that's the one. Isn't it super elegant."

"Belle, you are right. The shimmer of the amber and clear teardrop crystals create quite an effect. I'm pleased. I don't know why, but I'm glad it's here."

"It reminds me of you Katherine, tasteful and chic. Sorry, but I hated the foyer's red bulbs with dangling red pendants. For me, when I walk through its illumination, the lights cast a red-light district over everything. Feel I could take on the character of a night shift street walker."

She wrapped her arm around my shoulder. "Arabelle, I didn't know. I could have changed the bulbs."

"Katherine, when we first arrived, I couldn't share with anyone how that chandelier revolted me. I knew everything would be better if you replaced the light fixture. Then by accident, I found this light."

"Unfortunately, I saw the price, and it is not within the foyer's budget. Or, are you telling me that you are?" Katherine asked.

"Yes, oh yes." I forget where we are and give a hug, and she returns it. Once the carton is in the trunk, I drive home a happy camper. We arrive in time for Katherine to discuss the installation with Charlie.

ঌঌঌ

A week later I'm carrying her breakfast tray and stop. Katherine is looking upward and twirling like a child under the new chandelier.

"Spin with me, Belle. It's fun."

I put the tray on a foyer table. Then, I tilt my head back and join her in twirling until we crumble to the floor. "Wow! It felt like we were spinning under a galaxy of diamonds glistening in the morning dew. Belle, that sparkle is too much, I mean, too elegant."

"I agree." I lie there and enjoy the view.

"Belle, if this is personal, tell me. However, I'm curious why Mr. Boyd bartered his fee for the installation by taking the old chandelier. He did Clare's dumb waiter, pro bono. And, he reduced the cost of a powder room and greenhouse by a thousand dollars. He only charged for materials to do the interior painting, nothing for his labor and included laundry and kiln as part of the kitchen bid. The entire project is well below budgeted figures. Did his kiss mean something more than satisfying a teenage boy's wish?"

"Probably not, we were like big brother and kid sister in school. He's a great guy, who always protected me."

"He is a good man to have as a friend."

"The best friend ever, Katherine, but, he's not my Charlie. Good guy and nothing more."

Katherine hooks her arm into mine and heaves a sigh. "Belle, let me think for the record, I like this young man, more and more."

I wonder if Katherine is right, could there be something more? Is there still a meow left in me for Charlie or Neil? My life is becoming a roller coaster ride, and I'm nowhere closer to finding Adam's will.

"Honest Katherine, he stopped church going after his dad died. Believe me; Mr. Boyd is hardly a saint." We tiptoe toward the kitchen to surprise Clare in her new domain.

Within the casual atmosphere of her kitchen, Clare plates hot roast beef sandwiches for lunch. Charlie kissing me replays in my head until Katherine's voice brings me back to reality.

"I'm inviting you ladies to join me in attending our Guild meetings. I need moral support for my proposed fundraising project in July. It's for a home for unwed mothers and . . ."

Anson barges into the kitchen and interrupts her.

"Clare, please turn on Channel 12 News."

We direct our attention to Clare's new seven-inch portable television. The picture clears and the weathergirl points against the local area chart. Clare increases the volume.

"Warm air and water combined with shifting winds, we can expect heavy rains inland and severe winds along the upper East Coast. Tornado warnings with severe winds are forecasted for the following counties. . ."

With the sound of shattering glass, transmission dies. In a commanding voice, Anson issues orders. "Clare, lower the window coverings. I'll engage the main generator to the house and check the greenhouse. Katherine, see to Belle over in the corner."

I sit on the floor with my knees tight up against me. Don't know how I got there. Only know hands are cuddling me. I release mine from over my head and grasp the other hands in a death grip. Someone is encouraging me to get up, yet my feet can't support me. I'm unable to stand.

"Belle, listen to me. You are safe. It's not a hurricane or a tornado. Come now, come with me. There is a violent wind outside, as in Jeremiah. Remember you are safe here. The winds will only disturb the peace for a short time."

Katherine gently pulls me up, and we walk out of the kitchen. The wind rushes against the shutters. I cling to her side as we go to the sitting room and the nearest chair.

A leather book is placed in my hands. "It was my mother's Bible. A portion of Jeremiah could be my family's history."

"Where? Katherine, where?"

"Jeremiah chapter five, verses 26 and 27."

I flip through the pages, and the words fall from my lips. "'For there are among my people, criminals, like 'fowlers they set traps.' Clare once told me there were secrets here but criminals?"

"Secrets?" Katherine sounds surprised.

I can't run. Shutters are still rattling, and I'm holding a Bible. I confess. "Well, right after I came here, Clare mentions that this house is full of secrets. One day, when the construction dust settled, she and I wiped down the books in the library. Found a small crayoned, photograph of a red hair and black goatee man. He resembles an angry Anson minus the goatee. Since it was stuffed inside a book, I kept it a secret."

"I forgot I colored Adam McCutchen's photo. I hated this so-called grand patriarch but not his two bastard children. With no will, I have no evidence to prove Neil is his heir."

"I don't understand. Adam creates then hides his will. You tell me that Jeremiah's reference to criminals is Adam's legacy. Good grief Katherine, what did I get into by saying 'yes' to your offer of employment?"

From her desk drawer, Katherine removes a worn, leather-bound album. She sits down in the wingback chair. Her face is drawn as if a heavy weight presses upon her. She takes my right hand into hers.

"Arabelle, this family tree is generations old. Please, bring over the footstool and sit before me."

I want to know more and look around the room. A tapestry footstool, large enough for me to sit upon and hold the album across my lap, is in the corner. It's heavy, and I use both hands to push it closer.

"Before I open the album, let me tell you about the earliest McCutchen's birthrights. Great-great-grandfather Luke married Anne Bean. She had twins, Lionel, and Lucy. Lucy ran off with an English peddler and no further history. Lionel married Elizabeth McDugal. Their only daughter, Florence, died at seven. Three sons were Leroy, Samuel, and . . ."

The even monotone of Katherine's voice is masked by the outside noise of Anson covering a broken window. The generation family tree soon becomes boring, and my interest fades with an 'uh huh' murmur.

"Arabelle, are you with me?"

I nod.

"Excellent, now here is the last McCutchen group." She opens the album on my lap. There is a sepia drawing of a somber, unsmiling woman. It's dark brown-gray color has aged her more that the hair style of the tight bun, drawn back away from her face, and the lace collar is worn subtly hide her double chin from view.

"Whoever she is, she'd be someone I wouldn't want as an enemy."

"This is Martha McCutchen-Boyd, who refused to take her husband's name. While Martha wasn't the only one, she followed Lucy Stone's example. Lucy was the forerunner to be recorded in using her maiden name even after marriage."

"Why did she do that?" I ask.

"Martha and Edgar had no siblings. They were the only one to carry on the family name for their parents. They agreed Martha's first boy would bear the McCutchen name and all other children would carry the Boyd name."

"Do you think Charlie is part of the Boyd's family?"

CHAPTER 13
TOO MUCH INFORMATION

"In the Lord's kingdom, we are related. However, I doubt it. I knew Charlie's parents. They adopted their sons. Now if I may continue, they married and began the manor's construction. In 1905, a fatal accident took Edgar's life. Although expecting their child, Martha saw the construction completed and delivered Adam, their son, in this home. So began the estate's legacy."

"Wow! She was some woman. Imagine the criticism she experienced."

"She did and bravely went against the norms of the day. However, Martha for proprietary reasons kept her name as McCutchen-Boyd. Nevertheless, she never added 'Boyd' to Adam's birth or baptismal record. Yes! I'll agree. She was remarkable."

"Do you think that's what Clare meant by secrets?"

"Arabelle, Clare knows everything about this family. Some may call them secrets, but to me, life is the way it is. Your curiosity reminds me so much of my Emily, always wanting to know more."

Emily? I don't interrupt.

Katherine flips several pages in the album until she lifts out a five-by-seven photograph. "These are my children, Neil, and his baby sister, Emily."

"Emily? Is she with her father? Katherine, I'm curious why you don't have any photos on your desk?"

"After Miriam died, mother's grief was intense. According to Clare, she went out of control. In a frenzy she ransacked every room and any family photos she found, she burned them. Instead of committing her to a hospital, Clare became her nurse."

"This album, your mother never found it

"Clare found it and hid it under a floor panel. When Mother died, she removed it, and I've added to it. The album now rests on my desk. The defaced picture you found, I buried because I feared Adam."

"He hurt you. I can see it in your eyes."

"Belle, this is not a wholesome story. It is one I'm not proud of being in it." Katherine grips the arms of her chair and her face pales. "Following Miriam's death, he changed, and I had first-hand knowledge. He played the part of a Casanova, a flirt, a womanizer; and eventually, was my children's father."

Katherine voice is flat, no rise but a monotone when she said that. Then vents her anger when she knocks the album to the floor. Tears spill over her cheeks, and she tries wiping them away.

"I'm sorry, dear. Forgive me. It was long ago, and I've no more room for those memories bottled up inside me."

"T. M. I., Katherine. Should I forget what you just told me?" Dear Lord, I'm praying she'll say 'yes.'

"No, write whatever you'd like. You knew Cam, and I grew up in this same household. One night on the way to a picture show, Cam bragged that Adam took him to a brothel to learn the ropes of lovemaking. Would you believe Adam asked Cam if I was a virgin?"

I'm uncomfortable with her confession. "Katherine, too much information, this isn't any of my business."

"Don't worry. T the most truth he could ever say is we did kiss, but, never did the dirty deed. The worst thing is Adam asked his permission to see if I was experienced. When he told me he agreed to Adam's proposal, I slapped Cam's face. He only laughed and said he told the old geezer that I took sex education in high school."

"That was so wrong. Didn't you tell your parents?"

Katherine rises and walks toward the television. "Father was dead. Mother showed me a Servant Contract that they signed. I never read them, just listened to her. He told them that whoever worked for a McCutchen had to sign this contract. It meant if they accepted work from his family and lived under this roof, they and their children became the owner's personal possession to do as he wanted."

Without warning, Katherine slumps to the floor.

"Help! Anson! Clare! Help!" I shout and hope one of them is nearby as I go to her side. No one heard my call for help. As she comforted me earlier, I do my best to console her as she regains consciousness.

"Katherine, this is the twentieth century. People aren't chattel. No paper gives anyone, especially Adam, the right to violate you. Didn't you tell anyone?"

"I told my mother. Back in '56, with his wealth, Adam stayed away from the hearing. He had his attorney do the dirty work when we went to our lawyer's office. I was 15 and extremely terrified. So much so, I trembled next to my mother when the attorney pointed his finger at me. He said I flirted with Adam before and after Miriam's death."

"Yeah right, a 15-year-old flirting with a man. How old?"

"Sixty. When Attorney Weesel looked at my mother, he said my hug and goodnight kiss told Adam McCutchen I cared for him. The attorney looked directly at Mother. I tried to explain, and he told me to remain silent until he finished."

"Entrapment, Katherine. Didn't your mother say anything?"

"She sat frozen, like a block of ice. I shivered when he came right close to her face and said that Cameron told him that I let him touch me. She looked at me with cold, lifeless eyes. I wished I was Miriam . . . dead."

"Whoa, at that age I can't even imagine what you went through. Katherine, I'm so sorry."

"The attorney was so close to me; I smelled his cigarette breath. He said because of my actions and their testimony I was sexually aware of the act before I experienced it with his client."

I help Katherine to her feet and sit down beside her on the settee. "Would you like some tea?"

"No thank you, dear. Belle, I did whisper to Mother that when we took baths together, sometimes Cam and I touched each other."

"But that shared bath time was when you were young, right?"

"Up until I was eleven. One night he grabbed me up here, and I kicked him real hard on his pecker. That was our bath last time together."

"Good for you, he deserved it."

"That's not how his attorney took it. When he

slammed his briefcase closed, I jumped off my chair. He stared at me, then looked at my mother. He told us to leave because Adam McCutchen was innocent because he proved I had sexual experience before Adam's encounter with me. The pregnancy did not indicate he violated me."

"Katherine, come on. You didn't say anything to defend yourself?"

"I tried, but he ignored my stammering. He stood over my mother. Questioned her if she thought Adam McCutchen corrupted her daughter. She shook her head no. He asked if I was responsible. Her answer drove a knife through my heart. She said, 'Fully responsible' and that I would apologize to Adam when we arrive home."

"Neil was the result." I hope she'd deny it.

Katherine lowers her eyes from mine. Her trembling body leans forward, and she weeps. I find tissues and place several near her hand. In a few minutes her sobs stop, she straightens her back and clears her nose. I know she'll be okay, but then I couldn't release her hold on my shoulders.

"Belle, when we got back, I overheard Mother and Adam arguing. Her voice was loud when she repeated 'pervert.' Each time she said it, he would laugh. It became frightening. I ran from the hallway and vomited in a big vase. Belle, that night Mother came to my room. Told me that within the next two days, Cam and I must sleep together in the biblical sense and the following Saturday, we would be married."

"But you told her."

"Yes, I knew what the words meant, but two wrongs didn't make it a righteous act. Oh, she knew it. But, she insisted Cam should think it's his. He wouldn't doubt his fatherhood, providing I did as she told me."

What can I say? Just be here for her. I squeeze her hand, and she relaxes. The peculiar way these people lived and thought is beyond my grasp; I have to know why. "Katherine, why would she insist on such a thing? Once you're pregnant, you're pregnant."

"Mother reminded me of the protective upper class. How would the social structure of that class benefit my unborn child? If Cameron thought it wasn't his, he'd divorce me and put me out on the street. I understood her logic and did the act. After all, she was my mother, and I obeyed."

"Katherine, does Neil know?"

She loses her composure and laughs hysterically. "I hope not, but I don't know. As ironical as it may seem, Cameron never questioned a premature birth even when Neil's birth weight was eight pounds. At the christening, my mother told me that she blackmailed Adam into signing a paper that allows my child and me to remain here until we die."

"And Cameron, does he still believe Neil is his?"

"Did, but no longer. Years ago, Cam insisted we have the Company's family health insurance, and physicals were required. His report indicated sterility, by then I already had two children. Adam grieved when an accidental drowning took Emily's life. He died of remorse the following year. Cam showed no grief at either funeral. He knew."

"It's okay Katherine. Your secret is safe. Let's see what Clare has for lunch or maybe some tea with lemon? What do you say? I'm here, and you're not alone. I'll take care of you."

“The album . . . Mother mustn't see it.”

“It’s hidden in your drawer. She won’t burn the children’s pictures.”

I leave for a short while and bring some lunch. We eat. Emotionally, her past took a lot out of us. Afterward, she relaxes and dozes off. I sit with my knees close to my chest and sway back and forth, much like I did with Mom when she cried about her best friend, forced upon and then married off to cover the horrendous act.

When Katherine awakens, her composure no longer exhibits her anxiety, and she apologizes. “My heavens, Belle, I hope you’ll forgive an old woman’s fears.”

Before I can answer, rapping on the door brings reality back to the sitting room. Anson enters and Katherine looks up. “Anson, is everything okay outside?”

"Grounds and buildings—all secure. It looks like the worst of the storm is over. We might get rain tonight. Need anything before I return to the carriage house?”

She shakes her head, and he leaves. “Gracious, it must be late. Would you please inform Clare that I expect Cameron home tomorrow. Then, she’ll pull a roast for tomorrow’s dinner. Even with the nap, I believe I, too, will retire.”

“Do you want to review my notes after breakfast?”

She rises from the settee. “No, we won’t be meeting until Cam leaves. Goodnight, dear. Get a good night’s rest.”

“Good night,” I say and watch her walk to the stairway.

CHAPTER 14
THE CHEATING HUSBAND

As I near the back hallway with the news of Cameron's arrival, the smell of fried chicken hurries me along.

"Clare, a message from Katherine, Cameron arrives tomorrow, pull roast for dinner, and she has gone to bed. Not sure if she wants anything to eat. Want I should take her a tray?"

Busy at the kitchen counter, Clare ignores me and continues mumbling while seasoning a piece of beef. "Never mind tomorrow—arrived today. I'm not a mind reader. He's the most inconsiderate person I ever met. Not even a 'Hello Clare'. Instead, he barks like an old sea dog, 'Cook, where's the pot roast.' Explainin' dinner wasn't ready, and he waves me off."

"Clare, if the chicken is ready, I'll take Katherine her dinner."

Clare's silence has me wondering. Is Neil like his father? No, wait. Adam was his father. Good grief, Mom, were you one of Adam's conquests?

Clare fills Katherine's tray. "Takin' her dinner would help me to get his roast in the oven. Tomorrow, I'll need you in the kitchen early. Have an appointment and you'll need to do breakfast."

"No problem, Katherine's dinner."

"I put it into the dumb waiter. Take the back-stairs.

The second floor, to your left, the door is on the inside wall. Katherine's room continue to your left, all the way back." Clare gives me a gentle shove towards the stairs while mumbling under her breath, "Wants a roast, does he? Well, it'll be ready at midnight."

"Okay tomorrow. 6 a.m., do breakfast," I say to remind me of tomorrow's chore. I sprint up the stairwell and reach the next floor before the dumb waiter arrives. After unloading the tray, I walk the long hallway to her room. As I near it, a loud bang and Katherine's voice breaks the silence in the hall.

"Stay away from me. Cam, you reek of alcohol. You're drunk."

A slurred voice raises goose bumps on my forearms. Within steps from her bedroom door, I recognize the voice. What is C.J. doing in Katherine's bedroom?

"So what if I'm drunk? It's my liquor. Another thing, do I have to tell Cook everything. Return tired from my travels and found fried chicken on the stove. You know I hate chicken."

"Cam, have some respect for the woman that raised you. Her name is Clare, Clare Collins, not Cook."

"Yah! Yah! Know that. What ticks me off is—it's me, not you, Katherine, that has to remind her I don't like chicken. Humph! She's cooking a roast now. And are you becoming senile with remodeling this monstrosity? Have you forgotten my sweet? I don't like change!"

"Stop shouting and be reasonable. Your phone message said you were to arrive tomorrow and lower your voice; I'm not deaf."

"Reasonable? I'm shouting because a servant knows more than I do. You're lucky I hit your table and not you.

Away from home, only a few months and Kate, you presume too much. Hire strangers. Redo house interior and what did it cost me? This place without any changes guarantees me privacy. What do you have to say, Kate, or, does the proverbial cat have your tongue?"

I knock on the door frame. Maybe this will interrupt him. My heart races and I hit it harder.

"Calm down Cam and listen to me."

"Listen to your excuses. Why? This estate is ours until his will is found. By the way, what's with the new toilet? Whose idea, that secretary or those servants? Don't answer that. Someone brainwashes you into thinking the estate needs modernizing, and you spend thousands of my money. You listen to me, Kate. If you want me out of your sight, get rid of her tonight."

Although I hear her voice, I decide to knock until someone comes to the door.

"Cam, remodeling shouldn't eliminate your privacy. Second, don't need your permission. I got the right when Adam violated God's law, as he did with me. Go, check public records. You'll see in '57, specifically October 4th, my name went on the property deed—with the right of survivorship extending to my heirs."

It's quiet. The time to hit that door is now, and I pound hard. Lord, please let her hear me. I know things about C. J. that she doesn't.

"Come in, Clare. Oh, it's you, Belle. Just put the tray in the window alcove. Thank you."

I'd never been inside her bedroom and unsure where the tray should go, look around and see the alcove is left of a four poster bed.

"Excuse me, Mr. McCutchen." With my back to him, I

pass between them. In front of me is the alcove. Within it, an oversized desk holds ornate frames with her children's photos. An ebony writing box lies on an adjoining marble table. I put down her tray and back up trying not to face him.

"Arabelle, this is my husband, Cameron. Cam, you recall my speaking of her mother, Dorothy Lacey. Recently Dorothy died, and Arabelle is now my secretary."

Cameron ignores the introduction and goes to the window. "Kate, think we might have gale winds, have Anson check the grounds tomorrow for damage." He then stands beside her and without a trace of recognition on his face or in his voice, he extends his right hand. "Miss Lacey, welcome to the McCutchen's household."

That's for Katherine's benefit. But I know how your cheating husband double-dealt even my mother when he whispered to me, 'If Dot looked more like you, your mother would have been a kept woman on Park Avenue.'

Even the memory of him makes me uncomfortable. I nod in his direction and struggle to sound natural. "Thank you. Anything else I can get for either of you?"

He shakes his head and walks back to the window when a small tree limb hits the clear glass. The sound startles me, and I turn. Cameron's long-limbed body appears to be within the storm's eye. Lightning flashes give the impression they discharge from his silhouette into the swirling debris of leaves and twigs that dance in the wind.

I bite my lower lip. To meet him here in her bedroom is nauseating. If I don't leave soon, it's likely I'll throw up. "Excuse me, Katherine. Clare . . . Dishes, you know. Good evening, Mr. McCutchen."

Even though I want to rush out of the room, I take baby steps between them and the doorway. How could he take advantage of Katherine and Mom? Then trick me into taking those pictures. Why?

Before closing the door behind me, I overhear a passing remark.

"Secretary? Why she's a child, but dear Kate, by all means, it's your decision. I've other matters to handle. Enjoy your dinner. Goodnight."

Once in the hallway, I run to the dumb waiter. Thankful for its size, I get inside. His footsteps fade in the other direction. I climb out and continue to my bedroom; I lock the door, Once in my bed, emotions confuse logic and reason for what I just experienced. It helps when I pray. "Know you'll keep me safe, Lord, but I have a tiny question. Do I tell Katherine about Cameron? Yes? No? Okay, I know, in your time."

CHAPTER 15
ICED CINNAMON ROLLS

I find a comfortable position in bed to listen for footsteps and welcome the silence. I close my eyes for a minute when the smell of cinnamon buns has me look at the clock. I see it is five o'clock and realize I fell asleep. Does Clare ever sleep? If I go down, and I'm lucky, I get a bun before breakfast.

With a quick loop, I fasten my bathrobe and run down the stairs. Once more, I collide with Neil McCutchen. The impact reveals my legs beneath the baby doll nightgown. I'm embarrassed and push myself out of his grip. "Mr. McCutchen, you startled me. Shouldn't stand by an open stairway, when someone might suffer a concussion. However, no damage was done. May I make you some coffee?"

Neil steps aside. His move allows me access to the kitchen. I pass by and notice he lifts a white covered spatula, and a small grin spreads across his face. "Wait a minute; Clare never lets anyone ice her buns. Where is she and when did you arrive?"

"Well good morning, Miss Lacey. With you around, a fellow needs accident insurance. Not that it's necessary, but I arrived around four and Clare decided to go earlier to some appointment. I was hungry and made my rolls. I had no conceivable reason to anticipate being blindsided by a vision. You spilled down that stairwell like a Tsunami and right into my arms. If you think of it, a 'Good morning, Mr. McCutchen' or 'Excuse me, Mr. McCutchen' would be far more acceptable than a litany of questions concerning my arrival and Clare's departure. Nevertheless, how may I serve you?"

At first, I'm stunned but undaunted by his condescending remarks. I laugh and say, "Me, a vision? Take a cold shower because at five in the morning, you're either half asleep or have a vivid imagination. By-the-way the collision—your fault because the smell of those cinnamon buns woke me. Black, no cow or cane, and I can't believe Clare would share her recipe."

"Not hers, the recipe came from a sweet young lady in Athens."

"Like in Greece?"

"You are bright," Neil says and removes cups and plates from the cupboard.

I can't hold back my frustration with him. "Well Mr. McCutchen if you expect a warm, cherry morning from me, don't. When without a single word, you're gone for months. Do I side step your absence and consider this another visit? Or, will the sire and son be here for a longer duration?"

"Point taken, Miss Lacey. What a surprise, I didn't realize he arrived. In the past, our travels kept us miles apart. Should say hello before he darts off again. Would you accept a peace offering of black coffee, no cow or cane, and a delicious iced cinnamon roll?"

"Sure. There's one condition to accepting it. It's good for this morning. You have a secret which keeps you on the run. Any I should know to protect my reputation? Should I be afraid your buns have a connection between you and a Jeremiah's fowlers?" Am I asking too many questions, he's jiggling his car keys? With that aggravated expression, I think he's ready to choke me to keep me quiet.

"Miss Lacey, are you always this rude? I gather Mother related our family's history, and you accuse me of potentially harming you. Do you wonder if I added a secret ingredient while in the wee hours of the morning, I bake mouth-watering morsels to do away with you?"

"Not in the least, I apologize. However, your family's history is loaded with drama; and besides, I am trying to find Adam's will."

"Are you delving into the dark and dirty, Miss Lacey? Ha! Ha!" A strained laugh leaves his face unsmiling.

This is not what I hoped our next meeting would become. "Mr. McCutchen, this household isn't the usual run-of-the-mill variety. May I suggest your rolls and coffee become a sunrise breakfast in the gazebo?" He's smiling. That's a good sign.

"Why not, that is if you won't be too cold wearing a bathrobe."

"This morning, when compared to last night's storm, is a sun-filled, balmy day where this dingy robe is fine. So let's go."

He plates several rolls, and I fill a thermos. When he takes the cups, I wipe the flour off his face before we go out the back door. We look at each other and laugh.

"Lacey. Thought I'd drop the miss. Do you mind?"

"Not in the least McCutchen, sometimes I do the same."

"Well, Lacey it's your party, lead the way."

I start out and block the sun from my eyes as we walk toward the gazebo.

"You're more beautiful than before. It's amazing how the morning sun . . ."

"Cold shower McCutchen. Take one."

I hear his laughter as I hurry along the footpath toward the gazebo. When he arrives, he taps the top of my head. "Five feet?"

"In bare feet, I measure 58 ½ inches."

A long, low whistle comes forth. "A sense of humor, too. Must say, Lacey, you lack very little to intrigue a man."

I turn my head in his direction and smile. Can it be? He returns it with a sheepish grin and says, "What fierceness in those green eyes and the. . . "

"Hey remember. I'm the writer, so back to your mother's memoirs. She referenced this Jeremiah about criminals being among his people. Any thoughts on what she meant?" I take a chair opposite him when I recall he is Adam's son and keep a safe distance?

Neil stands and walks around as he surveys the surroundings of the bungalow and gardens below. He pours the coffee and sits near me. "I was fourteen when Anson and I finished building this. We designed a circle for Mother to view her gardens. Anson did the roof dome. It looks the same, but little different."

"Well, fresh paint, hanging baskets, and all. Neil, you

stalled long enough?"

Neil moves his chair closer. The spicy scent of his aftershave drifts closer, and I look upward. His return glance makes me turn my eyes away. Wonder if he'll kiss me? Good, grief! No problem in the kitchen, oh that's right, we were arguing. Sit still. Nibble on the bun. Yikes! I can't take his silence.

"Sometimes your mother brings her ladies from the Community League here for lunch. This year, they voted Katherine, Vice President."

"Thank you for Mother's exciting news. She works hard to make things right." He sits back and stretches his long legs toward mine.

I grow impatient while he finishes the roll and coffee. A cooling breeze blows, and I reposition myself in the wicker chair to cover my legs. He's not interested in small talk, so I say, "At night, it's quite beautiful. Oh, you can't see the azaleas or wisterias, yet their essence is there. Soon the silence is alive when the frogs and crickets echo each other. When there's moonlight, it filters through the branches of the weeping willow. I'm no longer alone. I belong here."

"Lacey, to you, this place is alive. I'm surprised at your romantic nature." He takes my hand and kisses my palm. "If I repeat a tale, let me know."

"McCutchen, I believe the manor's eyes, you know the windows, look into and beyond Katherine's memories. They are the stories of those who live and lived here, including Cameron's drinking problem. What I didn't expect, was the rapport I feel would sidetrack you so that you'd kiss my palm. Thank you. Katherine said Emily died without details. Mr. McCutchen, I'm asking you for childhood memories of your sister."

I can't read him. His face is blank, except for his eyes. Preoccupied , he looks beyond the garden. Minutes later he points toward the bungalow.

"See that well. Only Grandfather wanted one. He insisted and had it dug over their objections."

"Okay, but it's covered and locked tight. How's it connected with Emily's death?"

"That's where it happened. At four, Emily loved to play 'hide and seek' with me after I got home from school. She would squeeze into the smallest space and not make a sound until I found her. Then she'd spin in dizzy circles. Stop on a dime and let gravity take over. Lie there laughing, enjoying her private joke."

"Saw the photo where she stood beside you in Katherine's room. She was a beautiful child. There's even a picture of the three of you in the family album."

"According to Clare, when Emily heard the car return, she'd run and hide. That day she went outside." Neil takes my hand. "From the carriage house, I heard her screams. Anson and I raced in that direction. We were too late. Grandfather stood there clutching the garden hose.

The good bucket wasn't in sight. Police guessed she must have climbed into it. If it weren't secure enough, it'd drop into about five feet of water." McCutchen kneels on the ground. I hold him as he cries. It eats at my heart when he says, "Emily drowned."

"I'm so sorry."

"Mother never forgave Adam for digging that well. Soon after Emily's funeral, I was hiding behind the couch when the doctor told them Adam died. Cameron secured the well and forbade anyone to talk about Emily's accident. Guess he figured if he erased any memory of Emily, it would be easier for Mother. I keep Em's picture under my mattress."

I try to hug him.

Instead, Neil leans into me and lifts my chin for a kiss.

"Ahem!" From behind an overgrown boxwood hedge, a baritone's voice startles me. I push away his hand and sit at the table.

Neil rises, turns, and extends his hand to Anson. "Checking the grounds for strays, old man?"

"Yes, the two-legged variety on the prowl for fresh meat. Don't usually find them this early in the morning. You never know. Didn't mean to intrude, Miss Belle, I do apologize."

"Anson, would you escort Miss Lacey back to the house? I have to visit someone. Lacey, may we continue, later?"

"Later." I do a goodbye wave.

Neil heads toward the cemetery.

"Miss Belle." Anson pulls my chair out from the table.

In an attempt to hold my tongue, I roll my eyes at him with a look that would kill a lesser man. "Anson, your timing sucks. I can walk back myself. 'Two-legged variety,' I'll take my chances."

We walk back in silence. However, Anson stops me before I climb onto the porch. "Miss, you should never offer meat to a starving man. Not sure what, but something about you, intrigues men and that includes Neil McCutchen. Remember, you must not stir up love before its time."

Pleased that Anson is concerned for my well-being,

and yet, I find it annoying. I coyly put my hand to my mouth. "Anson, whatever did you mean? I never give him any encouragement, even though, our meetings usually result in a collision. Tell me, Anson, in Neil's minuscule visits, where he would find time to think of me. Let alone consider devouring me like a piece of meat.

"For your own good, I gave you some excellent advice. Hurry along. Get dressed because Katherine's breakfast is cooling, and so should you, Miss Lacey."

He leaves me standing on the back porch and returns to his apartment above the carriage house.

Anson was correct. Time for breakfast is two hours overdue. Still in my housecoat, I find Katherine dressed and pouring coffee for herself.

"Sorry, I have to leave so early. I have a hair appointment. I was so glad; coffee was made, and Neil left me a note beside his cinnamon buns. "Let's lunch. Love Neil"

After she leaves, I go to my room and dress to impress McLaughlin with a yellow sheath dress. Through the cold air vent, I hear the grandfather clock chime nine. Then I recall his note to Katherine; he left with her. But maybe, I can catch them.

CHAPTER 16
CORNERED ANIMAL

To surprise him, I make an entrance from the grand stairway. Coming down to the first floor, I smell Katherine's signature perfume, **Arpège**with it clean, floral fragrance and notice the front door is ajar. A slight breeze pinpoints her location, waving to someone leaving in a cab.

"Katherine thought you left. Forget something?" There's no reply. "Did Neil go without you?"

"Yes, he left fifteen minutes ago with his car. Dropped Clare off at the strip mall and went to the office. It is a shame Neil missed seeing you in that outfit. You look lovely. That was Cam in the taxi. Doesn't drive for any business trip and said he'd be gone for several days." She closes the door.

"I thought you had a hair appointment."

"Such confusion with everyone leaving decided to go last. Belle, why don't you join me? With Clare gone and Anson driving me, I rather not leave you alone. I'll get my hair was done and we could have lunch or shop a bit."

"It's okay. Thought I'd read for pleasure. With all the cars, we have here, why does Cameron use a taxi?"

"Belle, he always calls a cab. While he has a driver's

license, told me he's not sure of himself behind the wheel. Since you won't join me and you're looking for a book, then you must see my personal library."

"A personal library? Thought my mini-office was in yours. You have a separate one. Outstanding! Has Clare snooped in there for that will?

"Think she did. However, you'll find the room's location is hidden. Follow me. Behind the main staircase rise, a portion of the manor juts out over the rear drive. The oak panels hide a pocket door. While it is slightly larger than my sitting room, I forgot to mention it. Wasn't sure if you would remain."

She knows the prints contain the answer to undisclosed areas. "Is that why you wanted another pair of eyes to check the prints?"

"Of course and one day, you'll tour the west wing. Not in use since Miriam died. Belle, with so many rooms in this house, we must continue the search. I'm certain you'll find something. I must show you the library and leave before I lose my appointment. Don't worry about dinner; Neil promised, he'd return with Buffalo wings."

We walk the entire corridor in silence. Behind the expansive stairway, ornate animal heads decorate the outer wall. Katherine strokes a raised lion's head, and a panel glides into a wall pocket. Trembling in anticipation, I take a deep breath and enter her refuge.

"Wow Katherine, that mirror. I can't believe the reflected images. Hardbound books, porcelains and those dish rails, you've so many plates on display. It blows my mind."

"I come here so often I'd forgotten its magic. Today was seeing the floor-to-ceiling mirror through your eyes, I agree it makes a statement. In our early days, Cam and I traveled and each souvenir holds a memory. His cynicism shows little interest in my décor and sentimentality, but, I enjoy its isolation and independence it gives me. Come here whenever you want."

"Katherine, that's so cool."

"I'm pleased you like it. Find a good book, relax and enjoy. I must leave, Anson is waiting."

I take it all in and exit for a cola. The panel closes. As if the 'Twilight Zone' awaits me, I reenter with my drink through a wall where a mounted lion's head guarantees entry.

This place, under my nose and out of everyone's sight, is heaven. 'Relax and enjoy.' Katherine is so right.

I'm excited. Not to mar a table surface, I put my glass on a waiting linen doily. When I run my hand along a shelf's edge, I find nothing needs dusting.

The small writing desk holds a picture frame of a mother and infant from another century. I recognize the woman. She's Martha McCutcheon-Boyd and her son, Adam. I trail my hand over the blue velveteen nap covering the settee. It adds contrast to the waxed, polished wooden floor. Cream-hued silk pillows supply support along the back and arms. The setting beckons me to enjoy the luxury and comfort it offers.

Still curious, I look behind heavy, lined draperies. Bright sunlight streams through the etched glass window and spotlights a glazed ceramic vase filled with huge leafy green ferns. They bend low and touch the soft ivory wool carpeting running the length and breadth of the floor.

Above my head, I run my hand across book spines, pausing long enough to select something to read. Then stop. "Hello, Katherine, is that you?" Okay, my mind is playing tricks. I sense every move I make is being watched.

Soon a raspy voice brings reality to my imagination. "Hello, Belle. I figured you'd be with her, spending my money."

I've no idea how he entered the room. "C. J., the taxi took you. I saw Katherine wave. She told me you'd be gone for several days. The pocket door is closed. How did?"

"As a boy, I learned the ins and outs of this house from my guardian. Like I know Katherine's real reason you're here. Hah! She doesn't need a personal secretary. She wants a wife for her precious son. I left to fool her into a false security but didn't leave the grounds entirely. Why? Because I know your kind, you and your mother are alike."

"What are you're talking about?" He approaches and blocks my escape. My throat constricts, and I swallow hard to relieve a mounting fear.

"Adam told me of his conquests. Your mother was a sanctimonious gold digger. She didn't know that I knew she prostituted herself with Adam, my unscrupulous guardian. Like Neil, you are one of Adam's bastards. When I took your picture, I saw his evil ways in your eyes."

"You cheated on Katherine. Mom was Katherine's best friend. C.J., you're a deceitful worm. And, my father is Troy Lacey. You knew I only let you take the shots to help with rent money."

He shoves me onto the settee near the bookshelf and grabs my wrists to prevent another attack. My self-preservation turns him fierce. His eyes look glazed, and he lets loose one hand to strike me.

"I love how you're dressed for, my so-called-son?"

His slap stings and I struggle to free myself from a hold that tightens when he pulls me to my feet. His gaze lingers too long. I recall how his eyes followed his draping Mom's boa over my breasts to reveal cleavage. Now I wish I hadn't worn a dress that outlines my body.

"C.J. let me go. Don't know what you're talking about so let go of me!"

"Don't think so. Your pictures are hidden for now. I'd say they're worth a million words of denial. Do you think Kate would believe you aren't a gold digger after seeing your nudes? Even fully clothed, I like what I know lies beneath. Sweet Arabelle, you can't help but notice my swelling. Speechless are you? Thought you might be. Let's pretend I'm Neil and you are my personal bimbo."

The sound of skidding tires along the rear driveway stops him. For a brief moment, Cameron's grip loosens. I pull away and back up a step. With a swift kick to his groin, he crumbles to the floor.

"Help! Somebody, please help!" I scream and make an attempt to escape. Somehow Cameron manages to take hold of me and with his fist, he hits me again.

I fly backward against the bookshelf and dislodge a book onto the floor. I pick it up and take aim. Still unsteady, the book slips from my hand, and I fall to the floor.

"You're on my turf, Belle. Ten years ago Katherine told me this room was hers. Then, I put her in her place like I did you. No one is coming to your rescue, little girl. No one.

Katherine is a two-faced piece of work. She carries

herself aloof like a queen for that women's group. She's defiant as a devil to me. For her, I play nice in polite society with one condition. No one uses this room. It seems she's forgotten our agreement. A reminder may be necessary.

But for you, Arabelle, I'll let you be the exception. Come whenever. Remember we can always use your bungalow for our photo sessions."

With the unfamiliar taste of blood in my mouth, I struggle to get the words out. "Cameron, think again. I won't pose."

"Hello, anyone there? Miss Belle?"

I turn. It's Anson's voice coming from the corridor and Cameron's whispering behind me, "He mustn't spoil my fun. Try to hide? I'll find you. Count on it."

I look back. He's gone. Only the movement of the tapestry gives evidence of his being in this room. At the same time, Anson enters.

"Thought I heard two voices, you okay?"

"Cameron, . . He disappeared behind that tapestry. Anson, I'm so glad to see you, but why did you come back?"

Anson offers me his handkerchief to wipe my lip. "Sit down, Miss Belle. I drop Katherine off, and she tells me to return to see if you need anything from the city. Told her I'd call; but, she insisted I drive back to the house. Sorry, I didn't arrive sooner. Here, please sit down on the settee."

He sits beside me. I'm shaking and lean against him. His arm like a protective shield is around my shoulders. When the trembling stops, I explain, "C. J., I mean Cameron, I knew him from the old neighborhood but never saw him angry. Honest, I was terrified. Other than the lip, I'll live."

"Miss Arabelle, when that man is cornered, he becomes vicious. Are you sure you met him in your old neighborhood and he disappeared beyond the hanging? Then Cameron altered the renovation specs. They weren't to scale."

"What do you mean?"

"Don't concern yourself Miss. Think the fresh air might do you some good. Why don't you join Katherine for lunch at the Country Club? She ordered Susan B. Anthony coins to distribute to the Guild women. I need to deliver them to her."

"I heard on the radio, how she empowered women with the right to vote. Please tell Katherine to save one for me and that I'm okay. Do not tell her of Cameron's action." I pick up the book from the floor. "See I'll be chilling with this book. I'm fine."

Before he leaves, we examine the wall behind the tapestry and find nothing suspicious. "Later, we go over that blueprint with a microscope. Miss Belle, promise me, you'll take that book to your room and lock the door until we return." Still shaking his head Anson leaves but his advice rings in my ears.

A look at the book's title, Introduction to Psychology, makes me laugh. What did Anson mean? Renovation specs are not to scale. He didn't answer my question—Anson, knows more, but, what? With everything that happened, I find I'm hungry and go to the kitchen.

Within ten minutes, Anson enters the kitchen. "Back so soon, want a sandwich?"

"Nothing, thank you. Only a mile and Neil calls. He needs the paperwork in the briefcase he left. Stopped at the Arch, woofed down a Mac, and here I am."

"Gosh, Anson, you're a yo-yo man. See you got his stuff. Oh, remind Neil to bring back enough blue cheese dip. I love it."

"And you, off to your room and lock the door."

When Anson opens the rear door, we hear the rolling thunder in the distance and for August, the incoming air is sharp and cold. With an after-thought, Anson steps back into the kitchen.

"Miss Belle, I know for a fact, Neil may not return tonight. The estate is his top priority. Join us for dinner at the Country Club. Chef Red is well known for his signature dish."

"Anson, I'll do us a favor and call for home delivery by six p.m. You should be here around 5:30, Right?"

Anson places his hands on my shoulders. "Miss, Cameron's past precedes him. Don't want to alarm you but be wary of staying here alone."

"Anson, I'm fine. Stop worrying."

"That is impossible. After I leave, make your phone order. Take several books from Adam's private library in the West Wing."

"There's another library?" I don't believe it.

"Yes, plus a gallery of historical portraits. Most interesting and you can lose yourself there. Unless, you'd enjoy a visit to the company office and see Neil at work."

I smile and hug his massive frame. "Don't worry; it's been a strange summer. Today's TV forecast is unbelievable for August. It includes possible hail and icy rain. So drive safe and pump your brakes."

Anson pulls his coat collar up. "You are stubborn, Miss. And for once, the weatherman is correct. Those aren't cumulus clouds out there. Come. Take a look through the window. See along the horizon."

"They look like giant anvils."

"True but they are cumulonimbus. Sometimes they reach a vertical altitude of 30,000 feet and can dump some foul weather—rain, snow, hail, lightning and even tornadoes. A bit strange, as you said earlier for this time of year. However, I think the worst we'd get would be heavy rain."

"Anson, if I get bored, and the hail storm stays away, I'll join everyone for Chef Red's specialty."

"If you do, Miss, don't use the Ferrari. I left the keys for the tow truck driver. Tell him that the engine is misfiring and its leaking brake fluid. You let Katherine know you're coming and take the Porsche. Left the key in the ignition."

"Okay, okay. Now go!" I give him a big pouty look and shoo him out the door. The incoming cold air shocks me, and I rub my upper arm to warm it. "Anson, I will order dinner unless I change my mind. If I come, I don't drive the Ferrari. Instead, I use the Porsche. By George, I think I've got it."

He laughs and waves back, and I quickly shut the door.

From the foyer, I watch the on, off departing brake lights as Anson maneuvers the curved wet driveway. When he nears the entry gate, there's an open area of sky that exposes gray underbellies of mountainous clouds. A foreboding skyline is escalating its way to the manor.

With approaching crazy weather, I trust my instinct and place the take out order. Next, I fill a carafe of hot chocolate to take with me and retreat to my bedroom.

Lock the door and try reading 'Introduction to Psychology' for what seems like an hour. Nothing I read makes sense with the intense winds outside. Thoughts of the impending storm plus the memory of Cameron striking me puts fear foremost in my mind. When hail pelts the shutters, I check the time, one more hour until they return. I put aside the book and curl up beneath my coverlet.

An ear-splitting thunder clap is too close, and it startles me. My clock indicates I have only a half hour more to wait. I throw back the quilt and hear the soft sound of a knob turning.

"Click. Click. "Barely audible; but when it stops, the whispering of my name breaks the silence.

"Arabelle? Arabelle, I know you're in there. Open your door. It's me, your old Uncle Jerry. Come on sweetheart, open the door."

"C. J., what did any of us, do to you?"

"Belle, you don't know the whole story. Let me tell you."

"Tell me your story. I know you get a monthly allowance from profits. Know your lifestyle ends once Adam's will be found. Know you cheated your wife and my mother. Know you bully people or use physical force to get your way. Know you don't use the estate's vehicles because you can't drive. Did I leave anything out, C.J?"

"Adam's life of vice intrigued me. He promised I'd be in his will if I married Katherine. She bores me. I enjoy older women; they pleasure me. With his money, I delight in my lifestyle. Then the wet blanket learned of my indiscretions; I endure the resulting outcome. Outside, the world sees a playboy. Here, I'm subservient to her whims, unless I'm threatened—like today."

"Cameron, you toyed with Mom's feelings. You knew she was best friends with Katherine, your wife."

CHAPTER 17
CLARE'S SECRET

"Hah! Your mother's friend is a blackmailer. Because of her illegitimate brats, her name is on the property deed along with Adam's offspring named in the will. I'm not. Adam bragged how proud he was in keeping the McCutchen name alive for another generation. The man was sick, believe me."

He stops talking. I get closer to the door and with confidence say, "That's old news. It's already in her memoirs. Cameron, you screwed my mother and took away my innocence."

"Belle, you're right. Listen, open your door. I'm sorry I slapped you."

"I don't believe you. Please go away." What's with you, you're locked in, and you're saying please.

"Dear Belle, within these stately walls, I'm ridiculed."

Once more he twists the truth. I'm infuriated and throw caution aside when I open the door to face him. My blood boils as I poke his chest, "Same cock-and-bull sympathy stories you told Mom and me. I know Katherine. She is nothing like that. I know." It dawns on me. I did what he wanted.

When Cameron grabs both my shoulders, he pushes

me into the room and kicks the door shut. "To me, Katherine is no angel. She controls the purse strings. I tolerate her treatment to get what is rightfully mine. Then, your precious Kate sacrificed her friendship for my benefit."

I spit in his face and scream, "Liar! Liar! Liar! Another one of your lies, Katherine wouldn't do that to her best friend."

"But she did. She did." Cameron taunts me.

I shrink backward until I meet the wall and wish I could melt into it. Lord, I got myself into this pickle, could use some help when I can't forgive the hatred I feel. He towers over me, and a smile crosses his face. "Cameron, you're like a venomous snake in this house."

His smile is erased, and I look beyond his eyes filled with contempt. I've seen that look before, and it panics me. With the little courage that remains, I apologize. "I'm sorry. I agree this is your home. Although, Katherine would never betray my mother."

"Not intentionally," he says with a change in his voice. "I found an envelope on her writing table, addressed to Dorothy. I recalled how she flirted with Adam. I thought, what irony, your mother knew nothing about me. I'd have Kate's friend, as my personal oasis away from her. In time, your innocence and youth became refreshing water. When Kate advertised for a companion, it was my solution to solve Dot's money problems and bring you closer to me. After I told your mother about the Ad, I left town and let nature take its course. I never expected her heart would go."

He strokes my hair. The touch makes me nauseous, and I move my head away. He laughs so hard, he coughs.

This gives me time to make my way from him and soon feel the doorknob. I'm so close to my escape and turn the knob. He pulls me away from the door.

"Let me go and I won't tell Katherine the truth."

"Sweet, sweet Belle, tattling won't help. I told her to keep you, to give you refuge. How generous of me to welcome you, the little orphan. Keep me happy Belle. You'll live in the lap of luxury. Now where would you hide my favorite outfit, correction, her feather boa?"

"You gave her that boa. You told Mom it was a remembrance of your love. She believed you. I don't. I destroyed it."

My eyes give me away, and Cameron turns to his right. A firm shove and he moves the wardrobe and takes it from the floor. As if he held a snake, the feathers slip through his fingers.

"Belle, your photographs show your beauty. I might be selfish and not share them with Neil or Katherine. Providing, we schedule future photo sessions."

Vehemently, I shake my head. "Never again, you promised."

"Lied. You were so naïve and trusted to believe that I'd take shots of an innocent nude and not realize their commercial . . .."

His words are silenced by hail hitting against the manor and my window. The barrage causes the veins in his neck to stand out in livid ridges. When Cameron pulls me against him, I scratch his face until he shoves me away.

"You will see that Kate gives me a share of this place, or I'll have a judge contest Adam's last codicil that he signed under duress for his well-being. Now it's a shame I don't have my camera, but let me help you try it on for old time sake?"

"No. In the past, when you positioned the feathers against me, I felt each quill's shaft was punishment for what I was allowing to happen. You took advantage of our situation, Cameron."

"Boohoo! Took advantage, humph! Even for a short time I got your mother out of that hole-in-the-wall. Now she's dead, and you live the life of a socialite. Where are your tears now, little woman? When I gave her this boa, she was grateful and showed me a great time. Couldn't believe how I reaped double benefits from a cheap neckpiece."

Cameron begins draping the dusty object around my neck. I feel the boa tighten as he says, "Before I go, Arabelle, I must have you." He tries to kiss me. I scratch him and wipe away any trace of his lips and foul breath.

I yank the feather noose away and throw it to the floor. "It's over. I'm not your pawn. Don't plead or threaten me, Cameron. I'm no longer a scared teenager, who thinks that without your lecherous generosity, I'd have nothing."

A loud boom shakes the window and from the front of the manor, a resounding crash follows. My anger is magnified by the mirrored flashes of lightning across the evening's darkened sky and I plea, "Leave me alone. You can't hurt me anymore."

"Bam!" Something hits the roof so hard that the impact resonates to the floor beneath my feet. Lights go out. This happened once before, and I remember the generator will take over in seconds. Escape, but where? The lights come on, and I'm too late.

"Arabelle, I want to capture you with my camera lens. As an adolescent, your shots were unsophisticated, so innocent. How you've developed into a beautiful young woman. I need to experience the flesh of that woman. Belle, when I kissed your mother, only a few feet separated us. Doing your school work in the kitchen, you'd see us and knew what was happening."

"You're sick!" I shout to drown the sound outside where the hail storm intensifies. I worry for Cameron blocks a direct exit. He wets his lips like a stalking cat that has its prey cornered.

"Belle, believe me. Your youth and beauty handcuffed me to your mother. You don't understand." He appears nervous as he frequently glances outside while the winds intensify and debris flies.

During the distractions, I soon open the door wide enough to escape. "Leave now. I won't say anything. Then you'll still be able to enjoy your present life. However, should you ever take legal action against Katherine, you won't like the repercussion."

"The timid mouse threatens me. You won't get the chance, little girl."

"Be assured Cameron, it's not a threat. It's my promise, and I guarantee you. I keep my word." I race to the stairwell. Once in the kitchen, I hear heavier footsteps in pursuit and run to Katherine's private library. With the bungalow's key safe in my hand and the storm outside, I realize it is the nearest safety through the damaged patio door.

Cold air and hail blow through a broken pane, while I fumble with the latch lock. While my face and arms smart from the incoming weather, I'm fine until I feel feathers tighten around my neck. Once again, Cameron mysteriously got into this locked room. I gasp and tug at the feathers. The noose falls free, and I take a breath.

"It's not over Belle. You'll remember that I always get what I deserve." He turns me around. His slap reopens the cut on my lip. I reel back with his second blow and fall against a chair.

Now free, I spit blood in his face. "Get out of here Cameron, I'm not afraid of you, and I'm not leaving. You are."

Unsteady, I walk away from the terrace door, stepping onto several pieces of glass. Startled by the sound, I lose my balance and fall against the door frame. A glass shard cuts into my hand. Blood spatters onto the rug.

Cameron laughs and gives me a farewell salute. "Understand sweet Belle, I get what I deserve. By the way, Anson left you the car keys in the kitchen."

"Yes," I want to warn him, but he pushes past me and kicks the terrace door open to take the shortcut into the kitchen.

The adrenaline has left, and I pull hard to close the door. I sit, lowering my head, until the lightheadedness leaves. With a table doily, I wrap my hand. It stops the blood flow. I'm relieved and relax. Through the shattered door, I hear tires peel out and the sound of flying hail and gravel hitting against the back of the house. He's left. Tears of relief come and I glance at my watch. "Almost six, everything will be okay once they arrive."

I stagger into the foyer and unlock the front door. I need to see the car leave the estate grounds to feel safe. Still trembling from my experience, I peer through the storm door's frosted glass.

A blinding flash hits somewhere along the estate's driveway. Soon flames lick the sky. Horror-struck, I go to the nearest phone and dial the operator.

"Hello, fire at the McCutcheon estate.—Yes, Near the entry gate. I see flames from the house.—Please hurry.—thank you." I wrap a coat around me and grab an umbrella. Then rush toward the inferno.

High eastern winds propel leaves and branches into the air. Because of the gusty winds and slippery wet grass, my progress is slow. When I arrive there, volunteer firemen connect hose lines to put out the inferno of combined gasoline and a giant oak. Charred limbs burn against the vehicle embedded in the vast tree trunk.The earlier lightning strike caused the tree to split, leaving a portion of it on top of the car's hood.

I come close to the fire chief's vehicle. I see Katherine, who has her mouth covered. Beside her, Anson shakes his head and says, "Arabelle took the Ferrari."

I wave to them, and Katherine rushes to embrace me. "Thank you, God. Anson thought you went out to get the wings," Anson said. "But, if it's not you, who is it? Belle?"

Katherine's eyes meet mine, and I hesitate for a moment. We stare as the firemen freed and now removed the corpse. It's burnt beyond physical recognition.

"Cameron came back. He was upset and left in the car."

Katherine faints. After the ambulance medic checks her vitals, he suggests she be removed from the scene and taken to the house. Turning back for one last look, I watch as Cameron's incinerated remains go into a body bag. I walk alongside the gurney until we stop on the porch before entering the manor. Anson remains behind to speak with a police officer.

From the porch, we hear the grating sounds of the truck's crane. I rub my jaw as the strained, agonizing struggle between machine and a hundred-year-old tree, reminds me of a dental appointment. Behind the porch railing, I watch it remove the sports car from the charred oak and go across the lawn. That opens the driveway for a funeral hearse and other vehicles.

We wait in the sitting room for Anson's arrival. Katherine is conscious, calm, and silent. After a while, Anson enters and relates a shortened version of the officer's report.

"Their conclusion it was an accidental death. The Ferrari's speedometer stuck at 85 when he hit that tree. Without further inspection, they figure with wet driveway; he hydroplaned on the curve. With the lighting, he could have been blinded, lost control. Car overturned. No sign of his wearing a seat belt. On impact, Cameron's head went into the windshield."

"The Coroner, did he do his report?" Katherine asks as the color in her face comes back.

"Got a copy. He wrote that it was an accidental death due to blunt force trauma, accompanied by incineration."

Katherine paces back and forth. "Why did he come back? Told me he was leaving on business. He always takes a cab, never drives. Why was he driving?"

Anson and I look at each other. There is a silence between us, and I try to erase earlier scenes with Cameron from my memory.

"Anson, Clare and Neil? They should hear from us, and not the late news."

While she talks, the front door opens, and a trail of cold air follows behind Clare, who rushes to Katherine's side and hugs her.

I'm in the background and view the scene with questions. Jeepers, why is Clare crying? Maybe this is one of those times; it's better to be seen and not heard. But why is Clare more agitated than Katherine?

Katherine embraces the sobbing Clare. "Clare, it was an accident. How did you hear about it?"

Between sobs, Clare says. "Police band radio, my friend has one. Puts it on when she drives and we heard the address. She drops me off at the front gate. Police have the tape up, but he lets me in. What happened?"

Finally, I can help. "I'll fill you in, Clare. Was going to get Katherine some tea, join me?

"Cup of coffee would help," Anson says.

Before we reach the kitchen, Clare knows the details. She looks haggard, all too quiet for someone who complained about Cameron. Touching my hand, she says, "Migraine Arabelle. Please tell Katherine I'm sorry." Still crying, she goes to her bedroom and closes the door.

I make the tea and a small pot of coffee. Before I return to the sitting room, I check on Clare. She is curled up, and I hear her sobs, although muffled by her pillow. I leave and wonder why.

When I reach them, Katherine looks up as she finishes talking to Anson "Did you call Neil?"

"No, left word at the office. Got what he wanted from me and we drove away in opposite directions. Neil said he'd return within the week. Knowing him, if he sees the local news, he'll be back. If not, I alerted highway patrol to look out for him."

I look over. Katherine sits straight-backed. With folded hands in her lap, her eyes look downward. Without showing any emotion, she raises her head and looks from Anson to me. “Belle, please call the funeral home. I want Cam cremated. Yes, his final hurrah. I'll scatter his ashes away from the estate. He never stayed here long, never actually belonged. If you don’t mind, I’ll take my tea to my room.”

Anson leaves his coffee. Then juggles the tea cup while he assists Katherine to her room.

Minutes later, I return to the kitchen and find Clare crying into her hands. I wrap my arms around her for comfort. “Clare, it must be hard for you. His death, I mean. Katherine mentioned you cared for him almost nine years.”

“It was more like thirteen, Arabelle.” She blows her nose. No longer sobbing, yet keeps crying for like forever.

I recall Clare's remark. ‘It was more like thirteen.’ In her memoir, Katherine told me Cameron was four when he arrived. She indicated Clare kept him under her wings until he turned thirteen. Oh no, Clare was his mother. My embrace becomes softer as I stroke her temple. I know Clare’s secret and why she mourns far more than Katherine, his wife.

Anson returns with the teapot and hands Clare a shot glass. “Here, it’ll calm you. Sleep is best for a migraine. Arabelle, help the girl to her bed?”

Her hand trembles as she grasps the glass. Clare spills some of its contents but finishes the drink. “Not necessary Anson, I’m a grown woman. Know how to go to bed. Alone!”

I give him the nod and wait outside Clare's room until

I hear even breathing. When a light snore tells me she rests, I leave. How do I add this to Katherine's memoirs?

Following the police investigation, it's a week before Cameron's ashes arrive. That same day, Katherine decides I should drive her to a bluff above Lake Erie. There, a north-western wind has an occasional updraft.

"Belle, come closer. With the white caps below, it's a magnificent view."

Terrified of the drop I hang back from its edge. Katherine carries the urn and appears unafraid when she's within inches from the precipice. She slowly removes the lid as if she has something to say to his remains. Then, with an extended arm and deliberate movement, she takes a handful and scatters Cameron's ashes out over the precipice.

I'm amazed at her detachment when an unexpected updraft slams his granular remains into and against the slate rock crevices.

"Katherine, be careful. You'll fall if you lose your balance."

"Don't worry Belle. I finish what I start."

I watch her empty the urn into the water below. I'm surprised when Katherine turns around. She is smiling.

"Katherine, I don't believe you're grinning."

"Why Belle, the winds paid a perfect tribute to Cameron. He always desired to make a statement away from the manor."

I thought of his last words to me, 'I get what I deserve.' I smile unashamed but believe even he shouldn't have died the way he did.

On our way back, Katherine uses the car phone and calls the Country Club. "Yes, this is Mrs. McCutchen. I'd appreciate it if you would assist me. — Yes, I'd like you to open a two-hour memorial at the bar. I'll cover drinks for his acquaintances to convey their feeling at Cameron's passing. — Yes, it was a private ceremony. Please advise my secretary, Miss Lacey, of the cost and she'll send you payment. — Thank you, goodbye."

She places the phone on the console. Neither of us talk and we drive in silence until I pull into the estate's drive, and Katherine says, "His conversation was odd."

"Whose?"

"Well after the manager expressed his condolences, he said that Cameron was a humanitarian to many of the members. It seems he had ready cash to give if a member needed a considerable amount. The manager said that Cam handed him the money for the closing on his house. Then told him that it wasn't a loan only a gift to a friend. Well, I'm glad he had some redeeming qualities. Shame he didn't show them at the manor."

Neil chose not to attend any farewell ceremony. Under sedation, Clare stayed at the manor. Before we return, Anson had Cameron's personal things removed from the manor. When we return, I leave Katherine off in the front and drive to the rear. As Anson parks the Beamer for me, I feel, as if, Cameron never existed. Only memories remain.

Since we spent half the day with Cameron's cremated remains, Katherine looks in on Clare. While I see what's available for supper, Anson storms into the kitchen and Katherine closes the bedroom door.

"That kid, he's home because the Firebird is gone. I didn't wake Clare, did I?" Anson pours himself some coffee and sits down.

"Anson relax you didn't wake Clare. Neil called my private line and left a message. Upset he couldn't do the service, but Company pulled him back to the office. I forgot to tell you that he'll be here around six to go over Cameron's will. It was in the paperwork you brought him yesterday."

"He'll be here for dinner? Clare's frozen meals are gone, and I don't know what to cook."

"Belle, don't worry. He wants to take me out to eat. Has something he wants to discuss in private."

"What?" I say. "In private? Another secret, sorry Katherine, I had it with this dysfunctional family group. Enjoy your meal with your son. As for me, I'm going to the bungalow. Goodbye, all."

CHAPTER 18
BLAME THE CHERRY SUNSHINE

After several days, Clare recovers from her depression. With one drawback, her usual cooking routine lacks enthusiasm as she orders more take-out meals than she cooks. Today, she had Anson take her for groceries for a special dinner. I'm hoping they stop for burgers when the sound of the back door banging shut gets me curious. The intercom is out of order, so I must listen from the stairs. It's Neil. He and Anson are discussing business.

"Anson, fantastic job handling the HP account for me, be sure to remind me at bonus time."

"No problem. Wish life would pass out a bonus instead of disappointments. Can't complain too much. After all, one in almost twenty-seven years must be a record."

"You disappointed? Must have been a whopper for you to remember it. What was so devastating?"

"Believe me, Neil. It came from a particular young woman when she said 'No.' to my marriage proposal. Have hopes, she'll change her mind someday."

"Anson, her answer will remain the same," Clare said from her doorway and left the two men laughing.

"Kidding aside Anson, I asked our attorney to advise how Cameron's death affects the business and the estate.

Also, we need to discuss Mother's renovations. Costs were in line, but I'm concerned you believe there was tampering with the original drawings. Why would Cameron do that?"

"With Cameron, it would be anyone's guess, Neil."

Good grief, Neil's only interested in blueprints. I turn around to leave and lose my balance, falling into the stair riser. I freeze. Did they hear me? No. Anson is still talking.

"It's a gut feeling I have about the meeting with your mother. If it concerns you and Miss Belle, would you mind a bit of advice?"

"Advice, about what?"

"Your instincts, trust them. When in doubt as to whether or not to react, just do it."

A soft laugh comes from Neil. "Okay Anson, sounds quite profound. On an estate matter, we need to discuss Mother's plans. They inflated your garden expenses."

As I climb the stairs, their voices become distant. I'm depressed that Neil didn't mention me. Nothing, I mean nothing, is happening between us. Okay, plan A failed so onto plan B. Maybe he'll be with her when I bring in the afternoon tea.

I freshen up and slip on a floral sundress. Delighted with the thought of meeting him, I hop down the stairs two at a time.

"Hi Clare, know if Neil's staying for his birthday this year?"

She straightens the tea service on the cart. "Don't think so. He's with Katherine now. She's trying to convince him. I set it for three. By the way, you look lovely."

"Thanks, Clare." That woman constantly surprises me. I push the cart forward until I hear them talking. So before entering, I rap on the door.

Neil answers it and gives me a wink to accompany his grin. "It's okay Mom, or as Miss Lacey would say, 'It's cool.' Therefore, I leave a week from Sunday with no changes, even if it is my birthday. Anson has the power of attorney and can handle the unexpected."

Quickly I put the extra cup and saucer on the cart's lower shelf. I try not to intrude on their conversation but the cart jiggles the tea service. "Do apologize for interrupting, but you can't leave."

"Lacey, don't want to censor your manners but I must. As to your opinion regarding my departure, it is unnecessary. It does not concern you and inappropriate, when you stalk me, wearing such a cute outfit."

I step to the side and fill Katherine's cup. From the corner of my eye, I see him giving me a once over and can feel my cheeks warming.

"Mr. McCutchen, I don't tempt nor follow you. You happen to be wherever I have to go."

Katherine comes between us and stretches out her arms around our shoulders. "You are no longer children. So I say, don't fight. Play nice. Neil, on afternoons Arabelle doesn't search for Adam's will, we work on completing my memoirs. Today she is early. So, will you join us for tea or take a walk somewhere."

"Katherine, I thought you'd like some family time today. So, I've plans for a bit of fall cleaning at the bungalow. The weather is perfect for airing it out."

"What an excellent idea, Belle. Neil and I will have tea. Or, he'll come to help you. In case, the furniture needs to be moved."

I can't help but notice Neil's nonchalant maneuver toward the door. And so did Katherine, when she gives him a flick of her wrist.

"Oh, go. I'll enjoy the tea myself."

I suspect this was prearranged. For when we pass through the kitchen, Clare hands Neil a basket and something he puts into his back pocket. She said, "Katherine had a suspicion and warned me earlier. In the basket, there's a thermos of chowder—bits of clam, mussels and lobster chunks. Made sourdough bowls—just scoop out the bread and pour in the soup. No spoons. Eat medieval."

When I give her a quick peck on her cheek, she hands me the bread bowls. Armed with a meal fit for royalty, I wrap an arm around her and give a hug.

She whispers in my ear, "Maybe you can convince him to stay 'til his birthday."

"Will try, thanks for the lunch." I jump off the porch onto the path where Neil waits.

"Which do you want first, the medieval fare or hard labor?"

"Before Mother comes by for an inspection, I may as well get the work done. However, would like your opinion. Anson gave Clare a little something to add to our meal, his cherry sunshine. I enjoyed it the last time I came. Will you mind?"

"No, if it's good enough for him, it's okay by me. Mind if I add the bread bowls to your basket?"

Neil shrugs and opens the lid. Then smiles and offers his arm. I take it and we go along the path. We stroll past the gazebo, and now see that the bungalow is a stone's throw away. I stop him and look up into his face.

"See here McCutchen. I've no claim on your time or muscles. You know, don't feel obligated because your mother said to help."

"Neil, the name is Neil. Only my enemies call me McCutchen."

"Okay. Well, friends call me Belle and the special ones, call me Lacey."

"Then Belle, it's no imposition. Besides, I'd like to see what you've done to the place."

With the lunch basket on the kitchen table, he smiles like a Cheshire cat. I can't make up my mind if he's conveying me the message, Don't you think I'm the catch of the season? If so, I return a not so much, well maybe a little smile.

"Neil? The windows, how about you cleaning the outside? Neil?" I turn to face him and am spellbound. His lips approach mine, and I respond to his touch in raising my face to meet his. The sensation of his five o'clock shadow, as it scrapes against my cheek, awakens every nerve ending on my face and climaxes when he kisses me long and hard.

"Lacey, you're a sweet girl, and you can blame Anson. It's his fault that I kissed you right then and there." When he relaxes his hold, I breathe deep and rest my head on his chest and hear his heart beneath my ear. Or is mine, beating so loud? I need to regain control. "I don't believe Anson told you to do that."

We work for the next few hours. Window cleaning and fall cleanup become a new fascination for me. Only hours before we bickered, now his slightest touch against my elbow is a pleasurable experience.

I'm getting hungry and want to enjoy the meal. So I ask him point-blank, "When you kissed me, are you leaving again and playing your ace in the hole sooner than later? And promise me, you're staying longer for me and your birthday."

He twists away from me and opens the picnic basket. Then turns and gives me a quick wink. "Hard to say with hunger pangs affecting my decision. Maybe some lunch and a little libation of Anson's sunshine would help me choose."

Neil extends me the open flask. Never drank from a metal container before, but, I want to act cool and tip a mouthful from its lip. Too late. My eyes water and the vision blurs for a moment. I know I made a mistake when I gasp, "Oh my, can't get my breath."

"Sorry, thought you'd know anything homemade has a mule's kick to it. You okay?"

"Well, there's an excellent cherry aftertaste. Didn't think I'd go blind momentarily. Think it's time for Clare's chowder. Agree?"

"Agree." Neil takes a drink from the flask, tightens its cap and returns it to his back pocket.

In the meantime, I scoop out the large rolls soft inner bread for dunking into our soup. Then, pour the piping liquid into them. The chowder, bread and bowls disappear in minutes. I abandon thoughts of another kiss. After a sigh, I get back on track to get an answer and finish the cleaning.

"Neil, either you're avoiding my question. Or you can't reach a conclusion on a full stomach. Or your mind evaluates the question of whether the space program gets funding or not. So, will you be here for your birthday?"

"In time Belle, should I stay . . . what meal would you make for me?"

This man is trying my patience. I go to a drawer then to the cupboard before handing him an opener and a can of precooked ravioli in tomato sauce. Smiling, as sweetly as I could, I offer a fork. "Bon appetite."

"What—no bacon and eggs? Coffee with burnt toast? Bowl of cereal?"

"If I don't have to do it, don't. Once, I burned out the water while making coffee. Although, Clare keeps trying. There may be hope somewhere in my future. But don't expect it."

"Interesting, Lacey."

He pushes the flask toward me, and I find the next sip more comforting than the other. I hold the container out until his hand covers mine. Neil laughs and takes a healthy swallow and offers me another sip.

I try a swig to prove I can handle it. "Whoa! The room seems like a sauna. Anyone for some fresh air?"

"Not the room Belle. It's the cherry sunshine because that outdated space heater won't heat beyond low. I do think you need cooling down, so let's enjoy the night air."

I make myself comfortable on the porch swing. Neil follows and for a short time, I nestle under the crook of his arm. When he offers me another drink of Anson's brew. I refuse, and Neil begins to hiccup.

My hand remains on his chest. While he gulps for air, I can't believe I say, "Oh brother, Neil, your heart is thrumming like an engine."

"Well sweet child, if it keeps me from dying, take my heart, my love or give them back." Before he raises the flask again, I take it from him. I'm nervous and his reference to me being a 'sweet child' annoys me.

"McCutchen, I am short in stature, but I'm not a child. You're well aware of that because I kissed you back. Also, note, there are only two years between us. So take a look." I move off the swing, suck in my stomach, and twirl on my toes until I land in his arms.

What are you doing? This isn't you acting like that. Or is this the time to surrender?

While I wrestle with my conscience, Neil with one hand brings me closer to his lips and on the contrary, gives a simple tug to a metal zipper. He lifts me to my feet with very little assistance from me, and the sundress falls to the floor.

"Forgive me Lacey but this is happening with your permission."

This wasn't how I dreamed about it. Do I blame the cherry sunshine's influence? I could say 'no,' instead, I step over the crumbled garment beneath me and disregard all boundaries. The alcohol made this much easier to embrace, and I lead him by his fingertips to the sofa inside.

"Hmmm, you know Baby Soft shampoo leaves an intoxicating fragrance." Neil nibbles my ear and his kisses progress along my neck. I stir beside him, so he's able to kiss my throat hollow, but he stops.

"Belle loved you from the first crashing moment we met. Earlier when holding you, I wanted more, but, didn't want to rush you into anything, you would regret."

"I won't."

Our lips meet again. I close my eyes until the unexpected touch of his hand on my bare skin makes my breath come up short. I sink deeper into the pillows beneath me when the sensation of a warm liquid trickles onto my breast. I spoil the moment by laughing when his tongue and lips remove the droplets. He stops.

I sit up and trace my fingertip over his well-defined cleft chin. “Neil, tell me. Why would a man force himself on a woman?”

“What? You are a strange one, Belle. Thought my fondling you would show; I don’t consider you a child but rather a beautiful woman. At sixteen, I learned a lot from my Grandfather's birthday gift. The experience taught me how to give you pleasure without intercourse. When and if we should, I know when to withdraw before I ejaculate.”

“Whoa! I’m not ready for a family without a ring. Sorry Neil, I gave you the wrong idea.”

“Belle, I promise you won’t get pregnant. You can remain a virgin and experience a fantastic journey with me aboard. But if you’re squeamish . . .”

“Guess I’m a curious coward, Neil.” I surrender to his petting until I climax. Afterward, I rest on his arm. “Neil, what I asked you earlier about. . .”

“Arabelle, please lie still beside me. I’ve something to tell you.”

Something isn’t right. Should I have done him? He has a hurt expression and leans upon his elbow.

“Don’t believe you’ll want to put this into her book. A memory, I think she’d rather forget. Mother knew the weekly poker game would last until morning, so she’d come to say goodnight and tuck me in. She never caught me creeping out of my room. I’d go to Grandfather’s library upstairs. I’d hide behind Cameron’s smoking chair without anyone seeing me.

That night Grandfather won. They played without

money, just chip values where the biggest winner made the worst loser do some crazy thing. They swore, drank and made fun of the loser. Before the game started, Grandfather whispered to some fellow that Cameron said Mother wanted another baby. He laughed and leaned over Cameron's shoulder, didn't whisper this time. Only told him that he better win if he knew what Grandfather's loss would gain him."

"Neil, you had to know something was going to happen."

"Lacey, think about it. I was four. I heard she wants a baby, and it stuck in my head. And if a new baby comes, well. . ."

"Emily?"

"Yes, but I didn't know that then. Arabelle, this is hard enough for me. Will you let me finish?"

"Sorry." I lean on my side and brush aside Neil's curls.

"After hearing about a baby, I crept up the servant's stairway. Climbed into her armoire, like the one in your room and closed it."

Neil gets up from the sofa bed and walks around the room. When he sits down, he leans forward with elbows bent and hands holding his head. "Belle, before I could climb out of the wardrobe, her door opens. I thought it was my father. But then I hear her voice, and she's angry. A man laughs. It was Grandfather. He is laughing at her. Like at the poker game, he's swearing and yelling that she'll get a new baby just like the last one."

"Didn't you yell or go to her rescue?"

"I was little and afraid. I tried, but the door was tight. Belle, I did nothing but crouch into a corner. Heard her crying over the bed springs squeaking. Still remember his words, 'I lost and got my winnings.'

Then the door slammed. I wanted to be brave because she was crying real loud. I pushed on it so long. It opened. I crawled out. Mother lay so quietly; I thought he killed her. She smelled like whiskey and stinky cigars and looked like a crazy ghost lady. When I touched her face, her eyes stared back at me."

"Neil, I'm so sorry. Did you get Clare?"

"No, I covered her with a fluffy cover because she looked cold and dead. After that night, I didn't sleep with her anymore. But each time I see her, the memory plays over and over in my head. To this day, I never told anyone but you."

He stares at the ceiling. I pick up my clothes and go onto the porch.

CHAPTER 19
STALL TACTICS

I shiver as I dress in the moonlight. Silent tears stream down my cheeks, I compose myself on the walk to the manor. Neil runs after me.

"Lacey. Wait for me. I shouldn't have told you the way I did. I'm sorry."

"McCutchen, I wasn't shocked by what you said because your story caught me off guard. I can't believe he would plot to molest her again. It was too much for me. Never met Adam and I despise, no I loathe your father."

"Arabelle, wait. What did you mean? Did Mother tell you something about him?"

"By accident, she blurted it out. You need to ask her. Family album, baby pictures, I shouldn't tell you. What happened today should never have happened between us. I'm sorry."

I rush ahead and reach the porch before him. Meeting Katherine there, I try to wipe away the tears but can't. "Good night. Neil's on his way."

"Good night dear, I so hoped a romance might grow between you two. However, seeing you tonight, love seems out of the question."

For three days, I feign a flu attack and Neil distances himself from the manor. This weekend, he returned. We are distant, like ships passing in the night. Our moment of passion doesn't change Neil's mind. He now insists on an earlier departure. He makes arrangements with a local furnace company to install a combination unit of heat and air before Halloween. Katherine is desperate and enlists all of us to delay him.

"Anson, I know you can do it. His birthday is the 24th with a surprise party on the 22nd at the Blue Moon. This way, he won't think it is happening. Then surprise by a few of our friends but Neil must be there. Do what you have to, keep him from leaving. Fake a heart attack, if you must. Run off with Clare, get married. Tell him the IRS is sending you to jail unless. You all know what I mean, think of something."

"Rest assured. He'll be here until then." Anson says. Clare and I nod in agreement.

I leave Anson's apartment with Katherine and try to get her mind off the situation. "Katherine saw my friend Decima at the new Prenatal Clinic. She said to say 'Hi!' and sends her thanks for your group's help."

"Yes the clinic, we contributed to the building fund. Anson has business with my son and I must leave. Don't offer to drive because Anson called for a cab. Later, he'll pick me up. Do try to see if you and Clare can help to keep Neil here. Okay?"

"Sure, maybe he'd like to help to dig up the bulbs. Something will come up. I'll see her about brainstorming."

A car's horn announces her ride is here. She walks the curved driveway to the front of the manor while I climb the steps once more to Anson's apartment. "Hey,

Katherine sent me to help stir the brain pot. Ready?"

"Not exactly," he says, "have a seat. Instead of Clare, I prepared lunch, PB&J. Care for one?"

"Sure, make mine strawberry jam. What if we say we found a missing piece of paper regarding a stock transfer to Cameron's with only one signature?"

Clare shakes her head. "Won't work, Neil will be sayin', "Call Francine. She's our attorney, let her earn her salary."

"I could delay him a few days with the HP business and his stock options. But then, we'll still be short a day."

I do believe I could pretend an emergency existed to keep him here if necessary."

"Whoa Clare! Don't want that happening, even if it isn't real. Guys, I'm out of here. It's raining. Thanks for the lunch."

HP stock options, Clare's emergency, I haven't the foggiest idea. Instead I daydream and watch the rain sheeting down the window. Did we share more than the heat of the moment? That's it! I've got to talk to him, like today. Like right now.

I dial the carriage house's phone line. "Hi Anson is the Firebird back?—Great.—Yep, that's all." I press the intercom button. "Clare, where's Neil?"

Through the small box, I get the answer. "Arrived earlier, but has an evenin' supper engagement with the attorney. Went over to see Anson about the car. I'll let him know; you want to talk."

"Thank you. It's most important I speak with him before he leaves tonight. Thanks."

Forty-five minutes later, I hear his footsteps on the stairwell. Time enough for me to set the stage. A light tapping on my door precedes Neil entering, and I've timed coming out of the bathroom once he calls my name.

"Hey, Lacey."

"Hi." I wipe my face with a washcloth and sit on the bed.

"Clare told me that you want to see me. I presume, it's to thank me without a collision at the bottom of the stairs. Have you seen the unit? It heats and cools the air. Am I right?"

"Gosh, are you self-centered? The world revolves around the sun, not around Neil McCutchen."

"Sorry for my rudeness, I have a lot on my mind, and I'm running late for a dinner engagement."

"Apology accepted. And yes, thank you for the unit. What I wanted to tell you is that I'm late too. Have a morning appointment the day before you leave with the doctor. Thought you might like to know the results of the rabbit test."

"What rabbit test? We only did it once, and you wore your underwear."

"I did, and you were wrong because I read it's possible if the fella's semen has good swimmers. Look, you were my one and only. You promised me I wouldn't get pregnant. I'm not trying to trap you into anything. Just thought, you might want to know test results."

"Miss Lacey, if this is you grabbing at straws . . ." Neil goes toward the doorway. Stops and turns on his heel. His jaw is set, and the thin line of his lips lets me know he is thinking. "We'll discuss this tomorrow, Arabelle Lacey."

ഈഈഈ

For two days, I play Emily's favorite childhood game. I hide, and Neil just misses me at every point. Katherine and I enjoy our afternoon tea in the sitting room, and she says, "Keep up the good work, Belle. That son of mine is desperate to see you. He's due to be home in a few minutes. Go out through the terrace to the bungalow. Once you're there, open your intercom to receive, and I'll have mine on send."

I leave and with intercoms in working order, I relax on the sofa with the Psychology book. It still is confusing, and I put it down when I hear him.

"I don't understand this woman, Mother. She wants to talk, yet, flits from here to there. According to Clare, I just miss catching her. We need to talk. Although I have a feeling, something else is in the wind."

"What can be so important, Neil? I understand Anson has some HP stock division to discuss; but, I can't think of anything Arabelle would want to discuss with you."

"That Mother is a personal one, which I will take up with her, as soon as I can corral her."

"I didn't mean to intrude on your personal life. Neil, please stay with me until the end of September. I would so like to discuss your birthday party."

"You know my feelings about birthday parties."

"All right, you won. I'll cancel my party. Will you, at least, stay until the 24th?"

"Yes, that's agreed. No party and I'll rebook my flight to the next day. However, you promised me, no party. Anson does have paperwork for me to sign. I'll take care of that today, and hopefully, Belle and I will finish our conversation."

"Wonderful. I promise no party. Could we all go out to dinner before you depart? You can make the reservations wherever you want. That way we won't know where we are going until we arrive there. Good idea, yes?"

"Good idea, yes! Now be so kind and tell me what errand is she doing for you?"

"No errand dear, she has a headache. Gave her some aspirin and presume she's lying down in the bungalow."

"Love you Mother. You are beautiful and all-knowing. See you at dinner."

"Love you too, son. Remember if she's asleep, don't wake her."

"No guarantee. No guarantee. I noticed your intercom was open."

I laugh at his discovery and get ready for his arrival. While I don't hear any footsteps, the porch deck speaks to me with a squeak here and there and his cologne tells me he stands nearby.

Earlier I lowered the shade. Now with a washcloth over my forehead and eyes, I lie there. The cedar scent from Stetson grows stronger. He is so close I can almost taste his lips when he whispers into my ear. "Miss Lacey, is your headache gone?"

"No, it's not. Can't I even get a few moments to myself? Felt guilty going to church services, so I didn't. I know when you're near because I desire to lay with you again. It's hard for me because I won't want to stop you. Abstaining while you're here doesn't erase those feelings."

"Look, Belle, do you think God is going to send you to hell for going to second base? You sure, you're late? Don't look pregnant. Talk to me."

I remove the washcloth and look up. "All I know is what I told you. I'm late with my period. I'm never late. God might not send me to hell for what we did. Just think he understands our physical needs and that's why he prepares us for marriage through abstinence. I believed your promise that nothing would happen. Since I don't know why I'm late is why I have a doctor appointment. You say you've got to leave. Go. If I am pregnant, I'll fax. What else is left to discuss at this point? Not a thing. Feel free to leave anytime even if it's before your surprise party."

"Not until I ask and you say yes to marry me, I'll bet on God's forgiveness. So she did have a party planned? Think Katherine is suspicious?"

"Hasn't a clue. She thinks we have a budding romance, yet we confuse her because we don't act like it. And yes, your surprise party is on the 24th at the Blue Moon. Don't understand why you don't want one, and personally, don't care if you ever celebrate one or if we ever tie the knot. Now let me die in my misery."

Before I cover my eyes, he kisses my forehead. "Sure sure, sorry you feel miserable and for disturbing you. F. Y. I. I've changed my flight. I'll go with you to see what ails my favorite girl." I feel him pull the blanket up over my head. "Pleasant dreams, Lacey."

CHAPTER 20
ECTOPIC PREGNANCY

It's his birthday and Neil insists on driving. After an hour, Anson questions him. "Sir, you seem to be going in circles. May I assist in navigating to this new restaurant?"

"Although I appreciate the offer Anson, a few miles more, and I'll get us there."

Thirty minutes later, Neil pulls over. "Folks, I should have taken that last right or was it a left? Can anyone get us home?"

After they exchange seats, Anson takes command to order Chinese delivery and drives home. Tonight, Mr. Sung's catering truck awaits our arrival with our meal.

"Sorry Mother, I did my best to keep us together for a private celebration."

Neil escorts Katherine to the manor's front door. "Neil, don't be disappointed. It's okay; I like surprises—unlike you."

Before going inside, he says, "Folks, Francine arranged this merry-making. Welcome to my surprise party."

We enter the foyer where a maître d escorts us into the main dining room. Neil's friends and business associates wait to meet us, the unknowing guests of honor. He dashes ahead of Katherine and joins in the applause. While echoes of 'surprise' fill the room, Neil holds up his hand.

"Folks, thank you for coming. However, the surprise, an un-birthday party, is for everyone who isn't celebrating a birthday today. Tonight for your enjoyment, Chefs from my favorite restaurants will prepare their signature dishes. Enjoy the festivities."

"Neil, what an idea, you included wrapped presents at all the tables."

"I can't take the credit Mother. It was Francine's icing on the surprise party to have gifts for everyone. Let's celebrate your surprise party."

Away from the crowd, I admire this man-child, who indulges his friends with his version of a surprise party.

The foyer's grandfather clock chimes midnight and the honorary celebrants bid farewell to their host. Alone with him in the foyer, I'm surprised when he picks me up and twirls me around in his arms.

"I pulled it off, Arabelle. Party was a success and for once on my birthday, I even enjoyed the gathering." He kisses me softly and puts me down.

"Neil, I hope this next year will bring you happiness, as well." I return his kiss and leave.

ജജജ

The next afternoon, I pull Neil aside and into the butler's pantry. Once inside, he tries to kiss me, but I turn my head, and he kisses my cheek. "What's up Lacey?"

I keep a cool head and take a deep breath. "Neil, it was a false alarm. My period started. I hope you've no regrets."

"None, if you don't. Will you still see the doctor?"

"No. Canceled the appointment and had Anson reschedule your flight out for this afternoon. By-the-way, thanks for waiting it out with me." I crush the temptation, to throw my arms around his neck and kiss him, with a handshake and say, "Have a safe trip."

"Belle, you mean safe return! Can't abandon you for too long, or you might look in another direction."

"You're so right." We go onto the front porch where Clare's and Katherine's goodbye delay Neil's leaving.

The sound of the Beamer's horn signals it is time for his departure. Anson hits the horn once more and lowers the passenger side window. "Airplanes leave with or without you. Go ahead, kiss your darling and get in the car."

How I wish his lips would meet mine, but when Neil takes me in his arms, he kisses my forehead. To the others, he waves and gets into the car.

I did shake his hand, but my forehead. What with that? Wait a minute, Anson said, 'your darling'. I'm not a roll in the hay. He isn't like his father. I shout out, "Hurry back Neil."

At our teatime the following day, I confide in Katherine. "Don't think I should have canceled my appointment. Since midnight, I've had sharp pains and . . ."

Inside an ambulance. I'm on oxygen and an IV is in my arm. The siren hurts my ears. Time and presence are out of harmony. A man's voice states, "Prep for surgery. Get Dr. Roche."

A warm hand holds mine. I focus on a voice. It sounds confident.

"I'm Doctor Roche, Katherine's obstetrician. Miss Lacey, I want you to know she called my private line and asked me to help. You require surgery. If you have no objections, may I be your surgeon and primary physician?"

Katherine had his private number, and I hurt. "Sure. Fine, but about the surgery, I want it kept secret. Please, nothing is to reach Neil. What happened, why the surgery?"

"We'll discuss that later. Now relax and let me do my job."

The surgery brings relief and I have visitors. Katherine, Clare, and Anson stand around my hospital bed. During their time there, the doctor enters. He's not smiling as he says, "I would like some privacy with the patient. I'll be just a minute or so."

His look is scaring me, and I fear the worst. "No Doc, let them stay. They're the only family I have."

"If you don't mind, with all this female talk, I'd like to wait outside." Anson goes and Clare moves closer to Katherine.

Before he tells me the worst, he talks to Katherine. "Mrs. McCutchen, she is a brave girl. Before the surgery, Arabelle insisted your son should never know about her condition."

"Condition? Neil must know if she was pregnant."

He shakes his head. "No longer, I'm certain of that." He looks at me. "Arabelle, you suffered from what we call an ectopic pregnancy, or in laymen's language, a tubal pregnancy. Normal pregnancy usually starts in the uterus. Unfortunately, any number of reasons may have blocked or slowed the movement of a fertilized egg. Miss

Lacey am abnormal pregnancy could rupture and bleed. With this condition, the baby cannot survive. Your miscarriage resulted in my doing a D and C."

I lost Neil's child.

"Belle, Neil must know if you will ever have a baby?"

"Katherine, maybe I was wrong letting you stay. Minutes ago, I heard I lost my baby. Leave and please back off in taking control of my life and your son's."

When Clare squeezes my hand, it hurts, and I know the reason. I cry as I say, "Okay, you can stay." Clare releases her grip.

"Miss Lacey, in some cases, another pregnancy might be impossible. Personally, I believe there is a good chance you can. And Katherine, butt out. This is Arabelle's decision and not yours. It's hers to tell him in her time. I believe you should respect her wish.

Arabelle, I'll discharge you within a few days providing you don't climb stairs, do the heavy lifting, and eat a moderate diet. Now if you've no other questions, I'm due for a consultation."

"None, thank you for everything," I said and shook his hand before he goes.

They stand there, looking at me and then at each other. I press the call button. The nurse arrives, and I whisper to her. "Please have them leave, I want to be alone."

ഌഌഌ

When Anson brings me home, my bed replaces the overstuffed furniture in the sitting room. Dusty tapestries and worn draperies are missing. Instead, sheer panels allow a rainbow from the stained glass windows to decorate the repainted walls.

"Gosh, this room is too much. It's beautiful. But I could have stayed in the bungalow."

"Following doctor's orders to the letter. No stairs, here you'll rest. No heavy lifting, so I left my desk in case you'd like to continue your studies with Anson."

"Katherine, I'll tell Neil in time, just not now."

"I don't agree but doing my best to understand. Rest now, Clare is making lunch and will bring it to you."

She leaves. I change my clothes and get into bed. Lying there I know what I have to do. But how do I get Neil back in my life?

Without Neil's presence, even the bygone holidays gave no promise to explore any room to find the will. My physical and emotional strength finds its niche once I realize holidays were not a part of Neil's lifestyle. The routine of manor living has imprinted a non-judgmental attitude onto my thinking and learning to bake doesn't fulfill my dreams.

"If it weren't for you, Clare, I'd be happy to find a corner and let cobwebs cover me. I've lost interest in hunting and joined all of you in not caring. Katherine is so busy with other activities. I only exist to remind her we need to continue her memoirs. Neil dropped off the surface of the earth. Clare, did you hear me?"

"What? Arabelle, I was estimatin'. This year we have more than one hundred people comin' from East Aurora. I need you to bake and frost three more chocolate cakes. Maybe some more brownies wouldn't hurt."

I shut off the mixer, taste the buttercream frosting and add a bit more cocoa. "Clare, we already baked six dozen brownies, four chocolate cakes, and three dozen almond flavored cupcakes."

It's her glare across the room that adds emphasis to her words. "Your point is?"

"Clare, besides this household there are twenty other women baking for the Valentine box dessert. So, I don't think we need more brownies. What I do need is a piece of advice."

"Spit it out. I need five minutes to rest my feet."

"Since Cameron's death, Decima told me she has dreams with me in them. Think that palm reader on Broad can help her?"

While I wait for her reply, Clare shuts off the oven and sits beside me. "Don't let her go to one of them imposters. I decipher dreams. Yes, I do."

While I don't doubt Clare's ability, I need someone to make sense of my dreaded nightmares. Without disclosing everything, I relate portions of a recurring one.

"Is this for you or your friend? Never mind, don't need to know. Let me tell you a dream's sensation of fear foretells someone has to make a decision and do it alone. Know that once it's made, there's no turnin' back. It's final and that person's happiness hangs in the balance. Your friend must take particular care not to do anythin' that may hurt anyone includin' herself."

"What about . . ." I'm interrupted by the repeated sound of a car's horn and a door slamming. The distraction puts my dreams on a backburner when Katherine bursts into the kitchen from the back porch.

"IRS is questioning Neil using stock options or something with the stocks for running the business. Uncle Sam needs more documentation. Please come to the car, need help to carry boxes. Anson can't do everything."

Fifteen minutes later the last computer box is brought inside along with loose papers, journals and accountant's books. Finally, we rest when everyone sits around the overloaded table.

"Oh, I forgot to mention the IRS gave us 24 hours to prove his figures. I am sorry Belle; our afternoon get-together will have to be rescheduled."

"That's okay. What can I do to help?"

Anson directs a sheepish grin in Clare's direction. "I only need some coffee and a slice of chocolate cake. Then, I'm fine."

Clare and I look at each other and in unison we laugh and say, "No problem."

While she prepares Anson's snack, we tote everything into the control center and begin sorting papers into various categories. After seven hours and Clare's delicious meal, we organize the individual piles for IRS's inspection. I call it a night and high five the others before returning to the bungalow. Tomorrow should be an exciting day.

The inspector leaves and a fax to Neil advises him that the inspection went well, and the IRS collected the difference in taxes. When Anson wrote the check, I learned the importance of whether to place a comma or a period when you deal with numbers.

CHAPTER 21
WEST WING SECTION

For the past seven months, determined to erase any doubt Neil might have, I concentrate on learning everything about the family business. Anson tutors me with books from Adam's library, and I enroll at the local college.

Spring is on the horizon, and daffodils and crocus brighten the landscape. Katherine has kept her word. Communication between her and Neil is limited to business faxes or messages of regrets. There is no word for me from him. All outward signs indicate he forgot me. With so much time passing between us, I wonder if I made the right decision in not telling Neil about our loss.

The hunt, once more, is shelved. My exploring is intermittent based on Katherine's interest in finishing her memoirs and me finding time to study. Today she lacks any motivation, and that's fine when I consider classes demand my full attention. I try to see if Neil is on the road home or traveling to parts unknown.

"Spring break is on the horizon, Katherine. Think that son of yours might break through the ground like May flowers."

Katherine shakes her head back and forth. She hands

me a leather binder. "There is no apology I could say that would make up for his behavior. Belle, he should know what you've been through? Are you certain you don't need to relax a little? Maybe a slight diversion from your studies might cheer you up. Please, look inside."

I open the folder. Pictures of Disney World and traveler checks are tucked inside. Between being tutored and carrying specific courses, it prompts me to consider the dream every student looks forward to enjoying. Spring break. "Katherine, it might help a little if someone will join me. Should I send Neil a fax? No, it's his move if he has any feeling for us."

"Yes, my exact sentiments. What I thought was Decima Gordon would be a perfect choice to go with you. Please ask her to consider this opportunity. All expenses paid."

"Was planning to see if she'd help me clean the bungalow before I move back. You shared your sitting room too long. I'll check with Deci after Clare and I do our shopping. Thanks, Katherine."

It is asinine when I look forward to loading the dishwasher with lunch dishes and help Clare in preparing her spaghetti sauce for tonight's dinner. She never stops in keeping the home fire glowing.

"Clare, Decima is bringing some paint I ordered. When she arrives, please let her know that I'm at the bungalow."

She nods. "Ask her to stay for dinner. Have plenty now that Anson is working on a new diet."

"Okay, thanks. I know she loves your cooking."

The afternoon hours zoom and shutters are painted white. The fresh look adds a bold look to the fading blue exterior. Following dinner, Deci and I relax on the terrace, when I tug my ear. It's our high school's secret signal that we are not alone.

"Hi Clare didn't hear you approach. Colonel Sanders would enjoy your chicken."

"You're welcome Decima. The once distressed shutters look much better with the matching trim. Maybe Katherine will consider another color for the manor. Well, good evening girls."

We're exhausted, and Deci heads toward her car. With an hour drive ahead of her, she says, "Hate it but I've got to go. It's early hours at the clinic. Don't you forget to ask her." We hug, and she leaves, waving her hand out the car's window.

I wave goodbye and recall our earlier conversation. Knowing Katherine's schedule, I bring the folder. The weather report is over, and she clicks the television off. "Weather sound is promising for next few days."

"Katherine, is there a reason the third floor is closed off?"

"Closed off? Not all of it, only what isn't used for storage. Why do you ask?"

"Doing the shutters, I glanced toward the manor's upper floor. Anson mentioned there was another library with a gallery of ancient family pictures. But from below, it isn't easy to see which window lights it up. I didn't see any. Was he wrong?"

"No, he is correct. They are in the west wing section. I was about seven and Mom told me never to go there. Clare was allowed to go there and sweep the floor. When I asked, she said, 'a man's book place for smoking and drinking.' From the way she talked, I wasn't interested. I never visited it."

After Miriam died, Adam spent more and more time there. Months following Adam's death, Cam wanted to modernize several areas on the upper floors.He said that the sitting room and two downstairs' libraries would belong to me. So I didn't see any problem to his puttering around to create his personal space. As far as I can see, he only worked at it when he returned to the Estate."

"The gallery, have you ever seen it?" I ask when I return her vacation package.

"Must be Cameron's photographs from his hobby. That must be the gallery Anson mentioned. He said that the corridors were dark and narrow. They lead to the 'man library'. However, if you want to go, get the key from Clare. She has keys to every room in this place. You're certain you don't need to relax, Spring break and all?"

"Can't, Deci doesn't have vacation time. Maybe you can rebook for next year."

"Marvelous idea, find out when she takes a vacation, and I'll change the ticket date."

I turn. Neil is within arm's reach, and I shake his hand. "Congratulations, Mr. McCutchen."

"Say what? Congratulations for what?"

I didn't care that Clare is in earshot of our conversation when I force the crushed clipping from my pocket into his hand. "Sorry, I didn't read this before our tryst. Made a fool of myself in the bungalow thinking, I was more than a quick roll in the hay."

"Whatever are you talking about?"

"Don't con me Neil. Pictures don't lie. Plus, I have a photographic memory and will repeat the local society editor's article. I quote, 'Quick-stepping into the crowd, our enamored betrothed, Ms. Francine Bellsworth, local attorney, and Neil McCutchen, CEO of M Enterprises, dodge my question on their upcoming wedding date.' End quote."

"What? Where'd you get that article? It wasn't supposed to be in any of the local papers. I have no idea why you're so upset. And let's not air dirty laundry, if any, in front of Clare. Outside! Now!"

I exaggerate my walk with a march onto the back porch where I make certain the screen door hits him. He takes my arm and forcibly walks me to the gazebo. I'm steamed, and his dumb reaction fuels the flame.

"Fine, we're out of Clare's earshot. What did I do or not do to light that fire under you? What?"

"What? Guess I didn't measure up to your high standards. What'd you think? I was an easy conquest for you, just another notch on your belt."

I kick his shin and pound his chest with both fists. He takes hold of my hands and stops my attack.

"It doesn't matter Mr. McCutchen. Wish you were honest enough to tell me before you took advantage. The truth isn't easy, but, it is important when you seduced me. Now please, until we have total honesty between us. Let go of me."

"Now I'm Mr. McCutchen? Belle that time you ran into me, I fought the strangest urge to pull you into my arms and kiss you until you'd beg me to stop. Months ago, you asked me to make you a woman, and, we reacted together in confirming that fact. Then three days ago, I get a telegram from you. 'It was a girl.' There was no explanation. I drop everything. Catch the next connecting flight and you read me the riot act on total honesty."

"Neil, let me go."

"Okay Lacey, crying won't help you until you're truthful with me and let me explain."

Fondly he dabs my tears before he kisses my eyes. When he reaches my lips, his passion intensifies, and before I can surrender to his kiss, he stops. The moment is gone when he forces me into the lattice framework.

"I'll kiss you all night until you listen to me. Agree?"

"Yes, but. . ."

He kisses me for a longer time. "Agree?"

I nod.

Neil takes my hand and leads me into the living room, where we sit. "Four months ago this society busy body, saw me at a California Fundraiser. Yes, Francine and I, we acted close. It's good for the Company image to be seen at important charities. Also, I keep the lid tight on Fran's alternate lifestyle."

"California? Alternate lifestyle?"

He kisses me again. "No talking. Agree?"

I nod my head once more.

"Hell, Lacey. I don't owe you or anyone else an explanation for what I do for a good friend. And our afternoon together, didn't you feel the chemistry work between us. You know. It's that little gut feeling that lets you know the sex would be good."

I shake my head back and forth before I whisper, "Maybe."

A light peck caresses my lips. "It was better than good. I knew you were the one. Not sorry for my actions. My only regret is not calling you afterward. Nevertheless, you were always in my thoughts. So why weren't you honest about the baby months ago? When your fax came, it tore me apart. What do you want, Belle?"

"Thought the cramps were normal. You left. I found out, the fetus died because of a tubal pregnancy. Didn't see any reason to let you know because you didn't say you wouldn't call. I only hoped."

"Belle, there's no explanation why I didn't call."

He was right. I left him no reason to do so.

I head for the bungalow and Neil catches up with me near the gazebo.

"Lacey please stop. I apologize for not calling. I'm a free spirit. You understand that from my coming and leaving. Don't know what you want from me so late in the game. Didn't realize you need someone to lean on when times get tough, but, that's not me."

His superior attitude irritates me. "Look, I'm a survivor Neil. After I felt better, took college classes with Anson's help. So when you'd return, I'd impress you. I already read that article two days ago. You can't know how much I hated you then. I was glad. No overjoyed that the pregnancy ended. I wanted you to feel the loss, as I did all this time. Yes, I sent the fax to make you suffer."

"Belle. Thought you felt the same as I did without my telling you. Yes, I am sorry, I wasn't here with you to mourn our loss. Maybe, we don't know each other. Maybe, it is best that I'm out of your life."

I move away, but Neil takes a firm hold of me. His embrace and tenderness are what I need. It eases the loneliness I've felt. Now he knows the truth, and we share our daughter's death. Katherine was right. I should have told him long ago.

"Belle, shall I walk you back to your home?"

I can't believe he called his guest house, my home.

"Oh, you mean the bungalow. Sure why not, you're a free spirit and all. Let's have another fling, and you're gone again. No, thank you. McCutchen. I fight daily with myself because I don't just want to like you."

Neil presses his mouth to mine. No more words of anger pass over our lips. Instead, they fill a physical need for lovers—too much time apart. When we part, I lean against him. My tears mark his silk shirt.

"Neil, I'm so sorry. With no word from you, the worst suspicions filled my dreams. When I lost our baby, I wanted to tell you what emptiness filled me. That afternoon, we lost ourselves in giving everything and asking for nothing but the warmth and pleasure of our bodies. Although angry after I sent the telegram, I forgave you if you felt you needed a one-night stand?"

CHAPTER 22
FRANCINE BELLSWORTH

"Lacey, you forgive me for a one-night stand. Is sex all you think about when you think of me? Well?"

What irony? What right does he have to say that to me? I step back and shove him. "I apologize. I forgave you. And you're getting upset. Yes, I wonder if you score with other women. But, do I care about your sex life? Well, maybe sometimes. Oh heck, Neil, it bothers me all the time. At night, awake in my bed and at scattered moments every day since we did it. I care about us."

"Us? Haven't you noticed Belle, although two years don't seem much, I look much older than you, and I'd probably be the October shot in a calendar. Plus, there are other problems you can't comprehend."

As if that newscast could dampen the fire I feel inside, I hold my breath. When I stand tip-toe, nearly eye-to-eye, almost lip to lip, I was never so aware of a man in my life—his scent, his breathing. I can't shake the desire to love him.

"You once called me a child, yet you made me a woman. I agree you are two years older, and sometimes, you act sixty. You could fill all the months on my calendar. You never said you love me. Maybe I care so much because I'm dumb enough to hope you will."

"Lacey, so you do love me?" He tilts my head back and gives me a moist, succulent kiss on my neck. "Been thinking Belle, it's been too long. I want you right now here, but I won't. Hell, I won't."

What is his secret? I do love you, Neil. Please say you love me, too. I feel his arms pulling me to him and close my eyes. His hands move upward over my hips, raising the soft material of my skirt. With each upward movement, strong fingers press against my thighs and work their way upward. With his hold on my buttocks, he lifts me until his intimacy with my body brings my head and lips closer. I find resisting him when passion rises; it suspends my inhibitions.

"Love you McCutchen. Do you love me?" I open my eyes to trace his lips with my tongue.

Abruptly he lowers me to the ground. "You love me, and you still act like a tease. Am I wrong?"

Confused, I step away. We look at each other when Clare shouts from the back porch. "Neil; a Mr. Rangar is in the living room. Has an appointment."

I look at Neil. His neck muscles tense and his face hardens, yet, he gives Clare a thumb's up. She nods and disappears inside.

Unsure of all that happened, I apologize. "Guess I did tease you. Thought you'd like it. Won't let it happen again."

Neil chuckles and gives me a peck on the cheek. "Don't worry that pretty head of yours. However, I wonder what might have happened if Clare didn't interrupt. Must leave you today and be away for a few days. Excuse me now; Mr. Rangar is waiting. Promise, I'll return if only for another taste of your peach lipstick. By the way, mark your calendar for a January wedding."

I'm stunned by what he said and remain there for a short time. After I straighten my clothes and finger comb my hair, I return to the kitchen to face Clare's inquisition.

However, she isn't there, but Anson enjoys an afternoon coffee break.

"Well did you say 'yes'?"

"To what? He didn't ask me a thing. He's leaving again for a few days. Business I guess, maybe with that Francine or Mr. Rangar. Later Anson, I'm off to the bungalow to do laundry."

I skip down the pathway and sing at the top of my voice, "He loves me. He does. He wants to marry me." I stop. Or does he?

After our breakfast meeting, I sit across from Katherine. She reminisces about Emily and puts her memoirs on hold as I gnaw a pencil. I need to talk with her. Unfortunately, she is preoccupied with her daughter's beauty and rocks back and forth in her office chair.

"I can't wait any longer. I can't sit and be silent."

Katherine looks up and puts down her croissant. "Belle, what can't you do?"

"I don't know for sure. At least, I think I'm certain. But maybe, I misinterpreted the meaning. Maybe what I heard wasn't what I thought I heard. Or. . ." I get up and go to the window.

"Belle, slow down. What do you think, know or don't know? Tell me, what did you hear?"

I walk back to the table and lean over it so no one else will hear what I say to her. "Schedule your calendar for

January wedding. I checked every calendar, no mention of marriage on any of them. It doesn't make sense. Who'd plan a wedding without a date?"

"Okay, I have one piece of the puzzle, a January wedding. Now who said it?"

"Your son, he'll be gone somewhere with Mr. Rangar or was it Fran Bellsworth for several days. However before leaving, he tags the invitation onto the end of his goodbye."

"Well since I'm his mother, I'm usually the last to know anything that affects Neil or his life. Although you know a few of his associates, a wedding could happen. This Mr. Rangar, I don't know him and Francine is the Company's attorney. Whether Neil is asking you to go or be in the wedding, have no idea. Why don't you just ask him?"

"Did ask him about the attorney, not much info other than she lived on the west coast. Did you say she works here?"

"Yes, about two years ago, Neil told me he met her at some California seminar and that she used to live near here. When she found out California residents could study law by correspondence, she moved there. However, to take her bar exam, she needed to apprentice for a local attorney. When Neil met her, she was promoting her legal firm to prospective clients."

"Oh, that's why she's here. His invitation still bothers me. Katherine, I couldn't ask him. What if it's 'to go' to her wedding and not 'be in' ours? I'd die."

"Has he hinted in the 'be in' category?"

"You mean like I love you. Want to look at rings or how does Niagara Falls sound? Nothing! Gosh, maybe he wants me to be in the wedding."

"I'm getting a strong message that you want it to 'be in' your wedding. Am I right?"

"Yes! Yes! Yes! I fell in love with your son that night he thought of me as a woman and not a pesky child. Aagh! I'm losing my mind."

"Dear Belle, we know Neil's few days could be longer. Be prepared for his absence. But if he does return soon, you subtly ask, do I bring your mother's fur muff or my bridal bouquet? If he tells you the bouquet, shout loud and clear for joy as the acoustics here are marvelous. Then I'll be the second to know instead of the last."

I can't believe we are both laughing at our private joke and give Katherine a hug. "Whew, that just might work." I retrieve my pad and pencil and title the page—Mrs. Neil McCutchen and said, "Whenever you're ready Katherine."

"Belle, from here I can see you are doodling and from the look in your eyes, I have a good idea what you wrote. No memoirs today. Call Decima, and have lunch at LePeek. The Company has an account there. Just sign my name."

My mouth falls open. Wait 'til I tell Deci, free lunch with an all-male review. "Thank you, maybe lunch with a friend is what I need. Thanks, Katherine."

The afternoon meal lasted well past dinner time for I arrive home after eight. Before going to the bungalow, I let Clare know I returned.

"Hi, lunch went into overtime. Sorry, I'm late."

"Don't fret. Katherine said you went to meet Decima. Is she, the same one with the dream?"

I give a little nod as there was no need to answer with

a lie. I start to leave.

"Arabelle, friends are important. Need to keep them close. If you're hungry, there's meatloaf in the cooler. If not, see you at breakfast."

"Thanks, Clare. Goodnight."

I go onto the back porch. From here, the moon spotlights the well. For some strange reason, I'm drawn to its construction. The stones irregular surfaces pay tribute to my life. Raised and receded, fragmented and smooth I find understanding in the cold resilience and look skyward. "Hi Lord, little confused because Neil, well he's a mystery. Love him but why isn't he saying he loves me? Don't expect an answer, just needed to talk to you.

There in the darkness, I hear Neil's voice. "Belle! Meet me at the gazebo."

My heart pounds and I want to fly into his arms until I recall their words.' Don't offer meat to a hungry animal.' 'Ask him, muff or bouquet?' Instead of moving, I wait at the well for him to come to me.

He soon stands beside me. I take a deep breath and slide my finger along the underside of his collar.

"Neil, good evening, it's been ages since you paid a visit. So, I have a question."

"When don't you have a question in that pretty little head of yours?"

He tries to kiss me. I put up my hand between us and back away. Want a clear head before his kiss will muddle my words.

"About this January wedding invitation, do I borrow your mother's sable muff or keep my hands warm with a bride's bouquet?"

Neil grins. After he chuckles, he holds me by the

waist and lifts me onto the well's cover. "Depends, you could do both. Although, I believe the muff would be better on the honeymoon. That is if you say yes to an unasked question."

I can't believe it. Katherine once told me he sometimes talks in riddles. "Neil, did you bring me high enough to kiss me or play your mind games? Why? Because I never answer a question I haven't been asked. So don't expect me to say 'yes' to hear your question."

"Arabelle, instead of studying music or going spelunking to overcome a fear of deep holes, I considered mergers, acquisitions, and problem resolutions. Works well on short term goals, except for a collision-driven girl. You turned my life upside down. Can't focus on what I want to say."

"McCutchen, didn't think anything would disturb you?" I shake my head. "Riddles won't work Neil. You ask, and I'll answer."

"I had hoped you'd go to the gazebo. Had a soft pillow to kneel on, but, if you insist, I'll say it here under the moon and starless sky."

"McCutchen, what are you doing? I waited for you to say you loves me, and now you are asking without saying it. McCutchen?"

CHAPTER 23
BLACK PANEL

Neil soon finds a soft grassy knoll and gets down on one knee. He opens a blue velvet box and shows me the ring. "Miss Arabelle Lacey, will you do me the honor of becoming my bride? What's wrong?"

I smile at him but close the box in his hand.

"Wasn't sure what you'd like, so Francine picked it out. If you prefer, I'll get you a solitaire or a larger diamond."

"It's gorgeous. She has good taste."

"I'm confused Lacey. Something is wrong."

Okay, take a deep breath before you say anything. "Neil, I want to say yes, but not once have you said you love me. Isn't that a part of the equation? Love! And I'm sarcastic in saying I'm overjoyed your California girlfriend picked out my ring. Just ecstatic you had so much input in what you wanted to give me."

Neil reaches for my hand. "Arabelle Lacey, how do I love you? Let me count the ways. I love you to the depth and breadth and height my soul can reach. I love you with the breath, smiles, and tears of all my life! And if God choose, I shall but love you better after death." I fall to my knees beside him.

"McCutchen, you quoted Elizabeth's words. I love you, too."

Neil places the ring on my finger and kisses my hand. "This girl, Francine Bellsworth, is a friend for many years. She returned here to open her law office. I met her again at the Women's Clinic to discuss handling their legal matters."

"Really?"

"Yes. When we finished, she offered to accompany me to several jewelry stores for your ring. That reporter caught us coming out of Michael's and jumped to her conclusions. The tabloid picture was taken at a fundraiser while I was in California. Don't know how she got it. Do you think it's gorgeous?"

"It is the most spectacular engagement ever."

"It goes with your wedding band. The jeweler who came here is Mr. Rangar. He said that it was a half karat and white gold."

"He interrupted us the other day."

"Yes, wanted to deliver the rings. When you are ready to select the other gifts, he'll come here. Now Arabelle, will you answer my question because my knee is killing me. Will you do me the honor?"

For Katherine's benefit, I shout loud and long, "Yes. Yes. Yes."

Minutes later we burst into her sitting room. I hold out my left hand while Neil stands nearby.

"Katherine, he did, and I said yes. Look, it is official."

"It is a beautiful ring and that January, I presume is your wedding. Neil, will you be staying awhile to help arrange the details?"

"Yes, Neil, will you?" I hope and look forward to Neil

saying that he'll remain.

"I have in this room the two most beautiful women in my life, and I can't say, I will. Both of you handle the details with three provisions. One, the wedding will be an intimate, informal wedding aboard a yacht on the eighteenth. Second, the venue will be somewhere near the Barrier Reef. Third, honeymoon plans, you will leave to me. Have fun, my darlings. Tomorrow, Anson and I are interviewing a Texan CEO. He's interested in buying out our HP shares."

Katherine looked incredulous at her son's wedding proposition. I'm dumb struck until my brain and mouth join forces. "Mr. McCutchen, your delegation skill reached a new level. So, if you ever thought I'd marry a man that comes and goes like a traveling peddler, you're greatly mistaken. I believe the vow goes 'for better or worse, richer or poorer, sickness and in health.' I don't think it was rewritten to 'here today and gone tomorrow, with a slam-bam and thank you Ma'am marriage."

I take off the ring and return it to Neil."McCutchen, I acknowledge your proposal and thank you for asking, but my response is no thanks. Good night Katherine, Neil."

"Belle, Anson and I will be back within the week, a month at the most. Please, think it over. When I return, would you be willing to discuss the matter?"

I turn my head and give a wink to Katherine. "I would be willing to discuss it. Katherine, excuse me. I've some editing to do on your memoirs." I eavesdrop while exiting.

"Mom, think she'll say 'yes'?"

"Neil, nothing would make me happier than your getting married. However, what little I know about Arabelle, you'll have to convince her."

Over the week, I see a transformation in Katherine. Even with my refusal, with Neil out of sight, she becomes a controlling pre-mother-in-law imposing venue change and revising Neil's wedding plans into a three hundred plate dinner.

This morning we gather in what Clare calls the second-floor dining room. Katherine announces it will be a small, intimate ceremony for about fifty guests. Katherine runs her hand over the polished table top, walks to the doorway and surveys the room.

"Belle, if we move the sideboard in front of that banded panel and remove the furniture, we could seat forty-eight for the ceremony and hold the reception on the terrace. What do you think? Or choose Plan B. Everything is at the Country Club with enough space for two or three hundred guests. Have you started your guest list?"

"Katherine, it's a beautiful idea, but Neil wants an intimate group. Never been in this room. It is large and what's that black panel all about?"

"It used to be the focal point in the ballroom. I was a young girl, when Adam renovated the room and commissioned the piece. He wouldn't allow anyone except the artist and contractor in here until the room was finished. He always felt the graphic design was sufficient. Personally, the pewter banding never seemed to belong. Wouldn't you agree?"

"Personally, I'd get rid of it. Katherine, Neil wants it on a sailing vessel which might permit maybe eight or ten guests."

"Belle, he just doesn't understand how weddings work. Wedding excitement is in planning the venue, menu, and displaying a five-tier wedding cake. It is something I always wanted to have. Of course, dear, whatever you and Neil think is best. Oh, Arabelle, you've given me such pleasure in allowing me to help you plan."

"Katherine, we are not on the same page. Think about it, intimate wedding aboard a ship or the Country Club with half the population west of Buffalo."

"For the bridal shower, I think a five-piece string ensemble. They'll play in the gazebo with speakers leading to the terrace."

"But Katherine." The click, tap sound of the tea cart is music to my ears. After Clare enters, she pours each of us a cup and sits down.

"Excuse me, Katherine, if I might refresh my mind. Neil told both of you that he wants an intimate, informal affair on a ship in Australia and he would handle the honeymoon."

"That's right Clare. I remember Barrier Reef and a yacht." With Clare on my side, maybe Katherine will listen.

"Yes, he did say a ship. Although you popped my dream of Neil being married here, you are right. Forgive me, Belle."

"It's okay Katherine. I guess it's exciting for everyone. It seems we have much to do in so little time. Need a list to get organized. Thanks for the reminder."

"Excuse me," Clare said, "who knows how many can fit on a boat deck? Does someone know a livin' soul in Australia? If not, I have a friend at Miller's Travel. He'll find everythin' you want to know. Belle, call him. Let him do your homework and Miss Bellsworth agreed to handle the legal paperwork."

"Clare, we bickered, and you did the job as a truly

marvelous problem solver. Belle, now we can look for your trousseau and wedding gown. That is if you don't mind my intrusion."

"Excuse me, Katherine. I forgot to tell Belle something. Mr. Rangar called yesterday. Neil told him to come here today at one o'clock."

"Won't work Clare, please call him later to reschedule until next month around ten. Katherine, I'd love to have you join us when we go gown shopping, but not today."

"Wonderful, let me know when. Now Clare about the shower's menu."

I leave Clare describing her champagne punch with frozen fruity slush.

An hour later, Clare's voice comes through the bungalow's intercom. "Belle, I tried to reach him. But by the time I left Katherine, he's ringing the front bell. He's in the foyer."

"Clare, need five minutes. Escort him to the mini-office library. I'll be there shortly."

I change from the wrap-a-round to a Fifth Avenue business suit. Walking back, I mentally refresh my list. One, guest list is under control. Two, have to nix bridal shower. Three, a string ensemble . . . I know. I'll delegate music to Neil. Four, greet Mr. Rangar. Not sure about this meeting unless I put that management class to the test.

From the terrace, I station myself outside an open library window. Soon Clare brings him into the library, where for a minute or two I observe Mr. Rangar. He looks around the room and rubs his hands together. Under a table lamp, he places a black velvet cloth to display an array of expensive looking jewelry. I wonder if it's the costume pieces he leaves in his open leather case. Once he is satisfied with his displays, he sits back straight in the wingback chair, folds his hands, and waits.

I watch. He checks his gold pocket watch for the second time. I leave the terrace and enter the room. Once again, he looks at the time.

"Mr. Rangar, good morning." I wait for his reaction to meeting me because I've dressed for the occasion. A white business suit accentuates my figure and the emerald green silk blouse brings out my hazel eyes. His cursory glance lingers longer than necessary. He smiles and readjusts his eccentric plaid, sports coat.

"Not at all Miss Lacey, it is my pleasure to serve you. If it's no trouble, might I have some water? It was a long drive here, and I must remark, you are beautiful. Mr. McCutchen is a fortunate, young man." He comes forward, takes my hand to kiss it. I immediately shake his.

"Of course, Ms. Collins should arrive shortly with some refreshment. Mr. Rangar, I may appear naïve. However, I see your manner is meant to flatter a customer into spending more than she intended. Am I correct?"

His answer comes from a silent gulp that escapes from his lips. When he steps aside, with his right hand, he gestures to the table display, then moves back, not to invade any personal space I might need in making a selection.

"I assure you. It is meant as a genuine compliment. You'll see I've brought my best jewelry selection."

With those gold chains around his neck, he looks like a trained mouse with a receding chin and squinty eyes. I hand him a diamond ankle bracelet. "Mr. Rangar, stock numbers without cost?"

"No problem, Mr. McCutchen desires you to choose without cost in mind. He'll cover your purchases." With his lips, he smiles broadly, but his eyes go straight to my left hand.

"I understand Mr. McCutchen popped the question. Is there a problem in his ring selection?"

"Personal matter, sir, and now what have you in men's jewelry?"

He points to his case, and I rummage through its contents. After several minutes, I notice he selects a ruby choker necklace from the table display.

"Here is a lovely set, complete with earrings and bracelet, Miss. He thought you might wear it on your honeymoon."

"Sorry, I have my mother's pearls." From the case, I remove SCL190 and hold out my hand. "These will be perfect. I'd like two pairs."

"You've made an excellent selection for a formal occasion, a classic sterling silver cufflinks with cubic zirconia gemstones, and for your attendant?"

"Nothing strikes my eye.

Mr. Rangar covers his mouth in disbelief. In his nervousness, his gold chains get entangled in his pen.

He removes his case from the desktop. With the incoming sunlight, the precious stones cast a prism effect on the wall.

"Please have another look, top quality gems. Also, allow me to get my case containing birthstones. Your birthday is in September, Miss Lacey?"

"No," I said, and he leaves.

During his absence, Clare places the tray with pitcher

and glasses on the end table. Mr. Rangar is so fast in his retreat and return; he reminds me of Deci's dog, Buddy when he plays fetch.

I pour him a glass of water, and he takes a long drink. "Most refreshing, thank you."

"Yes, it is. We have an artesian spring."

He refills his glass while I look at the birthstone selections.

"Remarkable water, yes indeed. I notice you've selected a piece."

"Yes, these sapphires earrings. I like how there's a heart within the frosted crystal. The sapphires center it. Take two, no three pairs of E155 and add R881WS for my fiancée. My total?"

I can't help but note, his crafty smile now extends to greed in his eyes. "With his ring, the total will amount to a little over six thousand plus tax. The ring, you selected, is eighteen karats white gold with a karat blue sapphire. Will it replace Mr. McCutchen's wedding band?"

"No, I will pay for it separately. By the way, have you billed Neil for our rings?"

"Including tax, ninety-five hundred would be sufficient." After a resounding click on the metal case, he says, "No, I wanted to see what selections you made before any billing would occur."

"I know you can work something on the total cost of our joint purchases. Including tax and a forty percent discount, I calculate six thousand as a round figure." I drop the earrings into his palm.

He looks at me and puts them in his vest pocket. He continues packing his merchandise as his thin lips form a singular line. Once he finished, he straightened his jacket and said with much control in his voice, "Of course Miss Lacey, your selection will be discounted by twenty percent, and I'll apply the same discount to his total cost with delivery in two months."

With no trace of emotion in this transaction, I no longer smile and look directly into his eyes. "No, Mr. Rangar. I have his blank check for what he presumed would be a deposit. However, with a cash purchase today, a forty percent discount is expected and delivery within five weeks."

Mr. Rangar appears uncomfortable. He plays with his tie; and once more, straightens his sports coat before he extends his hand with an adjusted bill of sale. "Of course, within five weeks and I'll personally advise Mr. McCutchen of the generous discount."

I write the check and give it to him. "Thank you, Mr. Rangar."

He accepts my handshake, then, picks an imaginary piece of lint from my sleeve. "Your fiancée is very fortunate. His bride-to-be is very 'street smart'. Miss Lacey, I'll see myself out."

"Have a good day, Mr. Rangar."

CHAPTER 24
THE DULCIMER

It's hard to go a day without Katherine and I differing on wedding priorities, and she is getting on my nerves. As an escape, I go to the mini-library and call the clinic. I left Decima an invitation for an afternoon lunch. Today, I need time away from Katherine and her latest idea.

"Arabelle, Katherine is on the terrace. She asked me to remind you about."

"About what?" I ask.

"I forgot. Go see her. Maybe it's about her memoir."

There she is, reading a book on the terrace. When I get there, I say, "Katherine, we need to talk about your memoirs, which I find you spend less than an hour with me in fine tuning it."

"Belle, there are others things that should worry you. There is only so much time before the day arrives. You haven't tried on a single gown. I left you a bridal magazine. It hasn't been touched."

"Katherine, for all I know the eighteenth is a random day that he picked out of a hat. I spend several hours a day trying to locate Neil, to learn when he'll return. You recall I gave back the ring on the sixteenth. If he doesn't walk through that door soon, there will be no wedding."

The telephone rings twice and stops. Again, it rings twice, and I take hold of the receiver.

"Neil. Speak of the devil and who calls.—Yes, she's fine.—When do I pick you up?—Okay, the guest room is ready.-- ? Do I need to pick you up? Okay, the guest room is ready.—Me too, see you soon.—You do know two weeks max in Texas is a week in arrears. So I haven't decided.— Love you."

"What did he say?"

"Day after tomorrow, here for the fourth and ordered a rental. The attorney is coming with him, plans on staying here until she gets her place. Well, I'll call Deci and set my appointment at the boutique."

"Will you accept his proposal?"

"Good possibility, Katherine. Good possibility."

I dial Decima's number. "Hi Deci, green light all the way.—You're kidding. Eleven, we'll meet you there. Bye. "

"Katherine, I'll get Clare because in forty-five minutes we're going bridal shopping."

Traffic is light, and we arrive early. Inside Rachel's Boutique, I greet Decima's aunt. "Shalom Aunt Rachel, so glad you agreed that Decima would look fantastic in blue. Hope, she'll agree?"

"Hey, don't I have a say in the matter?" Decima asks. "Besides, thought we came here for your gown."

Aunt Rachel takes Decima and Clare by their arms. "Come with me, my darlings, you'll see. Blue is your color." They disappear into another room.

Katherine stops looking through the gowns. "Arabelle, why are they trying on a dress? Dear girl, you need to get your priorities in order."

"Katherine, no matter how out of normal it seems. I

know what I'm doing."

She goes to the wedding gowns and ransacks Aunt Rachel's inventory with comments of 'ordinary', 'run-of-the mill', 'nothing couture'. I'm uncomfortable and sorry she came along. A few minutes later, Deci and Clare return. Their smug look tells me a lot when each one climbs onto the risers and wait. Even though Katherine speaks softly, I know Clare and Deci are listening.

"I am speaking for your mother. Arabelle, you have no idea of priorities. We came here for your wedding gown, not an attendant's dress."

"Katherine, I already found mine. It was the second one Miss Rachel selected. I knew instantly. However, finding just one for both of them took a little longer. Katherine, take a look. Aren't they too, too gorgeous? That elegant silk crepe chiffon flows around the body and the bodice has something Miss Rachel called rushing."

Clare steps off the riser. Deci, still standing, said, "Well?"

When Katherine looks in their direction, she puts her hand to her mouth. "Ladies, words fail me. You both are beautiful."

Like a gleeful child, I clap my hands. "See, told you so. Deci, your Aunt Rachel said the design mimics a 'Jean Desses' creation. With your endowed body, Clare and that tasteful scoop beaded bodice, at least, Anson will have something to look at besides breasts. Well, what say you?"

Katherine rises and walks around the two women. Then says, "Belle, their outfits are delightful. I'm not sure how well they will flow on board a yacht?"

Deci lifts the gown below her knees and says, "No problem!"

"Ladies, the gown comes in calf-length. Do you like the color and design?" Rachel smiles into her hands, when their heads nod in unison and Deci says, "I love it." Clare looks at her reflection. "Me too, I feel a bit sexy in it. But where is Arabelle's?"

"I'll be back in a minute. Just wait," I dash to the fitting room, and Rachel follows me inside and takes my hands, "Need to talk my darling."

"Aunt Rachel, what's wrong?"

"Your boss has a pre-conceived opinion about you. When you arrive, she tells me that you have simple tastes. When she doubts your vision of what is appropriate for a McCutchen bride, I know narrow-mindedness. I think she looks down her nose at my shop when she wants to see my couture designs. I have a few, but they are not you. She will not be happy unless she picks the gown."

I say nothing and rely on Aunt Rachel to save my gown.

Minutes later, I leave the dressing room and twirl like a ballerina into the salon.

Decima is shaking her head. "Oh, Belle, you look, well, you look at least ten pounds heavier."

I look directly at Katherine. "Ten pounds, no way. Neil would kid me unmercifully. I'll be back."

When I return, I stand in front of my best friend. "Well, am I ten pounds lighter?"

After she lowers her head, I sense I embarrassed her by what I said. I try to apologize when, Katherine says, "Arabelle! Sarcasm doesn't fit you."

I'm surprised Katherine has raised her voice and made a face when I looked in her direction.

"Belle, we all want you to shine brighter than your attendants. Please be gracious." Katherine said and stood beside Deci.

In turn, I go over and hug Deci while I whisper in her ear. "Sorry. Guess Katherine has some balls after all."

We both giggle and then I climb onto the riser.

"Well Katherine, what do you think? I'll dye it and wear it again without the beaded bolero jacket."

She sits back and says, "Déjà vu. I've seen that design before. Different color and with a little pillbox hat, it was Jackie Kennedy's picture in the newspaper. Like you, slender hips allow for a bell-shaped skirt. I'm delighted?"

"Katherine? Jacqueline Kennedy? Don't think so; I'm a Republican, and this dress is out. Back we go Aunt Rachel to the other couture you selected. Although, I look like a flapper in that one."

"A flapper? Miss Rachel, is she joking?" Clare asks.

Aunt Rachel shakes her head. Then she approaches Mrs. McCutchen. "I'll have Arabelle wear several couture gowns from my collection. This designer admires Vionnet's fringe look of the 30's. In this creation, the fringe covers the full length of the skirt, with an extra five inches of trimming trailing the back train. Chi chi, Mrs. McCutchen."

"But she is not a flapper. Is she, Miss Rachel?"

"No, Madam, she is not. However, I believe there is one gown in my establishment that will meet with your satisfaction and Miss Lacey's."

I shrug. With my enthusiasm gone, I half-heartedly follow Aunt Rachel. "Maybe Katherine is correct. I'm not good enough to be a McCutchen bride if no gown satisfies her."

“None my darling, except the one you liked from the moment you saw it. This time, we add a simple veil. Trust me, dear.”

I feel like a bride when Aunt Rachel fastens a blusher veil to my head with a wedding tiara of white pearls and diamond chips. I do not enter the salon one foot in front of the other; I seem to glide over the floor in this white jersey, trained gown. I’m almost there when I overhear Decima. I stop.

“Mrs. McCutchen, this is not an apology. Nor, am I being a tad disrespectful when I say, you don’t know everything because my Aunt knows the business.”

“Indeed. Tell me Decima, what type of gown would you see her wearing?”

“Me? I see her in a gown that is quietly understated. Definitely, no frills and no waist at her hips. Empire waistline would work. I see a neckline that accentuates her long neck and oval face. That’s what I envision. Wait, here she comes.”

A shadow of Mendelssohn’s “Wedding March” echoes in my mind. I enter the showroom.

“Belle, you are drop-dead gorgeous. That ‘v’ stitching accents your bust. You look like a goddess with arms in those long slender sleeves. Oh, this is you.”

“Katherine? Are you okay because you’re crying?”

With her handkerchief, Katherine dabs her eyes. “This is your wedding gown. That is if this is the one you want.”

“Don’t know, Katherine. Maybe on board ship, jeans and this veil is all I need. Certainly, would be more comfortable. Think I’d love it too. But there is one more couture gown.”

"You can't be serious, Belle. That is your dress. Mrs. McCutchen, tell her."

"Decima speaks the truth. The look is yours, and Neil will love it."

With a wink to Aunt Rachel, we return to the dressing room. "I love you, Aunt Rachel. Please check with Deci and Clare on which length they would prefer. Then order them. One more favor, would you please let them know I'll be out shortly and that I'm starving."

When I come out, I discover Clare and Deci have gone to the car, and Katherine is shaking Aunt Rachel's hand. "Adieu, Miss Rachel."

"Shalom, Mrs. McCutchen, it was a pleasure meeting you. By the way, here is your book."

Katherine nods and takes her notebook. She leaves the boutique.

"Thank you. Shalom." I say and got into the driver's seat. "Katherine, is your planner a portion of your memoirs?"

"Not quite, Belle. More like thoughts and impressions of my impositions in your life. Now Decima, with the Blue Moon closed, where is the nearest eatery?"

"Burger King! Two blocks straight ahead, then turn right."

ꕥꕥꕥ

The next day, Clare prepares a celebration dinner. The venture to Texas is a success, and both men are glad to relax in their home environment. The house hums and I head back to the bungalow. When I hear a car door slam, I see Neil get out and go into the garage portion of the carriage house.

I'd love to have a one-on-one with him and enter the

garage. Muffled voices cause me to move into the shadows, where sight unseen, I listen.

"Anson, join me for a drink. Those women are driving me crazy. Mother wants strings. Francine says that Belle and I should decide. Then I couldn't believe Belle when she tells me I should choose the music. Clare didn't say a word; she left the room. Anson, I need a quiet moment. Join me?"

"So they know you're here. However, won't you join me with a social lubricant? There's an unopened bottle of 12-year-old Scotch upstairs. I saved it for two gentlemen to survive a house full of women. Then, I'd like to share something you might find useful."

They climb the stairs, and I get braver in finding a new listening place.

"Nice surroundings, Anson."

"Thanks, works for a bachelor. Before I pour, let me play this tape. Think you might like the sound."

With the stereo system on, I enjoy what I hear and hope Neil does too.

"That music . . . It's . . . It's different. Who are the artists?"

"Neil, in 1974, I bar-hopped and heard a group called "The Trapezoid". Following the band's set, I was curious about an instrument. I go backstage and meet Sam Rizzella. He played the dulcimer. With Rizzella's encouragement and months of lessons, I mastered it. The tape you're listening to is me on the dulcimer, playing 'The Parting Glass'. I converted the second bedroom into a recording studio, so I can record a duet or listen for my enjoyment. That music can soothe the savage soul, don't you agree?"

"I do. Anson, you are a genius. This solves their, nay my problem. The Trapezoid's, have their number? I'll hire them."

"Not exactly what I had in mind. Neil, I want to do this as my wedding gift."

"Thanks, Anson. Sounds intriguing but how will you do it when you're going to be my best man."

"Told you, have a recording studio. You and Belle pick your songs, and I'll tape them for the ceremony and later will play live at the reception."

"Not only are you a genius, but also, you are a life saver, Anson. Now cheers!"

"Cheers, Neil."

After four toasts and beautiful music, I return to the bungalow to relax.

CHAPTER 25
THE WEDDING BOUQUET

Two hours later Neil interrupts a heated exchange in Katherine's sitting room.

"Belle, you exasperate me. Why won't you understand, you'll find the best-traveling wardrobe in Toronto."

"Don't need to go there for a trousseau."

Katherine throws her arms up. "But the rate of exchange Belle, it's at 25 cents on our dollar. We can explore Alfred Sung's collection. Couture designers are so impressionable. They create with your vision in mind."

"Katherine, their creation is no longer my vision. If I need to see my vision custom made, we could go to Chaybana's Custom Tailors."

"Chaybana's? Never!"

"Katherine, I love my wedding gown, and I've enough clothes for a trousseau. Buy me something new and exciting, like lingerie that disintegrates in water. Now I'm off to find that son of yours."

I stop when Neil rushes into the room. He waves a small black tape in the air.

"Did someone call me? Mother and Arabelle, I found your musician. He will perform, and Belle and I get to select the music later. So I'm off to take Francine over to Decima's place. She thought it best to stay with her until they find her an apartment."

"Neil, I'd love to go with you."

"Can't my love. After Francine drops off her things, we finalize the paperwork at her office for the Australia government, the yacht, and selection of an alternate honeymoon spot. Don't ask where. I haven't decided. Will it be Paris, Switzerland, Africa, Colorado or Disneyland?"

He pecks my cheek then Katherine's. Retreats from the room and out the front door.

"Excuse me, Katherine. Disneyland? Neil wait." I shout and sprint after him. Somehow, he disappeared.

For the last four months, his fax messages indicate all is well, but, no further information. Francine knows his whereabouts but is tight-lipped on sharing. She handles daily business affairs from her office and tells me Neil's agenda is on schedule. Darkness shrouds my participation in my wedding.

Time moves forward, but news of Neil's location becomes non-existent until a glimmer of hope surfaces with his last fax that we'll finally meet in Sydney on second of January. I call Francine for details.

My new year begins in Australia. Although docked, I still work at gaining my sea legs. Everyone is aboard the schooner, and I make my way to Francine's and Deci's cabin.

"Francine, your handling the legal details for us is appreciated. Thank you from the bottom of my heart. The Captain informed me we just made it under the wire in completing that Notice of Intention of Marriage.”

Francine takes a quick glimpse out the porthole then moves away. “You’re welcome. Tying up loose ends is part of the job. However, when you both signed her wedding register that Justice is the one you needed to thank. She was on the ball in cutting through the red tape and processing the paperwork. Efficient and so pleasant, too bad she’s married.”

I clear my throat. “Fran, without you coaching me, I would have freaked out when Neil and I met with her. Were you aware that declaration had us stating that each of us believe there is no impediment to the marriage between the two of us? Well before I signed my name, had to think about that.”

"Why? You are single, and Neil loves you."

“Once thought, you were the obstacle. Then Katherine tells me you’re their attorney and that I shouldn’t worry. Attorney, okay, but . . .”

Fran is quiet for some time. So I fiddle with the room’s floral arrangement. I touch the long stem of a hairy, six claw-like flower. “Fran, did you know this is called a kangaroo paw? And, how did you and Neil become so close?”

“Business. Think Decima, would prefer a pink diamond?”

That's a question; I didn’t think I’d ever hear. Does she know Deci’s secret? It’s not your business. Answer her question. “Have to ask her, I guess. So why did you leave your lucrative career and move to New York’s suburbia?”

“Originally, lived in Rochester. I met him when I was a guest speaker at a Seminar on Contract Law. The estate's California business was undergoing some changes, and he approached me. Later became a client. On his trips to Los Angeles, we'd talk, discuss business at dinner. Told him I studied law by correspondence."

"Does New York allow that?"

"It doesn't but California did. So I moved there. The day he decided to find your ring, I spilled my heart on how I loved working with non-profit organizations, but our firm increased my workload with paying clients and stopped taking pro bono cases. With a change in office politics, I felt an insidious rain was melting who I am and Neil . . ."

I finish her sentence. "Knew Katherine wanted the estate to provide pro bono service to the Women's Clinic and that the attorney would also be on retainer for the estate's business."

"Yes exactly, I accepted Neil's informal offer. Primarily did it to practice law like I want and get away from being an ambulance chaser. Recently passed the New York Bar and will open my practice once I return."

"That newspaper picture of you and Neil almost destroyed any thoughts of me wanting to marry him. How I wanted to scratch your eyes out that is if I ever met you."

"Arabelle let me put your mind at ease. Katherine was correct. I like men as friends, some even as good friends, but that is as far as I would want any serious relationship to develop if you get my drift."

I walk over and give her a hug. "I didn't know. Thanks for putting my mind at ease. I know Neil values your friendship. Now let's eat. I was so nervous to confront you, and now, I'm starving and glad you accepted our invitation."

"My pleasure," said Francine and she returns my hug. "I'll tell you. I wasn't coming because I hated wearing dresses and didn't have a tux or even a formal looking suit. However, a rare jewel, your friend, Decima, found this cool outfit from a little bridal boutique."

"Rachel's?"

"None other. You know the place."

"Sure do but I think we'd better go to the dining area before the food is gone. Deci does have an appetite."

We laugh and walk arm-in-arm to the dining room and join the rehearsal dinner.

ജജജ

The following day, Anson and Clare do their best in keeping us from accidentally meeting each other aboard the yacht. As twilight approaches, the dulcimer's recorded music of 'You're the First, the Last, My Everything' is our signal the ceremony would begin in five minutes. I hide from his view of the processional line. From a tiptoed stance, I watch a few guests speaking in hushed tones. Katherine wears a gold and silver beaded fringe dress and is seated last.

Deci leans closer. "That woman is a knockout. She has the making of a Vegas showgirl. Although, not as beautiful as a bride I once loved."

Our exchanged glances take on a new meaning for me of the friendship we shared. I hope she'll find someone to love again. The recording stops. Everyone, including crew members, turn, and the wedding procession begins.

When the Justice of the Peace leads the way, Anson and Neil follow him to a makeshift railing. Clare manages the small swells as she walks.

Decima turns to arrange my veil and tucks a loose

lock under the tiara. "Belle got to ask you something important. Be honest, it's important. When I met Francine, I couldn't breathe. And well, she is looking for a roommate to share expenses. She asked me if we could live together. What should I say, you know—about me?"

"Deci, I would tell her, 'You take my breath away every time I meet you.' See what her reaction is to you and see where it goes. You may be surprised. Now Wagner's "Bridal Chorus" is playing for the second time. I think Neil may be waiting for our entrance."

"Think I should tell her?"

I look at my best friend and wonder which one is more nervous. "Yes, I do. Now go. Smile. Relax. Deci, you're choking your flowers."

She loosens her grip on the bouquet of scented wildflowers. In passing Francine, I see she tilts her head and notice a smile crosses Fran's face.

It's my turn to join the wedding spectacle. I wait. Two crewmembers unwind the white acetate roll for my walk through the dining room into the salon to Neil.

He's so handsome standing at attention and so nervous. He rubs his palms together. There, he gave a weak nod toward Katherine. No, he's trying to put his hand into a sewn pocket. Oh, he sees me. What a smile and he's mine.

Even with the small rolls of the yacht and high heels, I maintain my balance. Throughout Mendelssohn's wedding march, my bouquet of white orchids, ivy, and several kangaroo paws for luck shakes. I have a flutter in my throat as butterflies seek to escape. I look over to Deci. She understands and takes my bouquet. With as much grace as I can muster, Neil join hands. With the exchange of rings, my new life will begin when I hear the words.

"Dearly beloved. We are gathered here today . . ."

Following the ceremony, Neil and I stand in place as everyone rush in for hugs and well wishes. Once back on duty, crew members pour champagne and serve our guests the sparkling liquid.

Recorded dulcimer music of our favorite songs adds to the festivities. Anson lifts his glass and offers a toast. "Dance, as if no one is watching. Sing, as if no one was listening. Live every day as if it were your last."

A round of applause comes from the Captain and his crew. Others tap their glass as we kiss. The late evening catered reception is in the sky lounge. Crystal bowls contain fruity mimosa of rose champagne, orange juice, and tiny fish-shaped melons. The galley chef's selection of cheese and finger foods satisfies everyone. The wedding cake is cut, served, and Neil and I dance under a starlit sky.

Thoughts of Adam's malicious act in hiding his will; Katherine's dream on the brink of extinction; the futility of Clare and Anson, our star-crossed lovers' relationship, I toss overboard with the next swell. Love conquers my heart.

When Anson strums a lively number, Neil says, "Let's sit this one out." We cuddle in a floral decorated loveseat. "Look Deci's sneaking away with a wrapped piece of the red velvet wedding cake. Bet, she'll be putting it under her pillow. Better hurry or she'll miss the bouquet toss."

Of the six women invited, four clusters together and one stands apart. I stall until Deci races onto the deck. I turn, throw it high, and back. To my surprise, Clare catches the wedding bouquet.

The midnight hour grows closer, and Anson on the upper deck energizes the reception with his rendition of a lively set of 'We Are Family' and 'Dance to the Music'. Exhausted from dancing, we watch and smile at each other as the wedding guests sink back into their cushioned chairs. With Clare as his partner, Anson dances to his tape of the 'Arkansas Traveler'. The guests enjoy the slower music, and it covers our escape to leave the merriment.

Off with the wedding dress, I put on a navy suit. My heart beats with excitement the closer I come to meet my husband on the forward deck.

"Mrs. McCutchen, the moonlight casts an aura around you. You remind me of a sea nymph with your mother's string of pearls still entwined in your hair."

"Not an aura, my husband, but a spell I weave into your heart."

The first mate assists our boarding the yacht's dinghy. Within seconds, we slip away from our guests with the music fading into the night air.

I feel complete. "Neil, life doesn't get better than this. What a beautiful sky, no clouds and stars like diamonds light our way. Are we singled out by destiny for lives of infinite happiness?"

"If it was worth the wait, Mrs. McCutchen, we are."

At the dock, a taxi waits to drive us to a private plane intended for a red-eye flight out of Sydney.

Once aloft, I take his hand and place it inside my carry-on bag. "Traveling is nice but not what I envisioned for our wedding night. So, you'll have to imagine what I'd look like as you feel your way along the lace."

"Still teasing me, I see. Twenty more hours and we'll

be in Vail. I hear the nightclubbing and skiing is incredible. Picture us snuggling au naturel by the fireside and munching on rattlesnake appetizers."

"Rattlesnake . . . Mr. McCutchen, if this is your idea of a honeymoon . . ."

His kiss ends my sentence, and I cuddle into the warmth of his arms. "Love you, Neil."

"Love you more, little woman. Did you know Pike's Peak was the inspiration for 'America the Beautiful'? Belle?"

I keep my eyes closed, and he stops talking.

CHAPTER 26
BLUE-RINGED OCTOPUS

After the long flight and sleigh ride, it's mid-day when we arrive at an alpine village in the heart of the Rocky Mountains. Neil carries me over the bridal suite's threshold. I'm in his arms, and he kisses me with a few pecks on my cheek with his eyes open.

"Come on, Lacey; the slopes await us."

"Neil McCutchen, I slept and spent our wedding night on two planes. I dozed on the ride to the resort and received a lukewarm carry over the threshold. I hoped I'd be corrupted by your lovemaking. Instead, I get, 'Come on, Lacey, the slopes await us.' Neil, they'll be there tomorrow, and the tomorrow after the next tomorrow. If truth is known, I want a twosome shower. I want to get into or out of something sexy and have unending sex 'til the following afternoon with my husband."

He lowers me to the bed and lies beside me. "Belle, conditions are right, fresh snow today. Even the bellboy said so."

Wrinkled travel clothes separate our bodies from becoming one. I play with the buttons on his shirt and expose his chest. When I recall our last encounter, I giggle and say, "Mind if I remove your tie?"

Laughing he leans back and folds his arms behind his head as if to punctuate the point. “Be my guest, I haven’t been undressed by a woman in at least . . . well, too long.”

I undo and remove his tie. Unbutton his shirt to rest my head against his warm body. Without Anson's cherry sunshine, I refresh his memory and warm his torso with my tongue until I straddle his body and feel stiffening beneath me.

“Didn’t know you liked bare-chest riding, Lacey?”

“It’s better if we both are bare, McCutchen.” I begin humming a song from ‘Gypsy’ and a knowing glance exchanges between us. “Neil, I believe it’s time we start acting like married lovers and not opposing camps. Wouldn’t you agree?”

Our lips meet, and his French kiss foreshadows his penetration and the pleasures his experience brings. Lying there beside him, I snuggle into his arm and whisper, "Neil, forgive me for thinking aloud, but, I'd welcome you aboard many more times. So when you go skiing and should meet anyone, tell them I couldn't change your mind, even though, there's a large, heart-shaped tub. Plus, your wife is taking a bubble bath.”

I get off the bed and take the carry-on into the bathroom.

From the bed, Neil calls out to me. “Belle, hey listen to this. Vail, nestled in the heart of the Rocky Mountains, is North America’s biggest and most popular honeymoon resort. It is a favorite of jet-setting celebrities and a young, snowboarding crowd. Skiing is king, but the area’s vast splendor is perfect for hiking, snowmobiling or scenery-gazing at any time.”

Wearing a peek-a-boo black lace gown, I stand against

the doorframe and give him a seductive smile. "Speaking of scenery, darling would you help me? I heard the material vanishes when it got wet."

"Guess the slopes can wait. I need to buy some ski wax anyway. For now, let me help you see if it does disappear."

The brochure drops to the floor when Neil picks me up and carries me into the Jacuzzi. Slowly with care, he wets the sheer straps until they disappear from my shoulders. The gown drops away beneath the bubbles.

"It disappeared Lacey, and I must say, wife. It was worth the money."

"Katherine gave it to us as a wedding gift."

Neil's kiss brings us together, and before we submerge into a watery bed, he says, "Thank you, Mom!"

ജജജ

A week passes before Neil makes his way to rent some skis. "Have fun getting your souvenirs. I'm definitely on the slopes this afternoon."

"Love you too." I walk away and pass the hotel's concierge. He's calling my husband.

"Mr. McCutchen."

I turn to see he is talking to Neil and leading him into the Manager's office. I hurry over to find out what is happening.

"Good morning, Mrs. McCutchen. Please join us in my office."

"Is there a problem?" Neil asked while he put his arm around my shoulder.

"A Mr. Redman called and asked to speak to you or your wife. He said it was important."

We follow him to a small office, and he hands Neil the

phone. "Mr. Redman is on hold. Press two."

Neil takes a deep breath before he presses the speaker button, then the line. "Anson, what's wrong. Is everyone okay? "

"Neil, we are so sorry. It's Katherine. Neil, we should have stayed with her, but she said that the Chef had provided picnic lunches for those of us going ashore for snorkeling lessons. She wanted me to take Clare and enjoy our last day."

"How is she? What happened?" Neil's face turns white, and he squeezes my hand.

"You know how her energy pulls in so many directions. We never imagined this would happen. Insistent about her invisible tan line, she went to a nude beach. When we returned, it was almost twilight. We couldn't find her and checked with the Captain. He said she never returned for lunch. A search party went out. Clare and I found her, fully clothed and slumped over a tidal pool."

Neil is stunned and can't talk. I wrap my arm around his shoulder and say, "It can't be. Anson. We'll book the next flight back."

Neil interrupts me. There's a tremor in his voice. "You've my power of attorney, order an autopsy. Ask Francine to handle matters until we arrive. See if she found out whatever has to be done to have Mother's body shipped home? Are the authorities involved?"

"Local Police and the Coroner's office are looking into the matter. American Embassy was contacted. They're doing their best to move things along. Clare is in shock. Belle, your friend, Decima, is caring for her. I booked you a private jet. It departs as soon as you arrive at the airport. We're off the schooner. Francine booked us into a hotel. When you arrive, a limo driver will pick you up. Everyone here is sorry for your loss. Goodbye and a safe return trip."

Neil hangs up. Without words between us, we hug each other long and hard.

The Manager begins to leave to give us privacy. "Mr. & Mrs. McCutchen, we are sorry for your loss. As soon as you are ready, our car will take you to the Airport. Is there anything, we can do to help, let me know."

Neil looks at me, and I nod, knowing we both want the same thing. "Yes sir, there is. Take us now. Our belongings, ship them to our home address. Here is my charge card, run the number, and I'll notify them of upcoming charges. Thank you."

We leave the hotel, still numb from the news. There is nothing to say. At the tarmac, we hold hands and go aboard the jet.

When we arrive at the Sheraton in Sydney, hugs and tears are shared. Then with Clare and Anson, the limo takes us to the morgue.

"Anson, did they find anything new?" I ask. Neil sits in a stupor. I think he is still in shock.

"Coroner's office sent some paperwork. Decima is giving it her attention."

Clare interrupts, "We found her collapsed on her side and her fist clenched to her chest. She must have waded along the shoreline because they found seaweed between her toes. After we had identified her body, they told us to leave."

We are ushered into a private room where Decima

waits. She holds the report. After we embrace, she says, "The autopsy indicates the cause of death as asphyxiation through poisoning."

"Poisoning? Don't believe it. No one dies from seaweed. The report must be wrong. Let me see it." Neil takes the paper from Decima.

"Neil, I'll give you the Reader's Digest version. Your mother was poisoned by a blue-ringed octopus. The Coroner found one in her clenched hand. I saw the wound in her palm."

Neil skims the report. "A what? Deci, an octopus bite can't kill a person, can it?"

"Neil, this report indicates that while it is about the size of a golf ball, it produces a potent toxin that is lethal to humans. One milligram can kill a person within minutes."

Neil put his head into his hands and begins crying. "Can't believe it . . . how could something so small?"

"Darling, last year, I watched a broadcast on the Public Broadcasting Channel. The marine scientist said that this small octopus sometimes is found in tidal pools. When touched, it changes its color, which makes it appear to be playful. However when agitated, they flash their ring colors from dark brown, to gold, to bright iridescent blue."

"Knowing my mother, she'd be curious enough to touch it with something, maybe her finger. If that caused it to change its color, she'd pick it up."

"If she did that, it would defend itself by biting. Its saliva releases the neurotoxin into the open wound."

The Coroner comes into the room and says, "Mr. McCutchen, will you come with me. We need you to identify the body."

After Neil identified her corpse, everyone returns to the hotel. I see how unexpressed grief is masked by light chitchat regarding our flight and what Vail's weather was like when we left. On the drive, I hold his hand and squeeze it to keep tears from coming.

Later that afternoon, Decima takes me out to the hotel's pool. "Belle, it was over in minutes for Katherine. It wasn't peaceful. I would never tell Neil, and I'm only telling you, so you won't try to find out anything by yourself."

We sit, and she takes my hand. "Although I am curious, I understand. Why don't you want Neil to know the details?"

"Katherine would become nauseous. Within seconds after, her vision becomes hazy and then she'd go blind. Her sense of touch is now gone. Katherine couldn't speak or swallow. Within three minutes she'd become paralyzed, unable to breathe and die."

Decima embraces me in a crushing grip, I swallow hard and begin crying. "I promise, he'll never know."

At the hotel and throughout dinner, everyone has stories of how much they loved Katherine. We are finally alone, and I realize the numbness hasn't left either of us. Overtired, we retire but do not sleep near each other. After a few minutes, I pat his side of the bed. He isn't there. "Neil, come to bed."

"Belle, need to take a walk. Night air clears the head."

"Wait a second and I'll join you."

He gives me a weak smile and goes to the door. Once outside, we walk to the front of the hotel and down through the courtyard.

"Belle, I spoke with Francine. She and Deci are leaving tonight. I told Anson and Clare to return as well. Belle, I have a lot to consider. The additional cost is inconsequential. It's the time element. Could be as long as ten weeks to take care of what is required."

"Required? Can't we ship her body by air or something?"

Neil shakes his head. "Not that I can't do the paperwork, but it takes the officials time to register the death. Plus, the coroner is required to sign off because of the autopsy. Then, we get things done in the States, to secure permission to transport the body in a sealed casket."

"No other options, where we could leave sooner?"

"We could fly back in two days. Francine found a body shipping service that works with licensed funeral homes here and at home. They take care of the paperwork. Her remains would leave in a couple of weeks. If we leave without her, I'd feel I abandoned her. That doesn't seem the right way to handle her remains."

I see the anguish on his face. The decision is tormenting him. "Neil, what if her body is cremated, can we air it back with us. Then we could leave maybe in less than a week. Neil, Katherine once told me she wanted to be buried near her little girl. A sealed urn would fit beside the gravestone. How do you feel about that choice?"

The relieved look in his eyes gave me my answer. With the medical report signed, the cremation is done, and her ashes travel back in the hold. The evening we arrive home, Francine arranged for her memorial service to be held at the Estate. The gathering room, once again, is converted for her friends to offer their condolence.

I stand apart from the urn and answer their questions about her accidental death. Neil thanks, those who give testimonials of how the late Mrs. McCutchen made an impact in their life. I notice his discomfort when a lady from the Guild brings him closer to Katherine's urn.

From across the room, I wave to get his attention. Our eyes meet, and he blows me a kiss. This small interruption is enough for him to come over to the pocket doorway. The grandfather clock chimes and I know everyone will soon leave. When his arms wrap around me, I feel secure.

"Belle, you are a life saver. I couldn't think of a polite way to get away. Any more than I can think of a way to tell you I must leave you alone for a short time."

"What? Neil the room is spinning."

I cough from the ammonia smell and hear a familiar voice. Now conscious, I try to stand, but my legs feel like rubber bands.

"Take it, easy darling, you fainted."

"I'm okay. Stop with the smelling salts, Neil. I'm okay."

Anson hands me a glass of water. I take a sip and lean against Neil. "Miss Belle, your color is coming back. That's a good sign. Clare informs me there's a lull in the parade of visitors coming through the door."

Neil has me recline on the settee and slips off my shoes. He begins to massage my foot and says, "You've become quite the woman, Mrs. McCutchen. I hope you don't hire a masseuse when I leave."

"And your departure tactics are becoming more apparent, Mr. McCutchen. You'd better stop because if you look down the hallway, there's Mr. Rangar."

I slip on my shoes, stand and smooth my hair. I know Neil would leave shortly on business, and Mr. Rangar's visit is ill-timed and undeniably questionable. I smile. He nods and Neil escorts him out the door.

Within minutes, Decima comes into the sitting room. "Everyone has left except for us. Thought, you'd like her ashes in this room until the burial."

"Thanks, Deci. Please excuse me."

I go to Neil's side. "What happened? You rushed him out so fast, thought the police was looking for him."

"Nothing so dramatic, he contacted me in Sydney and insisted I give him the opportunity to appraise Mother's jewelry. Told him we weren't interested. I lost it when you noticed him."

Francine peeks around the doorway. "Okay folks, the kitchen is spit spot and Clare went with Anson. Neil, if you're packed, I'll drive you to the airport. Neil? You did tell Arabelle, didn't you?"

"No, because I won't be going, Anson is my replacement. Fran, Decima, Belle and I appreciate all you did for us."

"Labors of love belong in the definition of friendship. If you're ready Decima, I'll get Anson." Fran said.

He's staying with me. I've hope for our marriage.

ꙮꙮꙮ

Married life is typical of newlyweds minus a proper honeymoon. Because of what has happened, we promise each other a reunion at Vail for our first anniversary.

Every morning Neil leaves for the office and extends Anson's away-from-home time via phone calls, faxes, and overnight mail with his passport enclosed to conclude the sale of the McCutchen's European market share.

We move the mini-office to the sitting room, and I devote several hours a day to ready her memoirs for publication. However, any bequests she mentioned earlier to me go to the wayside because of her missing will. My search, though limited, now includes finding Katherine's. Many afternoons are spent closing Katherine's social commitments.

The evenings and weekends are ours. It begins Friday at six p.m. and then we're off. Secret rendezvous, weekend escapes, jet to Europe for croissants at breakfast or to hideaway beaches for underwater swimming. I look at the best of all this, Neil and I are together.

It's mid-March and airplane tickets to Vail are my surprise for Neil. I leave our bungalow and notice a light comes from the window in his former bedroom. I'm curious why anyone would be there. Without a word of warning, I find him packing his suitcase. Our together time ends in an argument, which should have never started.

CHAPTER 27
PLAY THE STOCK MARKET

"Hi, going somewhere without me?" I ask while poking him in the chest.

"Belle, you know I never remain here for this long. I'll be away four months tops. Anson arrives this evening. He'll file early this year. If a problem arises, have him immediately fax it to me from the office. I'm sorry, Belle, but I must leave tonight."

"Four months? That's longer than our marriage. Neil here at the Manor, we had a little time for each other. Can't you postpone this meeting? Or better, I'll travel with you?"

"Belle, don't try to save what you can't. You would be bored with business and board meetings."

"Breakfast in bed, shopping, sightseeing, midnight cocktails with my lover, I could handle that part of the trip. And wouldn't you be happy with a willing bed partner every night?"

"No, Arabelle! I put my foot down. You cannot go with me."

If he's looking for an argument, wait until he sees me on the warpath because I'm furious. I push him down onto the bed and straddle his chest.

"Think again lover; our marriage won't work with you off and traveling at the drop of a hat. There's no sense arguing or raising your voice, McCutchen; I'll have Anson make all the arrangements. Passport is valid, and an overnight bag takes five minutes to pack."

"No! Darling, what don't you understand about those two letters—n, o? There will be a no to arrangements and no to packing. This time, you cannot go with me. End of discussion."

The tenor of Neil's voice is firm and lacks emotion. "Belle, I love you more than life itself. However, I thought you were too young to marry. Believe me, if you can't handle a marriage with the craziness of my lifestyle, tell me. And we'll end it. Please understand, I need to make this trip alone."

"Neil, I love being married to you. I don't want our time together shortened by your trips. Absence doesn't always make the heart go fonder, and you get used to the separations. Until one day, you read the divorce paper in your hand."

"Divorce papers, how little is your faith in me? Belle, I desire you this moment and will want you until I die because it swallows all my reasoning."

"I'm a jinx, Neil. People that I love, die, and I don't want that to happen to you without our spending as much time together as we can."

"Okay, you need to believe me. You are not a jinx. Heart attack and accidental toxic poisoning were not preordained deaths because you loved them. Right now, you can't go with me. If you still want to in the future, Anson will brief you on upcoming ventures. European holdings are sold. Texas is a hand-holding situation for a year or so. Go to the office; you'll understand where I need your feedback. Then on my next trip, you'll join me."

I attempt to sweeten my position and stroke his temples. "Don't agree with you, but, you're right. I mean, how could you keep your mind on a successful merger if you were thinking of me languishing in bed and eating chocolate-covered strawberries?"

He laughs and kisses my cheek. His smile tells me he won the skirmish but not the battle. "Mrs. McCutchen, you're right as usual. I love you and want to leave you something to remember me."

A car horn resounds outside. Neil calls from the window. "Be out in ten, Anson."

Before Neil opens the car door, I shout from his bedroom, "Safe return, McCutchen. Love you."

He waves and throws me a kiss. "Love you more."

I look around the room and already am lonely. Get a hold girl; it's you who must learn to let go to survive. That's it. If I concentrate on her memoirs, the time will pass. I go to the sitting room and begin typing, 'Life includes superfluous things – including a blue- ringed octopus. Katherine Greene McCutchen's life is a story of a remarkable woman. As her confidant and daughter-in-law, I will tell it. It includes her joys and victory over the darkness she kept hidden as mentioned to me before her death.'

I work until midnight and shut off the lights. Instead of the back kitchen stairs, I climb the front staircase to my former bedroom. Time is in my favor. With Anson's help, I resolve Neil, this will be the last business trip you take alone.

Following breakfast, a trip to the in-house libraries results in several books that will further my education. I'm prepared for self-education when I bring along a pitcher of iced tea. I get comfortable on the settee and look at the book titles, 'Understanding the Business World', 'How to Play the Stock Market', and 'Seven Ways to Keep Your Husband Happy.' I scan the jackets and begin reading until my head starts nodding. I close my eyes until voices stir my consciousness.

"Thought she was reading. She isn't."

"Okay Clare, you wake her."

I feel a gentle shake and open my eyes.

"Arabelle, you had us worryin', absent from sight and sound all day. It's almost five o'clock, and your dinner is on the stove."

"Thanks, Clare you prepared my dinner? Have you plans?

"Need somethin' at the Mall. Then maybe we'll get a bit to eat or maybe a movie. Anythin' I can get you while we're there?"

I rub the sleep from my eyes and arch my back. "Don't think so. Wait, a couple of spring rolls from Mr. Sung's place would be fantastic. Go. Enjoy your evening. By the way, has anyone from the woman's group called?"

"Mrs. Yaple did. Said she'd call again. Katherine always wanted to do something positive for those young girls. Shame how unfortunate circumstances happen to good people. Good night."

"Good night Clare and dinner is on the stove, got it."

Clare starts to leave and stops. "Arabelle, don't like talkin' about the dead and their misfortunes. However without Katherine's will, I think it's time I tell you about

Mary, her mother. One night we got to drinkin' some of Anson's blackberry wine. After a while, she's confessin' to me about her secret shame. Said that it happened the time her husband left for a two-month trip for Adam. Not sayin', it was right or wrong because I don't think her mother ever told her about that. I think that's the reason how Mrs. Greene blackmailed Adam into addin' Katherine's name onto the house deed. Somehow we must find their wills and learn the truth. Goodnight."

I don't add anything to her admission of the past because I know the truth. I say, "Past is past, Clare. We can't change any of it. Well, goodnight Clare."

The sun is setting on the horizon, and I watch shadows skim over the floor. I grab the Stock Market book and head to the kitchen. I wonder about Mrs. Yaple. Does she know about Katherine's hope to ease the burden of single motherhood?

"Brrring....Brrring..." The telephone ringing startles me and answering it brought happiness for I recognize his voice. "Neil, have a safe flight?—Good, miss you already.—Uh-huh. Working on Mom's memoirs,—Yes, it does sound good, calling her Mom. I'm having some difficulty thinking of a name for her last project.—That's it.—Love you more. Bye."

On the kitchen's memo board, I print the words, NEW BEGINNING. The name tells it all. I feel fantastic and suddenly hungry. Soon, a thick ham sandwich fills my hands. Before I take a huge bite. I open the book to "Chapter 2 – The Way to a Man's Heart".

This chapter makes me wonder if that is all I hope to become—his wife. There is so much to do and so little time. I search the libraries for any information on building a non-for-profit organization from the ground up. Can one person can pull this together?

The telephone rings again as I reach the second-floor library. I'm thankful for the widespread phone system Cameron had installed throughout the manor. "Hello—Francine, are you clairvoyant?—Why? Well, I need help in organizing paperwork for Katherine's dream. —Where?—Okay, see you around three."

I leave a note on the refrigerator to cover my absence. "Clare, Attending meeting at Francine's office. Having dinner and spending the night at Decima's apartment. Neil called. He had a good flight and will call again later this week. Belle"

Before leaving, I search Katherine's desk. There is nothing about her project in any drawer. Wait her writing desk is on that shelf. Neil kidded me when he said, 'I deliver the traveling desktop to you.' While the inside is small, the limited space is filled with notes and ideas for giving a single, new mother and baby a safe home for an extended time. I hope this is what Francine is expecting.

In closing the lid, my sleeve gets snagged on the catch. With a slight tug, I free it. A side tray comes out. On it, is a lavender piece of paper. A quick glance reveals a child's handwriting. I push the tray back, drop the note into my purse, and leave.

The traffic is minimal, and the drive-in is under an hour. I knock on their door.

"Shalom, Belle. It's been a while since you visited. Fran said that you were doing something to resurrect Katherine's dream. I'm happy about that."

"I just learned of it a month before our wedding. How did you know?"

"I'm the guilty party," Fran says. "I told her. At our initial meeting Neil mentioned it, Then Katherine, told me when I became the estate's legal representation as I did pro bono work for the Guild's community activities. That led me into checking things out for her."

"Then you know about the non-profit for charities?"

Deci gets up and takes me by my arm. "Belle, enough business talk, I want you to see how I decorated our place."

Following a tour of the condo, we relax in the living room and Francine fills me in on everything Katherine and she did before she died.

"The world of non-profit organizations has its file. Most of the work was done before your wedding. Monies to fund the non-profit corporation came from private donations. Plus, a grant is available once tax exemption is received from the IRS. Katherine spearheaded activities toward getting it. At present, the documents are in limbo due to her death."

I rise and walk around the room and count the issues. They must be resolved if New Beginnings has a future. "How do we get out of limbo? Will everything fall apart if there is a time deadline? Where do I fit into the picture? How do we continue securing donors?"

"Potential for funding is a viable ingredient for a non-profit. Tax exempt status, I'm working on that problem because our hands are tied without it. Donations and even grant money for operational funds can't be touched until we get one. There is one problem we face as a group, a lack of leadership."

"And this means what to Neil and me?"

"Like I said, New Beginning is now a corporation.

Before your wedding, Katherine did a detailed budget using available outside funds. In layman's terms, she registered the Articles of Incorporation with the State of New York."

I'm suspicious. Neil knew the name. Waited for my reaction and played me for a time. Why? I ask her, "Did Neil know what was going on?"

CHAPTER 28
NEW BEGINNING

"Well, the Articles outline basic principles. On board after the ceremony, you and the Board signed IRS Form 1023, plus some others. Once submitted, it takes about three to four months. Mailed them the death certificate and that may delay it.

Yes, Neil already knew there is a registered name. In her notebook, the last few pages read like a mission statement."

I bite my lip and imagine furrow lines crease my forehead. I'm furious with Neil and lock my arms in front of me. "Francine, you are his confidant. I'm sure of that. Tell me, what else should I know?"

"Now that you're married, your name is listed in the Corporation. Remember the papers you signed on the yacht."

"Yes, you said some legal mumble jumble for an Australian wedding,"

"Arabelle, a part of my job is to tie up loose ends with the State. You and Neil will handle implementing her goals for the next four-to-five years."

"Well Fran, it may seem trivial, but I wonder how we raised enough to get 'New Beginnings' up and running.

Even if the Guild did some fundraising, where did the other money come from?"

"Okay, both of you will have to excuse me because I'm off to the bedroom to call and check the clinic's schedule with the night nurse." Decima gets up and stretches. "Later Arabelle."

She leaves and Francine explains to me the beautiful world of grants and benefactors.

"Ah, your concern about starting costs. Yes, it was expensive. You know he's out of state, and I'm not telling you this as an attorney, but as your friend. Legally, you should be aware his and Anson's investments and stock holdings were liquidated to cover start-up costs. He also established trusts for it from selling several of the estate's domestic businesses. Plus, Decima, secured several grants while small--but every penny counts. Also, Katherine found a few sponsors."

"So that's why Katherine never worried about Neil's coming and going."

"For sure, he traveled to pro-life agencies and Homes under the umbrella of public welfare programs. Right now that umbrella is receiving criticism."

"Why Fran? There is such a need." The serious look on Francine's face tells me how important the matter is.

"As a rule, people dislike giving money. Instead, our residents would work here to repay expenses. Katherine wanted a home where welfare funds would never be used. With all our gathered information, her work plan for the IRS functioned without requiring resources from the system."

"Neil never told me. I didn't know any of this. Is this why he told me to understand the business?"

"I apologize, Arabelle. Unknowing, you have been part of this since your wedding. Corporation is small, and the Board consists of you, Neil, Anson, Clare, and me. Eventually, a mother-to-be will be added as a needs and acquisitions manager."

"Neil travels too much. I worry so that even now, I have a headache."

"Arabelle, before you two became a number, Katherine worked on this project. Unincorporated, we took our time to set ground rules for soliciting money and cash flow. We wrote the responsibility role each of us would undertake. A one dollar per year salary was agreed upon and once incorporated her budget would prevail. Is there any question?"

Her explanations resolve many of my concerns. The wills must be found. "Before I ask, Francine I want to tell you something that should be sent to the others. I find the Board's secrecy despicable. Neil's involvement using me as a pawn is shameful. Look, I can carry my weight in this endeavor. My question is more of a request. Teach me Principles of Incorporation 101."

"No problem. Stay the night and come to my office tomorrow. I can lend you several books. Welcome aboard. Your first meeting is right around the corner."

We play a game of Monopoly, and I go bankrupt, losing the bet for the guest bed.

ཀཀཀ

After breakfast. Deci goes to the clinic. I follow Francine to the courthouse. Her office is on the third floor. After meeting her, we check the public records. Maybe, I'll find if the records disclose any additional clues to my parents' marital history.

I found nothing new. What was there, Fran already brought the information to me. The records indicate Neil and my name were added to the property deed. We walk to the elevator. Inside, she pushed her floor button and said, "The curious public have access to those records. Since Katherine added your names a month before she died, the codicil should remain. Unless someone contests, finding her will is not imperative. Continue looking for Adam's and relax on your way."

We reach her floor, and she gets off. I return to the manor, relieved and full of hope that New Beginning is more than a dream.

ജജജ

Since Neil's departure, I've conquered any business obstacle because of Anson's and Francine's grueling tutorage. I'm confident I would block any objection Neil could give. Free time for studying is spent on her autobiography or rummaging through every inch of Katherine's bedroom, library, and sitting room in search of anything from her past. At times, the search seems futile, but at long last, I've searched the entire west side. The east wing's bedrooms are done, and the upper floors are my next challenge after I spend a few hours typing her memoir.

I find working in the sitting room comforting. Sometimes I feel an unseen presence, no, it is more of reassurance that what I'm doing is not in vain. This morning my train of thought is broken by Clare's message coming over the intercom.

"Neil is arrivin' today, feel it in my bones. Be ready."

When the doorbell rings, I run to answer it. The mailman has a registered letter from the Mayo Clinic. I sign for it and call from the foyer, "Clare, it's a letter for me. Be on the terrace if Neil should arrive."

Patches of winter remain on the outer grounds. While the afternoon sun makes it bearable for me to rest there and read the letter. The contents smash an anvil's weight against my chest.

"He is here, Belle. He's here!" Clare yells through the kitchen window

I'm paralyzed from the Clinic's report. I can't seem to rise from my chair. I sit, trying to understand the letter's unsettling news and Neil's announced arrival. I fold the letter and press it into my pocket. When I turn toward the manor, I see he is not coming to me. Instead, he's on the telephone and Clare is squeezing his arm. Why is a phone call more important?

I go into the kitchen and overhear a part of his conversation.

"Yes, I was told a Courier delivered a letter.—You didn't?—Yes, goodbye." He replaces the phone on its receiver and greets Clare with a customary hug.

"She was on the terrace. Told her you were comin'. Just turn around."

Neil turns and sees me leaning against the wall. "Belle, my love. Where's my kiss?"

I don't break my stare and throw the letter at his face. He reaches for me, and I pound his chest with all my strength. "Neil, you are a gutless wonder. I have second thoughts why I ever agreed to marry you."

Caught off guard, he retreats a few feet. Unable to dodge my blows, he wraps my arms behind me.

"Let me go. You're the worst sort of human being, I ever loved." I can't look at him. My arms are at my side, and I begin crying. "I'm so sorry Neil. I didn't mean it. Yes, I did. How could you keep that from me?"

"Belle, what in heaven's name is the matter with you?"

"Neil, don't side-step this. We talk about our future life together. You, however, save yourself the anguish of telling me that you are dying."

"Oh my God!" Clare exclaims and leaves.

Neil releases his grip and takes me into his arms. I feel his hand gently rubbing my back.

"Darling, let me explain. Here, wipe your tears away. I'm home. I'm here for you. Lacey, I wanted to spare you as long as I could. For several years, I've searched for a cure or treatment that would give me, then us, additional time. Some words that would provide us hope. Please calm down."

I blow my nose using his handkerchief, then punch his shoulder. "In sparing me, did you ever consider how I missed our time together, particularly these past three months?" I trembled, and my hand hits the table. "What kind of a wife do you take me for?"

He reaches for my hand and kisses the palm. "I know what we need. A week away at No Name or maybe the mountains, lots of fresh air would do us wonders. What do you say?"

"Neil, don't change the subject. Remember 'in sickness and health,' I meant that vow. How could you be so cruel?"

"It wasn't intentional, Belle."

"It was! How long do I have before I place the notice in the Obits? You big lug, I love you and will share with you whatever life dishes out. Neil McCutchen, I don't understand. You have me at my wits end. Why couldn't you tell me?"

There is a wall between us. He lets go of me and turns away as he says, "Selfishness. Thought if you knew sooner, would you have married me, knowing in time I'll become impotent. I wanted what time remained to be free, ours without care. That's why I needed this last trip to take care of something. Please say you'll forgive me."

I push him away run outside, off the porch and toward the gardens. Blinded by my tears, I turn my ankle and fall into the bordering boxwood shrubs. I feel nothing as the bare branches and twigs tear at my skin. It's only his words which cut into my heart. 'I'll become impotent.' I'm a hypocrite. I forgot the vow, '. . . in sickness and health until death . . .'

I brush myself off and return to our bungalow. He's there on the recliner. Eyes closed and his head deep into a pillowed headrest. I owe him an apology. I kiss his eyes, then his lips. Neil opens one eye.

"Darling, I love you. I promise I won't ever hit you again unless you forget our anniversary."

"Of course, Mrs. McCutchen, now join me so I can kiss you properly." I jump into his arms and the recliner collapses. We both laugh.

"Okay my husband, while you relax, close your eyes."

Instead, he holds me close. "Belle, no one knows how long we have. When I kissed you, I knew you were the one. While I was gone, I checked with the doctor. He suggested a sperm bank. I took care of that before I left on the estate's business. I wanted us to have a child even with your problem. That is if you're willing to try in vitro."

I nod my head. His lips against mine have nerve

endings transmitting the message. A baby will happen one way or another.

During the following month, Neil and I enjoy a worldwide honeymoon. Free of responsibility we abandon the estate but not Katherine's dream. Anson remains to handle business matters; and under Francine's watch New Beginning goes forward. Clare agrees to put on another hat and becomes the lead in revamping the manor to accommodate the new residents. Our only concern is natural conception.

CHAPTER 29
PALLIATIVE CARE

Our month alone brought hope and surrender. During this time, Neil's stamina weakens as the disease manifests itself internally.

"Belle, I researched the chance of genetic transfer to our child. Don't want to take that chance. While there is only a small percentage of our baby or future grandchild suffering as I do, I won't debate the issue. Would you consider our adopting?"

"I would if I weren't already pregnant."

"What? When? How? I mean I know how but when did you find out?"

"Guilty of selfishness, something I learned from a wise man. Upon our return, I had your doctor check if the fetus showed any genetic trace. It doesn't. We're having a baby, darling. We're having a baby."

ꙮꙮꙮ

I'm nearing the end of my second trimester; and as the fetus thrives, I see how the disease robs him of his spirit. His appointment at Mayo Clinic is bittersweet. The short flight back takes its toll. I'm relieved to see Anson's friendly face at the airport.

"Good to have you back. What news from the clinic,

Neil?" Anson asks.

"Same as the last visit. On the positive side, the latest report indicates the baby shows no signs. The fetus is fine."

"Neil, Belle, that's great. After all this time, doesn't the clinic have any clue what causes this disease?"

"I asked the doctor the same thing. After his lengthy explanation, it boils down to this. Neil's immune system has its private war with itself. So let's head home because there's nothing like sleeping in your own bed."

Back at the manor, I raid its refrigerator and return to the bungalow with bowls of chili. While we ate, we reminisce. "Lacey, you knocked the wind out of me. I never had a chance."

"I think not McCutchen. Why even Anson knew, you'd be mine within a year. Did he even know how sick you were when you visited?"

"I didn't even know. Didn't have dry skin, which is an early sign of localized scleroderma. Only cold weather affected me. Fingertips would turn white, then blue. Needed to rest frequently, had heartburn and overall body aches, blamed all that on work and the laws of nature."

"That would explain why you're not here for the winter holidays." I give him a peck on the lips and clear the table.

"My, you're becoming quite the homemaker. Graduated from an unopened can of ravioli to feeding me with leftover chili and whatever surprise you have inside that bag."

"I raided spices from Clare's cabinet and flushed the remaining pills; you're not to take."

"Vitamins were a joke. I'm their guinea pig. Now they

want me taking that spice mixture you stole for me."

"You should have seen the look Clare had on her face when she caught me in her cupboard."

"I can picture it. Belle, before we left for our second honeymoon, the Doctor ordered a chest x-ray to see if any internal organs were affected."

"What? Another thing, you weren't willing to share. Neil, why didn't you confide in me?"

"If you'd let me continue. From its onset, I should have had six maybe seven years before I'd be at this stage. So without knowing how long before they might find a cure, I made a decision."

"Couldn't trust that I would stay around?"

"Quit kidding. I went to the sperm bank before we left on the whirlwind honeymoon. If what they said about impotence was true, I wanted us to have a child. Now, the little fellas will wait until we, well, need them."

"Okay, I'm happy you thought of the future. Am I up to speed on your medical reports?"

He nods his head. "Yes, except for the doctor's appointment coming up. Presently I'm weary. Care to join me because I'm going to bed."

"I agree. Lately, I've aches and pains unrelated to my pregnancy. So, I made an appointment on the same day as yours. Anson will drive you and Deci is coming with me."

"Coming?" Neil asks.

"Yes, coming." I take his hand, and we go to the bungalow.

ꙮꙮ

Because of the distance, Neil and Anson left for the Clinic yesterday. It's six a.m. and the phone rings. "Morning darling.—Love you too. See you tomorrow."

Clare's voice comes over the bungalow's intercom. "Belle, you're late for the appointment. Belle?"

I hear but can't seem to respond.

"Belle, it's me, Clare. You're in an ambulance. Doctor's going to meet us at the hospital. You'll be okay." She reassures me, and it is comforting when she strokes my head.

"Belle, stay with me. It's time. I have to do a C-section, need to avoid you having a seizure," Dr. Roche says.

"Nurse, IV with magnesium sulfate and prep for surgery. Belle, your BP is 190 over 130. Worse, the baby is showing signs of distress. The heart rate is low."

I nod. It's too soon, we need you, Neil. It's too soon. The overhead lights are like spotlights and close my eyes momentarily as they prep me for a Cesarean delivery. I turn my head to avoid the brightness and see eight units of blood are nearby.

"Who gets the blood? Me?"

"Arabelle, we always have some ready for a possible transfusion should internal bleeding occur. You're going to feel a light pressure on your face. Want you to count back from ten."

"Doctor, BP 150 over one . . ."

"Ten, nine, eight . . ."

Through a hazy consciousness comes the sound a human voice. In a half-awakened state, I ask, "The baby, girl or boy?"

"Doctor will see you soon." A distant female voice said.

I'm conscious now and lie on my left side. A nurse in green scrubs moves me to my back. "Mrs. McCutchen, I need to catheterize you. You'll feel a slight pressure.

Good, she's emptying. Take her upstairs."

In recovery, I wait. Once I'm in bed, and the drip is set, I relax and touch the flat of my belly and doze off. Limb shadows bounce against the wall when I awake. I try sitting up, but the movement is restricted by the intravenous tube.

"Take it easy, Arabelle."

A man's voice, I heard it before. Then, it comes to me. "Doctor Roche, the baby. How is the baby?"

"I'm sorry Belle, the infant died. I'm sorry for your loss. We did everything we could. I ordered a drip. It should help you sleep. You need the rest."

"Girl? Boy? Who died?"

"A boy, I am sorry I couldn't prevent it. The nurse will stop later to see if you want anything. I'll see you tomorrow."

He shuts the door. One song runs through me, and I begin to sing. "Hush little baby, don't you cry. Mama's going to love you until I die. Hush little baby. . ." Tears stream down my cheeks onto the pillow until the sedative lulls me to sleep.

ೞೞೞ

Although I'm discharged from the hospital, our baby remains in the morgue until I make funeral arrangements. I stay at the manor and find it peculiar that Neil or Anson do not call. Even Clare changes the subject when I ask her. Have I lost both a son and a husband? Depressed to make funeral arrangements alone and afraid of what happened to Neil, I wander out of the sitting room and see Francine in the foyer. "Francine, may we talk for a moment?"

She joins me. "Hi, Belle. We're sorry about the baby.

What's on your mind?"

"Thank you. I need your help in finding out what has happened to Neil. If he's dead, I'll bury our son beside him. If he's not, I want to comfort him. Please, help me."

"Will try Belle, give me a day. Got to go, Decima is waiting on me for a pickup."

She leaves and I phone the Minister to make the arrangements.

Francine calls that afternoon. Clare and I are in the solarium, so I press the speaker button. "Okay Fran, we're here."

"Hi, I've bad news. Neil's last lab results were serious enough to put him in I.C.U. at the hospital. Because his medical record doesn't show he got married, no word to you. The doctor sends his apology. Neil will be discharged with restrictions this afternoon. The doctor will do a house call on Friday. Belle, once he's home, I know you'll both feel better."

"Fran, he doesn't know about the baby. I failed him twice. I can't have his children."

"Knowing Neil, as I do, he will understand. Deci and I will try to stop over this weekend. So until then, goodbye."

"Bye Fran and thank you for everything."

Clare disappears before I have a chance to ask about Anson. I turn on the stereo system. The melancholy music of rhythm and blues matches my depression. I can only whisper an apology in the hope it'll reach his ears. Neil, how will I tell you? The phone rings. I ignore it.

Clare approaches with the portable phone. "It's Neil."

"I can't Clare. Tell him I'm sleeping."

"There is a season for all things, Arabelle." She places the phone in my hand and leaves.

"Hello, darling—Missed you too, McCutchen." I attempt to be cheerful until lightheadedness takes over and I slump in my chair.

There is a hand caressing mine, and I open my eyes.

"Hi beautiful, I love you, and I know about our son. When our line was disconnected, I was calling you on the way here. Anson told me about the preeclampsia. We couldn't know everything would go wrong during the pregnancy. He wasn't getting enough oxygen. Not anyone's fault. It happened. Mom told me that sometimes life throws you a twist."

"Throws a twist? I don't understand, Neil?"

"You might say a twist of fate. Guess we both were in line at the wrong time. It's going to be okay. I promise. It'll be okay."

I clung to him, relieved he understood.

"Promised, didn't I?" He holds me close. There in his arms, I relax and believe everything he tells me.

"I contacted the minister. Tomorrow our son will be buried here. Come with me; this is something we need to do together," I say and take his hand. We walk to the gathering room, where a tiny coffin rests on the sideboard.

"I named our son, Gregory."

"That is perfect, Lacey."

We stand for a time with our hands covering our son. Then leave and go to the bungalow.

ജജജ

The Reverend closes the service with a prayer. "Choirs of angels await your coming. May they take you, Gregory, to your cherished family in heaven? Today you are with God, who loved you long before your parents knew you existed. Amen."

Our son is buried in a small piece of land above and between his grandmothers' headstones. Five people return to the manor. While Neil and I remain, my mood turns sullen. I want to get even with the unfairness of life. I kick a clump of dirt as we stand beside his grave.

"Feel better or do you want to stay longer?"

"No to both. Was thinking Neil. It's becoming a family affair to rest here in peace."

"Lacey, ever wonder if our memories will bring you some good ones, joy rather than tears?"

"If I think our son is there with family, I can feel some joy. Don't understand why, darling, but I'm exhausted."

We stroll to the bungalow's porch to rest in the evening's quiet. That night Neil's breathing becomes labored. I use the intercom and have Anson get a wheelchair for our trek back to the manor.

Anson converted the sitting-room once more into a bedroom for Neil. We sit beside each other on the loveseat. His restlessness and labored breathing make me realize his health is rapidly deteriorating. I bring us a light meal, and we share it.

"Lacey, would you open the window. Some fresh air will do me good."

"Have to agree, McCutchen." With the turret windows open, a breeze stirs the air. within. Returning to the love seat, he reclines against me and takes a deep breath.

"Don't understand darling, why can't everyone get a second chance?" I say.

"Belle. All I know, it's what you choose to do with what life deals you makes the difference. It's always your choice."

“Then, can’t we fight it, Neil. Isn’t there a witch doctor that will help? We don't accept dying without a fight. Reject it with all your heart.”

"I'm passed that stage, Belle. Now you know what I have been doing since last summer at No Name. That is what drove me away time-and-again in search of hope, a cure, or even time out for good behavior. But, it was you that brought me back home. I couldn't help loving you, and yet loving you so much drove me away.”

My free hand touches his face, and I push back his hair and smile. Neil kisses my palm. His lips lack any warmth.

"I'm at peace with it, Belle. Doc's arriving tomorrow around six p.m. and he says palliative care is next step. He’ll be staying for the weekend. Please let Clare know.”

"You rest, and I'll tell her." I start to walk away.

“Wait a minute, Lacey. Ever tell you how I went head-over-heels in love with a wipe-out midget. But after she naughtily invited me to be her overnight guest, something put it into my head; she cared for me.”

I try to stop his story, but he puts his finger to my lips.

“Then my love, I became concerned about my health. I had this wild dream that she’d somehow become my wife. That's why I proposed the way I did. If you had said, ‘No.’, I couldn't bear it.”

I giggle into my hand and confess. "You should have waited. I danced all around the room. I was so flustered because wasn't sure if you did or didn't propose. Neil McCutchen, you put my heart into hyper-drive every time you came into viewing distance. I was always worrying you'd met someone else on those trips away. In light of everything, felt anxious you'd never come back. You should have waited for my 'Yes.' and given us both something wonderful to dream about."

Neil moves away and faces me. I lean forward for a kiss. Instead, he asks a favor.

"Belle, Anson is going to close No Name for the winter closing. Please, go with him."

"Now?"

"No, silly! This weekend would be perfect, and you'd have some time for yourself, even with Anson tagging along. When you return, you can tell me all about your adventure, and should I need you here, you'll be the first one I call."

"Neil, you are frightening me. Sending me away when I should be at your side."

He takes my hands and presses them to his lips.

"Sometimes, darling, getting a grip on life's problems means you know when to let go. You'll know when. I promise. Francine and I settled the business matters. You are not to worry. The house and business are in your name. I've seen to that. Anson continues as CEO with you, as President."

He hums and I see his fingers play along an invisible keyboard. "I love you McCutchen, but know this. You're not giving me a job while you travel. I will go with you as the Company President or as your wife. Because I love you, I'll go with Anson and bring back some fresh cider. Tonight, I pack an overnight bag. We leave tomorrow. Sooner I go, sooner I return to make you sorry you sent me away."

I lean over to kiss him. He returns it with a squeeze of my hand. Knowing I'm the one to leave; I hold back my tears.

CHAPTER 30
WIFE'S INTUITION

The three-day weekend in October at No Name puts color on my cheek and some energy to my step. It still bothers me how we disagreed on my taking this short trip. Neil's persistence won in the end with my concession to bring home fresh apple cider and a Northern spruce sapling for Clare's Christmas garden.

"Anson, I'm leaving today. Come with me; you can handle closing out the utilities over the phone on Monday. I have a cab waiting outside. The train leaves within the hour. Have a gut feeling; something is wrong, and Neil's not telling me. Anson, has he always put forth such effort concerning the estate's future?"

Anson sits down on the front step and motions me to join him. "You remind me a little of him. Neil sowed a few wild oats growing up. Too soon, Katherine put him in charge of running the family business while she managed the finances. To please her, he got a degree from Harvard. The hands-on education from his grandfather, I passed along. With his life experiences, he was successful in pulling it off. Hate to admit it, but, you soak things up easily. However, I understand your concern, Belle. I'll contact Clare to be there to pick you up. Give Neil my regards. I'll be home soon."

I arrive at our station and am surprised to find a local cabby waiting for me. Why does he hold a sign with my name on it? "Excuse me?"

"Yes, ma'am. A lady paid in advance, Mrs. McCutchen. I'm to bring you home right away."

The front door is unlocked. Something has happened during my absence. The knot in my stomach tightens when Decima comes across the foyer.

"Arabelle, he's failing. The doctor gave him a sedative to ease the pain."

"Deci, he can't die alone. I need to be there with him. The truth, Deci."

She takes hold of my shoulders. "I'm sorry Belle. It's just a matter of time. Go to him."

I rush through the doorway and stop. Neil remains in bed, connected to a heart monitor. It registers forty. I want him free of suffering but know that mine will begin without him. When I take him into my arms, I think of Michelangelo's 'Pieta.' I take his hand into mine and kiss it. His stillness accepts the inevitable. I kiss his lips, and he stirs.

"Honestly McCutchen, you'd think I'd be battle-scarred from our history of your leaving me. Wait for me, darling. On your journey, give our boy a big hug and kiss from his mommy. Neil, I promise you, Mom's dream will become a reality. Yes, I'm cuddling you. I'll miss you and that wink you'd give me. I'm okay with you're leaving. We winterized No Name and Anson going to plant the spruce near the cemetery. It's okay to let me go, darling. I want your pain to end. Love you more."

Not a syllable comes from his lips, yet I know my touch, and words transmit to his brain as the monitor spikes to sixty. I lie beside him and whisper, "You have a new beginning darling. Can't say goodbye, it's too final. It's a good night McCutchen. Know that you'll always be my love."

With my head on his chest, I face the machine. I watch as his heart rate drops. From his last silent words, I kiss his forehead, his eyes, and finally his lips. Tears have pooled in the corners of his tightly shut eyes; I wipe them away. He knows I heard him, as I do not cry until the monitor displays a flat line.

Clare helps me up from the bed. "Doctor gave him some drug. Said he wouldn't suffer in the end. Guess Neil, needed you home before he died. When's Anson comin'?"

" He'll be back tomorrow. Utilities, he had to wait until Monday. Clare, did Anson know how soon it would happen?"

"Neil, like he sensed it, asked us not to say anythin' to you. What made you come back?"

"A wife's intuition." I look away from the cooling body and see Decima holding an envelope, which she hands me.

"Neil wrote it long before you left and asked me to give it to you. By the way, the Doctor is here to see him. He'll sign the death certificate."

I need him by me and climb back onto the bed. After I put my arm under his head, I open the letter and read. His shaky handwriting gave evidence to his declining weakness.

'Lacey, you were mine for a brief moment. Farewell does not mean goodbye, nor does it mean forever gone. My farewell darling says until we meet once more. Promise me to live and love again. For all I want, is your happiness. Honestly, my love for you is eternal. McCutchen.'

The sun's rays came through the window, and I watch dust flecks in its beam until a cloud covers the sky. Like us darling, they did one last dance. I feel an arm beneath me, removing me from your side. Your doctor helps me rise from the bed.

"Arabelle, I gave Decima the death certificate. I've asked her to contact Lave. She's familiar with the procedure and information they need. I'll leave you a prescription for Valium."

I extend my hand. "No, I'm fine Doctor Williams. Appreciate your concern, just need some time. Neil and I, we were prepared. Although, we hoped for a little more time. Thank you so much for making him comfortable in the end."

Like a robot, I shake his and look beyond the faces in front of me. Their pained expressions touch my heart. "Clare, would you get the Doctor's overcoat?"

She nods and returns with it. He drapes it over his arm, and I walk him to the front door. He begins to leave when Clare and Decima hover behind me.

"She'll be fine ladies. Decima, I'll call in a script for her. I'd suggest someone be with her tonight."

"No problem," Clare said, "I'll stay with her tonight. I called Anson, and he'll be here before midnight."

The evening is cool but is comfortable enough for me to remain on the porch until the hearse arrives. Within the hour, the funeral home removes his body. Deci is on the phone with Fran. Clare goes about the manor, cleaning what doesn't need to be cleaned. I know it's my time to go home. On the bungalow's front porch, I sit outside and wonder which star I'll choose to be his. Except for the back porch, the manor's lights are off. The darkness behind its eyes holds a melancholic fascination that matches the emptiness I feel. Once inside our home, I locate his robe to take in the remembrance of his cologne, of him. Tonight our bed is off limits to me, and I stretch between the bolster couch pillows, clutching one the closest to me. The room is so silent, I hear the click of the door knob.

"Belle, are you awake?" Clare whispers. I pretend to sleep.

"She's okay, Clare. Cover her and let her rest." Anson says faintly.

"Anson, adjust the heat. Come morning; I'll call Decima to stay with her. She shouldn't be alone."

I peek through my eyelashes. Clare shakes her head when the afghan covers me. She goes by the doorway while Anson shuts off the light. They leave me as I wanted to be—alone.

ഇഇഇ

"Decima thank you for coming over. Knew I had to call you when I saw how Belle was doing yesterday. Went in the morning and found her sitting on the rocker outside the bungalow. Brought her breakfast, she shook her head. Just rocked, silent in her thoughts. From the kitchen window, I saw she stayed that way throughout the afternoon. Tried again to convince her to come to the manor for a cup of tea, she said 'No thank you.' She went inside and turned on the lights. Nothin' unusual about that, but at midnight, lights were still on. We go over before retiring and find her asleep. She's in a fetal position and has his robe beneath her. Not right, so that's why I called you to come over today."

"She'll be okay, Clare. Belle got dumped on big time. If you get me a phone, I'll call the Doctor and see what he wants to do. Mind if I stay until after the funeral."

"Not in the least. You stay as long as you'd like."

I can't say how Deci convinced me to dress, eat lunch, and go to Lave's Funeral Home. Only that she did as we walked together, up the few steps, through the door and into his viewing room. From across the floor, the ravages of Neil's diseased body are evident. I'm in control and know what I must do. Family funerals taught me that.

"Mr. Lave, Neil's viewing and service will be with a closed casket. I realize he had a wide range of friends and associates. However, I want a one-day viewing. Continuous hours from noon until nine o'clock. The burial is family only at the estate the very next day around ten."

I remain calm and show no emotion in selecting the casket. Sign over the insurance and other necessary paperwork. Then Deci and I join Fran at their apartment. I remain there until the funeral.

ꙮꙮꙮ

The one-day viewing has a steady flow of visitors. At 9:15 p.m., I'm ready to leave and run my hand over the coffin lid. With the subdued lighting, my wedding ring reflects on the smooth, lacquered cover. Seeing its mirror image, all my anger, kept hidden, erupts. I pound my fists onto the lid as my tears spatter the glossy, ebony finish.

"I know I said it was okay for you to leave, but I hate it being so soon. Not fair, Neil, to lose everyone you love, especially you, my knight. We were robbed, Neil. He stole our time together."

Anson pulls me away. With his arms around me, I bury my head in his chest. "It wasn't supposed to be, not the way we hoped."

"I know Miss Belle. Before we left for No Name, his tears indicated he felt the same. I hope Isaiah 38:5 will bring you comfort as it did Neil. Because he gave me a smile when I said, thus says the Lord. . .I have heard your prayer and seen your tears. I will heal you."

He holds me until the trembling stops. Then wipes my tears with a tissue. I take a deep breath and exhale before my final goodbye.

It is a quiet ride back to the manor. There is nothing more to say. Except on our arrival, I notice Clare wears a new outfit and Anson goes to his apartment.

"Clare, God has a lot of healing to do within me. I don't want to sleep in the bungalow tonight. If neither of you don't mind, I'd like to sleep in my old room."

"Belle, you do just that. Promise we won't disturb you when we return. Here's your pill. Think you left a nightgown in the sittin' room. Anson darlin', it's your turn to pick the restaurant. Good night Belle."

"I'm glad to hear you're going out. Have a good time. I'll take Doc's medicine and lock up after you leave. Dinner and a movie, terrific, have fun."

With the sound of the BMW leaving, I know what must be done. Tonight, I drop the Valium into the garbage disposal. Since we left the funeral home, I know Neil's spirit is no longer there. I sense his presence nearby. He's hiding like Emily did. I walk from room-to-room and call out "Marco." Strange how the house seems to echo my voice. I know he's somewhere near. "Marco," I say and return to the empty kitchen. A cold draft comes through the open door. I shiver. Neil, you forgot to close it. You went to the bungalow.

I grab a jacket off the hook and go onto the porch. In the distance yellow and orange lights dance in the air to background music of bells clanging and the shrieking wail of police sirens. I race toward the light, but it and the night air becomes hazy with smoke from burning leaves. The acrid smoke makes breathing difficult and my eyes water from the holocaust in the distance. The flames are beautiful and so close that I realize the bungalow is burning. I run toward the flames and shout, “Neil, wake up. Get out of there. I’m coming.” I near the porch. The heat is unbearable as glass windows break and gas from the burning wood gags me. Sparks ignite the dry grasses beneath my feet. He is in there beyond the porch. I cry out, “Neil; I can't reach you. The fire, you’re dead.”

CHAPTER 31
LEATHER JOURNAL

After two days and recovering more from smoke inhalation and the first degree burns I received, I'm discharged from the hospital. Wheeled out to the car, Anson and Clare greet me with repeated tales of the night it happened.

"Like it was the ending of a horror movie, the embers and charred ruins still were glowing when we returned. The fire department remained and kept the fire from spreading. A police officer said they found a lady wandering around. She looked dazed and was confused as to what happened. A fireman said that the woman had trouble breathing and burns on her feet. She remembered walking, but her eyes hurt and couldn't recall anything more. They figured she fainted near the blaze and came to in that dazed state. An ambulance took her to the hospital for treatment. Once again, on the trip back, Clare repeats her story. Some of what she says remain with me as the pain medication lull my senses.

"Arabelle, it was you in the ambulance. They reported you were mumblin' about Neil's illness but couldn't help him get out. I was so scared that night. Thought you were going to leave us." Clare reaches over the front seat and taps my arm.

"Miss Belle, we were so grateful you decided to stay at the manor. Well, when the fire inspector came by, he told us he discovered a trail of smaller burns that went back to a neighbor's bonfire. When the dry grass caught fire, it spread along the porches' undergrowth. You were so lucky."

"Yes, I was fortunate to get only first degree on my arms and feet. Anson, how much further is it?"

"Few more miles, we've readied the sitting room for you."

Clare begins retelling her story. I close my eyes until the Beamer stops at the rear of the manor. After climbing on the back porch, I see that a blackened patch of earth is all that remains. Rubble was removed, and the ground turned under. An acrid smell floats across the gardens and onto the terrace. Yes, I was lucky, except for the melancholy setback.

ഋഋഋ

For the next week Anson, Decima, or Francine drive me to sessions to deal with the experience I have in waiting for his return home. It helps when I see how life in the household undergoes a change with Anson and Clare being nice to each other.

"There's nothin'," said Clare, "that I could do to bring you back Arabelle. You kept to yourself. We lost the Arabelle we love. Welcome back. Now that Anson and I are together, my life couldn't be any sweeter. You sure you're okay to help decorate this year? Anson put everythin' in the storage closet. We weren't sure you'd want anythin' up for the season."

"Clare, you are right. It'll be hard this year and maybe

next. But Neil would want me to go on even if it begins with one decoration at a time. Let me change clothes and I can help dig into the closet's log jam of boxes and cartons."

A short while later, I'm standing on the step stool. I stretch to remove a shoe box from the shelf above my head. "Got it," I shout until it slips out of my grasp and I'm showered with an assortment of mini-decorations, vacation pictures, and a leather journal.

I sit on the rug to repack the box. When I pick up the journal, a name is embossed on the cover, C. Collins. I flip through it and find fragmented thoughts about the children. Question marks surround Adam's death or his suicide and several miscellaneous scribbles for women needing respite. There's only one person who'll fill in the blanks with gentle frankness.

"Clare!" I yell. Stepping over the floor's assortment, I hurry along to the pantry. Its shopping day, and Schwann's delivery brought boxes of goodies.

"Clare, let me help with the groceries. Then we need to talk."

She looks puzzled but, in record time, we finish. I pull two chairs together and open the journal in front of her.

"Look here. This C. Collins wrote, 'to live together in the community to help each other. To offer emotional and social support within a family environment. To include God as she understands him in taking responsibility for the life she carries.' Was this how Katherine hoped New Beginning would function?"

"Yes, she did. There was one bottleneck for her. She needed to find the loophole to allow a group home within estate grounds. Especially, since she didn't know who else might be mentioned in the will."

"But we found out earlier that the public records had Katherine's name on the deed."

"Yes, you're right. Where did you find this?"

"Storage closet. Mixed inside a box on the top shelf. This person mentions a key that unlocks a treasure. Had question marks for Adam McCutchen death whether suicide or murder. This is not Katherine's, but whose writing? Yours? What's the scoop, Clare?"

I caught Clare off guard. Her face becomes white, as the walls behind her. She avoids my inquiring eyes and gets up to make some tea. After she paces the room doing this and that, she changes the subject.

"Belle, don't need to worry about 'New Beginnin'. Miss Francine figured a way for it to be here inside the manor and certain areas of the grounds. Everythin' came to a standstill with all that has happened since past January. Some of the renovations are already done. Transformin' this place like Miss Katherine wanted is doable if you involve your friend, Mr. Boyd."

"Clare, I can't focus on what to wear tomorrow. You knew Katherine's vision. Your ideas are marvelous, and, I know you can delegate from personal experience."

"Okay, allow me a few days, I'll get the ball rollin'. Will need someone pregnant, it might help in knowin' what's important to her and her baby."

"I'll call Deci. She might know someone at the Clinic. Anything else, boss?"

"Yes, Anson saw two. Neil added your name to the property deed. Without Adam's will, not knowing other rightful ownership, this could hamper further reconstruction. Second, without the tax exemption status, there's no home. When Anson's right, he's right. Love that man."

She walks out the back door, and I have to agree with her about Anson. Wait a minute 'love that man'. When did her attitude change and why? I look outside, but she was out of my sight. I can't wait until I find out the answer. I put on her work coat and retrace Clare's foot tracks through the snow to Anson's apartment. There's music in the air when I knock on his door.

Anson shows his surprise when he opens it. "Well Miss Belle, so glad you're back. Come in. Come in. Clare, we have a visitor."

I follow Anson into his living room. "Didn't know if you noticed how everything wasn't real to me. It seemed like I couldn't get awake. But I'm better now. So what's going on with the two of you, eh?"

"Arabelle, Anson and I were worried. Thought we lost you too. With the two of us wanderin' around this place, well it was spooky. There's something we wanted to tell you when you got better."

"Please go on. It's been a while since I could think clearly about anything."

Clare holds onto Anson and cries out, "We eloped! We're married. It was at your weddin' that he was hypnotizin' me into lovin' him with his steady gaze or his hold on me when we danced."

"Wasn't no dance hold. Arabelle, it was all her fault. Miss Belle, I looked at her and didn't know if my queasiness came from her nearness or the pitch and roll of the ship. Or, how my pulse races whenever I smell her cologne. Wedding was over, Katherine's death and getting us to the U.S., well, I dismissed any love thoughts. Until, you became ill. Then, I saw Clare was my anchor. She gave us solid footing to get through all this."

"We were lookin' to help you, you know . . . for somethin' of Neil's. So durin' the day we searched these empty rooms, and . . ."

Anson surprises me when he interrupts her. "Clare let me finish. Miss Belle, once she took my hand, I felt a sense of inner strength, unlike mine. Her smile wound me as tight as a clock spring. You know I'm a controlling person. So, I had to know. I proposed and she said . . ."

I clap my hands in joy and smile at the couple holding hands but shocked when Clare interrupts Anson.

"Darlin', let me tell Belle. At first in a jokin' way, I said to him, 'Go on?' Honestly by the look, he gave me, I knew he was serious. So I hurried and said, 'Just kiddin'. Course I will.'"

"Why'd you say 'no' the last time?" I ask.

"I thought he felt guilty because we did it and that he didn't mean sayin' he loves me. Belle, guilt won't take the place of lovin' someone. Anson, workin' so close all these years I pushed down a lot of desires. I couldn't believe you were askin' me again."

"Clare, I felt the same way. However, I was glad to hear you were joking."

"So lovebirds, whatever happened in the past is over forever?"

"Yes." They said in unison and without any embarrassment, they kiss in front of me.

"Congratulations! I love you guys."

A group hug follows. When Anson leaves to wax the cars, Clare starts to follow, and I stop her.

"Clare, you got the best of me earlier. Side-tracking

me the way you did but you never answered my questions."

"Don't recall any other question Belle. I should help Anson."

"Oh no! Why would you write and wonder about whether Adam McCutchen was murdered? Is it important that it should be included in her memoirs?" I show her the notebook.

Clare takes it from me and pulls me down on the couch beside her. "It's mine. You diggin' up the past, can't say what's true or not. It started after Emily died. Adam's depression was worse than yours. Cameron ordered a night nurse for Adam so he wouldn't somehow kill himself. If it were anythin' other than natural causes, his insurance policies wouldn't be worth a plug nickel."

"So, how did Adam die?"

The night he died, his nurse and private secretary were with him. Personally thought his secretary, squirrelly in appearance with buck teeth and bushy hair, had a motive, dotin' on his every word. I wondered if she had designs on his money."

"Clare?"

"Well, as I recall, the mornin' nurse called the doctor around eleven because she smelled ammonia. I was curious why his secretary didn't come with her. I went into his room to see what's what. There were two dead bodies. The room smelled more like cherry blossoms, not ammonia. I called the police."

"The police!"

"Yes, police and fire department ambulance came. When Doctor arrived, he wrote, 'Stopped breathin', died of natural causes.' And signed their time of death between ten and eleven o'clock. Police and some detective came with the coroner. Katherine asked questions. Detective took Katherine aside and asked her lots of questions. Both the doctor and coroner agreed an autopsy would confirm the cause of death. Before they bagged the bodies, the coroner sniffed their mouths. Heard him mention cyanide to the detective. A few days later, Katherine told us Adam died of natural causes."

"I imagine Katherine was relieved to hear that. But what about the secretary?"

"She said that the medical examiner's report found traces of arsenic under her fingernails. You understand we tossed it around that maybe the secretary tried killin' him and somehow inhaled the powder. Did you know inhalin' the dust can block your breathin' until you choke?"

"Why murder him? Clare, what aren't you telling me? Wouldn't it be better to know if the secretary killed him and herself?

"Went to the hearin' with Katherine and they brought the secretary's diary out. In it, she wrote 'His depression increases. Do I assist in his suicide, losin' him mercifully?'

I tell Katherine that I guess she didn't want his sufferin' to go on. Lord knows, he asked me to end it almost every day after little Emily's funeral. While the secretary's diary raises doubt, it wasn't conclusive that she attempted to murder him with his doctor's report indicating he died from natural causes. Katherine decided without findin' the will to let the report be the reason. She thought if she pursued a murder conviction on the deceased secretary, it may have caused irreparable damage to the codicil and the business. So, she let a dead dog die. If you wouldn't mind, I'd like to take Anson some coffee."

"Clare thanks for the facts, Don't think your notes add anything to Katherine's memoir. It's back to the manor for me." I leave the notebook behind. With all this information to think about, I stroll through the house and look out onto the terrace at them enjoying the unusually warm weather.

I take the short cut off the gathering room and say, "Hi there, may I join you for a minute?"

Anson slides over another chair for me. Instead, I stand on the walkway for a moment before sitting.

"Not too many more of these days before the holidays. Clare, in your notes you mention a mysterious key. So you two tell me, with all the days, no months I spent searching for a hiding place what clues have either of you found to reference this key? What other clues need to be uncovered?"

Anson motions me to sit with them. "When I was younger, I remember seeing Adam dropping wax onto a paper and then putting his ring into it. Asked him what that was and he answered that it was his signature on relevant documents. Never saw him wear that ring again."

"Where were you when you saw it the first time?" I ask.

"Main dining room, after his meal, that's where he read his mail. Why?"

"Don't know, but could be a clue. I have an errand today. Think about what I said, any memory of his ring or a key he used. Are we in agreement to find the will or his ring or the mysterious key?"

I stretch out my arm so Anson and Clare can complete the pledge by adding theirs to mine.

“Enough of this,” said Clare, “I have a floor to clean.”

“Ladies, ladies so much work to do in the greenhouse. I’ll see you both later.”

While they exit in different directions, when I return to the manor, I notice a pair of snow prints that lead around and back to the carriage house. I laugh and think of a wedding gift, I'll buy them a bedroom set. Wait, Katherine once remarked ‘spent most of his time, in bed,’ A clue? Did anyone look there? I hurry back inside to check. Disappointed again.

With the arrival of a Chinese lunch delivery, I go over to their apartment. Clare excitedly hands me a book that she found earlier while cleaning Katherine’s floor.

"After her funeral only did a light dustin’ once a week. Today, I moved her night table and found this. Thought it might be a diary, but, it’s not. Here, maybe it’ll give a clue.”

“Thank you, I’ll read it later tonight. Now . . .”

“Miss Belle, don’t mean to deflate your enthusiasm with Chinese food; but, I forgot to tell you. We got a celebration dinner to get ready for tonight. Guests are coming.”

“Guests? Do I know them?”

“What Anson means to say is that Decima and Francine, they were our witnesses, are comin’. They are such a cute couple. Got this feelin’ she and that attorney got somethin' goin' on between them. Tonight is our month anniversary. That’s why I want a rib roast. Dinner at six thirty, don’t forget.”

“Sure Clare. Go shopping. I’ll freeze what I can.”

Not wanting a sandwich, I fill my plate with orange chicken, rice, and vegetables. At the table, I open Katherine's notebook. Drawings and cryptic entries fill the lined pages. Repeated words, cherry blossoms, ammonia, and arsenic are underlined. A folded copy of the medical examiner's copy of Adam's death certificate had dirty socks written on it. By the time they return, I'm ready with questions and show the certificate to them. "Dirty socks? What do you make of it?"

"Don't know, Miss Belle. There was tension in this place with Adam dying and Cameron insisting on an autopsy. Neil was quite upset, and Katherine fought Cameron on having it done. And well, you know why. She exploded and told Cameron that Adam's depression and lifestyle lead to his death. What were her exact words? Yes, 'Adam would never stop to die. I'm so delighted death stopped for him.' Those were cruel words for her. I swore an oath to never tell anyone what she said. Until today."

"I thought maybe there'd be something hidden in his bedroom? I looked and didn't find anything unusual."

"First room I did after he died. Never thought to look for somethin' that might be a clue."

"His death makes sense as to why she left so many empty pages after he died."

"Don't understand Arabelle. How's his dyin', makin' sense?"

"Clare don't you see, Katherine stopped writing in her journal because that man took everything he wanted, including the life of her daughter. In her mind, Adam's death was evidence that justice was served."

Clare looks befuddled, and I clasp my arms around her. “I can hardly wait until tonight’s dinner.” I try to give Clare a big hug, and she pulls away. Now, I’m confused.

“Sorry Arabelle, we must be goin’. Our appointment is for three o’clock.” Anson waves and follows behind his bride.

CHAPTER 32
KEY OUT OF KEY

They leave and I go to the first-floor library. The settee is most comfortable for reading. I notice a pattern of four pages between drawings and eight between her notes.

On the inside hard cover, she drew a simple floor plan drawing of the two floors above. The foyer's broad staircase leads into the upper corridor. The blueprint indicates a slant downward to the flooring. That coincides with the narrowing hallway for Cameron's photo lab and to the upward spiraling staircase.

Four empty pages then she wrote, third-floor staircases. One shrinks in size up to the black ceiling; a light escapes through the floor board. I attempt to touch the ceiling. Can't go beyond the third step, feel suffocated. One is a spiral and leads to dead end. One goes downward to nothing. I turn over another eight empty pages until Katherine continues with tag lines not expanded, written alone on its page. Are these the prompts I need to follow?—'no will in his library – family portrait hangs – uncomfortable in seeing his children – writing desk, something shakes, can't open – keep looking.'

In the next section are drawings. The woman fills the

entire sheet, and I feel as if I've seen her before. On the next page is a writing desk. Arrows indicate several pressure points where secret compartment might be found.

I fan the remaining pages, and a lavender piece of ripped letterhead is tucked between two pages. Here is another riddle. 'Hidden treasures are yours to keep. Don't know where to look – not behind a picture or book. Found in space, so hidden from eyes, for me to know and you to find.'

I don't recognize the handwriting; maybe they'll know who wrote it. What treasures beside his will are hidden?

I do a quick rummage through Clare's catch-all drawer. Finding a flashlight, I go to the second floor and am prepared to walk through the dark narrowing corridor just past Cameron's photo lab to the steep stairway. I number each metal riser until I reach the fourth. I wonder why Katherine became anxious.

Nothing unusual happens. I hold tight onto the railing as the next few stairs are closer together and become narrower. The exaggerated spiral elevation reminds me of a coiled snake. I wipe my sweating palms against my side as if impending doom lies in the distance between my head and the blackness above.

I take another step and disappear into the black void that is not a ceiling but a concealed floor. It is an eerie feeling to climb onto a floor and have splashes of colored images create a mosaic over my arms. I pan left and right with the flashlight, then focus on the dormer's stained glass window. Incoming light creates a work of art to color my entry.

There's a door across from me. It faces the stairwell. A

splay of light to my left displays objects on shelves recessed into the inner walls.

Minutes ago, filled with apprehension my hands sweated. Now above the stairs, my fear is gone, and the air around me is fresh and comfortable as the library below. Cameron extended climate control to the third floor. A strange gesture that is most welcome.

I use the flashlight to view Japanese vases, figurines, cranes, and horses. Soon my eyes adjust to the natural lighting, and I turn the knob to the nearest door.

A storage room contains flat and domed travel trunks from the past. A massive portrait of St. Michael and a fire-breathing dragon rise above a steamer trunk reinforced with hardwood slats, metal hardware and baggage stickers from Genoa and Florence. While one flat trunk, upholstered with studded hide and leather, is stamped 'fragile' and leans against the wall. How'd anyone get all these up here—secret dumb waiter?

I close the door and take advantage of the catbird view of the estate's grounds. Even through muted colors, there is a panoramic palette of snow covered fields dotted with skeleton trees that extend where land ends and a glass surface begins.

"Wow! Katherine should have continued." I shrug my shoulders and hope I've better luck in the other room. I turn a brass doorknob and find the light switch. The room is so arranged that I can view its entirety from the door. It is totally a male sanctuary of stamped and gilded leather with trophy mounted animal heads. I'm amazed. Several wall shelves support a neat array of books braced together by brass bookends. Near a leather chair is a telescope aimed toward a skylight window. In a corner away from the sun's rays is a magnificent grandfather clock. Upon closer inspection, the tic toc, metronome sound, is absent. The room is locked in time.

I find the key to wind the springs and see the hands are immoveable when a lavender note is tucked under the minute hand. I remove it and read another riddle. 'While not here, don't despair—papers will be found elsewhere. Will the finder become the keeper?' I wind the mechanism; and with sound around me, I continue my search.

Near it is a colorful floral portrait of a fairy queen. Artfully pressed between a mirror and clean pane of glass, layered petals of pink and white honeysuckle characterize the blushing of her fair skin. I come closer and remove a stained card from its corner. Although faded by age the letters spell 'FIRST PLACEWINNER – GARDEN ART, Wood Nymph by Miriam Greene'

I move it, and tiny particles drift down. Respectfully, I leave the portrait as is. The vintage frame complements the nymph's features. The delicate hands and long fingers are turned under and lay against a forest green gown. Her heart-shaped face is tilted into the light and highlights a loose chignon. Miriam captured the merriment in her warm brown eyes as whimsical auburn tendrils expose the nape of her neck. I see why Adam desired Katherine. She's a mirror-image of Miriam's portrait.

Atop a drum table is an ebony writing desk. When I grip it to lift it off the table, I hear the movement of something sliding. I remove the drawer. It's empty.

Wait a minute. Katherine's drawing had pressure points. With trembling fingers, I trace along its edge to uncover a switch or lever. Nothing happens. I raise the box using the loose brass side grips. It slips briefly and releases a bottom panel. A passport and folded parchment fall to the floor.

Good grief, is this another riddle sealed with a waxed stamp? It is not a clue. It has his seal on it. Carefully I open it and read. 'Miriam, my love, I have only hoped you'll read this after I die. Loving you was its reward. Although my punishment because I could not sire a child between us. It grows hard for me to continue in knowing your needs rocket through my bloodstream, but nothing grows from us. Your devoted husband, Adam.'

I sigh and wipe away a tear. I replace the panel then tuck the letter inside the passport and into my pocket. Disappointed there was no clue, I return the writing desk to the table when an object hits against something. I'd need x-ray eyes to find it. That's it. Call Dr. Roche. Taking the box, I return to the sitting room and recall Adam loved Miriam.

ꕥꕥꕥ

The next morning, I reveal my findings to Anson and Clare. "Listen. It's not empty; something is inside. With Dr. Roche's intervention, I'm able to x-ray the writing box."

At the hospital, accompanied by the doctor, the technician does her job and prints out the x-ray pictures. The exposures reveal a hidden latch and pressure points to expose a hidden compartment with an envelope containing a key.

"Dr. Roche, not sure what we'll find, but it's another piece closer to finding Adam's will. Thank you. How can I ever repay you?"

"If it helps uncover the truth, that's all the payment I

need. However, I'm sure the hospital will send a bill. Good luck, Mrs. McCutchen."

Before our trip, we agreed discovery time should be at the Estate. Anson carries everything to the car, and we return to the manor. The three of us gather in the dining room. I push the writing desk over to Anson. "I can't do it, Anson. You knew him. Don't think he'd mind if you discover the contents."

With the negative prints, Anson releases the final latch. He unfolds the creased sheets onto the table top. "Looks like blueprints to me."

"Humph! A bunch of more lines, you got excited over nothin'."

"Darling, not lines but the original house plans. Look here, see where a substitution was made from walls to mirrored walls that moved like French doors to the terrace."

My encounter with Cameron had a beginning with that design. "Anson, those mirrors were covered with paneling. That's how Cameron went in and out of Katherine's library. Just look at this. Each drawing has a series of different spaces—all running into each other. Here are detailed views of open passageways and stairways from the vestibule up into the gallery."

"Hey, I found my half bath, there's a trap door. It leads to the basement. Here's a print dated January 9th, 1951. It's a shrinkin' triangle with a mini corkscrew on it."

I take it from Clare. "That triangle is the second-floor gallery. Adam closed off the hall's width and made a small hide-a-way room. That corkscrew is the spiral stairs to the third floor."

"Hide-a-way?"

"Remember Clare, Cameron's birthday. Adam told him he could have whatever he wanted. Remember?"

"Yes, a secret room, just big enough for him. Often wondered where Cameron hid, when he had homework. Adam, the skinflint, had no sense where to spend his money."

"Yes, with a steel grip as I recall. Although these other prints are dated after his death."

Excited I knew something, I interrupt, "Cameron . . . he updated plumbing, electric, heating and air to this all-seeing manor."

"Clare, here's the kitchen prints. No changes but, I'll compare it later to the updated one."

"It'll give you more room on the table if I move that box." When Clare leans forward, her thin gold chain falls behind the back panel. "Anson, Belle, I'm caught."

Anson uses the x-ray print and removes the top and a support panel. This uncovers a knob.

"Let me pull it. It's my chain." After freeing her chain, Clare yanks the knob, and it doesn't open. The warped wood won't budge. Anson uses his knife to loosen one side, and soon the drawer opens. Inside is lavender paper wrapped around a key.

"Belle, any riddle? Clare, what's this key?"

I'm glad I have the easier question and say, "The handwriting is sloppy, but it says, 'Prints and wood will lead you to it. This key unlocks the treasures. Not even C. J. would find in his leisure.' Wait a minute, teeny writing in the border. I go to the window for more light, and my hand shakes while I read. 'Key out of key profits beyond measure. No one ever will enjoy my treasure.' That makes no sense."

Clare interrupts, "Anson, this is a makeshift key. With all the keys I owned, never saw one made out of ebony. Adam, you devil, you're not hidin' a blamed thing. Only a bunch of clues that are givin' me a headache. Like Arabelle said, 'No one ever will enjoy my treasure.' No sense in his clues, no sense at all."

Anson takes it from Clare's hand. "Resembles a skeleton key but there's writing on it. Listen, "key-out-of-key'. Strange he'd repeat the saying, eh?"

"Although I enjoyed the adventure, I need to set tonight's table. Our company will be here soon. Arabelle, would you help to bring in flowers and candles to the main dining room. Anson, with the roast, please select Ridge Red's Bordeaux for tonight's celebration."

Anson carries the prints to the carriage house for further review. They leave me with a key and another piece of paper. I've all the pieces except the one I found on Katherine's desk. I hope they haven't left. The call arrives in time and Francine will bring the notebook. Walking from the sitting room, I turn the key between my fingers. The last message makes no sense, and I go to set the table.

The so-called month anniversary becomes a postponed wedding celebration complete with a tiered wedding cake and bridal bouquet for throwing. We linger at the table long after the flowers are caught by Francine and reminisce about the past few months and unsolved riddles. Afterward, everyone takes a turn handling the ebony key and guesses what the clues might mean. Until Clare takes hold of it.

"No, use to me. Have too many keys already, I'm goin' to bed. Decima, Francine, thank you for being our witnesses. Arabelle, I left my key ring on the kitchen counter. In case you want to try and match that one to one of mine. Good night. Anson, you comin'?"

He nods and says, "Still a mystery. Key out of key, well good night ladies."

They leave. I glance across the table, and notice Deci, and Fran exchange a sheepish grin.

"Belle . . . Belle, you are staring at us. Never see a couple before?"

"Excuse me Deci. Just thinking, it is getting late. Won't you gals stay and you'll get a fresh start in the morning. Please stay. We've plenty of beds."

"Sorry Belle, have to take a rain check. Fran's got an early court case, and I open the pre-natal clinic. You know that advice might be a good one for you to take. Get a fresh start in the morning. Thank you for a lovely evening. Clare makes us feel like family. Oh, you might want to tell her that her suspicions are correct."

"Okay. Sure." I give them both a hug. "Love you both." I walk them to the door and remain on the veranda. "Good night guys, safe trip." I yawn as I wave goodbye. Get a fresh start in the morning. How am I going to where there is something out of place? When is a key out of key? Sure, when it doesn't fit what? I shout, "Deci's eagle eye always spots a mistake."

In a half hour, I call and leave a message. Then channel surf until the phone rings.

"Deci. Smooth trip in?—Recall when we were growing up, how you always figured things out? —Well, I was thinking. You've been here so often, what doesn't belong in this house?—You're kidding me. The dining room? That's super. Thanks. Bye."

With the key safe in my jean pocket, I flick on the lights as I run back to the dining room. I'm determined to put an end to this mystery. I must see if what she suggested is true where an object contradicts the room.

I start with the windows and silk curtains, though faded, hang proportionately. The mural on the ceiling is okay except for the burned out bulb. Wallpaper borders complement the room's décor. The wainscot is in perfect condition and ends at that black fleur-de-lis' monstrosity. Taking everything into consideration, I decide the art piece isn't the focal point because it's hung too low for the room's height.

"That's it. Neither high nor low. It's out of harmony with the rest of the room. That panel is out of key."

I tremble as my hands touch its surface. Fingertips search for a keyhole around and in each pattern. I'm so involved, I do not hear Anson approach.

CHAPTER 33
ADAM'S JOURNAL

"Excuse me, Belle. We noticed the house lights are still on. Is something wrong?"

"Anson. Sorry, didn't hear you. I think this key has something to do with this black piece."

"Hardly think a decorative key is your answer to his riddle. Where you aware in Colonial time, it was called a level lock key? Later on because of its unique skeleton-like designs, became known as a skeleton key. It was in use up to end of World War II, then tumbler locks became famous."

Where does he come up with those facts? "Anson, sometimes I think you're a walking encyclopedia. So how does that information apply to what I said?"

"I. Q. is a hundred and thirty-five and I read a lot. Now, take a look at this. It has only one lever and a specific ward. That means yours can only open one hole, to do that, we need to check physically every inch of each cutout design. Are you up to the challenge at this hour?"

"I think it's about eleven. So, what do you mean by the challenge and what happens if we don't find one that long?"

"If we find one smaller, we keep looking. Let's get a

fresh start. Daylight will give us a better view."

"You're right. Yes, we meet here after coffee."

Anson nods and goes back. I follow suit and go to bed.

ꙮꙮꙮ

At dawn, I 'm anxious to begin and replace the flashlight's batteries before preparing breakfast. While Anson and Clare come through the back door, the foyer's doorbell rings. Anson leaves to answer the door. When he announces, "There are at least a dozen architects or contractors waiting in the gathering room.", Clare covers her mouth.

I drop the whisk and shake my head. "I forgot about this meeting to go over their ideas for the manor's conversion. Anson, please think of something. There's no way I can talk with anyone today."

Anson presses the intercom button, "Attention! Mrs. McCutchen conveys her regret in not being able to confer with anyone today. She requests you leave your presentation on the Rosewood table. After our review, I will call you sometime next week, provided, your renderings follow her requirements of an inviting atmosphere where each room retains its Victorian character. We thank you for the timeliness of your response. Madam, gentlemen, have a good day."

"Thank you. Please see how many followed directions."

He waits several minutes and goes out. When he returns with only two tubes and a single envelope, I'm at a loss for words. Thankfully, Clare isn't when she says, "Anson, my darling, you should become a diplomat." I give him a tiptoe hug.

"Yes well, I'm as anxious as you are to begin our search. Do me a favor Clare. Would you mind spreading these out by room in Katherine's library? If necessary, use the extra tables that are there."

A few minutes later, Francine knocks on the back door and comes inside. "Morning everyone, couldn't believe the congestion outside. Tried coming in through the front but quite a few men were clustered along the driveway. Heard a tall fellow say, 'Wasn't expecting that bombshell speech. Left mine. You're still holding yours. Sorry.' Well, I got back in my car and pulled around back."

"Francine, I'm prouder than a peahen. My husband put his foot down. You have time to join us for sausage and pancakes?"

"Clare if there's a coffee refill , I'll take it and a rain check for the rest. Have another appointment in Avonia. Stopped by with the notebook, I forgot it yesterday. Good luck in figuring out Decima's suggestion. Thanks for the coffee. See you all later."

Breakfast is over when Anson places his cup to be cleaned.

"Ladies, are we ready to match wits with the late Adam McCutchen and today's architects?"

We laugh. Clare is armed with tubes and paperwork and marches out of the room while Anson and I raise our flashlights and talk our way into the dining room.

"Your school friend stopped yesterday to see you, but, you weren't available. Strange he didn't show for Neil's funeral."

"He sent a card and explained he'd be out of town. So what did Charlie want?"

"Oh, he gave Clare lighting brochures for this room—added casual approach to his design."

"So, he wants to barter the antique sideboard for part of his payment?"

"No. He surprised me when he suggested we use it to display Katherine's collectibles."

Interesting, Charlie is one of the architects. In the dining room, I stand away and clasp my chin to study the detailed panel, tilting my head back and forth. "Okay, where do you want to start? Check for the key's opening or rip it off the wall. But Anson, what if it's not a doorway to anything, think Katherine's portrait would cover that wall section?"

"Possibly with a larger frame, I remember the day it was unveiled. Adam treated the event with great ceremony. He held up his arm and proclaimed, 'As Lord of the Manor, behold my seal and shield forever.'"

"Are you serious, his seal and shield?" I ask.

"Very serious. Clare found out he researched the family name and decided to give himself the title of Lord. After he died, no one ever questioned its removal."

I push hard against the piece. "Doesn't move, can it be a part of the wall? Guess, a night's sleep puts perspective on the reality of a hidden room. Not much space between the studs."

"There might be enough space for narrow shelves. However, before you rip it off the wall, I'd like to check the panel first. We feel our way and find a missing section of wood. Or if you insist, we call your friend, Charlie, and have him remove it."

"Nice try Anson. Dangling Charlie in front of me, like a carrot, won't keep you from helping me now. In the best interest of the common people, I think you start at the top because I'm closer to the bottom." I look up at Anson. He is shaking his head and from the look he gives me, I know this touching business isn't his choice.

On the floor at first glance, I notice the raised relief has a piece missing in the lower corner. "Anson, there's a missing wood section. See its been painted black to cover the broken portion near the floor."

"The key fits like a puzzle piece, but that's all. Maybe there's a keyhole somewhere close."

"Belle, start slightly above the indent and search for a circular one about a half inch. I'll work my way down from the middle just above your head. Wait, let me have the key. No, the hole isn't deep enough." He gives it back to me, and I see the disappointment in his eyes.

"You try so hard, Miss Belle, to keep Katherine's dream alive. Clare and I, we don't know why you do it."

"I arrived here, almost penniless and Katherine paid for mother's funeral. Because of her compassion, I was able to keep my chin up. A second chance meant a lot. Plus I found an extended family in the most unexpected people.So, I'll do all I can to make her dream become a reality. We check this panel until the key belongs or I cross it off my checklist."

Occasionally, we relieve the boredom with idle chatter about renovating the room. "Depending on how many come, Clare and I thought we'd need two carts. If we all eat dinner in here, we could use the kitchen for individual snacks. That's if you wouldn't mind eating with so many women."

"Sounds like a plan, but you might want to keep one holding cart loaded with clean dishes. With two serving carts used to carry off the dirty ones. However, I know Clare can't do it all, the cooking I mean. She'll need someone to help. Do you agree? Belle?"

"Anson? I'm not anywhere near that missing section, but I think I found the circle. It's a foot above the floor. Darn it. Keep looking, the key's ward is too small."

"Hand me the flashlight."

I watch him kneel, then lay on the floor to position the light for a closer look at the opening. "Wait, a small piece of wood is chipped. The rough finish is not like the rest of the groove. Let me try it. He smiled at me and said, "It turns, want to?"

"No, we call Clare. She's keeper of the keys. Let her do it."

"You ready, on the count of three. One. Two. Three."

"CLARE!" We shout in unison, and she comes running.

"You have the honor of turning the key," I said. This is the point of no return. As the key turns, there is a click. Anson touches the side of the panel and it moves toward us.

A cedar scent tickles my nose. "Who'd think this is a door?"

"Yes, and behind it, enough room for shelving."

"Let me see Anson." Clare pulls the panel closer to her and looks behind. "Belle look. There on that shelf is Anne's metal plane and a picture of Emily and Miss Katherine. Wonder what's in them boxes? Want me to call your friends?"

"Thanks, Clare but I'll call. Will you and Anson bring everything out and onto the tables?" While they begin, I go to the library to call Decima.

"Hi. Glad it's you.—Fran, need your advice on some legal documents. —Wait a minute. Clare is bringing me a box of papers. I'm not fooling, —We won't touch a thing. Both of you come as you are. See you in about an hour. I'll make a fresh pot. Come around back; the kitchen door is open. We're in the dining room. —Sure, bye."

Anson walks over to where I stand. "Found this. You might want to read it while you wait. It's Adam's journal."

I take it and slide down the wall before I open it while sitting on the floor. His entries are penned in ink.

'August 1931 There must be an heir. The Greene girls, Miriam, and Anne, are maturing. Have to see which one will oblige me in this matter. Once heir is born, I'll contract a will.

July 1936 Anne said she'll never marry because Miriam is older and should marry first. A foolish child of 14 is so young and has not begun her menstruation.

April 1938 Anne at 16 is a late bloomer. What a silly girl. So willing to play house and allow my affectionate nature. Says she is too young to marry and will have no part of being my mistress. Left before I could confirm her child is mine. Down-to-earth Miriam is 19 and more likely to agree to a marriage bed before she becomes a spinster.

January 1939 Marriage to Miriam is beyond my deepest desires. Even though childbearing is not yet hers to give me, I grow in love more each day with this woman.

July 1940 Today's child was a stillbirth

December 1940 I took him into my confidence before sending him to England. He understands his position in this household.

January 1941 Miriam has lost our twins. Her condition weakens. Getting older, need proof of Anne's child. Again, I tried wooing their mother, Mary Greene, a stubborn woman. Sent her husband on another trip, how many times do I send him away to get what I want from her?

February 1941 I confess to Mary that Miriam's health is a great concern for me and my physical needs will harm her. I comfort Mary in telling her I understand how her physical needs are important too. She is faithful but weakening. I will lengthen his trips away from her.

February 1941 He died on the last trip. I offer solace. Mary's tears weaken her resistance. I achieve my objective.

March 1941 Mary confesses she's with her husband's child. But will offers me physical comfort during Miriam's pregnancy.

November 1941 My son lives only six hours. I've still no heir from Miriam. Unlike her mother, who births another Greene daughter, Katherine.

December 1941 Miriam's depression worsens. Cameron Jerrod, a ward of the court, is brought here. Consider adoption, but not of my seed.

June 1942 Miriam died before the boy's adoption. My lineage expires. Did not adopt this child, Cameron, but given a family name to meet society's norm.

August 1952 Blood test confirms Anne's child is my son. Child, Anson Redman, doesn't know. I'll guide him in Estate's business matters. I've someone to share estate inheritance. I've rewritten the will.

December 1956 Ashamed of unwanted deflowering of the girl, Katherine—yet the estate requires a legitimate heir. Cameron's medical records indicate sterility--no heir. His impotence forces my actions. Have to manipulate circumstances, arrange copulation with arranged marriage, and I'll have an heir. Will, once more, is rewritten to cover my indiscretion and her betrothal to Cameron.

September 1957 Youngest Greene girl, Katherine, has a boy. The test confirmed Neil is my son.

March 1959 At 64, I'm still virile. Her fertility will give me another heir. Katherine is unaware of Cameron's illness, what a fool, he gambles her body away.

December 1959 Girl, Emily, is born. Illegitimate or not, she's my daughter. The three shall share my fortune.

September 1962 I see myself in Neil's unorthodox way of dealing with a problem. He and Anson will control the business.

June 1963 My sweet, beautiful gem is gone. At Emily's funeral, Mary Greene plunges a knife into my heart when she said, 'How does it feel to know because of your arrogance, your well murdered my grand-daughter.' Nay, I killed my daughter. Because of my sin, the land and estate are in Katherine's name only.

January 1964 Life has lost its purpose. Hell awaits me, and Katherine must never know because of her sister's likeness, I sired her children. My sons, my heirs, remain from Anne and Katherine's offspring. I have seen to my end with my secretary.'

I put it down. Then reread it, until I'm comfortable enough to return to the dining room, I tell them it speaks of a man driven nearly to insanity. All he's written is evidence of that. His will must be within the papers we found.

CHAPTER 34
TWO DIVIDED EQUALS THREE

Within the hour, clutching her coffee mug, Francine strolls into the dining room with Decima close on her heels. They find us with Anson carrying an armful of loose papers to the long table where I'm sorting.

"Whoa! That is a serious amount of paperwork. Hey, guy and gals don't be offended if I ask you to stop whatever you're doing. I'll be able to go through these quicker if I do it myself with an intravenous coffee supply.

I look at this jean-driven, bunny-mules drill instructor. All matter-of-fact, she centers herself in the middle of a large empty floor space.

"Clare, need a refill every half-hour. Anson, if you wouldn't mind, put those boxes and papers in a circle around me. Dee, keep Belle occupied and out of here for at least three hours. No sooner. Most of this will be sorted before dinner. Can't have this become an all-nighter."

Decima takes Fran's mug with her and disappears with me into the kitchen. With the aroma of coffee brewing, Clare prepared sandwiches and said, "Didn't see that trait in her, but it'll get the job done quicker. See that she gets her coffee. Here I made a few for her."

On our return, Anson is removing the last box before

he pushes the panel back against the wall.

With an extended arm directed to her coffee mug, Fran gets comfortable on the floor amid the piles of loose papers and a dozen letter-sized boxes. Before she begins reading, she gives a 'shoo away' signal and Deci, and I go out to spend some quality time together.

After two hours, the suspense is driving me crazy. On the pretext of bringing Francine something to eat, I rap on the doorframe. "Sandwich? Sweet roll? Piece of fruit? What's your choice?" Tray in hand, I wait and am surprised at the neat stacks in one part of the room and a bonfire worth of paper wreckage an arm's throw from where Anything worth consideration?"

"Important legal documents were thrown together with food receipts. Anson said that he gave you a journal."

Is she testing me? "Yes he did. A couple entries mentioned his heir."

"What about that legal stuff, any mention of an heir?"

Francine hands me a stack. "Here Arabelle, have a look, acquisitions, stock shares, property deeds, birth records, donated works of art and I left the weirdest thing on top. Early DNA reports on everyone whoever resided, worked, or visited this place."

"Go on, How about Dorothy Lacey?"

"Nothing. I did find one for a Dorothy MacPherson. She worked here as a nanny. Found her report attached to copies of a marriage license and an annulment document."

"No, her married name was Lacey, not MacPherson. My father died."

"Papers don't lie. Arabelle, she kept your identity away from your father. Annulment was processed seven months before you were born. Done through an attorney so your father would not know your mother was pregnant. Noted reason indicated one party was not entirely committed to the marriage."

Can't believe what Fran just showed me. Who is this MacPherson? He doesn't know I'm alive. Doesn't make sense, but records don't lie.

"Arabelle. At your feet are the treasures of Adam McCutchen's legacy? This one, I believe, is the document everyone wants."

My throat constricts as if Adam reaches out from his grave and tightens his fingers around my throat. I collapse into a nearby chair when Francine pulls out the original 1939 document, Adam's will with all the attached codicils.

"A quick read gave everything to Miriam. Later however, several changes may be notarized in these loose papers. If you've no objections, will take this box with me? I'll get back to you as soon as I unravel everything. Never know what you'll find that is written between the legal lines."

"No objections, it's a relief to know the search is over." I hug her and Decima as they leave. The future has promise for New Beginnings.

ᢒᢒᢒ

Whirlwind holidays are coupled with found treasures. While I battle the flu bug, the green light for New Beginnings' renovation take its toll on my health. Clare and Anson insist I spend time recuperating in the former solarium with a deck of cards. Before our wedding, Katherine decided to rename it to conservatoire for musical achievement. The CMA room takes advantage of the audio acoustics, and the upbeat stereo music helps me relax.

"Arabelle, would you prefer cinnamon toast and tea?" Clare asks as she removes my untouched breakfast tray.

"Not hungry." I raise my hands high above the table and let the playing cards slip through my fingers. "Clare, how often do you win at solitaire on your first time?"

"Don't play cards, but I've watched Anson. He'll play three times. If he doesn't win, he slams the cards down and leaves the room. Why are you askin'?"

"Just played and I won. Before I started, I finished. The story of how my life is going. I'm tired of losing who means the most to me. I want challenges and to start living again."

Before Clare can reply, I hear Anson's voice. "Belle, road construction has traffic backed up about two miles from here. Sorry, we'll need to leave a little earlier than planned."

I look to Clare, whose hand has gone up to her mouth.

"Didn't you cancel with Francine as I asked?"

"I called her several times, Belle, but no luck. Then I forgot. Besides, you told me that you wanted to start livin'."

"Vaguely remember what I said. So we both go."

"You can use the back roads. It'll only add a few minutes to the drive." Anson tosses me the keys. I toss them back.

"Clare, relax tonight. We'll bring dinner."

It's after seven when Anson gives a triple toot to alert Clare. When she comes outside, he carries in three bags of food. I park the car outside the carriage house and go into the manor.

Once inside, Clare's interrogation begins. "Did you get lost in China town's Forbidden Garden? Expectin' guests, because you brought enough to feed six of us? Anson? Arabelle? Which one is hidin' somethin'?"

With my most serious face, I try to appear disappointed as I walk over and take their hands. Instead, I grab both of their arms and begin jumping up-and-down beside them.

Anson's face has gone white when he looks at me. He didn't go into Fran's office with me, and I think he suspects something while Clare does her best to stop my jumping.

"Arabelle, stop it. You've gone stark ravin' mad."

I stop and hug both of them. "Not mad, Clare. It's wonderful. New Beginning is now tax exempt. End of January, we can officially open the door. However, there is one problem. All renovations must be done to get the occupancy permit. Fortunately for us, Fran thinks it might take couple months for that permit, red tape and all."

"Anson, honey, isn't that good news? Dearie, are you okay? You look like you saw a ghost. You sure you're okay?"

"Yes, okay. Give me a minute Clare." He walks over to the cabinet and pours whiskey into three snifters. He drinks his and refills the glass.

"Anson Redman, you lost your mind. Drinkin' like this. Arabelle, what's goin' on?"

"Clare, it's Adam's will and the codicils. Anson, do you want me to tell her?"

"Clare darling, please sit down and take a good hold of your glass."

Bewildered, she watches us and lifts hers to match our toast. "Okay, I'm sittin' and toastin'. Arabelle, he confused me. Will you start explainin'?"

"Clare, if you had one wish, what would you want?"

"Me? Oh, maybe a child or our place. Not that I'm not grateful for livin' here but . . .I'd wish for somethin' that's ours."

"Your wish is granted. You and Anson can have your house."

"Arabelle, don't be playin' with my wish."

"Francine found a tiny loophole in Adam's will, and with it, Anson and I receive a third of the inheritance."

Clare empties her snifter in one swallow and takes a hold of Anson's arm. "A third? Don't understand, only two of you and you each get a third. How'd that happen?

I reach across the table and hold her hand. "Adam left everything to Miriam, and later he willed an equal share to any child he sired within this household. He additionally included future spouses and their offspring. Nothing in his bequest included Cameron, his ward, or any charity."

"Never figured in over 30 years, he did a lot of matin' to get an heir. He should have stopped with you, Anson. Your mama could have acknowledged it right up front. Okay, that covers you and Anson but how does one-half become one-third?"

Anson stands to refill Clare's sniffer. She drinks it down as if the alcohol is water to a thirsty man.

"I still don't understand how two surviving heirs get only a third. Does the other go to pay taxes?"

"Inheritance, that's not the situation, dear. Last time we met with Francine, Belle and I agreed if we were considered heirs, we'd divide it to include a portion of it for Katherine's dream to become a reality. Clare in those papers, Francine found sheets from Adam's business journal stapled inside the will. A few had cryptic business notes and the mention of HP. Those she needs to review next week. With some financial planning and investments that third share will keep New Beginnings going on in financial perpetuity."

I glance at Clare, and her smile tells me she understands what can happen to all of us once New Beginnings open the manor's door. She lifts her glass, and we join her.

"Why didn't you say that in the beginnin'? I do think you two are nuttier than my holiday fruitcake. I'm proud of you. Just don't think this sentimentality is goin' to last. Did she have a chance to check Katherine's will?"

"Francine called me earlier when she read me her intentions. That, my darling wife, is how we get our house. In Katherine's will, you and I will receive a monetary bequest, enough to buy your dream house. And as Belle told you Neil's portion, is hers."

I look at them. "Anson, you and Clare, go out and celebrate. I'll have General Tso's chicken and then off to bed."

Hands joined, they walk from the kitchen, and I overhear her parting words, "Darlin', did you mean our own place?"

ꟸꟸꟸ

The next few weeks I spend time with two other architects beside Charlie. While all three are aware completion time is critical, a major problem confronts two of them. How to do a functional elevator to allow a redesign to the third floor?

I decide to make a call. "Hi Charlie, need help with a problem. We can discuss it tonight at the Civic Center. — Yes, I'm asking you on a date and don't get any ideas. It's a night with Christopher Bell. He's a fantastic supporter of pro-life. Hoping to get a few ideas for our project.— Okay pick me up by six. Good grief Charlie, that's an hour away.—Me too. Later 'gator." Did I just say that I love him too?

Charlie insists on driving and that becomes a blessing in disguise. We arrive back early enough to share the evening with Clare and Anson. A surprise to me is when Charlie asks about New Beginnings' financial start. It is an important issue for me as well. I'm so grateful when Anson shares his knowledge with us.

"Charlie, Katherine's income covered the initial renovations of which you had a part. Belle, you know of Neil's HP stock. That and his personal funds grew from his first birthday into a trust. That created an enormous nest egg. Before Katherine died, he knew she needed cash flow. He liquidated some of his assets to fund the extra renovations that you kept under budget."

"Charlie, after Katherine's will had gone through probate, Clare and Anson received a monetary bequest and the rest went to Neil. When he died, I received it and not aware of the amount. Or what funds Anson supplied. Francine has done her work pro bono. Now with the tax exemption, we can secure grant funding for New Beginnings use."

Charlie's nod is only an acknowledgment. I have no idea of his commitment to a dream becoming a reality.

"That shows the passion each one of you has. Clare,

Anson congratulations on the wedding. And Belle, I'll stop by tomorrow, around nine. Think I might have a solution to the third floor. Several ideas popped into my head while that fellow was talking about thinking outside the box."

"Chris' talk, also got me excited . It is getting late, and I look forward to tomorrow. If you make it eight, I'll make a western omelet for breakfast." I walk him to his truck.

"Eight it is." Charlie throws a kiss through his window. I throw one back. Strange, I didn't feel guilty about doing that.

Before I go back to the manor, I notice their lights are on and climb the stairs.

CHAPTER 35
BOUQUET OF DAFFODILS

"Hello! Is anyone still awake?"

"Do come up, Arabelle. Havin' a late night pizza, like to join us?"

"Love to and I've some fantastic news to share. If I don't tell you tonight, I'll explode."

Clare brings out another plate and sits beside Anson. "Well, tell us before you pop your cork."

"You know I went to hear Christopher Bell's talk on second-chance homes for women. Afterwards, we took a chance and went backstage to meet him. I introduce Charlie and myself and he asks me if I'm related to Neil McCutchen. Told him Neil died and that I was his widow. He offered his condolence and said he met Neil when he was abroad. What a coincidence, they had a similar concern. How to help single, expectant mothers."

"He knew our Neil." Clare grasps at her throat.

"Yes, he did. He told me about an agency, Good Counsel. They give unwed, pregnant girls or women a place to stay while expecting. Plus, if interested, G. E. D. classes or job training in life skills. Mr. Bell will send me some information about the place and gave me his private phone number in case Francine has a question."

Clare jumps from her chair and paces the room. "I can't believe. Arabelle, I can't believe you told us everything Katherine envisioned. Here, where we gave a second chance to have their baby, get a job, and a home until they'd find affordable housing. She even hoped to have a day care facility on the grounds."

"Tell us more, Belle. Were the ladies impressed?"

"Anson if, you guys, saw them, you'd think they were sponges just soaking up all that he sent. After Francine checks the legalize with their program, she'll set a meeting time. It has to be workable for us, as well as for them."

"When Katherine told me to figure where a daycare would fit on the estate, I didn't do anything. Maybe Charlie or Francine knows zoning regulations; then I could help."

"If that pizza tastes as delicious as it smells, I'll have a slice. Not to be too nosey, but did you two find a house?"

They look at each other and exclaim, "The bungalow!"

"Are you kidding? There is no way; the burnt debris was plowed under."

"Arabelle, miracles do happen. Yesterday, we met with Mr. Boyd and B&B Contractin' Both said that it is doable but will take a while. Weather permittin', in the next six weeks, the contractor will remove all debris. B&B will set the new foundation for a 1,500 square foot ranch. Mr. Boyd handles part of the construction and finishes the interior details. Will it bother you, if they build on the old site with extra acreage for a patio and a small garden?"

"Clare, bungalow memories are in my heart. Your home and any land you need will be deeded to you from the estate."

"Anson, joint teamwork, I like the idea. Could you tell if Charlie feels comfortable working with B&B?"

"Sounded like it during our conversations. Don't know more than that. The pizza is cooling. Who's hungry for another piece?"

༄༄༄

My alarm goes off a half hour earlier. I've time for a quick shower and selecting an outfit more feminine than jeans and tank top. Instead, I wear a blue gingham shirtwaist and my favorite pumps. With a bit of lip color and upsweep of my hair, I'm ready to impress Charlie with my culinary skills. By 7:30 a.m., coffee is brewing, and the omelet mixture is ready. The sound of car tires crunching gravel sends me to set the table.

"Charlie, Hi. You're early. Give me a minute and breakfast will be served. Help yourself to the coffee."

"Thanks." He gives me a hug and quick peck on my cheek. It's good.

"Okay Charlie, there's a bottleneck situation between you and B&B."

"Belle, feed this body before you tax the brain."

I should have remembered his appetite takes precedent, when he remains silent.

"Charlie, you know, you can talk between bites. So last night, what idea popped into your head?"

He shakes his head and finishes his toast by dunking it first into his coffee. "Great breakfast, remind me to give the cook a big tip. My idea can wait. Bottlenecks are my specialty. Now I understand, why you resist my subtle advances. You're in love with my quick solutions. How flattering that you love my build and also my mind. The workable solution is to find the way to get a person from floor to floor."

"Yes, Charlie, you're so right. I love your brain's extemporaneous view of life. Love you for you; now that's another story. I'm serious Charlie. Fran had to postpone opening the doors. B&B insists on a chair life to eliminate the spiral. Pro, it is the least expensive. Con carries one person at a time. What's your solution?"

We sit across from each other. Slacks and a great shirt make the most of his blue eyes and overall look. Without coveralls Charlie, you clean up good.

"An elevator is what I had in mind. The idea isn't novel and would involve little more cost but up to four people could use it."

"B&B mentioned using one behind the main stairway. Didn't like removing the powder room and the noise isn't acceptable. Where would you put yours?"

He pushes his chair back from the table. "Hate to eat and run, but, I must. Forgot my plans, be back in a minute.

I watch. He wipes his mouth, puts his plate in the sink and rushes out the back door. I lean into my hand. Can't believe how theatrical he still is. Guess there's enough time to wash the dishes. The fresh air behind me makes me turn around.

"For such a delicious meal, Arabelle McCutchen, I bring you exactly what you need this fine, fine day."

With a grin, a Cheshire cat would envy, Charlie approaches. From behind his back with a flourishing bow, he hands me a bouquet of daffodils tied to a small rolled blueprint.

"Thank you for the flowers Charlie, and if this print has the answer to my problem, I think I'm going to give you a kiss."

"I'll collect it, too." Charlie gives a wink before he unrolls the print and spreads it on the table before us. "Took me awhile, but at Chris' talk, I realized don't need to do anything to the inside, only the outside inside."

The door opens again, and the air blows the print to the floor. Anson picks it up, returning it to the table. "Sorry for the interruption. Wanted to find out if you need anything, we're going to Sears to pick our appliances. Morning Charlie, this here, another idea of yours?"

Charlie and Anson exchange the handshake of old friends. While he greets Anson, I notice his eyes make contact with mine.

"Yes, come look. Here is the attached garage. Stairs lead in and out of the house and to the next floor. We run a lift from here through the ceiling and the area above. Now on the second floor, I build up enough support for an additional inside lift for three that a child can run. It can be done, Belle. By using these conveyances, you'll have enough space for a mini-day care facility for the wee folk on the third floor. Anson, what do you think?"

"That is one bright idea. It's so simple, it would work. Oh, why I'm here. Clare's new assistant, poor girl, she sometimes leaves things unfinished and untidy. Clare doesn't think we should leave you with her being in charge of the household."

"Anson, I'm certain Kayla is ready to fly on her own. Finalize your house plans with Charlie and go on your honeymoon. When you return, you can carry Clare across the threshold into a completely furnished home. As Company President, I'm confident I'll handle matters here. And, Charlie will do the same on his end."

Anson leans up against the doorway. “Belle, never saw anyone grasp running a business so well. Sure, you weren’t a business tycoon in another life.”

“No, Anson, you taught me the simple rules. Have capital, invest. Receive gain, reinvest or minimize your loss. Find a teacher to point out alternatives. Or, apply a dash of common sense and fair dealing with people. The rest is child’s play.”

“Touché Arabelle. I’m off before Clare adds more items to our household list. We’ve packing to do. Then, au revoir.”

ℵℵℵ

Two weeks later, Clare sets off sparks and in some instances, fireworks explode at the manor. Anson is grateful business interests abroad will keep him from being underfoot while Clare deals with the two contractors.

“Don’t understand Mr. Boyd, your work is totally unacceptable. What did you do besides sit on your keister?”

“Clare, please calm down. It’s my fault your place wasn’t finished. To meet both schedules, Charlie subcontracted with B&B for the framing and remodeling on the two floors here. He took over the building of your house with volunteered hours. January first was the target date to open the doors, and it didn't happen."

“Why? Tell me what was so important at the manor that you push aside our home. Tell me, Arabelle.”

“I couldn’t have Fran postpone the opening again. We needed a certificate of occupancy. Without consulting the Board, I made an executive decision. You and Anson have a temporary home, and I'm asking a lot for you to be patient for another month. Hmmm!"

"A month, not a day more. I'll see to that. Executive decision, well you iron out the details with Mr. Boyd on my house."

No, he's still here, and I bet he's waiting to collect. Bite the bullet; it's only a kiss. I find he's trying out the lift's operation. "Hi, Charlie, Clare's inclined to give you a month but no more. Then, she'll enforce her penalty clause."

"Penalty clause? That woman will probably poison my food or at least decide not to feed us."

"Simmer down. I'll pay for the overtime if both crews start doing both jobs on the same day. Please, Charlie, she is not a happy camper."

"Start? Not until I collect an overdue payment, on the cheek, of course."

"Gladly." I lean over to give him his due. At the last second, Charlie takes my head and plants a long kiss on my lips.

I sputter, "Charlie, no fair."

"All's fair in love, Belle as all is fair in war with Clare." He gives a short bow and jumps onto the lift and ascends to the top floor. He shouts down, "Did you know, Belle, Clare watches everything the workers do at each place. They leave a smudge, and she's after them to clean it. B&B's owner complained that each day they start fresh, and he's not sure if she delayed the job or makes it easier. I'm glad they're nearing completion."

True to her agreement, Clare feeds the crews with home-baked muffins and comfort foods and monitors the work on both homes. To safeguard Arabelle's interests, she logs every overtime hour for the past three weeks, four days and fourteen hours. Her perseverance moves everyone in the right direction. In three weeks, the manor is completed and awaits the inspection. It's a pleasure for me to see her joy when her appliances are installed.

Both crews donate their time to convert five bedrooms into ten smaller, but adequate rooms. Plus, with Charlie's drawings for the third-floor lift, the plumbing subcontractor adds a half bath to each floor.

The last week of February, we gather together while the Inspector tapes the Certificate of Occupancy.

I bubble with enthusiasm and want to share this feeling of well-being with Charlie. I find him getting ready to leave. "Can't believe you did it and no penalty. Don't you just feel . . . I don't know what exactly. Only it's the best I've felt in a long time. Earlier today, I hired a teacher and will interview volunteers for the daycare this afternoon."

"Hope you didn't mind Mr. and Mrs. David coming here last week. She wanted to see my work before they hire me."

"I'm not lying, Charlie. His wife couldn't believe your compacted bedrooms and how well everything fit. She said that it was charming. The changing table was perfect for their nursery."

"Her husband called this morning and gave me the contracts."

"That's wonderful Charlie. The strangest thing happened before I found you. A Baby Land truck pulls up, and the driver hands me an envelope. Inside was a note. She wrote that she noticed several things were missing in each room and donated a dozen rocking chairs, rolls of wallpaper borders and ten different bedding sets for either bed or crib." I'm crying tears of joy and cover my face.

Charlie puts his arm around my shoulder. "People always amaze me. When he told me his wife's anniversary present would be delivered today, I never believed it would be a gift for New Beginnings because he sent his gift to my office. It's meant for your converted master bedroom."

"Charlie, that's the educational area and nursery nook. That idea of yours was sheer genius. What did they send you?"

"Office equipment included two computers and a printer. Belle, I told them about New Beginnings and how you catapulted Katherine's dream beyond a safe harbor into an opportunity for another chance. Well, they said it was something they'd like to support."

"The extra rockers are for the turret's nook." I stand on tiptoes to hug him, "Thank you, Charlie, for everything."

Instead, he kisses me. I find I'm locked in his embrace. "Belle, trust me. Don't say a word. Close your eyes and take my hand, I'll lead."

While his request is a bit off the wall, I'm not afraid. He holds my elbow, and we go outside. I feel a few raindrops and wonder where he is taking me.

"Hold tight; the ground is slippery when going up a hill."

I know where we are.

CHAPTER 36
FAMILY HERITAGE

He stops and places his hands on my shoulder and draws me down beside him. “Open your eyes.”

From the pagoda, I look out on a grassy knoll where an adjoining playground is near the other rose pagodas. “Charlie, this was Anson’s dream. A place for the little ones. I’m so grateful the crews built it. Anson is not good at hammering a nail. Never saw a thumb swell up so big.”

Charlie laughs. “Had one like that when I built a swing for my brother’s kids. Maybe one day I’ll make one for my own. So do you like?”

“It’s a terrific addition. It’s your creation.”

“Won’t change your mind about my brightening that hide-a-way room with a splash of color?”

“If you do, I’ll never speak to you, Charlie Boyd. That place always makes me feel detached from all that was sad in my life. I’d like them to experience another time with Victorian charm.”

“Okay, with the exception of helping Anson hang that banner, my job here is finished. So unless you have another engagement, join me tonight for a celebration dinner.”

“Charlie, in the old days, you treated me like your

little sister. You wouldn't let anyone tease me about my Terry Thomas smile. Because of you, I liked myself in those awkward years."

He frames my face with his hands and says, "You're a beautiful woman, Belle, not a kid sister. Don't think of you like that anymore. Will you join me as a consenting adult?"

"Sure! Can my friends, Decima and Francine, go too? You know, to celebrate."

Charlie's hands fall away from their caress, and a look of disappointment fills his eyes. "A double date. Sure. Seven o'clock at the Country Club. I'll get you around six. Let's hang that banner."

Charlie leaves to recruit Anson while Clare and I take the large sign out to the front porch. We stretch the banner between the two ladders. The men take hold of each grommet and climb high to the roof's façade. Now positioned with a flowing emblem, hammers, and nails, they await our instructions.

"Okay Anson, raise your end about five inches and Charlie bring your end down almost a foot. That's perfect. Hammer away."

Clare stands beside me. She fidgets and twists her handkerchief throughout the ceremony.

"He's okay Clare. Been on ladders many times, or is something else bothering you?"

"Was just thinkin' it would lower number of adoptions with you offerin' them an extra year's stay if they keep their baby and find a job."

"That's a possibility Clare and why is this upsetting you?"

"You see, Anson and I were talkin' about havin' a

family. So if one of the girls puts her baby up for adoption, well, we'd give the baby a good home if you would give the Court a good character recommendation."

"Hey, down there. How does it look?" Calls, Anson.

"Come see for yourselves." I take a moment to think about Clare's concern. "Clare, time will tell, but, with Francine's help, maybe not immediately but it could happen."

We go off the porch and onto the lawn where a blue bunting emblazoned with the McCutchen Coat of Arms billows out the flowing gold script, New Beginnings.

Charlie turns and gives Anson a smart salute. "The family crest makes a statement."

"Thank you, took me a year to research it for Clare. Helmet denotes wisdom, security, strength and protection. The boar's head reflects the hospitality and the arrow shows a readiness for battle."

"If I recall my darling, you said the green background stands for hope, joy, and loyalty in love." Clare quickly adds.

"Anson, your crest is your family heritage. Adam McCutchen would be proud of his son."

"Yah! Proud!"

Those were the last words I hear as Charlie heads to his car.

ഇഇഇ

Resident candidates were interviewed during the weeks that follow. With Good Counsel's assist, New Beginning residence is filled. Today Francine, as a witness, sits with me as I conclude Lehlah's orientation.

"Lehlah, all residents live here under a common bond, and we'd like you to read through it before signing the pledge."

"Mind if I read it aloud? Sticks better in my head when I hear the words."

Francine and I both nod our approval.

"I, Lehlah, pledge to bring hope by thoughtful listening to others. I promise to be attentive to the needs of others in this small community. I will embrace how forgiveness in giving and accepting returns my dignity. I promise to learn so I may better my life and that of my child. I pledge to bring hope to others by encouraging and supporting family values. I will do my very best to do these all the days of my life. Mighty strong words to live by Mrs. McCutchen. I'll do my best."

Before signing, she asks, "Mrs. McCutchen, think we'll make it?" Lehlah pats her stomach and looks frightened.

"Yes, I do. Sometimes life is easier when someone guides and helps you on the journey. But, it's your decision as to what you make of this opportunity. Now let's get you settled in your room. Okay?"

"Okay!" She signs the pledge and Francine, and I sign as witnesses. Lehlah picks up a Kroger grocery bag from the floor. "I travel light."

Once Lehlah is settled, we go to the office. Francine says, "Katherine. I'm sorry Araelle, we're filled. Will her plan work or did we take on more than we should have?"

I face her and say, "Only time will tell."

ꟹꟹꟹ

Activity in the business increases and I discover I'm pulled away from the day-to-day running of the home and its residents. I regret leaving an overwhelming responsibility in Clare's hands. While I hire a per diem grounds keeper to handle Anson work here at the estate, Clare's rigidity to training makes it difficult in finding her an assistant. She either believes the person is either incompetent or a run-of-the-mill short order cook or a cleaning women from the local high school.

As the company flourishes, New Beginnings unravels at the seams. Today during our drive into the city, a cold snap from Canada sends snow flurries across the roadway.

"Wonder how Clare is handling the extra work? Does she ever says anything to you, Anson?"

"You may want to have a cup of tea and sit a spell with her in the sitting room. She could use the sit-down if you get my drift."

I don't ask but wonder what does he mean by that remark. I call and make reservations at the Olive Garden.

That evening following the manor's dinner service, we leave for the restaurant. Clare slams the car door shut; and as if she wears a muzzle, says nothing. Once we arrive and are seated, she sits in a straight back chair and juts out her chin. Not a single complaint comes from her lips. She just sips her tea and waits for me to begin talking.

Not good, I think. She is a pot waiting to boil over. Okay, Lacey, get her to open up. You know her buttons. "It was beautiful this morning with the new snow falling."

"Seen better," Clare says. The dining room is air-controlled, but I sense ice builds between us. I change chairs to sit beside her.

"Since we opened, I miss our kitchen talks. You think spring will ever come?"

"Not soon enough for my arthritis." She stands and walks toward the restroom.

I wait for what seems an eternity. She returns and closes the clasp on her purse. "Bill, I paid it. You ready to go?"

"Clare, are you regretting the decision to open New Beginning, so early? Did I put a burr under you with all you have to do? Tell me. Clare, what is with you? We prepared well in advance and everything was going great over the past weeks. What is bothering you?"

"'More precise it started after our honeymoon. Belle, the extra work I needed to redo from the personnel you felt would take care of everythin'. Well, not to my likin', I calculated it took me fifty-seven days gettin' things back the way it was. A lot of my life passed under that bridge since we crossed over. Hate to say it's been rampagin' like a muddy Mississippi flood since we opened the doors."

I begin worrying about her health. The woman standing in front of me is not Clare, who bounces back with enthusiasm and quick wit. Is this the reason Anson suggested I have a sit down with her?

"Clare, one thing I noticed yesterday concerned your kitchen. With so many meals, it is always sparkling. How is your new assistant handling the workload?"

Clare stiffens her back and clasps her hands in front of her. She stares without blinking and recites a litany of a frightened child, who will forget something.

"After we returned, it started. Not complainin' but, she acted like she's the housekeeper and I'm her assistant. Glad you got rid of her until the string of women you brought in made me work all the harder in cleanin' up their work. And not complainin' but some of them act like this is a hotel, and Clare's their personal maid. Also not complainin', but with all the extra laundry, I don't have time for my husband. Besides his handlin' Company matters, not complainin', but they got him runnin' errands left and right. Said what I said because you asked me Arabelle, but I'm not complainin'. The one woman reminds me of you, burned the water out of my favorite teapot. Belle, I thank you for listenin' and for the tea. But, I'd like to go home now."

I'm too stunned to do no more than drive back and drop her off near the walkway to their home.

"Good night Clare. I'm spending tonight at Deci's. See you tomorrow." I go inside, grab my overnight bag and take the BMW into town.

Thirty minutes later a surprised Decima opens their door. "Arabelle? What are the odds, you'd be knocking?"

I give her a side-cheek kiss, pull off my coat and throw it onto the floor. "Help! I need your help. It can't be falling down around me. It can't be happening. I need help."

Soon I'm sitting between them. Deci holds my hand, and Fran has her arm around my shoulder.

"Everything is out of control. Clare spilled the beans on unforeseen problems that are now festering under the manor's roof. Although the business runs okay, I hate every minute I'm away from the girls. In Clare's frame of mind, I'm worried about her. Can't lose her or Anson. I'm in a pressure cooker, and the lid is about to fly. Don't know anymore." I let out a loud sigh and sink back into the couch.

Deci lets go of my hand and gives me a hug. "It'll work out, Belle. I know in time, it will. Francine, aren't the girls supposed to help?"

"She's right Belle. This shouldn't be happening. Each expectant mother is given our version of Good Counsel's sharing program. And what the contribution, however small, is outlined for them to remain there."

"They've little to no money, Francine. What are you getting at?"

"Money from them isn't how New Beginnings was established. It states they contribute time and talents while living there. They are responsible for their housekeeping and in sharing the household's work, as much as they are able. That could include light dusting of the furniture in a single room. Tomorrow after breakfast we'll stop by my office. I have plenty of reminders for you to pass along."

Decima takes me by my shoulders. "The situation that involves Anson, the first thing you do is make Clare happy. Tell her she has to get up on the kitchen foot stool. Look him right in his eyes, and, tell him verbatim. 'Arabelle said, You're the man of the house. You will learn to say 'No!' to the residents. Handle it or you, Anson, will hear me saying "No." when you get frisky.' That is their problem, Belle. And Clare must manage it to get control over her potential helpers."

"Guess that leaves one problem for me, firing Clare's last assistant. One chief, too many, brings down the teepee. Feel so much better. Except now I am ravenous. Where can we go? It's my treat."

"Tony's Pizzeria!" We yell together.

Two flights down and around the corner is Tony's. A 'Seat Yourself' sign is in the window, and a booth in the rear is our favorite spot.

"Belle, we . . . that is Fran and me . . ."

A gum-popping waitress holds pad and pencil in hand and interrupts Decima. "We're out of anchovies. So what'll you have?"

"A large veggie pizza extra cheese, no anchovies and three sweet ice teas. Check for a refill in ten and this should cover the bill and your tip. That's all."

The puzzled waitress snaps her gum. "Like thanks." She goes to the next table.

"Way to go, Belle." Said Deci. "Guess Katherine wasn't the only one who can kick butt." We look at each other. Cover our mouths and burst into laughter. "Fran, I'll explain later."

"Okay Deci, before rudely interrupted, you were saying?"

"We hired a private investigator after Francine told you that your father's last name was MacPherson. The good news is he found a Paddy MacPherson living in California."

"Sorry, it's not him Francine. Hope you didn't pay him."

"But Deci told me you once that your mother said, 'Paddy, he's your Daddy.'.

"Deci, you misunderstood. What I said was that Mom said he had a funny first name, and she couldn't rhyme it with Daddy."

"Well, it's not over yet. He's still on retainer. Fifty dollars a day plus expenses, I promise he'll find the right MacPherson."

"Fran. Deci. Thanks. If I could only remember, Mom would laugh and say the funniest Scotch name, I ever heard. Fizzypad, Fizzyrick, Fitzrick, Fitzpat. Sorry, don't remember."

"I do!" A male voice comes from an adjoining booth.

I look over my shoulder and to see if the face will match the voice. With no further comments, I place my attention onto enjoying my pizza.

Without warning, a familiar head pops around the booth's corner. "Care to share?"

Decima shakes her finger at him. "Charlie, you hated vegetables ever since you were born. Or are you looking for an excuse to be with Arabelle?"

"Just sitting behind you all and couldn't help but overhear the conversation. Thought I could help with the missing name. About a year ago, did some work for a McPherson. Believe she called her son, some ridiculous name."

"That's why the name wasn't right. Our P.I. said he found a MacPherson. Sorry for interrupting." Said Fran.

"Charlie. Thanks ever so much. Do they still live here? Maybe, they knew my mother."

"No longer, the house sold last summer. Heard the mother moved closer to her daughter. Thought it strange a Scottish family would call a son, Paddy. That was until I learned the reason."

He shoves, and I move over for him to sit. "Charlie please, not another one of your stories."

"True story Belle. Mrs. McPherson's daughter told me her mother was an only child of Irish parents. Married a Scot and they had a son. To appease her parents, she convinced her husband to name the boy, Fitzpatrick. That name meant son of Patrick and the family name of McPherson meant son of a parson. Close to Irish, but no cigars as far as I could see. However, it made her side happy when she nicknamed him Paddy."

"But where did they move?" Deci asks.

"Not sure, save your money Deci. I'll get the information for Belle."

"Mazel tov Charlie, you give us a blessing."

"Francine, you're Jewish? Deci? When did all this happen?"

"Not yet, Belle. Fran's on her way to becoming a Reconstructionist Jew, after that, then our Rabbi will marry us. Now would you like some pizza, Charlie?"

A young man appears carrying a pizza paddle. "Excuse me, sir, this your pepperoni and sausage pizza."

"Now that's pizza, ladies." Charlie slides away from me and goes back to his booth.

CHAPTER 37
CRYSTAL TOOK OVER

It takes a few days to bring harmony back to the manor. The kitchen assistant was laid off and given a letter of recommendation. Anson smiles more since Clare has time for them and she claims dominion over her kitchen and household. I schedule the weekend's informal meeting as a perfect time to go over Francine's brochure, highlighting the 'Time and Talent' section of each pamphlet I distribute. Questions and answers follow, and Clare is anxious without a volunteer coming forth. The tension reflects on her face until Lehlah steps forward.

"What's with you sisters, never washed a dish before. And I'll tell you; I'm tired of stepping onto wet towels left in the shower. Clare, need any potatoes peeled?"

A few young ladies step up to do light housekeeping. Gradually all come forth to contribute their time or talent to making this their place. Under Anson guidance, a few offer to drive to doctor appointments. Decision is made to retain the gardener on a full-time basis.

After several months, Clare and I evaluate the leadership skills she needs to assist her. Three become group leaders. Lehlah and Estelle alternate meals and assist in the kitchen. They surprise Clare with their culinary skills and use of the estate's garden. An unforeseen turn of events happens when Kayla emerges victorious as the assistant housekeeper. Her skill in delegating and organizing a staff of ongoing volunteers surprises us. Kayla remains after her baby is adopted and is hired as a permanent employee at the manor. There is light at the end of the tunnel when New Beginnings offers its residents a second chance.

Holidays and year-end business increase activities within the manor. Our Thanksgiving gave us two babies. Mary places her daughter for open adoption and has asked to remain until she finds a place to stay. Sharlia and her son, Sipho, return to her family. False labor happens with Braxton Hicks contractions and has Anson driving each one on separate days to the hospital.

ഇഇഇ

"Come, Mrs. McCutchen, you must see the stockings I made for Carolina and Carlos. Madres working on Daniel's and Angel's stocking."

We take the lift to their floor, and I see several girls make a construction paper garland framing the bookcases or string popcorn and cranberries for the tree, which arrives in two days. Rosario and Marcela are finishing their baby's stocking to hang beside the twins on the fireplace mantel.

"Hello everyone, your decorations are beautiful."

"Hello!"

"Buenos Dias!"

"Hi back!"

"Hola!"

"Morning!"

A blending of voices came forth with a variety of greetings which mae a beautiful sound. I smile for my morning starts off with love filling the air. Loretta leaves me and joins the others making a garland. I descend the back stairway as the smell of gingerbread cookies teases my taste buds. I go over to the icing table.

Lehlah is busy teaching new volunteers on how to frost the little people."Remember, some of you are expecting girls. Morning, Mrs. McCutchen."

"Morning Lehlah, ladies."

I watch Clare. Her back is to me, and she is busy instructing two teenagers in using her recipe for making nut bread batter.

"We're triplin' the recipe for the shelter downtown. Make sure you do the math right. Well hello, Arabelle. Do me a favor? Get him out of here." She points to Anson eating popcorn. "Anson, take your hand out of that bowl. Send it up on the dumb waiter along with the cranberries."

"Anson, do this. Anson, do that. My dear wife, you'd think I'd get at least a factory reject for all I do."

"Oh, poor boy, here's your cookie. Sorry, it's missing a section." Said Estelle as she breaks a cookie leg.

"Th**ank** you, Estelle. Clare, her reward is she goes with me when I go to select our trees."

Kayla and Lehlah hurry over with a cookie.

"Okay, the three of you can come."

My chest swells with delight. It's a busy kitchen and filled with laughter. From the housekeeping volunteers, Virginia keeps the room free of dirty dishes. I see Clare give Anson her look, and he responds to it.

"Off with all of you. The rest of us will slave away and

have everythin' baked, and spic span clean before you return. If you're bringin' back the trees today, we'll decorate at seven o'clock. Get a move on."

Anson gives her a bow and opens the rear door.

"Anson, wait a minute. Did you invite him? I'm countin' on you. Anson?"

"Clare, he said that it's doubtful. Let it go, Clare. Charlie and I are alike. Only take so much rejection."

ℵℵℵ

On Christmas morning, no one knew who did it or when, but three extra stockings have our names. Following breakfast, we gather in the living room to exchange homemade gifts.A soft whimper is heard coming from under the tree. When a bark is heard, those, who can, are on all four trying to find which box because it is mixed among the other gifts.

"Found it. 'To Clare from Anson,'" Betsy says. She brings out a box tied with a bright plaid bow and places it on Clare's lap.

Clare removes the lid and a black nose sticks above the box. It belongs to a tiny female poodle. Her collar has a dangling heart-shaped nameplate with Crystal engraved on it.

"Thank you, dear. She's our first."

Anson kisses her cheek and takes the puppy outside. Clare and I leave the group as they exchange their gifts.

"Belle, if you don't mind, I'd like to play with Crystal. Anson can't have all the fun with my present."

Three new lives join New Beginnings intercultural family.

I sit with the Board to review the past fiscal year when Francine rises. "Our records show five residents received their GED. We had five deliveries with two adoptions. Three want to remain for the extra year. One is due sometime this month. And one young lady left."

Francine put down her report. "Arabelle, how could Patty leave and no one saw her? The police are looking but aren't giving much hope with her runaway history".

"Well," said Clare, "my heart goes out to the two who left here childless. You can't cuddle tears and depression. I felt like slappin' Jeanne's parents. That sanctimonious pair stood right over there. Thankin' God for punishin' their daughter because of her sinful life. Or that mother, tellin' Dusty how it's for the best so now she can get on with her life, without a brat holdin' her back. What bothers me the most is there is nothin' I can say to them."

"You are correct Clare. It is our first year, and we might learn how to handle these problems when Mr. Bell arrives next week. So ends my report on New Beginnings."

"Thanks, Fran, next topic is the manor's recertification. Anson, have you heard from Charlie? I've tried calling him. The only message I get is phone out-of-order. He needs to inspect and certify the lifts for this year."

Anson shakes his head. "Not a word since last month Belle. Sorry."

"If no questions, meeting is adjourned."

"Belle, I'll ride over to his house with an invite to Clare's famous fried chicken dinner, he can't refuse."

With the morning mail, the postman delivers a registered letter. Clare brings it to my attention. "It's from Charlie, seein' the return address."

"How strange? The postmark is from Pennsylvania." I

use the letter opener and remove a typed document.

"Clare, it's in small type, and my reading glasses are in the apartment. Will you please read it?"

To Whom It May Concern: Repairs Made Easy will no longer service New Beginning's lifts. Effective January 1st, 1983, B&B Contractors will continue by transfer of all contractual agreements for a $1.00 consideration. Charles L. Boyd President/CEO Repairs Made Easy

Clare returns the letter, and I'm stunned by the news as if a bullet penetrated my brain. In a state of shock, I get up and walk to the fireplace, crumble the letter, and throw it into the cold fireplace.

"Another one of his jokes and I don't find it amusing. Please catch Anson and have him go now to Charlie's place to see if we can get an answer to that letter. Then if you wouldn't mind, schedule an appointment with B&B for tomorrow."

There is no further word from Charlie and B&B has certified the lift. As time passes, I push any idea of moving forward in a relationship with Charlie into a subterranean closet. His solo bit bothers me and by all that is right, it shouldn't.

When Christopher Bell faces the Board members primarily to recharge our slipping enthusiasm, the meeting is a success. With so few words, he gives the booster shot we need in the overall upkeep of morale and energy.

"Mrs. McCutchen . . ."

"Please call me Arabelle or Belle for short, feel I wasn't a Mrs. long enough time to earn the title."

"I disagree, Mrs. McCutchen, but if it'll make you

more comfortable Belle, call me Chris."

We laugh at the formality of the informal use of our names and go into my office.

"Belle, it was a pleasure seeing how well such a small group is doing. Please come with me for a month or so. After New Beginnings, I'm leaving on a tour of like facilities in New York and New Jersey. It would give you a first-hand overview of procedures and maybe a few policies you could implement here."

"Chris, will you excuse me for a few minutes."

With no communication from Charlie, I reschedule important meetings and cancel all others. Afterward, I discover Chris in the nursery. "If it takes a tour for me to be a 'hands-on director,' I need to take that a giant step forward to make this home succeed. Yes, I'd love to go with you. Give me an hour and I'll be ready."

"Anson, we got a good start last year. Mr. Bell offered me an opportunity I can't refuse. I know the Board will keep things running in my absence. I'm leaving tonight with him for a month to tour various facilities. Let Clare know I've taken care of my appointments. If anything is important, pass it along to Francine. I'm relying on you to run and maintain the business in your customary manner. Have to go now because I have a suitcase to pack."

"Do you need cash?"

"Saved a few pennies in the cookie jar and there's American Express. However, I love you for asking, goodbye!"

Packing my suitcase, I feel good about my decision to go. I call their home and Clare answers. She tells me that two girls came back because their parents' negative attitude made them want to finish their schooling and job training. She received my fax and Anson will be there at one o'clock. She included news of Crystal and how she took over the manor. Everything runs okay and I'm to have a safe trip back. I can't wait to get back.

The airplane ride is smooth, and a familiar face greets me in the luggage area. Although beneficial, I've spent two months traveling. On the ride back to the estate, I remain quiet with an occasional whisper, "There's no place like home. There's no place like home."

My murmurings have Anson pull off the next exit. "Arabelle, are you okay? Were there any problems on the trip?"

"I'm drained, Anson. This trip gave me lots of time to think. I feel whipped and keelhauled. Not sure of myself, of who I am, or of the decisions I'm making. Anson, when we enter the gates, drop me off. I'd like to walk a little."

Twenty minutes later, he parks the car and opens my door. I step out, and he drives away. While dusk hasn't arrived, the remaining sunlight guides my steps along small patches of remaining ice along the cleared driveway.

In the distance, a view of several girls warms my heart. They stroll along the snow covered garden path and from an aerial view of the Estate, a girl waves to them. Then there's an exchange as they wave to each other.

Smoke rises from the chimneys. Lights through the manor's eyes shine brightly. The peacefulness of the estate offers solace for their future.

I pass the cemetery and pause for a moment to say my farewell. I know what I must do. Fluff snow covers the pathway to the kitchen, and I notice Kayla stares out the window. On the porch, Clare and Anson wait.

"Arabelle, Anson told me how quiet you were comin' home. Is there anythin' we can do to help?

"Clare, I'm sorry if I worry you. While I learned a lot from visiting other facilities, I gave serious thought about New Beginnings. I decided to step down from the Board and asked for help in promoting you to director. I exchanged faxes with Francine and Anson the past week, and Francine made it all legal.

When I stepped out of the car, nostalgia blind-sided me. I questioned my decision. What I saw on my walk and how you guys tied the strings together. I was pleased. You blended our hopes and your love for New Beginnings into a success. I realized this chapter ended, and a new one begins."

"Where will you go?" Anson asks.

"Yes," Clare speaks up, "how will you manage without, well you know funds for livin'?"

"Technically, I own No Name, so thought I'd stay there. Until, I make other plans. As to managing, with Anson's investment advice and from Neil's bequeath, financially I will be more than okay. Since I haven't unpacked, think the time is right for me to say my goodbyes and leave today. Anson, would you call me a cab?"

Clare gives me a hug. "Arabelle, I've so much to share. Do you recall that time when I mentioned to you about adoptin'?"

I nod and take her hand.

"Well, I think we already did with one girl at a time. I'm happy to say we have five grandbabies to care for and love. In my heart, anyone who leaves will always call New Beginnin's home. Don't have time for a farewell party, so I need to give you somethin'. Come inside, stay awhile so we can talk."

We go into the kitchen. Tears come as memories leave us laughing over Crystal's antics and place within the manor. We reminisce about the good times when a voice calls me.

"Mrs. McCutchen, your ride's coming onto the grounds."

CHAPTER 38
WILL MY LIFE CHANGE?

I take in a final memory and pay my respects at the cemetery. I know they go with me in my heart. To say my farewells, I walk to the foyer where Clare gathered the women and their babies. We exchange tears, hugs, and kisses and for some in friendship, they let me hold their tiny blessings from God. One-by-one they leave and I join Clare and Anson on the front veranda.

The cool March breeze billows out my cape, and I wrap my arms around Clare in a hug. "I will miss you so much and all you taught me about living and loving. However, I must go."

Clare leaves my side before we both cry. Anson towers over me and extends his arm.

"Anson, I want to give you a proper hug. Mind stepping down a step?"

He does, and we take a long time hugging. Before I let go, I whisper into his ear. "The estate rightfully is yours and Clare's. I had Francine take care of transferring the deed. It's a new beginning for all of us. Thank you, good friend, for everything."

Anson kisses me on the cheek then wipes the corner of his eye. "You are making this a bittersweet departure,

Miss Belle. Thank you for what you've done. I hope you will have a successful journey in finding your father. I know it's the puzzle piece that is missing from your life. Remember my words. You will find him. Look there; the car is coming. If you don't mind, the driver will take care of your luggage. It's on the porch steps. Good luck, Arabelle."

He leaves me as an ill will wind blows. I look to the horizon for incoming clouds and my transportation.

"Belle!" "Belle!" Clare's familiar voice calls from the upper floor turret window.

I shout back, "What?"

"Thank you for your gift. If you're in the neighborhood, remember the carriage house apartment has a sign on it. Anson painted the name, 'Just for You'.

Anson's bass voice is louder, "Belle, your mother's boa. We found it while you were gone. Here, catch."

I watch him ball the feathers and throw it downward. In its short descent, it unfurls in the crisp breeze and floats like a red centipede. I laugh. Once it's within inches from my outstretched fingers, I grasp at the boa. Feathers dislodge. Some float to the ground, others are airborne. My movement and an incoming breeze, lift it above my reach and toward the horizon. Soon its red hues become highlights of a sunset. I'm disturbed by its departure and feel goosebumps rising on my arm. Boa, was that your purpose? Haunting me as a foreshadower of death to those I loved? You've flown away, will my life change?

"Sorry, Belle."

"No, problem," I say and wave good-bye. Bored by the car's slow progression up the driveway, I scuff my shoe along the frosted ground covering. I arch my back to stretch and notice a faded new moon making an appearance.

"Hey there, the man in the moon," I shout. "Think I'll make it."

The wind and the cold ground surface have me shift my weight from foot to foot. The fox cape and traveling knit suit keeps me warm but open-toed pumps weren't. I step back as a long silver limousine pulls into the front drive. I wait as a man exits from the driver's seat. It's Charlie.

"What the heck! You close your business to driving a rental. What gives?"

"Belle I didn't close the business. I sold it to B&B for lots more than it was worth, considering they got your service contract."

"So that's why Bruce acted so cocky when he came that day to inspect the lifts. Told me he's hot after working, could he have a drink. Clare was busy in the kitchen with the girls, so I invite him to the carriage house."

"Oh, I heard it was more like you seduced him with your invitation to see your love nest." His sneering infuriated me.

"My what! I did what! Who's spreading those lies? Bruce? Let me tell you, Charlie Boyd, we get there, and he asks to use the bathroom. No problem, until he stays in there a long, long time. So I go. You know, to check if he's okay. Pass my room and out of the corner of my eye I see him spread eagle on my bedspread with a red, cardboard arrow pointing to his privates. I wasn't amused, so quit laughing at me."

"That's not Bruce's story. He called and said that you

invited him for a drink. When he went there, you wore a flimsy baby doll and held two bottles of beer."

"Yes, I did have an open one waiting in the kitchen for him. When I screamed for him to get out, he grabbed his pants and headed for the stairway. I was so angry I threw his shoes at him and then threw that open beer bottle. Hit his right shoulder and beer foam was over him, the floor and a couple of stairs. Never saw a man move so fast while trying to put on his pants. Lost his balance and fell head over heels, ass side up, down a flight of stairs."

Recalling the scene and as angry as I was, I joined Charlie in laughing. "A very confused Anson got a call to reschedule the inspection."

"What'd you do with his shoes?" Charlie asks.

I point to the garbage can.

"Well done, Belle. There is one thing you didn't know. Bruce and I go back a long time. Didn't believe a word he said and figured he needed a lesson. So I socked him for you and requested his partner return your service contract after the inspection. He mailed it yesterday to Anson."

"Thanks, Sir Galahad, you are a man of action."

He opens the rear door, and I lean against the fender. "Remember that P.I.?"

He's changing the subject, and I want answers. "Yes. So what's up with the limo? And why are you driving?"

"It was his. I hired him to check out my leads in finding your father. One day, he drives it to my place with information. He moonlights with his rental business but has this gas guzzler up for sale. I had the cash and made a low ball offer. So I figure . . ."

"Charlie, you figured what? You had a successful

business and freedom to be your own boss. What more could you want?"

"Oh, I have contacts needing rides to the airport in style or marketing the best transportation for a wedding couple and entourage or any number of discreet tête-à-têtes in surrounding areas. I'll make a decent living and not have all the backache from a construction business."

"That's wonderful Charlie, was the P.I. worth the money you paid him?"

"Sure was. Earlier today, I had a conversation with your father's sister. And if you've no other plans, will deliver you there safely today."

"Charlie, don't try to bamboozle me, I'm not a kid."

He surprises me when he takes hold of my shoulders. "Arabelle McCutchen, what do you want from me or any other man? Is it someone who loves the ground you walk on, who'll leap a high building in a single bound, who will protect you from you? Or me, who will sacrifice what he treasures most to give you the happiness you seek."

"I know you, Charles Shawn Michael Boyd, what treasure do you possess that is so great?"

"My love for you, Belle, I'd sacrifice it if you tell me to leave. No matter what you say. The ticket and plane ride is yours."

"Charlie, you're not serious." I break free of his grip and move back.

"Belle, this isn't a game, and I'm not laughing."

"Charlie, I was afraid to tell you. I'm afraid to even now if I say it . . . I'll lose you. For me, loving someone is like an invitation for . . . death. I killed everyone I loved."

"Can't you see? I'm still standing. I'm still breathing. I'm still willing to take a chance on living with you as my wife."

I jump into his extended arms and kiss him.

"Is that your 'yes'?"

"Yes, Charlie. Yes."

A uniformed driver exits the back seat. He loads my cape and luggage into the trunk, returns to the driver's seat and waits.

I shiver, and Charlie wraps his arms around me. "Belle, look the sun's sinking into the horizon. Red sky at night erases the past and gives us clear sky and fair weather ahead."

I climb into the rear seat. When Charlie puts his arm around my shoulder, I snuggle against him. Well Lacey girl, in a few hours, you'll meet the missing piece. You'll have your father's love or the realization that life and love aren't evenhanded. In the comfort and warmth of his arms, I fall asleep. When I open my eyes, I'm in a strange room and in a bed that isn't mine.

I look beneath the blanket. My undergarments are intact and serve as a covering. My suit jacket and skirt are pressed and hang from a motel hanger. Two beds in the room and only this one was used. So where's Charlie? I wrap the blanket, like a giant shawl, around me and rap on the bathroom door. "Charlie, are you in there? Charlie?"

ઈઙઈઙઈઙ

I knock harder, and the door opens. The bathroom is empty of personal items except for one wrapped toothbrush and a sample tube of toothpaste. The digital clock on the night table flashes 5:30 a.m., and near it, is a folded piece of paper. It's a note from Charlie.

'Belle, limo broke down along the way. Made our way

to Ramada Inn and booked two rooms. You'd fallen asleep on the drive and were half-asleep when we arrived. Told the desk clerk we were just married and I carried you across the threshold. Couldn't believe you didn't fight me when I put you to bed. The room is locked, and I have the key card. The limo will be ready by ten o'clock. See you for breakfast around nine. Pleasant dreams Belle. Charlie p.s. XO'

I smooth out the covers and reset the alarm. Then crawl under the covers.

"Morning bright eyes, hungry? "Asks a familiar voice.

I nod and don't say anything. Not sure if I should be upset or thankful he didn't spend the night, quit worrying. Act cool. He has probably seen more than what he did last night. Change the subject—always worked with Mom. "I see the limo, but where's the restaurant?"

"Patience Belle, breakfast depends on Cleveland's traffic. That's all I'm going to say, so don't ask and get dressed. I'll wait in the limo."

Our ride is spellbinding, I watch traffic weave in and around the limo. We stop at the West Side Market. It's Saturday morning and the crowd mills around us. I've never experienced being in such a colossal building filled with shoppers, which spill over the aisle way carrying baskets filled with produce, meats, or sweets.

"You couldn't maneuver a cart through these aisles, and you say there's a restaurant here. Where is it, Charlie?"

"Over in that far, left corner is a crepe maker's stall. Look around, while I get our breakfast, coffee with no cow or cane. Right?"

"You remembered."

Charlie smiles and becomes lost in the crowd. Within a few minutes, he returns, “Breakfast is ready, now onto my favorite table.”

I follow behind him and look over the railing as I climb the metal stairs. “This place certainly outdoes a mega food market, with German sausage, chicken legs. Nope, not chicken but frog legs. Charlie, come and see them.”

“Your crepe is cooling. Later Belle.”

He carries our containers, and we make our way to the far end of the building on the upper floor walk-around. I'm so hungry; I wish he brought more. "Charlie, can we go to the bakery next. The strudel smell makes my mouth water.”

“Belle, enjoy the window sill and eat.”

Instead, I lean against the rail and look down at the crepe stand. "Charlie, that man . . . I recognize him. He looks like, well not sure, but I met him somewhere. He probably waited on you. Sure you don't know him?"

“Not really, maybe we passed each other coming here.”

While he finishes his drink, I take in the excitement and panoramic view of this hundred-year-old market. “Charlie, grocery shopping will never be the same, but, I can’t get that man’s face out of my head.”

“Let it rest and it’ll come to you. Come on. Before we visit the Museum of Art, I want to drive over to the McPherson place.”

I twist around and give a right jab to his shoulder. “McPherson’s?”

He links my arm through his, and we go outside where mysteriously the limo is waiting.

While I search my brain for a nameless face, ten minutes pass, and we arrive in the small community of Bay Village.

"I'm a little scared Charlie. What if this isn't my father's family" I don't want you chasing another wild goose in finding him."

"Look at today as an adventure. If we don't locate him, we step back and dig deeper. He's out there Arabelle. You might call it a guy thing, but, I feel it in my gut. You'll know who he is. I feel it."

I press the doorbell and a matronly woman about forty answers.

"Mr. Boyd, Mrs. McCutchen, come in, please. I'm his sister, Mrs. Blackman. My mother knows you by the name of Arabelle Lacey. She's in the living room. I told her you were coming, but with Alzheimer, sometimes she gets confused. Hope you understand."

"Mrs. Blackman, we do, and I promise if she gets upset, we'll leave," Charlie assures her.

Although Charlie walks behind us, he attempts some local chit-chat about the West Side Market. I walk and say nothing until we enter the living room. That face from the Market stares into the room. Its frame rests on the fireplace mantle.

I point and interrupt their conversation. "Sorry, but who's that?"

"I was just telling Mr. Boyd how my nephew works at the crepe stall. He's spitting image of my step-brother. God rest his soul."

"He's dead?" I look back and grab hold of Charlie's hand.

"About a year ago, heart attack the doctor said." She

goes to a woman in a rocker. “Mom. . . . Mom, here’s the lady I told you was coming to visit you. Remember?”

The blue-gray hair turns away from staring out the window. An ashen face looks at me, and her hand adjusts her eyeglasses. A smile slowly emerges on her wrinkled face.

“Well, I live and breathe. Why didn’t you tell me little Dorothy was coming to visit?”

Mrs. Blackman shrugs, “It’s the Alzheimer. She’s mistaken you for someone else.”

“It’s okay. She knew my mother.” Maybe my search has an ending after all. “Hello, Mrs. McPherson. My mother’s name was Dorothy. Did you know her?”

She looks at me and tilts her head back and forth. “I sometimes forget, but you look like her. Yes, I remember her coming over with Fizzy, like two little love birds they were. But after we moved, she didn't come to visit. Fizzy never spoke any more about her. I remember at his wedding to Carmen; he told me he got married a long time ago, but, it didn't last. He never said who it was. I never asked. Fizzy and Carmen gave me my grandson. She died young, and Fizzy moved back with the boy." She turns away to look out the window. When she looks back, she takes my hand.

“Dorothy, Fizzy should be coming home soon. The nurse tells me he’s on a very long business trip. It was hard for me. Fizzy became my life after Milly’s father died. Milly is my daughter, was only two when he had the car accident. She is at kindergarten.”

She relaxes and closes her eyes. It appears she is sleeping, and her daughter covers her with a lap rug.

“I’m Milly, not her nurse. I hope she helped you and

glad she knew your mother. Sometimes she talks about a Dorothy and my step-brother. Could I get you some ginger ale or water?"

"No thank you, Mrs. Blackman. We have to be going back to Buffalo today."

"Mrs. Blackman," I said and gave her a hug. "Thank you so much for letting us into your home. She knew my mother, and that is comforting. I'm sorry about Fizzy's death."

The old woman raises her head. "Buffalo, I used to live there. Say hello to your kinfolk Dorothy, nice people your family."

She turns again to stare out the window and waits for Fizzy's return. We leave quietly. Our visit lets me fit in the final piece. I have a step-brother and maybe one day I'll meet him.

"Goodbye Mr. Boyd, Mrs. McCutchen, hope you have a safe trip and enjoy your day." She closes the door, and we get into the limo.

"Charlie, I was thinking about the museum. It'll always be there. However, life as your wife would be interesting. What about a honeymoon at Niagara Falls with a rainbow which holds the promise of a wonderful future? What'd think?"

Jim tips his hat and opens the back door. "Where to Mr. Boyd?"

"Jim, you heard Belle. We're off to the Cleveland Hopkins International Airport, flight destination unknown. Okay, my beloved."

I nod and give him a smile as I think of my name. Mrs. Arabelle Lacey-McPherson-McCutchen-Boyd.

"Belle, Jim cleaned the wipers while we were inside.

Look what he found, red feathers."

Where breezes blew earlier, a violent, abrupt gust of wind snaps a part of a tree. We hear the noise and look up. The dead, canopy limb falls eight feet toward Charlie. I scream. The impact of the branch's fork is inevitable with Charlie's head. Jim rushes over to lift the extending leafless branches from me.

"Charlie, Charlie. You okay?"

It takes our combined effort to lift the tree's limb off and away from him. Is he unconscious or did the boa's feathers have its final revenge?

Jim calls for an ambulance, and I cradle his head in my lap. The wound appears shallow with little blood showing. "Can't do this Charlie. You can't give up. Move, open your eyes. Hang in there." I take his hand into mine and remove the red feathers.

The gusty wind leaves. A gentle breeze touches our faces. I open my hand and it carries away the feathers. His finger moves. Charlie opens his blue eyes. I see our future in them.

THE END

ABOUT THE AUTHOR

Before DVDs and iPads, to distract and amuse their five children on family trips, Patricia Petronella Balinski told stories. She would ask for characters, where the story happens, and should the story be happy or scary? Then, her imagination went to work. When her children were old enough to go to school, Balinski attended college part-time. In 1984, after nine years, she received a B.A. degree at Mercyhurst College, in Erie, PA. Completing courses from the Institute of Children's Literature, she wrote stories for her grandchildren.

However, something lacked in a personal dream to be a published author. In 1997, Balinski graduated from the Writer's Digest School; joined Jerry B. Jenkins Christian Writers Guild within the Word Weavers group.

Widowhood and an address move from Central Florida brought Balinski and her three dogs to South Central Florida. Here, she found aspiring and published writers within Writer for All Seasons and Florida Writers Group.

A secular Franciscan, Balinski traveled to Greece and Italy. She published articles in the Franciscan Canticle and published a short story in Writers for All Seasons anthology, **Stories for All Seasons**. ***The Manor's Eyes*** is Balinski first romance novel. Her current project is a mystery book.

Patricia Petronella a/k/a Patsy Balinski to family and colleagues admits her favorite quote is "Be brave in the Dreams that you dream for yourself." Laurie Rohner

She would love to hear from her readers: patsypen1@gmail.com

DISCUSSION GUIDE

1. How did you **experience** the book? Were you engaged immediately, or did it take you a while to "get into it"? How did you feel reading it—amused, sad, disturbed, confused, bored...?
2. What motivates different character's actions? Do you think those actions are justified or ethical? How has the past shaped their lives?
3. Do you find the characters convincing? Are they believable? Are they fully developed as complex human beings—or were they one-dimensional?
4. What motivates different character's actions? Do you think those actions are justified or ethical?
5. Who in the book would you like to meet? What would you ask, or say?
6. If you could insert yourself as a character in the book, what role would you play?
7. Are the main characters **dynamic**—changing or maturing by the end of the book? Do they learn about themselves, how the world works and their role in it?
8. Is the story plot or character driven? Do events unfold quickly or is more time spent developing characters' inner lives? Does it make a difference to your enjoyment? Were you surprised by complications, twists and turns?
9. What time period is it set in? Is this a period you know anything about? Would you have liked to live in this time? What would be the advantages -- disadvantages?

10. Talk about the book's **structure**.
   a. Is it a continuous story...or interlocking short stories?
   b. Does the time-line move forward chronologically?
   c. Does time shift back & forth from past to present?
   d. Is there a single viewpoint or shifting viewpoints?
   e. Why might the author have chosen to tell the story the way he or she did?
   f. What difference does the structure make in the way you read or understand the book?

11. What main ideas—**themes**—does the author explore? (Consider the title, often a clue to a theme.) Does the author use **symbols** to reinforce the main ideas?

12. What **passages** strike you as insightful, even profound? Perhaps a bit of dialogue that's funny or poignant or that encapsulates a character? Maybe there's a particular comment that states the book's thematic concerns?

13. Consider the ending. Did you expect it or were you surprised? Was it manipulative or forced? Was it neatly wrapped up—maybe too neatly? Or was the story unresolved, ending on an ambiguous note?

14. Has this novel **changed you**—broadened your perspective? Have you learned something new or been exposed to different ideas about people or a certain part of the world?

15. Does the book remind you of your own life? An event? A person—like a friend, family member, boss, co-worker?

16. Project into the future. What do you think will happen to the characters next? Does the author plan a sequel? Would you read a sequel?

17. Did you find the dialogue real and flow naturally between characters?

18. Between the protagonist's two loves, what sets them apart?

19. What surprised you the most from the events within protagonist's life?

20. If the sub-plot relationship between minor characters is eliminated, would you think it would improve story? If so, which characters' relationship would you choose?

21. What made you purchase the book . . . the price is right; the title and front cover; the author's bio; or, the reviews?

ABOUT PORTALS PUBLISHING

What We Offer

- ✓ We publish in three versions: trade paperback, e-book and audio
- ✓ We distribute worldwide in English.
- ✓ We offer standard royalties for each of the versions based on net.
- ✓ We provide the book cover by a professional designer.
- ✓ We provide the author 10 copies as the advance.
- ✓ We post the author's discussion guide on the nation's largest book club database.
- ✓ We promote the book to the media (the author's local newspapers and radio stations) and the representative editor of the book's genre at BellaOnline (second largest women's e-magazine in the world)
- ✓ The author is responsible to do the research, but we will announce the book to as many groups for which the author can give us email addresses and/or meet-up contacts in the United States, Great Britain, Australia and New Zealand.
- ✓ We can help set up book signings and speaking/lecture tours.
- ✓ We will nominate the book for at least one, but possibly several literary awards throughout the contract's duration.
- ✓ We can help set up as much of the author's platform as the author wants – the author does the hard work; we'll assist and advise.
- ✓ We continuously assist the author with promotion strategies throughout the contract's duration.

PortalsPublishing.com
"The Best Books are Portals to a New World."

An imprint of **Denouement Literary Agency, LLC**
DenouementLit.com

You may also be interested in **Bliss Books**
BlissBooksOnliine.com
"Building Life-Long Inspirational & Successful Strategies"